Through the Veil

"[A] hold-on-to-your-seat tale of demons, hunky warriors and witches served with a mix of love and betrayal. Fun! If you enjoy otherworldly, action-packed adventures with a hot and steamy romance, this is for you."   —*Fresh Fiction*

"A good read . . . Walker obviously has an unmatched imagination."
                                        —*Romance Reader at Heart*

"Walker does an excellent job of creating a world whose inhabitants are fighting for their very existence. Dark and evocative, this tale is filled with danger, betrayal and a destined love."   —*Romantic Times*

"Action, adventure and romance abound . . . an engaging tale."
                                        —*Romance Reviews Today*

"A fabulous action-packed romantic fantasy . . . Fans will believe that the world on the other side of the veil exists, which is key to this fine tale."   —*Midwest Book Review*

Hunter's Salvation

"One of the best tales in a series that always achieves high marks . . . An excellent thriller."   —*Midwest Book Review*

continued . . .

Hunters: Heart and Soul

"Some of the best erotic romantic fantasies on the market. Walker's world is vibrantly alive with this pair."   —*The Best Reviews*

Hunting the Hunter

"Action, sex, savvy writing and characters with larger-than-life personalities that you will not soon forget are where Ms. Walker's talents lie, and she delivered all that and more . . . This is a flawless five-rose paranormal novel, and one that every lover of things that go bump in the night will be howling about after they read it . . . Do not walk! Run to get your copy today!"   —*A Romance Review*

"An exhilarating romantic fantasy filled with suspense and . . . star-crossed love . . . action-packed."   —*Midwest Book Review*

"Fast-paced and very readable . . . titillating."   —*The Romance Reader*

"Action-packed, with intriguing characters and a very erotic punch, *Hunting the Hunter* had me from page one. Thoroughly enjoyable with a great hero and a story line you can sink your teeth into, this book is a winner. A very good read!"   —*Fresh Fiction*

"Another promising voice is joining the paranormal genre by bringing her own take on the ever-evolving vampire myth. Walker has set up the bones of an interesting world and populated it with some intriguing characters. Hopefully, there will be a sequel that ties together more threads and divulges more details."   —*Romantic Times*

Books by Shiloh Walker

HUNTING THE HUNTER
HUNTERS: HEART AND SOUL
HUNTER'S SALVATION
THROUGH THE VEIL

THE MISSING
FRAGILE

CHAINS

Anthologies

HOT SPELL
(with Emma Holly, Lora Leigh, and Meljean Brook)

PRIVATE PLACES
(with Robin Schone, Claudia Dain, and Allyson James)

Chains

SHILOH WALKER

HEAT
NEW YORK

THE BERKLEY PUBLISHING GROUP
Published by the Penguin Group
Penguin Group (USA) Inc.
375 Hudson Street, New York, New York 10014, USA
Penguin Group (Canada), 90 Eglinton Avenue East, Suite 700, Toronto, Ontario M4P 2Y3, Canada
(a division of Pearson Penguin Canada Inc.)
Penguin Books Ltd., 80 Strand, London WC2R 0RL, England
Penguin Group Ireland, 25 St. Stephen's Green, Dublin 2, Ireland (a division of Penguin Books Ltd.)
Penguin Group (Australia), 250 Camberwell Road, Camberwell, Victoria 3124, Australia
(a division of Pearson Australia Group Pty. Ltd.)
Penguin Books India Pvt. Ltd., 11 Community Centre, Panchsheel Park, New Delhi—110 017, India
Penguin Group (NZ), 67 Apollo Drive, Rosedale, North Shore 0632, New Zealand
(a division of Pearson New Zealand Ltd.)
Penguin Books (South Africa) (Pty.) Ltd., 24 Sturdee Avenue, Rosebank, Johannesburg 2196, South Africa

Penguin Books Ltd., Registered Offices: 80 Strand, London WC2R 0RL, England

This is an original publication of The Berkley Publishing Group.

This is a work of fiction. Names, characters, places, and incidents either are the product of the author's imagination or are used fictitiously, and any resemblance to actual persons, living or dead, business establishments, events, or locales is entirely coincidental. The publisher does not have any control over and does not assume any responsibility for author or third-party websites or their content.

PRINTING HISTORY
Heat trade paperback edition / May 2009

Library of Congress Cataloging-in-Publication Data
Walker, Shiloh.
    Chains / Shiloh Walker. —1st ed.
      p. cm.
    ISBN 978-0-425-22786-2
    1. Reunions—Fiction. 2. Madison (Ohio)—Fiction. I. Title.
PS3623.A35958C47 2009
813'.6—dc22   2008047107

PRINTED IN THE UNITED STATES OF AMERICA

10 9 8 7 6 5 4 3 2 1

Thanks to Joey Hill for her insight into the characters of Deacon and Renee. And to my friend Renee: You waited long enough. Hope you enjoy.

CONTENTS

BOOK ONE

Renee

CHAINS OF REBELLION

Madison, Ohio, 1994

STANDING IN FRONT of the mirror, Renee Lincoln adjusted one of the thin straps holding up her sundress. It was simply made white eyelet and against the golden glow of her tan, it looked damn hot. *She* looked damn hot. With a bitter smile, she wondered if that was her only reason for being born.

To look good.

It was the only value she really had, according to her mother. Not as bright as her dad would have liked—although her dad, at least, had seemed to love her. Just not enough to keep from killing himself two years earlier.

Her mother, though . . . Renee knew her mother didn't love her at all. Renee wasn't an "ideal" Lincoln, not by a long shot. Her faults were far too many; she wasn't ladylike enough, she lacked ambition, she didn't think enough of her place in society, she acted too common.

At least you are physically attractive, Renee. With any luck, we can find a suitable man who will overlook your shortcomings.

And oh, were there shortcomings.

What a loser.

Tears burned in her throat but she wouldn't let them fall from her eyes. She couldn't. Lincolns didn't cry in public. Or in private, according to her mother. Tears caused bags and wrinkles and lines. Renee wouldn't be young forever and soon she would have to find a man who would provide for her. The endless, *ceaseless* prattle of her mother's voice echoed in her mind and she could only imagine the disgust that would enter her mother's eyes if she could see Renee now.

Standing there with her hair a mess, her dress wrinkled and an ugly red mark on her face that was swelling by the second. Yes, her mother would be disgusted.

But not because James D. Whitcomb Jr., Renee's boyfriend, had slapped her. No, Mother would be disappointed because Renee looked far less than perfect. Lincoln women never went out in public looking anything less than perfect.

The vivid red mark on her face was certainly less than perfect.

What on earth did you do to provoke him?

Although Mother Dear wasn't there, Renee could hear her words as clear as day. When her mother saw her, the woman would want to know what happened, and why. If Renee told the truth, what would her mom's reaction be?

He hit me because I didn't want to sleep with him.

Mother would want to know why Renee hadn't slept with him. *You could do far worse than a young man like James, Renee.*

Yeah, Renee could see her mother saying something along those lines. Mother would be *shocked* that Renee hadn't given JD whatever he wanted. *You're lucky to have a respectable man like James interested in you, Renee. You could do so much worse.*

And that wasn't some imagined bullshit—no, her mother had actually said that to Renee, and said it repeatedly. Renee could do so much worse than JD. Worse than a guy who hit his girlfriend because she didn't want to sleep with him.

By *worse*, Renee knew Mother meant *common*. Lincolns didn't do common.

There were a lot of things Lincolns didn't do.

They didn't do common.

They didn't do emotion.

They didn't do tears.

Lincolns never cried. Renee was a Lincoln and she would *not* cry.

Not when she found out all of her top college choices had sent back rejection letters.

Not when they found out her father was being indicted for Medicare fraud. Not when he quietly took the easy way out and overdosed on a nice cocktail of sleeping pills, a little OxyContin and Grey Goose.

Not when Renee came home and found her mother drunk and unconscious on the floor of her room the day they buried her father.

Not when her boyfriend got pissed off when she said *no*. Not when he hit her.

Gingerly, she touched fingers to the ugly, red handprint forming on her cheek. JD had actually hit her. All because she told him she didn't want to have sex with him for the first time while a loud, raucous party carried on just feet away.

Actually, she didn't want to do it with JD at all. When he'd first started calling her, she hadn't even taken his calls. Then Mother found out. Renee was made to take the next call under her mother's watchful eye and when he asked her out, saying *no* would have been like moving Mount Everest. It couldn't be done.

The few times she'd tried to get out of dates, Mother had intervened—just like this party. Renee hadn't wanted to come, but her mother had *requested* it. *There's booze at these parties, Mother. The kids have sex. They drink. There are drugs.* That was what she'd wanted to say.

But none of it would have been acknowledged. JD was a good boy. Good boys didn't throw those kinds of parties.

Because she couldn't stand up to her mother, she was dating

a guy she really didn't like. Because she couldn't stand up to her mother, she was at a party that looked like the staging ground for an MTV episode of *Spring Break*. Because she couldn't stand up to her mother, she'd just gotten slapped when she told JD no.

Part of her wondered if she shouldn't have just done it. Gotten it over with. Sooner or later, she'd give in. She always did.

JD didn't have many people tell him no and when they did, the person ended up humiliated. If she'd thought being his girlfriend would save her from that, she'd been wrong. He'd followed her out into the hall and then when she headed past Boyd Fellows, JD's best friend, JD had shoved her at him. "Maybe you should have a go at her, Boyd."

Boyd had laughed and said, "Damn, JD, you did her fast."

"*Did* me?" Renee had demanded, feeling humiliated, angry— and nervous. Nervous the way a fuzzy little bunny probably felt when faced with a couple of coyotes. But the anger and the humiliation overrode the nerves and when she turned around to confront her boyfriend, he hit her. Backhanded her across the face and knocked her into the wall. Boyd had looked a little surprised, but had he said anything?

Of course not. Not Boyd. He followed after JD like a damn poodle, and he did whatever JD wanted.

Still staring at her puffy, aching cheek, she tried to figure out if she was surprised or not. Renee hadn't ever been hit before. The initial shock of it had made her freeze. By the time her brain had managed to think past the shock, JD and Boyd had disappeared down the hall and the others drifting in and out of the hall barely seemed to notice her.

Trailing her fingers down the mark, she realized her hand was shaking. *She* was shaking.

Renee had faced cold disapproval from her mother on a regular basis. She remembered wishing once that her mother would hit her instead of giving her the icy royal snub. But now, as her cheek ached and her head pounded, she decided the cold treatment was better than this pain any day of the week.

Tired, she straightened up and crossed her arms over her chest. Man, she wanted to go home. Just crawl into her big bed and pull the covers over her head, sleep for a week. Or two. By then, graduation would be over and JD would be gone with Boyd on his trip to Europe.

Maybe while he was gone, she'd figure out a way to break things off with him.

If you're going to do it . . . just do it.

Where that voice came from, Renee really didn't know. Emotional strength and self-confidence weren't really her thing. But oddly enough, staring at the bruise spreading across her right cheek, she realized she'd gotten damn fed up with her mother and her boyfriend controlling her life.

She was eighteen years old, damn it. If she didn't take control now, then she never would.

Then do it. Do it now.

Shaking and scared, in that moment, she made the decision. It was a terrifying one, but she was going to go out there, find JD and tell him she was going home. Without him. Squaring her shoulders, she turned away from the mirror and strode across the bathroom floor.

In the hallway, though, her resolve faltered a little as she bumped into Lacey Talbot. Lacey was an all-American kind of girl, wholesome looking, funny, sweet—and nice. Really nice, the way most people pretended to be until they could stab you in the back.

She was also the kind of girl who wouldn't be too afraid to stand up to somebody like JD. Renee would bet no guy had ever hit Lacey. And Lacey's mom was a total sweetheart—that lady wouldn't ever make Lacey go out on a date with a guy just because the guy was rich and popular. If Lacey's boyfriend dared to hit her and Lacey didn't kill him, chances were her mother would.

Lacey was like some kind of modern-day version of Marcia Brady, pretty, smart and genuinely kind. She went out with one of the best-looking guys in Madison, Ohio. Deacon Cross. He was a freshman down at the University of Kentucky, he had the most amazing blue eyes and he looked at Lacey as though he thought the sun rose and set on her. He looked at Lacey in a way that made Renee so jealous, it almost hurt.

Humiliated at the thought of Lacey seeing her face, Renee dodged around her and mumbled under her breath.

Lacey's hand caught her arm. "Hey, are you okay?"

Some polite lie formed on Renee's lips but before she could even squeeze the words past her tight throat, a shadow separated itself from the wall and approached. Sherra Salinger—okay, if Lacey reminded Renee of Marcia Brady, blonde, beautiful and perky, then Sherra was the teenaged version of Wednesday Addams, only scarier.

Blacker than black hair, natural black—not some grunge-inspired bad dye job, but inky, natural black. Dark brown eyes and skin so white, Renee wondered if the girl left the house for anything but school and kicking ass.

"He hit you."

Sherra's words weren't a question but a statement of fact, and there was a world of disgust in her dark brown eyes. Blushing furiously, Renee averted her face and mumbled, "I'm fine."

"JD *hit* you?" Lacey demanded, her eyes widening. But there was no disbelief in her voice—just anger.

It only made Renee feel a little less sick inside.

Averting her face so that her hair fell down and hid the bruise a little bit, she just shook her head. *Coward.* Her grand plans of standing up to JD were falling apart around her and she hadn't even seen him. Just two of the most confident girls in school.

"I'm fine," she said quietly, trying to slip between the two girls, but Sherra shifted her body and wouldn't let Renee pass.

It seemed Renee's humiliation was now complete. Sherra was a spooky piece of work. Not too many people actually wanted to be around her.

With her pale face, the black hair and eyes that looked a little too old for a high school senior, Sherra didn't just *not* fit in with the small high school crowd.

She stood out.

Smart, with a caustic sense of humor and totally lacking the normal teenaged need to fit in, Sherra alternately terrified fellow classmates and amused the hell out of them. Right now, with Sherra's near-black eyes boring into hers, Renee wished she could just sink into the floor and disappear.

Sherra reached out and laid a hand on Renee's arm. Her fingers, as white as her face and tipped with crimson nails, curled around Renee's arm and squeezed. Gently, though. All she seemed to want was Renee's attention. "Guys who like to hit don't stop too often, Renee." Her mouth twisted in a grimace and her voice was soft and mournful as she murmured, "Believe me, I know."

"Has he done this before?" Lacey asked.

That concern only made it worse. Yep. Her humiliation was definitely complete. This would have been hard and embarrassing no matter who she'd run into, but Lacey and Sherra?

There were two "popular" girls in the senior class.

Renee was one.

Lacey was the other. Peppy, funny, smart, the kind of popular girl everybody liked, everybody wanted to be—including Renee. Lacey had *real* friends; Renee was surrounded by people who didn't even know her well enough to like her.

Then there was Sherra, the meanest bitch in all of Madison High. The two of them gazed at Renee with sympathy in their eyes, and she would almost rather have taken another slap from JD than stand there.

She wanted to run and hide. But that would have just made this whole mess that much more mortifying. Lifting her chin, she said coolly, "This really isn't any of your business, is it?" Sliding her gaze to meet Lacey's, she added, "Either of you." Then she stepped around them and walked away without another word.

But instead of heading back down the main staircase, she headed down the long hall. JD's house was huge, even bigger than the big old house that had been in the Lincoln family for generations. There had to be someplace where she could find some privacy.

Hopefully, she could get a grip.

EVEN FROM THE blue guest bedroom on the third floor, Renee could hear the music. The voices. The occasional bark of laughter. She wished she were anyplace but where she was, and she desperately wanted to leave. But humiliation and shame kept her frozen in place. She wasn't leaving until there would be nobody left to see her leave. Remembering the sympathetic way Lacey had looked at her sent Renee's gut into spasms.

Lacey's concern, humiliating as it was, came as little surprise. Simply because Lacey was a nice girl. Sometimes too nice. She was the kind of girl who would interfere when one of the other girls from the popular crowd starting picking on other kids. More, she was nice enough that nobody was afraid to talk to her. It seemed everybody loved Lacey.

Not like with JD. Or Renee. Renee didn't get her kicks by making fun of other kids, but she wasn't the outgoing, sweet girl that Lacey was. She was a little stuck up and she knew it, but she couldn't stand to be cruel.

Still, not too many people outside Renee's circle were nice to her, just for the sake of being nice. She wasn't used to it, and she didn't really expect it.

But while Lacey's pity had Renee ready to pull the covers up over her head, it had been Sherra's reaction that hurt the worst. Renee wouldn't have expected it from Sherra.

There was a time when Renee had thought of Sherra as her mirror reflection. Neither of them had a bunch of people going out of their way to be nice to them. People looked at both of them kind of like they were barracudas or something. Sometimes Renee wondered if Sherra felt as isolated as Renee often did.

But Renee hadn't ever said anything more than *hi* to Sherra. Sherra had said even less than that, ignoring Renee with a single-minded intent.

Sherra didn't like Renee. At all.

So Sherra's sympathy was majorly unsettling.

Huddled on the window seat, she tried to tune out the sounds of the music, the laughter, and just wait it out. The party had to end sooner or later. But the ebb and flow of music and voices didn't show any sign of ending and Renee felt frozen.

The minutes stretched out into hours and she managed to tune out the music and the voices. But then there came something a little harder to ignore, a strangled, muffled scream.

Her gut churned and almost despite herself, she felt her body moving, coming off the window seat and moving toward the door. Ears straining to hear another sound, her eyes darting all over the place, she crept down the hallway on legs that shook and wobbled with every step.

Where . . . ?

There.

Downstairs. It had come from the second floor, probably the room right under where Renee had been hiding. Descending the stairs, she headed in what she hoped was the right direction—again. Another scream. Muffled, quieter.

It came from the library. A rarely used one, if Renee knew much about Whitcomb Senior. Just ahead, she could see Lacey Talbot.

They were both heading in the same direction, following the sound of a fight, the sound of a girl's muffled cries and male laughter. "Do you . . ." Lacey's voice trailed off, but Renee knew what she was asking.

Wordless, Renee nodded as she wrapped her arms around her midsection. Edging closer, she stood next to Lacey as the tall blonde reached out and opened the door to the library. Lacey moved slowly, almost as if she felt the same reluctance that Renee felt.

The door opened and the sounds of a struggle became clearer. Much clearer. A girl's voice, muffled and desperate, a harsh, angry voice that was disturbingly familiar. A dull thud, a sharp slap.

Pressing herself flat to the wall, she peered into the room, and what she saw was enough to make her want to fall to her knees and puke. It was JD.

And Sherra.

Boyd crouched by Sherra's head, holding her hands pinned to the ground. JD crouched over Sherra's struggling body and he sneered at Lacey, shouted for her to get out. Whatever else was said fell on deaf ears as far as Renee was concerned. She couldn't hear anything over the roaring in her ears—and the loud, insistent voice.

Don't just stand there!

She had to do something.

Something—like what?

The voice of self-doubt was an insistent scream inside her. *Coward. Worthless coward. Just leave—*

But as she watched JD swing out, backhanding Sherra, Renee realized she couldn't leave. Lacey kicked him and he tried to hit her back, but Lacey had already moved away.

Until her hands closed around the big, ugly lamp on the corner of the desk, Renee hadn't been aware that she was moving. Until she lifted it over her head, she didn't realize what she was going to do.

With all her strength, she brought it crashing down on JD's head. He went limp and flopped onto Sherra's body, pinning her down. Renee swallowed, staring at the back of JD's head and the bloody goose egg that was forming. She'd hit him. She'd fought back.

Her knees went a little weak and she sagged against the desk and struggled to stay upright. The roaring in her ears faded a little, just enough to hear Lacey say to Boyd, "Get away from her."

But Boyd acted as though he didn't even hear her, staring at JD as though he couldn't think, couldn't act unless JD told him what to do.

A movement out of the corner of her eye had her looking over and she watched, numb, as Deacon Cross came running into the room, stopping behind Lacey and taking in everything with one quick glance. His face went tight, his brows dropped low over his eyes and a snarl twisted his lips. Boyd still hadn't moved, but he did look up at Deacon as the older, bigger guy snarled, "Move. *Now*."

Slowly, almost reluctantly, Boyd let go of Sherra, and immediately the girl started squirming and struggling to get out from under JD's deadweight.

As Boyd stood up, Deacon said softly, "Lacey, call the cops."

"I'd love to."

Stunned, Boyd demanded, "What the hell for? Little slut was looking to party."

Deacon moved so fast that Renee jumped, pulling back instinctively as he lashed out, landing a punch square on Boyd's jaw. Boyd sagged backward, stumbling, bumping into the davenport.

Renee watched him warily, unwilling to be so close to him, but her legs were still too shaky for her to move away.

Boyd's hazel eyes rounded with shock as he blurted out, "We didn't do nothing wrong."

Renee's jaw dropped. Eyes wide, she stared at Boyd in disbelief. *Nothing wrong?* Lacey's thoughts seemed to echo Renee's, if the look on her face was anything to go by. But before she could say anything, she saw movement from the corner of her eye. Tensed. Tried to say something, but it was too late.

Horrified, she watched as JD shoved himself up from the floor and lunged for Lacey. Lacey didn't retreat the way Renee would have, and Renee watched, awed, as Lacey used her arm to block a blow from JD—and then hit him back, striking him in the nose with the heel of her palm.

Blood sprayed and JD bellowed, "You stupid bitch."

He spun away from Lacey, and instinctively Renee backed away, keeping a very large distance between them. Dread flooded her as she saw where JD was going. The desk. His dad kept a gun in there—Renee knew it, because JD had showed it to her just a week or two ago.

Shit.

"He's going for his dad's gun." She tried to keep her voice calm, but it came out in a panicked scream. It didn't matter how it came out, though, because Deacon understood and he rushed for JD just as the younger guy raced around the desk and jerked open the drawer that held the gun.

It went flying, ended up by Boyd's feet. A clear rush of knowledge flooded her and she knew, she *knew*, JD wouldn't blink over killing—and if JD told Boyd to pick up that gun, Boyd would.

Shoving off the wall, she made her way over to Sherra and Lacey and said, "We need to get out of here."

But Sherra didn't even hear her. She bent back down, weaving and stumbling, and she grabbed something from the ground. Little rivulets of blood flowed down her face and when she stood back up, Renee saw that the fear had been replaced by anger.

Sherra held a jagged, broken piece of pottery in her hand, a part of the lamp that Renee had broken over JD's head. The lamp had been a weird, urn-looking thing with handles on either side. Right now, Sherra had one of those handles in her fist and the wicked, jagged edge pointed out, making one very effective knife.

As Boyd lifted the gun, Sherra sprang, attacking with clear-minded focus.

It was over in moments. Lacey Talbot stood off to the side, the phone in her hand as she spoke to the police.

Renee collapsed onto the davenport under the window, jerking her feet up to keep them out of the ever-spreading pool of blood.

Deacon was on top of JD, holding him pinned in a wrestler's lock.

And Sherra . . . she stood still in the middle of the room, staring down at Boyd's lifeless face.

1

"Why in the hell am I here?"

Sitting in the rental car, Renee Lincoln tried to convince herself that she should just turn around and go home.

There really wasn't anything for her in Madison and it wasn't like she really wanted to see old friends or old flames. Old flames— her gut knotted on her the same way it always did when she thought of JD Whitcomb.

The town's golden boy.

Her boyfriend from senior year.

Would-be rapist.

Dear God, even after the truth had come out about what happened the night Boyd Fellows died, her mother had kept trying to push her at JD. *Mama, didn't you hear me? He was going to rape Sherra Salinger!*

Her mother's nose had wrinkled ever so slightly, the closest she'd come to frowning. *Honestly, that's not the kind of girl that any man would need to rape, Renee. Men do have their needs . . .*

Needs. Laughing harshly, Renee acknowledged that even fifteen years later, it was enough to make her sick. Breaking up with JD hadn't been necessary. He hadn't once tried to call after that, but that hadn't kept Claudia Lincoln from trying to push Renee after him.

The horror of what Renee had seen had given her the strength, though, finally, to stand up against the woman. After that night, Claudia Lincoln wasn't going to control Renee. Not anymore.

Not that she'd ever give up trying. Claudia continued in her efforts to ride herd on her only daughter up until she'd died three years ago.

Including dropping not-so-subtle hints that JD was still single.

Grimacing, Renee acknowledged that at some point, she would most likely see JD while she was in town. She'd arranged to spend two weeks at home, because she needed to figure out what to do with the house. It had been left to her after her mother died, and Renee kept putting off making any decisions.

Letting it sit empty made little sense but selling it would be hard. It had been in her family for generations. At the same time, Renee couldn't see herself living in Madison again—although she realized that she had missed the quiet, pretty little town where she'd grown up, and other than thoughts of seeing JD, Renee really did want to go home.

It would be nice to see Lacey. They'd stayed in contact since their freshman year of college. One night over Christmas break, they'd run into each other and ended up talking for hours about the night Boyd died. They'd gone to school in different parts of the country, Lacey attending Tulane on athletic and academic scholarships while Renee ended up going to the Culinary Institute in Pittsburgh.

A cook? You want to be a cook? To this day, Renee could still remember her mother's horror when Renee had announced out of the blue that she had changed her mind about going to Ole Miss. That she wanted to become a chef. She'd always enjoyed cooking, a fact that had mortified her mother to no end. But as long as it was kept quiet, like some dirty family secret, her mother had tolerated it.

Actually going to school for it? Training for it? As far as her mother was concerned, it was unthinkable. Lincoln women did not actually work. They went to school, they studied hard, they achieved degrees, but they didn't put them to use. Especially not in a *service* industry.

College was a hunting ground for finding an appropriate husband and all the rest was merely window dressing. Naturally, Renee had failed to get into the right kind of school, but money changed everything and Claudia had already made the arrangements to get Renee into University of Mississippi, just like Claudia.

All it had taken was a sizable donation. *Do be a good girl, Renee. We really need to find you a good husband.*

A good husband. So Renee could get married and go on to live out her life as some rich jerk's polite society wife. Except Renee had lived most of her life as *window dressing*. The perfect daughter. She had the perfect boyfriend and the perfect life already spread out before her.

Then the night of a stupid party in high school, her so-called perfect life had fallen apart. Her perfect boyfriend had slapped her. Her perfect boyfriend had tried to rape a girl.

And Renee had seen a man killed.

She still had nightmares. Nightmares where she ran into a room, but it was too late. Nightmares where *she* was the one pinned to the ground, screaming for help while two men held her down and raped her, but nobody came when she screamed.

The worst ones were about the blood. The smell of it, the look of it as it gleamed so red and wet on the floor. How Sherra had looked standing over Boyd, the jagged, makeshift blade in her hand coated with crimson. Renee didn't blame Sherra for those ugly, bloody dreams. Having read some of the horror books that Sherra had written over the years, she had a feeling the woman had more than a few nightmares of her own.

But Renee couldn't get over the smell of the blood, the way it had crept over the floor, covering everything with that wet, glistening red.

A truck came blasting down the highway and the sound of it broke through Renee's reverie. Her gut churned and she asked herself once more, *Why are you doing this?*

She really didn't have an answer. But Renee also knew as she put the car into drive and checked the traffic behind her that it didn't matter. The exact reason *why* didn't matter. It didn't matter that she hadn't gone to the ten-year reunion and it didn't matter that she really didn't want to go back for this one.

She was going back because she had to.

For some strange reason, she had to. She needed some sort of closure, although why she thought she'd find it at a stupid reunion, she wasn't sure.

However, before she went home, she was going to get a drink. Several drinks. And then, a hotel room and one more night to get herself prepared to face the past.

Getting smashed hadn't ever sounded so appealing.

SHE WALKED INTO the hotel bar looking completely removed, completely remote—and so fucking gorgeous that one look had Deacon Cross's body going on red alert. All the blood in his head drained south and it was amazing he had the brain power required to hold on to the pilsner in his hand. The beer in his mouth suddenly tasted flat. Swallowing it, he put the glass down to the side so he could focus on her.

There was something vaguely familiar about her, eyes that tilted up at the corners, that long, deep red hair—and he did mean *long*; that perfect, gorgeous hair fell down to her ass. Couldn't see the ass, but he'd bet it was nice, especially considering how sweetly rounded her hips were. He watched as she walked across the dark carpet, not looking anywhere but straight ahead. Several eyes drifted her way and he suspected she was as aware of their stares as she was of his own, but she didn't so much as flick them a glance.

The hotel bar was fairly crowded. It was Monday night in early August, which tended to mean a decent amount of travelers, people either on vacation or just on business.

Deacon wasn't exactly there on business but he sure as hell wouldn't call it vacation, and he also suspected he wouldn't much enjoy the trip.

But the sight of the long, sleek redhead had him a little more interested in something other than a few beers before heading back upstairs to have some room service and maybe watch a movie.

He'd much rather have her.

As she slid onto the seat next to him, he fought not to grin. The flirting couple on her other side didn't even notice her, and all the other seats at the bar were taken. But instead of turning to look at her right off the bat and hand her some cheesy line, he wrapped his hand around his beer again and took another long drink. When he lowered it, he watched from the corner of his eye as she smoothed down a long, close-fitting skirt and crossed her legs. The side slit of the skirt parted and let him see what was under it. Deacon had excellent peripheral vision, and in that moment, he was damn glad.

Black, sleek leather boots fit to her legs like they'd been made for her, rising up to just above her knee.

He felt her gaze on him but instead of looking at her, he took another drink. It wasn't until the bartender came up and took her order—a glass of white zinfandel—that he glanced over at her. She met his eyes briefly, and then looked away.

The bartender took forever getting the wine to her and after about two minutes, Deacon leaned in and murmured, "The guy had to look it up in a manual how to make a gin and tonic earlier. Hope you're not in a hurry."

A faint smile curved her lips. They were full and slicked with a deep, wine red. "No. No hurry." Her gaze dropped to the pilsner in front of him and then she glanced at him. "Did he figure out how to draw the beer without the manual?"

Deacon smiled. "Yeah. But I suspect he could need help working the corkscrew." He nodded down the length of the bar toward the bartender. The kid barely looked old enough to serve alcohol and he was using the corkscrew as though this was only the second or third time he'd done so.

Gorgeous smiled back, a bit ruefully. "If I'd known that, I would have ordered the gin and tonic. Maybe he'd have remembered from earlier."

IT WAS A bad mistake to flirt with a guy you met in a bar.

Renee knew this.

But as the minutes stretched into an hour, she knew that was exactly what she was doing and she also had no desire to stop.

It felt too good. Too right. That in and of itself was odd. She wasn't a flirt. She wasn't shy and she certainly wasn't leery of the opposite sex. It was just . . . well, not too many guys appealed to her on that level.

Not like this one did.

He was sexy, he was polite and talking to him felt easy, for some reason. Like she knew him, although Renee couldn't imagine meeting a guy that good-looking and then forgetting about it. Didn't change how simple and easy it was to sit there and talk with him, talk like she'd known him for years instead of minutes.

When he shifted on his chair and leaned over to murmur in her ear, the length of his thigh pressed against hers and instead of pulling back, however discreetly, she closed her eyes and breathed in the warm scent of him.

Heat whispered through her, warming her skin, tightening her nipples and leaving her with the urge to squirm and press her thighs together to ease the empty ache in her belly. Too long—it had been *way* too long. But even if it had been only a few days or weeks since she'd had sex, instead of years, there was something about this guy.

It wasn't just that odd sense of familiarity. There was a sexual pull, tugging her closer and closer, and she had no desire to fight it. He went quiet and from under her lashes, she looked at him. His gaze rested on her mouth and then he glanced up, met her gaze.

Renee honestly didn't know why she did it. But when his eyes bored into hers, she dipped her head submissively.

It wasn't shyness. It was a signal not everybody would pick up on, subtle enough that if it was missed, she wouldn't have to worry about feeling embarrassed or awkward over it. Even as she did it, she expected it to go right over his head. She hadn't been in the scene for years, but there wasn't a big likelihood that this *one* guy, the first guy to seriously interest her in years, would recognize that small signal.

From the corner of her eye, she could see his face. Judging by his reaction, it was pretty damn clear he knew exactly what it was. His pupils flared, his lids drooped low and everything about his attitude—light, friendly, flirtatious—changed.

Her mouth went dry when she saw his expression. She didn't know whether to be excited or terrified. She didn't know whether to kick herself or laugh at herself—or take off running.

What in the hell are you doing?

Back in college, Renee had played around in the bondage scene. Or maybe *playing* didn't quite describe it. Three years in the life-style went a little bit deeper than just *playing*, she knew that. Although a huge part of the reason she'd stayed so long was because of Billy—her boyfriend. The first guy she'd ever loved.

He'd only been part of why she'd gotten into it. It was the ultimate act of rebellion as far as she was concerned, something she could do that her mother had no control over, something that would make Claudia Lincoln explode if she knew—yet it was also one of the few things that Renee actually had some control over.

She decided how far she went; she decided when she'd had

enough. The sub in the BDSM lifestyle tended to have more power than an outsider realized and she'd loved having that power. She'd loved knowing that just one word from her could end everything.

But even as much as she enjoyed that, really living the life all out wasn't for her.

Rebelling might have been a huge reason why she'd done it initially, but Billy had been why she'd stayed. She'd loved him. In the end, though, it hadn't been enough for either of them.

Kinky sex games turned her on, and she loved the fantasy of submitting to a guy. But it was only fantasy—complete and total submission wasn't something she had any desire to give. She had lived too damn long under somebody's control, and even though she understood all the subtle nuances of a sub's role, understood how much control the sub really did have, committing to it seriously just didn't appeal to her.

And since things had ended with Billy, other than an occasional fantasy or hot, sweaty dream, she'd been happy to leave that part of her life behind her. Until now—until him.

The typical guy wouldn't have noticed her subtle signal, but when he leaned in closer, all but caging her with his body, she knew he wasn't the typical guy. He'd picked up on it with a deftness that came from somebody who did a little more than play the game. He dipped his head. He didn't say anything. All he did was press a hot, openmouthed kiss to her neck, and then he lifted his head. Renee kept her eyes down.

His hand came up, cupped her chin. His voice was quiet, but commanding all the same. "Look at me."

Slowly, she did. She stared into his eyes levelly and watched as a slow smile curled his lips upward. Then he trailed his hand down her neck, over her shoulder, down her arm, resting it on her thigh, just above the slit. Through the thin black material, she could feel the heat of his hand.

Already, she was wet.

Hell, she could smell it, feel it in the air, and she had no doubt that he could, too. He reached into his pocket, keeping his gaze on hers. He pulled out a key card and then murmured, "I'm in room eight-oh-one, on the concierge level. I want you in my bed, naked, in fifteen minutes."

She cocked a brow, smirked a little. "And if I'm not?"

He smiled back and bent down, bit her lower lip. "If you're not, it's both our losses." Then he dismissed her and straightened in his seat, staring straight ahead as he took another drink.

Common sense warred with want. She didn't even know his name. Renee had spent the past hour casually flirting with him, but that casual flirtation was all she'd been in the mood for. She hadn't wanted to know his name, his phone number, or where he lived—so why in the hell was she doing this?

Going to his room would be *stupid, stupid, stupid*. But as she slid out of the seat and stood on wobbly legs, key card clutched in her hand, Renee knew she didn't give a damn how stupid it was. She was doing it. The need was a hot, vicious song in her blood and she was most definitely doing it.

As she walked, she felt the cool air drift under her skirt, teasing her overheated thighs—and higher. Under her panties, she was as wet as a rainstorm and she had to suppress a whimper as the slick thong rubbed against her sensitized flesh. Before she could take a step away, a hand came up, cupped over her neck.

Obediently, she stopped but she didn't look at him. It had been a while, but she remembered the rules well enough. He squeezed, ever so gently, and murmured, "Leave the boots on." His breath caressed her cheek as he lowered his head and added, "Fifteen minutes, pet."

DEACON WAITED TWENTY minutes before he left the bar. Twenty minutes where he tried to figure out just what he was doing. Well, other than sitting there, drinking a beer he didn't want, while a gorgeous woman was up in his room, naked . . . waiting for him.

From the moment he'd looked at her, he'd felt something stir

CHAINS25

inside him. The desire to feel that sexy, perfect body moving under his, against his, had kept him at the bar, playing the light game of flirtation. It wasn't one he generally messed with too much, but he hadn't been able to leave, either.

Granted, some of that had probably been because his damned dick had been hard as pike pretty much from the get-go. But that wasn't all of it.

Brooding, he tossed back the rest of his drink and then stood up. She was waiting for him . . . Right now, that was what mattered. That was what counted. Hot anticipation burned in him as he strode out of the bar.

He was pretty sure he hadn't felt this kind of anticipation in years. Hell, maybe never. He couldn't recall the name of a single sub who'd made him feel this hot, this early in the game. There wasn't one—he knew it.

Because none of them were the one . . .

Scowling, he shoved that thought aside. Now definitely wasn't time to be thinking along those lines.

On his way through the lobby, he paused at the desk to get another key card, claiming he'd left his in his room.

After verifying his name and address, the clerk slid him another key card. He pocketed it and headed toward the elevator, his steps slow, unhurried—but all he wanted to do was storm the remaining distance, kick the door down and see if she was waiting.

She'd be waiting. He had no doubt of that. The answer had been in her eyes as she slid away from the bar, that sexy skirt tangling ever so briefly around her long legs. He'd seen the boots, remembered wondering how she'd look with just the boots.

And now, thinking of her waiting on his bed, spread out and naked for him, wearing nothing but those boots, had his cock jerking painfully under the tight confines of his jeans.

The elevator moved more slowly than Christmas and by the time he exited onto the eighth floor, he was gritting his teeth. Striding down the hall, his cock was already stiff, engorged and aching, and he knew if she wasn't in his room, he was going to end up spending the next hour in a cold shower.

What in the hell . . .

Deacon couldn't remember the last time a woman had hit him this hard. When he slid the key card in the slot, he watched the light flash green before opening the door slowly.

The sight of her lying there in his bed had about the same effect on him as if he'd sucked down a couple quarts of whiskey. His blood heated, his heart started to pound, but the only reaction he gave was a faint smile as he stepped inside and closed the door behind him.

Leaning his shoulder against the wall, he stared at her.

The dark red hair spread around her like a silken cape. He could see himself fisting a hand in that hair, wrapping it around his wrist and using it to guide her as she sucked on his cock. Other than her hair, her face and her neck, he couldn't see anything else of her body. She lay under the covers, and on the chair by the desk, he could see her clothes folded neatly. No sign of the boots, though, which meant she must be wearing them.

Cocking a brow, he drawled, "Did I say to wait under the covers?"

She shook her head.

"I didn't hear you."

A faint smirk curled her lips, a little bit mocking, a little too confident, and the sight of it had lust blistering through him. "No."

"No, what?"

And her response, it was so challenging, it took everything he had not to grab her, flip her onto her knees and take her just like that. "You want me to call you *master*, you'll have to prove you deserve it," she said softly. Then she slid out from under the covers, but she managed to move so that her hair hid much of her upper body.

He could see the slight indentation of her waist, the curve of her hip and between her thighs, the neatly trimmed patch of hair that shielded her sex. "You don't wax."

That smile tugged at her lips again and she glanced down, looking at herself. The grin widened as she looked back up at him and drawled, "Obviously not."

His lids drooped low. Damn, she was asking for it. "Why not?"

She shrugged restlessly. "Just don't care to."

Deacon nodded. Yeah, he could handle that. It didn't matter much to him—the curls between her legs looked soft and wispy and he imagined they'd feel like silk on his cock. He started to push off the wall toward her, but he had one moment of clarity. "You don't belong to somebody, do you?" Hell, it wouldn't be the first time some sassy little sub had gotten into a fight with her man and then rushed off to get it on with somebody else in a fit of pique.

Her eyes narrowed and she said in an arrogant tone, "I belong to myself."

That was answer enough, but that wasn't what he'd been referring to. She knew it. Shoving off the wall, he crossed over to where she sat on the edge of the bed. Softly, he murmured, "Lie down and spread your thighs."

Her chin arched up but she did it, lying back and letting her thighs fall open. Deacon shook his head. "Not enough, pet. I want to see that pretty pink pussy." She obliged and Deacon almost shuddered at the sight of her sex. The folds glistened pink and wet. He sat on the edge of the bed and smoothed a hand down her belly. The muscles there jumped under his hand and her skin was so silken soft. He traced her entrance with one fingertip and then pushed inside. She closed over him, snug, hot and tight. "You're wet."

Her lids drooped low and a harsh sigh escaped her. Watching her face, he finger-fucked her until her hips rose to meet each stroke of his hand, until she was panting and the muscles in her pussy went tight as the climax moved closer. Then—he stopped. Pulled his hand away and rose from the bed to stand in front of her. "Let's try this again. Do you belong to anybody?"

The outraged look in her eyes seemed totally at odds with the soft, breathy sound of her voice as she said roughly, "No. I don't have a boyfriend at home waiting for me, a master, a Dom, anybody. I haven't been involved with a guy in years."

Satisfied, he nodded. Then he hooked his thumbs in the belt loops of his jeans and said, "Stand up and undress me."

She moved slowly, almost languidly, and Deacon tortured himself watching her breasts sway with her movements. The plump, small curves were topped with nipples a deep, dark pink. She unbuttoned his shirt and then left it on his shoulders to reach for his belt. "No. Take the shirt all the way off. Hang it up."

He waited for some sign of resistance, but instead, she slid the shirt away and he turned his head, watching as she crossed the room, staring at the absolute perfection of her heart-shaped ass. The black leather encased her legs up over her knees and he wanted to see her tied to the bed, facedown, that perfect ass in the air while she wore those boots. "There's a black bag on the top shelf. I want it."

Deacon hadn't really planned on much happening for him on this quick visit home, but he'd been a Boy Scout. He did like to be prepared. He hadn't brought much, a pair of cuffs, some lubricant and a box of Trojans. It would be enough, but damn, what he would give to see her back at his house, bent over some of the restraint equipment he'd rigged up with his own two hands, to take a dildo he'd selected just for her and listen to her moan as he pushed it inside her ass.

She had to rise on her tiptoes to reach the bag. Deacon supposed he could have gotten it for her, but he didn't have that much time to establish some modicum of control over her. They had only the night.

Fleetingly, he decided that was a serious bitch. Somehow, he knew that one or two nights with this woman wasn't going to be enough.

She brought him the bag and he took it, tossed it onto the bed. Then he slid a hand up her front, trailing his fingers over one nipple, up, curling over the back of her neck. "Probably need to get a few ground rules out of the way," he murmured. "You got any lines you'd rather me not cross?"

Tipping her head back, she stared at him with dark, forest green eyes and replied, "I can take damn near anything you want to give me."

Deacon laughed softly. "You really ought to learn to watch that mouth, pet. It could get you into so much trouble with this kind of game." He pressed his thumb against her lower lip and repeated, "Got any lines?"

Her lids flickered. "I won't do another woman—and I won't do threesomes. One-on-one or I walk. I don't do hard-core pain. If that's your thing, then it's best I leave now. Other than that . . ." She shrugged her shoulders restlessly and then gave him that same cocky, confident smile. "Other than that, I can take almost anything you want to give me."

"Got a safe word you like to use?"

Again, that cool, almost dismissive smile. "I gave you my lines. I'm thinking I won't need one."

For some reason, her carelessness made Deacon furious. Hardening his voice, he said, "You'll pick a safe word. Whether you think you'll need it or not. And you really should be more careful."

"If I was careful, I wouldn't be up here with you, now, would I?"

He pressed his thumb against her lips again, harder, effectively silencing her. "That wasn't a question. That was a statement. The next time you speak without me addressing you first, you'll get down on your knees and suck my cock until I'm satisfied you understand the rules."

It didn't seem possible, but her forest green eyes got even darker and the smell of her seemed hotter. *She* seemed hotter. "Your safe word will be *green*," he said quietly, studying her eyes. "Do you understand me?"

One slow nod.

He turned away briefly, digging out the box of Trojans and tossing it on the bedside table. "When you first walked into the bar, I saw your mouth and I wondered how it would look wrapped around my dick. I want you to show me."

She started to sink to her knees in front of him, but he fisted a hand in her hair. "No. Bend over. The mirror is behind you. I'll be able to see that tight ass and your wet pussy while you suck me off. Spread your legs for me."

She whimpered. That soft sound of female hunger went straight to his head and all he wanted to do was push her to her knees, mount her and fuck her, but he didn't. The longer he held off, the better it would be for both of them—and he already knew it was going to be damn good.

Taking the rubber, he put it in her hands and said, "Put it on me. Nice and slow."

Nice and slow, that was exactly how she did it, bent over in that awkward pose with his hand fisted in her hair and her ass sticking out. Deacon had to adjust his position a little so he could touch her, see her the way he wanted. Yeah . . . under the fringe of his lashes, he stared at their reflection and felt his cock jerk with need at the sight.

Trailing his fingers down her back, he spread the cheeks of her ass and eyed the tight pucker there, thought of watching it flower open around his—

Day-um. She had finished putting the condom on, rolling it down his aching length and then, without waiting another five seconds, she took him in her mouth. Deep—deep—deep. He could feel her throat muscles working to accommodate him and when she swallowed, Deacon thought he just might come from that alone.

Reining himself in, he managed a bored, if slightly hoarse tone

as he said, "On your knees." If he kept staring at her ass, this would
be over way too soon. She sank gracefully, smoothly, to her knees,
keeping his cock in her mouth and stroking him with a skill that
threatened to eradicate any bit of self-control he might have.

By the time the skin of his balls went tight, Deacon knew that
they couldn't keep doing this, not unless he wanted to come before
he'd even started touching her. "Enough."

Obediently, she sat back on her heels.

"Push your hair back. I can't see your breasts." Her breasts
lifted and fell as she reached back, scooped her hair up. "You have
pretty breasts, pet." Leaving her kneeling before him, he turned
and studied the room. Not much to work with. Nodding his head
toward the floor by the desk, he said, "Go over there. Kneel down
and wait for me."

The cuffs and the leg of the desk would have to work. Digging
into the open suitcase by the wardrobe, he found a couple of ties.
One he balled up and pressed into her hand. "When you want me
to stop, drop it," he said as he crouched in front of her.

She glanced down and then back up. "I won't need it."

That was what the other tie was for. She seemed determined
to push every aggressive, demanding switch he had. "Open your
mouth," he ordered. She did so without hesitation and when he
used the tie as a makeshift gag, she still managed to stare at him
insolently.

"Fuck," he muttered. "No wonder you don't belong to anybody.
You're enough to try a saint, pet."

He shifted around behind her and guided her body into the position he wanted, lying belly down on the carpeted floor, her arms
stretched over head and held in place by the cuffs. The cuffs he
looped around one desk leg and he tossed his bag onto the floor by
her head. Grabbing the extra pillows from the dresser, he pushed
them under her hips and then said, "I'm going to eat your pussy
now. You can make as much noise as the gag will let you, but if you
come before I tell you that you can come, I'll punish you."

Trailing a hand down her ass, he stroked the soft, plump curves. "Would you like to know what your punishment is?" Without waiting for a response, he spanked her. Three times in hard, fast succession, and when he was done, her ass was blushing the sweetest shade of pink. Her breath came in harsh, ragged gasps—but she hadn't made a sound. A quick glance revealed that she still held the balled-up tie.

Stretching himself out between her legs, he pushed them apart and pressed his mouth to her core. She was shockingly, searingly wet, the slick, silky juices of her pussy coating her folds and even rolling down her thighs in glistening wet paths. He started there, licking that sweet moisture away, closer and closer, until he could fit his mouth to her entry and plunge his tongue into her sex. She moaned behind the gag. That soft, feminine sound of surrender fired the blaze burning inside him and everything inside him focused on her, on the sounds of hunger that came from behind the gag, her soft, strangled moans, the rocking rhythm of her hips.

She particularly liked it when he circled her entrance with his tongue while he used his fingers on her clit. And she liked it when he sucked on the sensitive folds, when he bit her ever so softly. So damn responsive—and controlled. He pushed her close to orgasm but each time, she held off.

The fourth time Deacon sensed she was near, he pulled away and crouched between her thighs. He ran his hands over the sweet curves of her ass and then leaned in, rested his chin on her shoulder so that his body covered hers. "You did good," he muttered against her ear. "I can't decide if I'm happy about that or not. I was really looking forward to spanking that pretty ass again."

She groaned and rolled her hips. Grinning, Deacon straightened and stared down at her quivering body. "You want to be spanked, pet?" he asked gently, resting a hand on her butt.

No response. He reached between her thighs and plunged two fingers inside her sex, stroking until he felt that climax moving near—and then he stopped. "I asked you a question. Do you like to be spanked?"

Finally, a slight nod. Almost as if she hadn't wanted to respond. Fuck, Deacon hadn't had this much fun with a woman in years. Hot, ball-busting and heart-pounding, but fun nonetheless. He'd yet to find a submissive who didn't bore him after a few days, a few weeks—but something about this woman told him that boredom would be a long time coming. Maybe even never.

Already he could feel something binding him to her—something that went deeper than sex, deeper than desire. Something he couldn't explain.

"Good girl," he crooned. Rising, he pulled up the table leg so she could pull her hands back, and then he scooped her up into his arms, carried her to the bed and sat down with her lying ass up across his lap.

"Let's see just how much you like to be spanked."

Deacon found out the answer to that was . . . *a lot*. Three carefully placed strikes and she was rocking and writhing on his lap, and he could feel the heat of her arousal penetrating his jeans. "Should I stop?" he asked, half wishing she'd nod—and drop the damn tie she still held clutched in her hand.

He wanted to fuck her. So bad he hurt with it.

But she shook her head, almost frantically, and Deacon slapped her ass again. And again. Her butt blushed pink for him, his cock got harder and harder and both of them were sweating. He asked again, "Are you ready for me to stop?"

She whimpered behind the gag. But continued to hold the tie. Okay—normally, Deacon would have kept going. His control was absolute—but not with this woman. Time to change tactics. Working the knot on the tie loose, he pulled it out of her mouth and hauled her against him.

"Are you ready to get fucked?"

Her eyes were wide and glassy, her face flushed a pretty shade of pink. "Yes."

"Tell me. Say, *I'm ready to get fucked, Master*," he ordered. And he prayed she would.

When she did speak, Deacon was so damn ready, he could have shoved her onto the floor, spread her thighs and taken her right like that. "I'm ready to get fucked . . . Master."

"Good girl," he praised, stroking her ass. It was warm under his hand and he imagined the flesh was stinging from the number of times he'd spanked her. Shifting their position, he bent her over the bed so that it supported her upper body. Then he reached around and snagged his bag, digging out his lubricant and tossing it on the floor beside him.

Leaning over her, he whispered, "I'm going to fuck your ass." Making sure she saw him over her shoulder, he replaced her gag and said, "If that bothers you . . ." Then he glanced at the tie. Her hands were in front of her, trapped between the bed and her body. Scowling, he moved away from her long enough to get the key, free her wrists and then recuff them at the base of her spine. Tucking the tie into her hands once again, he said, "You drop the tie if you don't want this."

Instead of dropping it, her fingers went tight. Chuckling, Deacon grabbed the lubricant. After coating his sheathed cock with the lubricant, he squeezed some into his palm, slathering it over his fingers. Resting one hand on the base of her spine, he pressed his slicked fingers against her ass and pushed.

Behind the makeshift gag, Renee wheezed for air. The sensations burning through her body were intense, more intense than anything she'd ever experienced. It had been years since she had done this, years since she'd gone this far. In the back of her mind, a voice warned that this was a little more intense than she usually went, and that this wasn't a game, wasn't some personal rebellion for the guy who knelt behind her, preparing her body for his use in a way so skillfully seductive, it was almost as arousing as his mouth on her pussy—or that spanking.

Renee liked being spanked. More than anything else as far as the kinky sex games went. She loved being spanked but she hadn't ever come so close to climax just from that. But this . . . oh, man, this . . . the years she'd spent acting the sub to her college boyfriend, it hadn't prepared her for this.

Anal sex before had always been more about the submitting, the control—the kink. The rebellion. This was hot—this was need—and yet, as his free hand smoothed gently up her back, stroking tense muscles, she sensed a tenderness that she hadn't been prepared for. She still held the tie clutched in her hands, and although she hadn't once thought of dropping it, he handled her with care, moving slowly enough that she'd have time to act before he went any further.

By the time he had fully prepared her passage for his cock, she was burning. Literally burning inside, outside, fire shooting through and through. The sensation of that thick, rounded head pressing against her anus was mind-blowing. He lingered for just a second and murmured, "Do you want this?" Behind the gag, she moaned. He ordered, "Nod if you want it."

She nodded so hard it was amazing the gag didn't dislodge itself.

Without waiting another second, he pushed inside. As tenderly masterful as he had been from the beginning, this sudden, near-brutal possession was shocking. Arousingly, almost painfully so, he pushed inside with one deep stroke, relentless and merciless, pushing deeper and deeper. Scalding hot pain ripped through her and for one second, she thought she'd reached her limit. Sex games were a power thing for her—proving to herself that she could take whatever a man wanted to dish out, as long as he didn't outright hurt her.

But as his thick cock pushed deeper and deeper, stretching her more and more, she almost dropped the tie. Then he reached around, hooked two fingers inside her pussy and scissored them inside as he rotated his thumb against her clit. Behind the gag, she screamed, thrust back—and came.

Hard and fast.

Behind her, he said in a flat, almost bored tone, "You weren't supposed to come yet, pet." He pulled his fingers out of her pussy and rested the flat of his hand on her rump. "Remember the punishment?" He didn't wait for a response, just spanked her. Harder than before, harder than she really liked, yet she loved it. He started to thrust deep, hard and fast, hurting her, making her ass clench around his invading cock, burning and stretching—and she loved it. He took her with a force that practically had her teeth rattling.

Slap, thrust. Slap, thrust. Deep, hard digs of his cock, followed by harsh, stinging blows from his hand, and each one made her burn more and more. She could feel her climax moving on her again and she started to push back, meeting his thrusts, desperate to come. But he stopped. He shoved in deep, forcing his cock completely inside her ass so that his lower belly was cuddled against her bottom. The hand that had been slapping her ass now rested on her hip. In a harsh, authoritative voice, he commanded, "You come when *I* say you can."

Then he resumed shafting her, bracing his hands on her hips, holding her still for the relentless, intimate invasion. She neared climax again, but this time, she whimpered and tried to hold back. Wrapping the tie around her still-cuffed wrists, she jerked tight, focusing on the silk biting into her skin and hoping that slight pain would ward off the need to come.

It didn't . . . oh, so damn close . . . Whimpering, mewling desperately, she swung her head around and stared at him pleadingly over her shoulder. A smile curved his lips. He slowed the pace of his thrusts and bent over, purred into her ear, "You can come now."

Slowly, he straightened, holding so still inside her body that she could feel the jerking sensations of his cock. And then—he moved. Slapped her ass—

Renee came, hard and violent, shuddering and shaking beneath the force of it. Dimly, she was aware that he was coming, too, his control apparently shattered as he growled and swore, his hands going to her hips and gripping her with bruising force. Her own climax seemed to last forever, and his—even longer.

By the time he stopped moving inside her, she had collapsed onto the bed, darkness washing over her. She sank into a void of unconsciousness, not even aware that he had finally stopped thrusting, and was cuddling around her and holding her close.

Holding her like she mattered.

When she came out of that dark, brief slumber, she was still on the bed and he was curled around her, holding her with gentle, strong arms. One hand moved up and down her back, massaging the muscles low in her spine and then, as he realized she was awake, he rolled her onto her belly and straddled her back, placing his hands on her shoulders and massaging them. "Your muscles are in knots," he murmured. Glancing over her shoulder at him, she saw a wry smile on his lips and he added, "If I hadn't fucked you into blacking out, I'd almost worry about my abilities."

"Hmmm. Oh, no need to worry there." She groaned as his thumbs found a particularly tight spot just a little under her neck and to the right. "How long was I out?"

"Ten minutes, give or take," he murmured. He nodded toward the bedside table and she saw the cuffs and the ties lying there. "Long enough to uncuff you and wash up a little."

She blushed, realizing he was talking about her, as well as himself. He grinned. She could see it from the corner of her eyes. "You just let me fuck your ass, pet. You really shouldn't blush because I cleaned up our mess."

Turning her face into the mattress, she muttered, "Says you."

A few moments passed and she felt the tension in her muscles melting away under his skilled hands. Damn, did he have good hands. She'd almost drifted back off when he stopped, pausing long enough to stroke his hand down her back. The bed shifted under his weight as he settled with his back against the headboard.

She smiled up at him, but one look at the serious expression on his face caused her smile to fade.

"What is it? You went and got all serious all of a sudden."

He combed his hand through her hair. "You need to be more careful," he said quietly.

Cocking a brow at him, she repeated, "Careful? You mean like 'not going with strange men to their rooms' careful or a different kind of careful?"

"A different kind." The hand in her hair tightened. "I get the feeling this isn't a serious thing for you. You play at it. If that's what works for you, fine. But if you aren't more careful, you're going to have problems."

Blood rushed to her cheeks, but she didn't let herself squirm or look away. "If I was *careful*, we wouldn't be here. And unless I'm mistaken, you enjoyed yourself quite a bit."

"Not exactly the kind of careful I'm talking about . . . Although, woman, you probably shouldn't be running off with some strange guy, Dom or no Dom. I'm talking about basic common sense that anybody who lives this lifestyle—or just plays at it—needs to know."

"Is this about a safe word?" she demanded. Rolling her eyes, she said, "If it will make you feel better, I promise I'll use one the next time you fuck me. Does that make you feel better . . . Master?" She dipped her head and trailed her lips over his thigh, smiling to herself as she heard the slight catch in his breath as her hair brushed against his cock.

"Just tell me you'll be more careful," he muttered, fisting a hand in her hair.

"I'll be more careful." She peeked up at him through her hair and saw that the serious expression in his eyes had been replaced by a different one—one of heat and hunger.

"Are you going to freak out if I ask you to spend the night?" he rasped, grabbing another condom from the bedside table.

A smile tugged at her lips as he tore the package open and put the condom on. Shoot, she hadn't been looking forward to leaving, truth be told. Lowering her head, she kissed the tip of his cock and then glanced back up at him. With a wicked grin, she replied, "If you want me for the night, all you have to do is say the word . . . Master."

2

Around ten thirty, Deacon replayed her words in his head and wished he'd said a few different words before they drifted off to sleep sometime around four in the morning. Something like . . . *Don't leave until you give me your name, your number, your home address and preferably your house key.*

They hadn't spent the entire night having sex. Although that had been so fricking amazing, he was still reeling from it. He'd even . . . Closing his eyes, he rested his head back against the door and remembered how they had been eating a pizza around one a.m. Some pizza sauce had splattered on his thigh. She had put her slice down and rolled onto her knees and crawled across the bed to lick it off.

He hadn't said a word. Not when she licked it off, not when she straightened long enough to grab a condom and put it on his rigid dick, and not when she'd straddled him. Deacon liked to call the shots when it came to sex. Not all the women he slept with were into the bondage deal, and he didn't always have to have that— but when he was with a woman, he made the moves. He initiated things. When he wanted a blow job, he made sure the woman got the point, and when he wanted . . . well, hell. He couldn't remember ever wanting a woman on top.

But she'd straddled him, staring into his eyes, almost as if she was challenging him to say she couldn't—and then she'd ridden him until they'd both come, moaning into each other's mouths.

Mind-blowing, all right. The sex had been hotter than anything he'd ever known, but there was something more. A connection. They'd watched a scary movie and she had squealed at the gross parts, but kept watching, and when it ended, she'd been as disgusted by the ending as he'd been. "Whatever happened to the good guy reigning triumphant?" she'd demanded.

They'd gotten into a discussion about movies, realized they had many of the same favorites.

Deacon wasn't so sure he believed in love at first sight, or at least he hadn't *thought* he believed in it. But there had been something between them.

If he didn't sleep like a damn rock, he would have woken up as she dressed and slipped away. Now it was too late. He'd spent the past two hours in the lobby, waiting for her.

But in his gut, he knew she'd already checked out.

Since he hadn't even gotten her name or her room number, he had no way of finding her.

And plenty of time to regret it.

FOURTEEN HOURS AFTER she'd walked out of the man's room—at six a.m., after less than two hours of sleep, Renee stumbled into the bathroom at the home she'd inherited from her mother. Kicking the door shut behind her, she stripped out of her clothes, leaving them where they fell as she headed to the shower.

Tight, sore, abused muscles screamed in protest and she groaned, thoroughly exhausted and aching. She hurt in the way a woman hurt only after a night of seriously *good* sex. She hurt in a way she hadn't hurt in years.

Even when the sex had been good between her and Billy, she didn't remember it being that good. Of course, her one boyfriend probably didn't make her an expert, even though he'd gotten better at it as time went on. Both of them had. Something had attracted Billy to the BDSM lifestyle and Renee, ready to do something she shouldn't, had followed.

It had held more appeal for Billy in the long run than it had for her. It had been fun—for her. For him, it had gotten to the point that her refusal to acquiesce and submit to his every need had pissed him off. The day came when he decided he wanted to have himself a little three-way action and he'd assumed *ordering* her into it would work. When it hadn't, they ended up having the fight to end all fights. They'd tried to make it work out for a few more months, but they were just fooling themselves.

He got hard-core into a lifestyle that was little more than sex games to her.

It sucked, especially because they really had loved each other. Love just hadn't been enough. Or maybe they hadn't loved each other as much as they'd thought.

She didn't know.

If her time with Billy had been anything like last night, who knows? Maybe she would have seen a greater appeal. She doubted it, though. She'd been purposefully arrogant, pushing—hell, she didn't even know what to call him—pushing that guy's buttons just to see how he'd react. She'd done likewise to Billy and it had pissed him off. This guy, though? All it had done was make him hotter.

And man, they could talk. He'd made her laugh; he'd made her think. He'd seen past the cool surface and saw secrets most people never realized were there. He saw her reservations; he saw her hidden anxieties . . . all from one night.

"Maybe it's better like this," she mumbled to herself. If he could see her that clearly after one night, how much would he see after days together?

Too much.

She didn't want him seeing the guilt she carried inside, the weaknesses and the anger. Bad enough she had to live with it. She wasn't going to share it with others.

Renee turned the shower on, letting it heat up and steam up the air before she climbed in. She used the bathroom and then headed into the shower, letting the hot water soothe tired, aching muscles. But she remembered the feel of his hands on her shoulders, kneading the tension away better than a week of hot showers could.

Staying under the spray until the water started to cool and her fingers had gone all wrinkly, she finally turned the shower off and stepped outside. The moment her feet touched the rug just outside the shower, she froze.

Something was wrong. Her skin crawled, the hair on the back of her neck stood up and everything inside her screamed out a warning.

Grabbing the robe from a hook by the shower stall, she shoved her arms into it and crept to the door. It wasn't that late, but the house had that dead silence feel to it. She'd sent the house staff home early, needing some peace and quiet. Although Madison was only an hour away from the Cincinnati hotel where she had stayed last night, she'd spent the entire day running around, driving here, driving there.

Meetings with the lawyers and two different Realtors, and a stop by her parents' graves had kept her on her feet all damn day. The rest of the week promised to be every bit as busy. So instead of accepting Lily's offer to cook her up a nice, hot meal, Renee had sent the cook, the housekeeper and everybody else home.

She needed privacy.

Privacy as she dealt with being in her mother's home for the first time in fifteen years. When she'd come back for the funeral, she'd stayed at the Inn, unwilling to come back to this house. Unwilling, and just not ready.

She had been ready this time.

But now she wished she hadn't had everybody leave.

Slipping outside of the bathroom, she looked up and then down the hall and saw nothing, heard nothing. She couldn't see any reason for the fine hairs on the back of her neck to be standing up on edge, but nonetheless, they were.

A warm breeze cut through the hallway and she turned her head, glanced toward the staircase. That was when she saw it.

The front door was wide open. She could see it from there.

Terror lit through her. She had closed it, double-checked twice to make sure it was locked. Habit, after living the past ten years in a much larger city. It had been locked. But now it was wide open and the warm summer breeze was blowing through the big, old house. Images from every second-rate horror flick she'd ever seen flashed through her mind, and instead of heading downstairs to investigate, she retreated back into the bathroom, locked the door and grabbed her jeans from the floor.

Her cell phone was still clipped to the waistband and she pulled it free with shaking hands.

SCREAMING SIRENS WEREN'T exactly the norm for Madison. Deacon didn't think that much had changed in the years since he'd left. During his frequent trips home over the past fifteen years, it had seemed as though very, very little had changed.

But this was definitely new—two county sheriff cars speeding down the quiet road and then turning down the drive that led to the Lincolns' home. Dr. Reginald Lincoln had died years ago—suicide, although that part of his death was kept hush-hush. Mrs. Lincoln had died a few years ago—Deacon remembered his mother telling him that, as well as the fact that the house had been left to their only daughter. Renee had come to the funeral, but hadn't stayed long enough to see to her dead mother's affairs.

Deacon hadn't ever had much interaction with Renee, but he did remember her and her folks. Cold-eyed, emotionless bastards who had been more concerned with appearances than with their daughter. Renee had been the picture-perfect prom queen, beautiful, aloof and arrogant.

Renee had been part of the 'in' crowd as much as his high school girlfriend, Lacey, had been, but they'd run in different circles.

Lacey . . . Man, he hadn't thought of her in years. She'd be here at some point and Deacon wondered how he'd feel when he saw her, wondered if maybe he should have rescheduled his visit home. He had graduated a year ahead of Lacey and the reunion deal wasn't his thing.

He hadn't even known about the reunion for the class of '94 until Seth had mentioned it when they'd e-mailed last, a few weeks back.

The reunion meant Lacey would be coming home.

Lacey. Renee. Sherra.

That night—shit. That night had changed his entire life. It had been the beginning of the end of him and Lacey.

Considering the witnesses—Renee, Lacey and himself—Boyd's parents hadn't had much luck convincing the DA to press charges against Sherra. But self-defense or not, it had been ugly, watching as a young man bled to death in a matter of seconds.

Curious about the squad cars, he headed down the hall and paused by his mother's bedroom. Her private duty nurse, Callie, had finished getting the older woman into bed, and Immi had already drifted off to sleep. Keeping his voice low, he murmured, "I'm going to run across the street. Will you be okay for a little while?"

Callie smiled, nodded and settled down in the armchair by the bed with a book in hand. Deacon had one second to register the author's name written across the top half of the cover in huge, bloodred font.

Sherra Salinger.

The reigning queen of horror, she'd been called. He'd seen her books on the bestseller lists online and he'd bought a couple, read enough to know that she was seriously talented—and seriously warped. The imagination that girl had was surreal. And against his will, he found himself remembering that night.

The night he'd heard his high school girlfriend screaming his name, pissed and terrified. The night he'd run in to see JD Whitcomb on top of a struggling, terrified girl while Lacey, Deacon's girlfriend, fought to help. Deacon hadn't realized it was Sherra until later—when he'd seen her standing over Boyd's body, her clothes and hands splattered with his blood.

How many of her nightmarish stories came from that night?

Hell, he had nightmares of his own about it. He hadn't realized just how much blood a human body could hold until Boyd's had come gushing out through the vicious gash in his throat.

What she'd done had been necessary; of that Deacon had no doubt.

Boyd and JD would have killed the four of them if they'd been able to. Deacon had seen it in JD's eyes, an utter lack of emotion, and he'd known there weren't many lines JD wouldn't cross. Boyd had been such a follower, he would have done whatever JD told him to and not once stopped to question whether it was something he *should* do.

Not until it was too late.

Sherra's actions had saved lives—possibly all of theirs.

But Deacon wondered now, as he had in the past, how much that had cost her.

It sure as hell had left a mark on Lacey, on himself.

The piercing wail of sirens intruded on his thoughts once more and he headed down the grand staircase at a jog, wondering if any of them had emerged from that night unscathed.

A faint smirk twisted his lips as he drew closer to the Lincoln house. If any of them had come through unaffected, it would be Renee. Definitely her parents' daughter, Renee was a cool, icy piece of work—a veritable ice queen—and he doubted much of anything could penetrate that icy shroud enough to see if anything worth finding lay below the surface.

Seeing a man killed right in front of her hadn't seemed to do that much damage; Deacon knew that. He could still remember the way she'd been that night, standing off to the side, her hands clasped neatly in front of her, and she'd answered the questions from the police in a polite, bored tone. The rest of them, they'd been a mess. But Renee, the picture-perfect prom queen, could have been discussing the weather for all the emotion she showed.

Even with a bruise on her face, one that looked vaguely handshaped, she had looked icy-cold and beautiful. Her dark hair had been styled in an intricate braid, her makeup perfect, unsmudged, highlighting ivory skin and dark eyes . . .

A shiver raced down his spine. He frowned as something illusive danced just out of his reach. Renee . . . ?

But he shook it off as he crossed the road and headed up the Lincolns' driveway. During the day, he imagined the grass would still be emerald green, manicured and trimmed and landscaped to perfection.

Perfection—that was what the Lincolns were about. They had their perfect daughter and they had paired her up with the town's golden boy, JD Whitcomb—would-be rapist. Smirking, he wondered what the Lincolns had thought of that, how Renee had reacted once the shock of the night had passed.

Taking the final curve of the drive, he took in the scene of sheriffs' cars, an ambulance and four uniformed deputies. Four—damn, something big must have happened, he thought. An absent, almost abstract thought drifted through his mind—he hoped Renee hadn't been hurt or anything.

Speaking of perfection, what lay before him would have been enough to totally incense the late Miz Lincoln. There was a flashy red convertible in front of the house but it would have to spend some serious time in a body shop because somebody had spray painted it, slashed the tires and the thick, durable material of the ragtop. More destruction spread out from the car, leading to the front door. Huge flowerpots upended, a couple of garden statues shattered and smashed. More spray paint.

It had been a quick job, as though whoever did it wanted to do as much damage as possible in a very short amount of time.

He crossed paths with Grady Morris, the chief deputy sheriff. Grady was studying the flower beds with his arms crossed over his chest and a faint frown on his face.

"Hey, Morris. What's going on?"

Grady glanced at him, his hazel eyes vague behind the lenses of his glasses. Then he blinked and smiled. "Hey, back." Jerking his head back toward the Lincoln home, he said, "Got us a case of vandalism, I guess."

Deacon blinked. "Four deputies, the sheriff and an ambulance for vandalism?"

Grady shrugged and grimaced. "The nine-one-one call was a little vague. Woman on a cell phone, panicky; then the phone just went dead. Better safe than sorry. Not to mention that this is the most entertainment we get around here."

Snorting, Deacon muttered, "Yeah, I bet Renee is real entertained right about now." He pushed his fingers through his hair, studying the destroyed flower beds for a second. "But since this is the entertainment, I might as well get a good seat." He waved to Grady and headed closer to the house.

A familiar voice reached his ears and he worked his way through the crowd to find Seth Salinger, Sherra's twin brother, standing in front of a woman with tangled, wet hair, wearing a robe and nothing else.

Seth had a disgusted, almost cruel look to his face, and that was enough out of character for Seth that Deacon found himself frowning.

With her head downcast and her shoulders slumped, she looked frail. Delicate—almost as if a good gust of wind would blow her right over. She stood with her back to him, arms wrapped around her middle and shaking her head in response to a question Seth had just asked.

"You didn't hear anything?" Deacon heard Seth asking as he drew closer to the sheriff and the woman.

She might look frail, Deacon thought absently, but it certainly wouldn't show in her voice. There was pure steel underlying her words as she gritted out, "Haven't I already explained this once or twice?"

That voice was familiar. Extremely.

Seth shrugged. "Just a little weird this kind of damage could happen without you hearing anything. So how much did you have to drink?"

"Not a damn thing," she replied. Her voice was strong and confident, despite the softness of it. That was when his body made the connection. His head was a little slower, but his body already recognized her. As she stood there with her head bent and her arms wrapped around her midsection, Deacon was struck by a wave of lust so intense and strong, he could have doubled over from the pain of it.

"You sure as hell don't seem very interested in helping me out, Ms. Lincoln," Seth said, and he leveled a glare at the woman.

Renee.

Shit.

He'd spent the night fucking the prom queen.

The glare Seth gave her had every protective instinct Deacon had growling and rumbling just below the surface. As Seth loomed closer, Deacon closed the distance between them in two long steps.

Just in time to see her shift a little and square off with Seth. In profile, her features were every bit as lovely, as timelessly beautiful, as they'd been last night. Her eyes, though dark and troubled, met Seth's stare without backing down.

Any appearance of frailty was gone. "You seem more interested in finding a way to blame this on me. Or is it something else you blame me for, Seth?"

Deacon edged closer. From the corner of her eye, she saw him, and her gaze swung around to meet his. The world underneath his feet seemed to crumble, time faded away and for a few minutes, life just stopped.

Her eyes widened when she saw his face, a soft blush rushing to her cheeks, but he didn't say anything to her just yet. Hell, he wasn't sure if he *could* say anything coherent to her—well, other than, *Why in the hell did you leave like that* or maybe *Get your ass back in my bed, now*. He had a feeling this wasn't the time for either of those.

So instead, he focused on Seth. If he spoke to her before he had a chance to absorb this, Deacon was likely to make a fricking fool of himself. "Somebody's been causing some trouble here, it looks like," he said.

Seth snorted. "Make that two somebodies. What are you doing here, Deacon?"

There was a faint, harsh gasp. Unable to resist, he glanced into Renee's eyes for a second, watched the pupils flare, saw the speculation in her gaze, followed by slow understanding. He wanted to reach out and touch her, pull her against him and stroke away the shadows, the doubts and the fear he sensed within her.

Instead, he responded to Seth. "Heard the squad cars from Mom's. Came down to make sure everything was okay." Taking a slow, deliberate look around, he stared at the seriously damaged car, the destroyed flower beds and smashed garden statues. "I'd imagine seeing something like this would throw a person for a loop. I dunno about you, but if it happened to me, and then a cop jumped down my throat, I sure as hell wouldn't care if I did a damn thing to make your job easier."

"I never met a Lincoln yet that was interested in anything, or anybody, beyond themselves. They don't give a flying fuck about my job and it wouldn't matter if I came in here smiling like a politician."

"I'd rather have the damn politician if I had my choice," Renee said, calling Seth's attention back to her.

"Hell, Seth, I've seen you be nicer to people you've arrested than you're being to her," Deacon snapped, pissed off. Pissed off at the dismissive, insulting way Seth treated Renee.

Pissed off—and damn possessive.

Brooding, he thought, *Not good. Not fricking good at all.*

A dull red flush stained Seth's cheeks and he jerked his gaze away from Renee, glaring at Deacon. Deacon glared right back.

He liked Seth, knew him well enough to know exactly what the problem was here. But he'd be damned if he let Renee bear the brunt of Seth's anger.

"You know something, Deacon? This doesn't really concern you, does it?"

Without batting an eyelash, Deacon responded, "Sure it does. She's entitled to legal counsel."

Curling his lip, Seth said, "She's not under arrest. Last I checked, only suspects needed counsel. Not the victims of a crime."

Deacon shrugged. "Then stop treating her like a damn criminal."

"Excuse me, boys," Renee interrupted. "You know, I'm capable of speaking for myself." She shot Deacon a narrow look, one that had him torn between frustration and reluctant amusement. Cocking her head, she gave Seth an icy glare. "Is there anything else you need from me, Sheriff?"

Snapping his notepad closed, Seth tucked it back inside his jacket. With a scowl, he said, "No, but they are going to be a while." He tucked his hands in his back pockets and turned his head to study the car. "That car of yours is going to cost some money to get fixed. Of course, I don't suppose that's a problem for you."

"Tell me something, Seth. Do you hate me because I was born with money? Or because of what JD did?"

She asked it softly, in a bland, polite tone. But Deacon already knew the answer, and when Seth's eyes cut to her face, Deacon could see the knowledge reflected in her eyes as well. "I don't hate you, Ms. Lincoln."

Snorting derisively, she said, "Yeah, and I'm going to buy that line, too."

"I hardly know you—I've got no reason to hate you," Seth said defensively.

Coolly, she said, "That's absolutely right."

Her large green eyes glanced over at Deacon, for just the briefest second, and then she turned back toward the house. "I'm going to get some stuff together so I can stay in town for a few days."

Like hell, Deacon thought, moving to follow. Renee paused in midstep and looked back at Seth. "I had nothing to do with what JD did to your sister, Seth. Nothing. I'm not going to pay for choices he made or things he did."

That dull red flush stained Seth's face once more, but he met her gaze head-on. "You might not have had anything to do with it, but you were his girlfriend. Sure as hell doesn't say much about your taste in guys or the kind of person you are."

A faint smile came and went. Renee reached up and brushed a hand over her cheek, and she looked incredibly sad. "And making the judgment calls you're making—what does that say about you?"

Then she turned and headed into the house.

"You don't need to be messing with stuff in there yet," Seth called after her.

She paused on the steps and looked back. "I'm just getting my bags and leaving. I promise, I can do that without getting in your way."

As she disappeared inside the house, Deacon looked at Seth. "He hit her, you know."

Seth blinked. "What?"

"When I saw Renee that night, she had a bruise on her face.

Somebody had slapped her, and I don't think we need to guess who did it," Deacon said. He paused, waited for that bit of information to sink into Seth's thick skull and then he added, "She was also there trying to help your sister, Seth. It wasn't just Lacey and it wasn't just me. Hell, I'm sure you read the reports about that night by now. You know what happened."

A muscle jerked in Seth's jaw but he remained silent. The rage in his eyes hadn't faded, though. Not at all.

Softly, Deacon said, "You want to hate her by association? That doesn't make you much better than the people who went around saying that Sherra deserved what happened because of who she was."

From the corner of his eye, he could see Seth's hand curling into a fist. Deacon waited, tensed, ready. But Seth just turned and walked away.

3

Deacon.

She was still trying to wrap her mind around that little piece of information as she dug through her bags with shaking hands. Renee grabbed the first things she could find, a pair of jeans and a tank top.

She'd spent the night in bed with *Deacon Cross*. Renee had thought there was something oddly familiar about him, but she hadn't really thought she *knew* him.

It took two tries before she could manage to get her jeans on, and her fingers trembled so hard, she could barely fasten the button. Renee was cold, through and through, frozen to the core.

The vicious, ugly destruction outside her house and into the foyer, all done so silently she'd never heard a sound. That she could be in the shower while somebody came in and cut into furniture, tore up her car, messed up the meticulous flower beds—and she'd never known. Never heard them.

Ugly images of those stupid B movies started flashing through her head once more. The girl in the shower, never aware somebody was in her house, not until somebody grabs her from behind and slices her throat—

"Oh, God . . ." she moaned and covered her mouth with her hand, trying to keep the whimpers silent.

She'd been handling it, though. She'd been handling it fine until the sheriff showed up. Seth Salinger. Of all people. She hadn't heard that he had taken over the job, and it wasn't something she would have thought would happen. Not in a million years. Right up until he opened his mouth and all his blatant dislike of her came pouring out, she'd been handling things just fine.

But the way he'd spoken to her, the way he'd looked at her, had ripped apart the shreds of her control.

Sure as hell doesn't say much about your taste in guys or the kind of person you are.

"The person I *was*," Renee muttered. "And I was just a damn kid." But it didn't assuage the guilt. She'd blamed herself for JD, for the actions of her parents for years, and she'd thought she moved past it.

Obviously, she was wrong.

There was no knock, no sound outside the door, but as she reached for the tank top, her skin broke out into goose bumps. Her stomach went tight and her breathing went shallow. Cutting her gaze to the door, she stared at it and swallowed.

Deacon was out there. She didn't even have to look.

"Open the door, Renee," he said quietly. Quiet but firm, as though he expected to be obeyed. And Renee guessed that was exactly what he would expect.

Renee's knee-jerk reaction was to ignore him. But instead, she went to the door and opened it, stood there half naked before him, totally forgetting that there were still guys from the sheriff's department wandering through her home.

Deacon's eyes narrowed. He stepped forward, forcing her to back up, and then he closed the door behind him. Something flashed in his eyes, something that sent a shiver running down her spine—it wasn't lust, at least not yet, but it was . . . something.

Possessiveness, maybe. Another knee-jerk reaction, but this

one was totally unexpected. Instead of her normal reaction, which would have been derisive amusement, she found herself liking it.

Enough that she just might have done something to bring it out a little more, tease him with, taunt him—but she was still shaking so hard, she was almost sick with it. Glancing down, she found herself staring at her semiexposed breasts with a little bit of dismay.

Her shirt. Forgot her shirt.

"Here." Deacon spoke gently, softly, reaching out and taking the shirt from her, and then he pulled it over her head, dressing her as if she were a doll or some small child. He caught the long ends of her hair and eased it out from under the shirt, smoothed it down.

Then he cupped her chin in his hand, angled her face so that their eyes met. "Are you okay?" he asked.

"I'm fine," she said automatically. Pride, years of manners drilled into her head, they wouldn't let her say that she really wanted to get out of this house, and maybe even fall apart a little. Stupid, though, wasn't it? It wasn't like she was hurt. It wasn't like she didn't have the money to repair the damage or replace what couldn't be fixed.

Seth's scathing voice echoed in her ears. *That car of yours is going to cost some money to get fixed. Of course, I don't suppose that's a problem for you.* Instinctively, she flinched. Plenty of people had given her grief for being born to money. It was nothing new.

Still, it stung.

Deacon's fingers tightened, drawing her attention back to him. "Don't lie to me," he said, an underlying current of steel in his voice.

She rolled her eyes and sneered at him. "Fine, then. I'm doing pretty damn shitty. Somebody busts open the front door, cuts up my furniture, tears up my mom's flower beds, tears up *my car*, all while I was blissfully unaware in the shower." An edge worked its way into her voice—she couldn't help it, couldn't help but sound a little bitchy as she added, "Then I see this guy that I fucked six different ways to Sunday, and find out it's somebody that used to date one of my best friends. Oh, I'm just peachy, Deacon."

A grin curled the edges of his lips. "Yeah, you're going to be just fine." Then he slid his arms around her waist and eased her against him.

Just holding her. Simple, comforting—and devastating. There weren't many people in her life who had ever been big on offering simple comfort. Not her parents, not JD, not even Billy.

It was her undoing. A harsh sob escaped her lips, followed by another, and another.

Deacon held her until the storm passed and then he eased her back, sat her down on the toilet, again treating her with the same care he'd use on a small child. He rooted through the cabinets until he found some washcloths and he ran the water until it warmed.

All the while, Renee sat there staring at him, watching the play of muscles under his shirt, staring at his profile and comparing the harsh lines there to the features of the younger man from her memories.

It was there—plain as day, she could see it now. Now that she was looking, she could easily see it. The hair shorter, a little darker. The dimples in his cheeks had deepened to deep slashes that bracketed his mouth. The lean, lanky lines of his body had filled out.

She hadn't ever said more than a few words to Deacon, even though they'd grown up across the street from each other. He ran in a different crowd and her mother hadn't cared for the Cross family—*common*—that was Claudia's outlook, even if they *did* have money.

It had been fifteen years since she'd seen him. That night. Too many of her memories from that night weren't exactly what she could consider clear. Before that, she hadn't seen him much at all since he'd graduated high school. Understandable, she guessed, that she hadn't recognized him.

Of course, she also didn't remember him being so damn domineering, either.

Even as her body went all weak and soft, thinking of his *domineering* the previous night, she tensed when he turned and tried to wash the tears from her face. Renee turned her head and reached for the rag.

"Be still," he ordered brusquely.

Narrowing her eyes, she said, "A night in your bed didn't turn me into your pet, Deacon."

That same sardonic grin appeared on his lips. "Yeah, that's a likely image." Then he cupped her chin in his hand—his skin was rough, but so warm . . . Shivering, unable to stop herself, she moved a little closer, seeking his warmth. "Just let me help, okay, Renee?"

It was the closest he'd come to asking, she decided. Although it was damn humiliating to sit there and be cared for as though she were helpless, she remained sitting on her butt as he washed her face.

Besides, if she argued with him, he might just turn around and walk out. Renee really wasn't big on the idea of being alone at just that moment.

"So you're a lawyer," she said quietly as he turned away to rinse out the rag.

He slid her a glance. "Yeah." Lifting a brow, he asked, "You got a problem with lawyers?"

Renee shrugged. "Depends on what kind."

A faint smile appeared on his lips. "Victims' advocate." He took an inordinate amount of time straightening the rag on the bar attached to the wall. His voice was steady, but she sensed a vast undercurrent of emotion there as he said, "I'd had plans for law school anyway, although I had pretty much set my mind up that I wanted to be a defense attorney." Wide shoulders strained at the worn seams of his T-shirt as he murmured, "But that night . . ."

His voice trailed and his gaze flicked up to meet hers. "Left a mark." Shaking his head, he said, "I just couldn't see going into court and defending a guy like JD. Making it seem like it was okay, that he didn't do anything—that Sherra had done a damn thing to ask for it."

In a derisive tone, he added, "And I'd get him off. I'm a damn good lawyer. But then I'd start to hate myself."

"So you help the victims instead," Renee whispered. Something warm, sentimental—and most likely foolish—took up root in her heart and she averted her eyes, hoping he wouldn't see.

Leaning back against the counter of the sink, he shrugged. "Just seemed like the right thing to do. I like it—for the most part. Helping people put their lives back together is a damn sight better than helping those who destroy lives."

Outside the door, they heard a few voices, one in particular standing out.

As one, they glanced at the door and then Deacon sighed, pushed a hand through his hair. "Seth can be a jerk, but he's good at what he does, Renee. He'll find who did it."

Seth—a bitter smile curled her lips. "Something tells me he isn't going to be too worried if he doesn't."

Deacon shook his head. "He'll find him. Seth's that kind of guy."

Renee shook her head. "I don't see him pulling out all the stops for this. He's going to write it off as vandalism. Hell, that's probably all it is, anyway." Even as she said it, though, a chill rushed along her spine.

"This wasn't just vandalism." Voice flat, Deacon said, "You know it as well as I do."

Renee suppressed a shiver. She had a bad feeling he was right. There was something—well, *wrong* about how the whole damn thing felt. But it wasn't like she'd ever had this happen before. Maybe she was just being overly dramatic. That Deacon sensed it, too, only made the dread inside her deepen.

"Even if I do know better, Seth isn't likely to care. He hates me."

"He doesn't hate you," Deacon murmured. "He just hates . . ." His voice trailed off and an awkward silence filled the air.

"He hates what he thinks I am. Somebody just like my mother, who will turn a blind eye to anything and everything so long as it doesn't interfere with my life or reflect poorly on me." She was still so damn cold—another shiver racked her body and she wrapped her arms around herself. It didn't do a damn thing to warm her.

A hand appeared in her line of vision and she jumped, not even realizing that Deacon had moved away from the dark blue marble counter and now stood in front of her. With his hand stretched out for hers, he stood there waiting, and she suspected he'd wait as long as needed. Warily, she eyed his hand. "What?"

"Come on. You need to get out of here, you need to stop thinking about this and you need to get some rest. You won't be able to do that here," he said, his tone implacable. "So come on."

Slipping him a nervous glance, she asked, "Where?"

Now he smiled. "To my house—my mom's. Don't worry, Renee. You're safe from me . . . for tonight."

"Safe?" she asked, frowning. "Aren't you going to be there—or are you staying at the hotel?"

"Oh, I'll be there. I came out to spend a week or two with Mom. I usually do during the summer."

"If you're staying there, why were you at a hotel last night?"

Deacon shrugged restlessly. "Needed some downtime first. Had a crazy few weeks." Then he blew out a breath and added, "Plus, I knew Sherra and Lacey were going to be back in town. Had me thinking about things I don't like thinking about. Wanted another day to get ready for it."

A wicked glint appeared in his eyes. "And I'm damn glad . . . otherwise I might have missed the pleasure of your company last night." He reached out and toyed with the ends of her hair. "That would have been a serious loss."

Renee blushed and glanced away from him. Damn it. He'd gone and complicated things. If she'd realized it was Deacon last night . . . Hell, she knew there was no way anything would have happened. "I think I'd rather go to the Inn," she said, fighting the urge to fidget.

"No, you wouldn't. You don't really want to be alone right now, do you?" he murmured.

She sighed and closed her eyes. "No. But I'm . . . I just . . ." Her voice trailed off and she floundered for words, not even sure what she wanted to say.

"Come home with me." He drew her against him and nuzzled her neck, then stepped back and offered a hand. "I'm not going to lie and say I'm not having any deviant, sordid thoughts, but I'm not a complete bastard. You need rest."

Slowly, she reached up and laid her hand in his. His fingers closed around hers and squeezed gently as she stood. Renee stepped forward, but Deacon continued to stand there, so they were close—so close she could smell him, so close she could hear the soft, slow pace of his breathing and feel the warmth of it on her brow.

His hand came up and brushed her hair back from her face. Lifting her gaze, she met his and it was as if she'd fallen into some void where nothing existed but him. The smell of him, the feel of him, the color of his eyes and the way he'd felt as he moved against her last night—the commanding, dominating cadence of his voice as he pushed her, took her deep and far into the unknown territory of absolute, blind desire.

She'd thought she understood desire—real desire. She'd thought she'd felt it before. But it had paled in comparison to last night. His pupils flared, eclipsing the pale blue of his irises. He sucked in a harsh breath and the hand holding hers tightened, pulled her closer.

Bracing her free hand against his chest, she leaned into him, felt herself swaying closer, closer . . . "Damn, Renee," he muttered, dipping his head.

Bracing for his kiss was an impossible waste of time. His mouth came crushing down on hers with near-bruising force and she loved it. Needed it. His tongue pushed past the barrier of her lips, seeking, claiming, and she met him eagerly, drawing him deeper and whimpering as he slid a hand down her back and cupped the curve of her ass.

He lifted her up against him and Renee whimpered low in her throat. Deacon growled against her lips and pulled away, but not completely. "You're going to drive me crazy, aren't you, Renee?" He raked his teeth down her neck and slid his free hand under her tank top. "Are you going to tell me to stop?"

His hands felt warm against her chilled flesh. Almost too warm. But she loved it. As he edged up closer and closer to her unbound breasts, she lifted her head and stared at him. She had no idea blue eyes could burn that hot. "Should I?"

A faint smile curled his lips and he glanced from her to the door and then back, staring at his hands as he shoved her tank top up over her breasts. "Considering you just had one hell of a scare, considering the sheriff was being an ass . . . considering that half the sheriff's department is standing outside the door . . . yeah, baby, you should tell me to stop before I bend you over the sink and fuck you until you scream."

Heat swelled inside her. So she'd had a bad day, so what? She had no doubt that Deacon could make her forget every last second of that. But . . . her lashes lowered over her eyes. She thought of the people standing outside the door, thought of the mess her life was already in.

Having a guy like Deacon come into her life right now wasn't going to make that mess any better. A night of anonymous sex wasn't going to throw her—okay, wasn't going to throw her *much*— but Deacon would.

Deacon could.

Giving him a cocky smile that didn't reflect at all how she felt, Renee stood a little straighter and said, "I'm not much for screaming in front of a bunch of guys I don't know."

He let her go, his arms falling to his sides. But the smile on his face didn't fade. "I bet I could make you forget all about them."

"Hmmm. And then we go out there and I have to deal with their smirks and smiles until this mess is cleaned up. What fun."

Deacon reached out and brushed her hair back from her face.

"You still spend that much time worrying about what people think of you?"

Okay. Wrong thing to say, Deacon realized, as she stiffened and pulled back. Not physically so much, but emotionally. A shutter fell across her gaze and that warm, sassy green was now aloof, cool and distant—the ice queen once more.

She stood differently, and he realized it was the same way she'd held herself the night Boyd had been killed. Guarded. The warm, funny woman he'd spent the night with, the soft, scared woman he'd held and comforted in his arms only moments ago had disappeared and in her place stood a faint, pale shadow. "Renee . . ."

"I'm tired." She interrupted him with a polite but chilly smile and said, "If the offer of a place to sleep is still open, then we should go. If not, I need to get out of here and find a place in town."

He reached out and cupped her elbow, drawing her against him. "You're not sleeping in a hotel." Lowering his head, he nuzzled her neck, tried to find the woman he'd held just seconds ago. But Renee stood still and stiff, as though she'd tolerate his touch but never enjoy it. Never respond.

Shit.

YOU STILL SPEND *that much time worrying about what people think of you?*

She should have slept like the dead. The past day had been hell, she hadn't slept more than a few hours the night before, and her entire body screamed for oblivion, but she couldn't sleep.

Deacon's words circled around in her mind. He wasn't the first to have ever said anything like that, and she didn't expect he'd be the last. But it had hurt coming from him. Renee had been raised to care very much about appearances, even though she'd hated it.

But it wasn't so much that she worried what others thought of her—not really.

She was just private. Reserved, she guessed.

It was who she was.

Speaking up, voicing her thoughts, was something she'd had to work on. It had taken years, but she had finally managed to find some modicum of self-confidence. She no longer thought through every last thing she did or said, worrying about whether she should do it, whether she shouldn't. She did it only with about *half* of everything now—that was a huge improvement in her mind.

Seth Salinger thought Renee was just like her mother, so concerned with appearances, but not at all concerned with what lay underneath. From him, she wasn't surprised. He saw her as a connection to JD, and anything that was a connection to JD, he was going to hate.

But apparently, Deacon viewed her on the same level.

And that *hurt.* Even though logically there was no reason it should. It wasn't like Deacon really knew her from Adam—why shouldn't he view her exactly as so many others did? A pampered, privileged princess who never had to lift a finger to work, who never worried about anything more than whether she'd be able to find a purse to match her attire to the shade.

Depressed, she rolled onto her side and huddled into the blankets. For the hundredth time, Renee found herself wondering why in the hell she'd come back to Madison.

Even when she finally managed to drift off to a restless sleep, that question danced in the back of her mind. Taunting her.

4

He wasn't going to sleep worth shit, he realized. Not until he'd talked to Renee. Of course, *she* might already be asleep . . . but he didn't let that stop him as he rolled out of bed and pulled on the jeans he'd tossed over the footboard earlier.

He tugged up the zipper but didn't mess with buttoning them as he left his bedroom. Renee was sleeping in the room just across the hall from his. He could have put her in the guest wing, but he hadn't been able to. Where he wanted her had been in his room, in his bed . . . even though he had no intention of trying to do anything tonight.

It had been a stupid thing to do earlier, moving on her like that, and then when she pulled back, his comment about appearances—

All of it stupid and thoughtless. She'd been so shaken already, the wisest thing to do would have been to just bring her to the house, tuck her into bed and make sure she fell asleep.

Instead he practically fucked her with a room full of cops only a few feet away, and then he'd hurt her. At least he thought he'd hurt her. He couldn't be sure, because that ice princess routine was complete. She showed no emotion on her face, in her voice, in her eyes. She hadn't pulled away and huddled in on herself, but instead she'd walked alongside him with her head held high, looking at nothing, looking at nobody.

Exactly as she'd been that night fifteen years ago. Aloof. Untouchable.

But still, he suspected that he *had* hurt her . . . and if that icy facade was just an act, then he hadn't just hurt her feelings; he'd been misjudging her for a good long while. He hadn't thought of Renee Lincoln all that much, unless he was remembering that night, and every time he thought of her, he'd been a little disgusted by her lack of emotion. Disgusted enough that if he'd known who she was when he saw her in the bar, he would have probably treated her the same way that Seth had.

Which is damn sad, because he had been there—he hadn't come in until after she'd busted the lamp over JD's head but he knew how things had played out. And he *had* been there as she warned them all about the gun. No, he didn't know her, not now, and not then, but that hadn't kept him from making his own snap judgments. That knowledge left him with a bad taste in his mouth and a heavy weight in his gut.

No. Until he'd apologized, he wasn't going to sleep.

Outside her door, he paused, resting a hand on the smooth, gleaming surface of polished mahogany. He could hear her . . . shit. Soft, sexy little moans. Was she dreaming . . . of him?

Arrogant much? Still, thinking that she just might be dreaming of him had his cock standing at attention—and acknowledging that she might be dreaming of somebody else was enough to have him snarling in frustration.

"Go back to bed, Deacon," he muttered. "Apologize in the morning."

That would have been the courteous thing. The polite thing. The *wise* thing. But Deacon wasn't a gentleman and courtesy only suited him when it served its purpose. Wisdom was probably something he could kiss good-bye if Renee was in the picture.

So instead of leaving, he opened the door. Moonlight spilled across the bed, highlighting her face, turning her dark red hair to inky black. Her breasts rose and fell under the thin fabric of her tank top. Sheets lay in a tangle around her waist.

As he watched, she heaved out a harsh breath. Another faint moan. All the blood drained south and he stood there staring at her with his dick aching and his mouth watering. He wanted to see her naked again, naked and under him. Hell, naked and over him sounded pretty damn good, too.

It was dark in the room, but his night vision had always been good. The moonlight was more than adequate for him to see the way her erect nipples stabbed into the cotton of her shirt. More than adequate for him to see the soft pout on her lips before another moan slid free. More than adequate for him to see as her head started to thrash back and forth on the pillow.

Caught in a haze of lust, torn between going to her and doing the right thing, he almost didn't hear it at first. As her soft moans became words. Soft, broken words.

"No."

"No . . ."

By the third *no*, his brain decided to turn back on and he shoved off the wall, the need to fuck fading as the need to touch and comfort rose to the forefront. "No . . ." He knelt down, braced one knee on the bed as he reached out and brushed his fingers down her cheek.

"Renee."

She jerked. Tensed. Her voice was louder, more tortured this time. "No."

He tapped her cheek. "Renee, it's Deacon. Wake up."

But the only reaction she gave was to huddle deeper into the bed, clutching the blankets like a life preserver. Deacon's heart twisted in his chest as she started to whimper, low and soft, in her throat. It was a choked, terrified sound—quiet. That only made it that much more heartrending.

He lowered himself onto the bed and laid his hand on her cheek. When he spoke again, it was louder. She came awake with a start. Moonlight splashed across her face, making her features paler, her eyes darker. But it was no trick of light that caused the fear in her gaze, or the horror. Blind instinct seemed to guide her as she swung out, and he just barely managed to catch her wrist before she decked him.

"Renee, it's me."

She jerked back away from him, staring at him with uncomprehending eyes.

"You were having a nightmare." He rubbed his thumb on the inside of her wrist.

She tugged against his hold. Reluctantly, he let go and watched as she scooted away and smoothed the tangled sheets and blankets down around her. "Did I wake you?" she asked, her voice harsh and rough.

"No. I wasn't sleeping." Reaching out, he threaded his fingers through the long tangle of her hair, smoothing it back from her face. "Do you have nightmares a lot?"

Renee shrugged, a jerky motion that lacked her elegant grace. "From time to time." She licked her lips, eased a little farther away from him without seeming to.

Narrowing his eyes, he watched as she put on that damned ice queen mask. With her face averted, she tucked her hair back from her face, smoothed the blankets in her lap. "I'm sorry if I disturbed—"

"I wasn't asleep," he said, cutting off her apology. Shifting around on the bed, he settled with his back against the headboard. Reaching out, he snagged the chain on the small bedside lamp. Pale light filtered through the deep, rose-colored glass. The circle of light didn't reach far, and somehow it made things more intimate than the darkness. He stretched his legs out in front of him and crossed them at the ankle. "What were you dreaming about?"

Renee huffed out a breath. Unconsciously, she mirrored his pose, leaning her back against the headboard and crossing her arms over her chest. Some of the polite, well-bred society girl manners faded as she gave him a withering look. "Deacon, do we really need to do this right now? It's late. I'm tired."

She wouldn't talk about it. Without even asking another question, Deacon knew that. Just as he knew that she had been dreaming about that night. Instead of responding to her not-so-subtle request, he said, "I have nightmares every now and then. Hate it like hell, but not much I can do about it, I guess. Boyd was an ass and I don't blame Sherra a bit, but still . . . seeing somebody bleed to death right in front of you, it will do a number on you, won't it?"

For a long moment, she was quiet. She stared off into the distance, but he knew she wasn't seeing the room or anything else— except maybe in her memories. "You have nightmares about it, too?"

Deacon shrugged. He wasn't even sure why he'd told her. He hadn't told anybody about them, not even Seth, and the guy had gotten to be one of his best friends over the years. "Yeah. Not as much as I used to, but yeah. Sometimes I can go months without one and then . . ."

"And then you come back here, or you talk to your mother, or you see somebody that vaguely resembles Boyd and *bam*," she finished when his voice trailed away. She reached behind and gathered her hair into a tail, finger-combing the tangles out.

Deacon found himself enthralled by the sight of her slender fingers gliding through the dark strands of her hair. So much so that he had to focus on her voice to understand her words as she continued to speak. "I never liked Boyd—hell, I didn't even like JD. I know what could have happened, what probably *would* have happened. But still . . ."

"Not liking somebody and being okay with it as they die right in front of you are two different things," Deacon said. He closed his eyes. It was either that, or grab her. And he probably needed to clear the air between them first. But he could work his way up to that. "If you didn't like JD, why did you go out with him? You were at the party with him."

"My mother." She drew herself up, sitting as though somebody had shoved a steel pole up her spine. In an arch, patrician tone that sounded dead-on like her mother, Renee said, "James D is a nice boy, Renee. Polite. Well-bred. Comes from a good family. You could do far worse than him."

Deacon smirked. "Yeah, that sounds like your mother." Then he winced. "Shit, I'm sorry . . ."

She glanced at him. "For what? Being honest?" Renee shrugged. "Don't be sorry. Mother and I weren't on good terms after I left for college—before that, to be honest. I don't know if we were ever on good terms. Maybe before my father died, things weren't so bad. After he died, though, we were like two strangers sharing a house. Worse. If she hadn't pushed me into it, I wouldn't ever have gone out with JD. I couldn't stand him."

Deacon reached for her hand, slowly, giving her a chance to pull away. But she didn't. Twining their fingers, he shifted on the bed until they faced each other. "He hit you that night."

She stilled—so completely still, it didn't seem as though she even breathed or blinked. Then she blinked. In the muted light, he saw her eyes go dark and thoughtful as she reached up with her free hand and touched her cheek, as though she could still feel the ugly red mark JD had put on her. "Yes."

"Had he done it before?"

Renee shook her head. "No. But if I'd stayed with him, I bet he would have. Mother kept *suggesting* I make amends with him, even after I told her what had happened. I told her he hit me. I told her what I saw when Lacey and I went into that room and found him and Boyd getting ready to rape Sherra." She laughed, an ugly, brittle sound. "Naturally, though, I'd done something to provoke him. And Sherra? White trash. Girls like that don't get raped, do they?"

Abruptly, she jerked on her hand, pulling free from him and climbing out of the bed. Either she'd forgotten that all she wore was her tank top and a pair of panties, or she didn't care, as she started to pace the room. Moving in restless circles as though being still made it that much harder to deal with the memories. "I never liked Boyd. But it was getting to where I *hated* JD. I was just too much of a coward to break up with him. To stand up against my mother. Until that night. That was what it took—seeing what he would have done to Sherra. Having him hit me."

She passed by the large mirror hanging over the bureau and paused. Turning, she studied her reflection. "Do you know what my main accomplishment in life at that time was, Deacon? I was passably attractive. That was it. I couldn't get into any of my first picks for college. I wasn't smart enough. I didn't have any real friends. The only boyfriend I had? I dated him because my mother insisted. I didn't have the courage to stand up to her, or to him. Until that night."

A muscle jerked in his jaw as he watched her stare at her reflection. He heard the echo of her mother in her words and he had no doubt that it was her mother who had put those pathetic ideas in Renee's mind. He slid off the bed and moved to stand behind her, resting his hands on her shoulders. "How old were you, Renee? Seventeen? Eighteen?"

She sighed. "Eighteen. But being eighteen is no excuse for being weak."

"You weren't weak. A weak woman wouldn't have gone into that room—you can't tell me that something inside you didn't realize what was probably happening in there. You didn't just go look out of curiosity. You went to help."

"A weak woman wouldn't have stood there when her boyfriend belted her."

"Would you have stayed with him? After that night even if . . ." His voice trailed off. He couldn't quite put the travesty of that night into a few simple words . . . *Even if our lives weren't totally changed? Even if that bastard hadn't tried to rape a girl? Even if he hadn't gone for a gun?*

Instead of trying to find the words, he reached around and trailed his fingers down the smooth surface of her cheek. "If the worst he did that night was hit you, would you have stayed?"

"In all honesty, I don't know." Then her shoulders slumped and her eyes closed. "I told myself it was over. I didn't want to turn into the kind of woman who'd stay with a guy who beat her. I want to think I would have ended it. But I don't know."

"I do." Deacon rested his chin on her shoulder and slid his arms around her waist. Drawing her back against him, he stared into her eyes through the reflection. "The girl I saw that night wasn't weak. You didn't run away when you heard Sherra and you didn't run away when JD went to grab a gun. You fought back. You're not weak."

She gazed at him solemnly, but he didn't see any confidence in her eyes. Smoothing his hands up her arms, he said softly, "You know, I came in here to tell you that I was sorry."

Her lips quirked up in a smile. "Now I bet you *are* sorry, walking in on me while I was at my absolute best."

Deacon shrugged. "I don't know. Hate knowing you have nightmares, but I got to say, I'm glad I'm not the only one who has some bad dreams about that night." Then, determined to see the misery fade from her eyes, he slid his hands down and cupped her breasts through the thin tank top she wore. "I want to fuck you. Right here. Like this. Should I get the apology out of the way first?"

For a moment, he wasn't sure she was going to respond—or be receptive. Then that arrogant smile curled her lips and she said, "Since when does your type bother with asking? Don't you just hand out orders and expect obedience?"

Deacon took his time sliding a hand through her hair, tangling his fingers in the dark, silky length. Then he wrapped it around his wrist, drawing her back against him. "Does that mean I don't need to mess with the apology?" he teased, wedging his knee between her thighs and widening her stance. Not enough, though. Letting go of her hair, he stepped back. "Spread your legs."

She did—maybe two inches.

Over her shoulder, he met her gaze in the reflection and said, "Not enough."

Deliberately, he used his foot to knock hers over. "Spread them, Renee."

Heat bloomed in her eyes as she spread her legs farther apart. Cocking a dark brow, she drawled, "Are you a lawyer or a cop?" Then she grinned and asked, "Where are those handcuffs?"

"You got a smart mouth on you," he murmured. Stripping his jeans off, he tried to figure out why in the hell that smart-ass mouth was so damn appealing . . . well, besides the obvious. Deacon had been with subs before who were more into playing the brat, pushing and pushing, just to see how far they could go—with him, not very far. It bored him. Deacon wasn't much for boredom.

But he wasn't bored with Renee.

She clearly delighted in challenging him on pretty much every level and he suspected that wouldn't change. More, he wasn't too sure he wanted it to change.

That was just confusing as hell. Damn it, what in the hell had he gotten into with her? And how?

Too confusing, especially considering it was the dead of the night and she was standing in front of him wearing nothing but a skimpy tank and a pair of black silk panties that rode low on her hips. He moved to stand behind her, gathering the silk in his hand and tugging on it until the silky fabric drew tight against her cleft.

In the mirror, he kept his gaze on hers, watching as her lashes fluttered low and a husky moan escaped her lips. "I didn't like waking up alone at the hotel."

He half expected some smart-ass retort, but there wasn't one. Her cheeks flushed a pretty shade of pink. "I really didn't feel like leaving."

Deacon let go of her panties, trailing his fingers along the skinny swath of fabric along her hips. He slid his hand inside her panties, staring at his reflection in the mirror, watching as he touched her. She was soaking wet and hot as he pushed two fingers inside her. "Then why did you?"

Her throat worked as she swallowed and she opened her lips to answer, but ended up moaning instead and rocking against his hand. Circling his thumb around her clit, he worked her until he could feel her silky sheath tightening as her orgasm moved closer. Then he stopped, pulling his hand away and pressing a hand against her belly to still the rhythmic motion of her hips. Her butt pressed snugly against his cock. Memories of the past night had the aching piece of flesh jerking in demand.

"Renee."

Her lashes lifted, just a bit, enough for him the see the vibrant green of her eyes. A sexy pout formed on her lips.

"I asked you a question," he said patiently. To tease her, and himself, he slid his hand down and cupped her through her panties, pressing against her, stroking her through the damp silk. Once more, he stroked her until she was shaking in his arms and on the verge of climax.

When he stopped this time, her eyes flew open and she snarled at him. "Damn it, Deacon!"

"Answer me." He turned her in his arms, needing to see her face, needing to see her eyes. What had started as a teasing little question was suddenly of vital importance. He cupped her rump in his hand, squeezed the firm, soft flesh and then spanked her, hard enough that his hand stung from the contact. "Why in the hell did you leave me?"

Temper and desire flared in her eyes and Deacon could tell she wasn't sure if she wanted to get mad—or push him to do it again. In the end, she snapped, "I don't do one-night stands. I woke up and didn't know what in the hell to do, so I left."

"I didn't like it."

Russet brows arched over her eyes. "Yeah, I noticed." Then, as quick as it had come on her, her temper faded away and she gave him a wicked smile. She smoothed a hand down his belly, staring at him from under her lashes. Cool, strong fingers closed around his cock. "Want me to make it up to you?"

Any response he might have come up with faded as she sank to her knees in front of him and took him in her mouth. Some half-formed thought of *condom* formed in his mind and he swore half-heartedly. He hadn't come in here prepared for this—*and you're thinking of that* now?

Her lips closed around the head of his cock, sucking softly. She eased down, taking him deeper, deeper, and Deacon groaned. Her fingers slid up over his thigh, then between, cupping his balls in her palms. He tensed.

Renee pulled away and settled on her heels, looking up at him. "Problem?"

Problem—well, he wasn't quite sure how to answer that. When he wanted a woman to touch him, he told her when and how. But that wasn't going to go over well with Renee; he already knew that.

Besides, his body had pretty much made a decision on that. If she wanted to touch him, hell, he was all for it.

But—yeah. *Problem*. Throat gone tight, he said, "I didn't come in here for this. I don't have anything with me." He glanced at her bag, still sitting open on the floor and although he seriously despised the thought that she might be going around ready to hook up with somebody, he also had a hope . . . "Don't suppose you have anything with you?"

That sexy pout came back. Under the thin fabric of her tank top, her breasts rose and fell. "No. Like I said, I don't do one-night stands."

"Shit." Deacon bent down and grabbed his jeans. "Wait here."

Instantly, her smile appeared. She tapped the floor and said, "Right here?"

"Right there."

It took just a couple of minutes to grab a couple of rubbers from his bag—the last two. Shit. Those couple of minutes were too damn long, though, and he strode back into her room, all ready to get one of the rubbers on and get inside her. She was exactly as he had left her, kneeling on the floor with her palms resting on slender, pale thighs.

He tore one rubber off the strip, tossing the last one onto the bed. Keeping the other one in his hand, he went to stand in front of her. Before he could push his jeans back off, Renee was already working on it, easing the zipper down over his engorged flesh, pausing to lean forward and kiss him, swirling her tongue over the head of his cock before tugging the jeans down his hips.

She paused again, sliding her hand up the inside of his thigh, teasing the flesh of his balls with her fingertips, stroking one along the length of his shaft. The cool, light touch was sheer torture. Deacon groaned and reached out, fisted his hand in her hair and brought her mouth back. She opened for him, staring up at him, challenging—and motionless.

Slowly, keeping their gazes locked, he moved, surged forward, watching as her lips stretched tight around his cock. He dropped the rubber and brought up his other hand and held her head steady as he moved, fucking his cock in and out of her mouth, keeping his strokes shallow and slow.

She tugged against his hold. Deacon went to pull away, but she brought up her hands, gripped his hips. He hissed as she raked the sensitive head of his shaft with her teeth. Slowly, teasingly, she moved forward and he let her, watched—until his eyes all but crossed as she took more and more, until he'd filled her mouth and the head of his penis nudged the back of her throat.

When she swallowed, he rocked up on his heels and just barely managed to keep from shouting. Warning hot/cold chills raced down his spine and his balls drew tight. Swearing, he tugged on her head. She resisted, pulling back and then sliding back down on him. The skin of his cock was ruddy, wet from her mouth. As she sucked on him, Deacon shuddered and groaned. He tugged on her head again, harder this time, and he didn't stop until she released him—but she took her sweet time about it, teasing the flared head with her tongue, cupping his balls in her hand and squeezing.

He was sweating and too damn close to coming—and damn it, the smug smile on her lips assured him that Renee knew just how close he was. "Turnabout is fair play," she whispered.

Standing over her, his hand fisted in her hair, his cock throbbing and demanding to feel her mouth again, he almost pulled her back to him, almost let her finish it.

Instead, he reached for some measure of control and said, "Get the rubber."

She did, moving slowly and lazily, reaching down and plucking it from the ground, holding it up to him. "Want me to put it on you again?"

Shit, no. If she kept touching him, he was going to lose control—and Deacon didn't lose it until he was ready. He was nowhere near that point yet. "No," he gritted out, grabbing it from her and tearing it open. "Lose the shirt, Renee."

She did, stripping it off as he rolled the rubber down over his sex. Her long hair floated down around her shoulders and back, hiding her breasts from him. The pinks of her nipples were just barely visible. "Push your hair back—I want to see you."

That's it; focus . . . Talking his way through the need made it a little easier. Not much, but enough.

Renee apparently wasn't too interested in making things easy on him. She gave him that smug grin and said, "You can see me just fine."

In response, he reached down, seeking out one round, plump breast through her hair. He pinched the nipple, squeezing until her lashes fluttered and a soft whimper escaped her lips. Her eyes gone nearly black with want, she stared at him. "I want to see your breasts, Renee. I want to look at your nipples, pinch them, maybe bite them or lick them. I want to see you, and your hair is covering you. Push your hair back."

She did so and Deacon saw with some satisfaction that her hands were shaking. Good. He didn't want this madness to be all one-sided.

"I want you to get up and stand in front of the mirror again. I'm going to fuck you there—and you're going to watch me. You won't come until I tell you."

Oh, the hell I won't, Renee thought, dazed. She was so damn turned on, if he'd just kiss her, she'd probably come. But he didn't kiss her and he didn't even touch her as she went to stand in front of the dresser.

His voice was a deep, sexy growl as he said, "Face the mirror. Put your hands on the dresser . . . Yeah, just like that."

Keeping her eyes on his reflection, she watched his face as he slid his hand down her back, over her hip. He cupped her ass, squeezed lightly, looking down—watching as he touched her, she suspected.

His gaze came up and met hers and she had just a second to brace herself before he spanked her. Lightly at first, but then harder, harder, harder until the pleasure became pain and the two blurred together. She was panting and whimpering, all but crying his name and ready to beg, but then he stopped. Leaned over her body and whispered, "You can't scream here. People will hear you."

He smoothed a hand over her butt and she whimpered. The skin was burning, sensitized from the spanking, and just that light touch was torture. "Can you keep from screaming?"

Shit. She didn't know the answer. Instead of answering, she just lowered her head, stared at the floor and tried to level out her breathing. Deacon moved away. She heard a zipper rasp and lifted her head, watching him in the mirror as he rooted through the overnight bag she'd brought. He stood, holding her black silk stockings in his hand. A wicked grin curled his lips as he rubbed the soft lingerie. "Nice," he murmured.

Smoothing the silk along her still-stinging rump, he trailed it up over her back. "I'd love to see you wearing just these, stretched out and tied to my bed. You wear things like this much?"

She had to swallow before she could even say a damn thing. "Not much." That pair was new—and she already knew what he was going to do with it before he did it. He used it as a makeshift gag, much like he'd done with his tie the night before.

The guy did know how to improvise. He slipped the silk between her lips and Renee shuddered, heat spiraling through her as he tied the silk behind her head.

"Fuck, Renee . . . I really like the look of you this way." He fisted his hand in her hair, using the hold to guide her head up so that she was watching herself in the mirror. Her face was flushed, her eyes glittering, overbright. The black silk was a dark slash against her cheeks and above it, her skin glowed pink.

In the mirror, their eyes met and Deacon smiled, a slow, confident smile as he gathered the material of her panties into his hand and tugged. The silk slid over the dewy, swollen folds of her sex and she shuddered, arched her hips. From the corner of her eye, she saw his hand lift and she braced herself. The gag muffled her moan and moments later, a strangled scream as he alternated tortures—sharp, stinging blows to her ass and slow, teasing tugs on her panties that slid the fabric over her aching pussy.

"Do you want me to fuck you?"

She nodded—if he hadn't gagged her, she would have begged.

Deacon moved behind her and just as he had earlier, he nudged her thighs apart, lightly kicked at her heel until she spread her stance. He reached down and pulled her panties aside, then pushed two fingers deep inside her. She clamped down around him and rocked against his hand when he would have pulled away. He chuckled.

If she wasn't so damn turned on, that confident, arrogant sound might have pissed her off. But right now she didn't give a damn about anything else but having him inside her, anything but riding and working against that thick ridge of flesh.

But the nonvocal cues weren't working quite so well. Deliberately, she shifted her stance, bringing her legs closer together. It had the dual, pleasurable side effects of tightening her sex around his thrusting fingers and the way his eyes narrowed on her face.

Tossing her hair back, she met his gaze challengingly.

"Open your thighs, Renee."

The gag kept her from speaking, but gave him a look that clearly said, *Make me*.

He stopped touching her. Stopped stroking. Crowding her up against the dresser, he whispered, "You keep pushing and pushing, don't you?"

In response, she did push—she pushed her butt back against the throbbing length of his cock and wiggled. Behind her, Deacon snarled and wrapped a brawny arm around her waist. With the other, he grasped his cock and, without waiting another second, he impaled her, moving in on her until she was trapped between the dresser and his body. Automatically, she tried to widen her stance to accommodate him but he spanked her. "Be still."

Whimpering, she arched back against him and tried to ride him, tried to take him deeper. He tangled his hand in her hair, jerked her head to the side and raked her neck with his teeth. "Be . . . still . . ." he rasped. He slid a hand around her hip, down over her belly, spearing through the curls until he could stroke her clit.

He took her with a force that knocked the breath from her body, plying her with devilish strokes of her clit and shafting her deep and hard. "Come—" His voice was a demanding growl in her ear. He slapped his fingers against her clit, a quick, stinging blow.

She came. She screamed against the gag and when it was over, she would have sagged against the dresser, but his hands on her hips kept her pinned in place.

"Come," he ordered again before she'd even had time to catch her breath.

Can't . . . She couldn't speak around the gag, but he seemed to know exactly what she was thinking.

His eyes narrowed on her face, staring at her with an intensity that shook her to the core. "You will. Whenever I tell you to. Won't you?"

Whenever I tell you to . . . The part of her that had been controlled for too much of her life wanted to rebel. She wouldn't tell him that. Couldn't. But then he dipped his head and brushed his lips over her shoulder, his voice a soft, seductive purr in her ear. "Tell me . . . just nod your head. *I'll come whenever you want, Deacon. I'll do whatever you want . . .*"

And to her dismay, she nodded. A satisfied smile curled his lips and he praised, "Good girl." He moved back, just a little, enough that her exhausted body could collapse against the smooth, cool surface of the dresser.

Inside her pussy, he throbbed and she shuddered, knowing he wasn't done with her, half desperate for more, half desperate for rest.

"I don't think I've ever enjoyed spanking this much before," he whispered, smoothing a hand over her rump. He settled into a slow, almost lazy rhythm, his cock pushing deep, withdrawing, followed by another slow, thorough plunge. "Does it hurt?"

Renee nodded.

"Is it good?"

Again she nodded and when he lifted his hand, she braced herself, tensing, her pussy locking down tight on his shaft as he swatted her ass. She bucked against him and he grunted, his lids drooping low over his eyes, teeth bared in a sexy snarl. "Yeah, it's good," he muttered.

He withdrew and as he thrust back into her this time, he swatted her on the other cheek. Falling into that rhythm, he alternated between one side of her ass and the other as he slowly, leisurely fucked her.

But the slow, leisurely fuck didn't last. As she panted and moved closer and closer to orgasm, she felt an answering tension in his body. He sped up, bracing her hips with one hand and using the flat of his other hand on her ass. The sound of flesh striking flesh, the labored sounds of their breathing and the scents of sex filled the air.

He bent over her once more, crowding into her. Sliding a hand around her body, he cupped one breast in his hand and pinched her nipple—tighter and tighter. "Come!"

She did, screaming around the gag and shuddering as the orgasm slammed into her.

DEACON FELL ASLEEP holding her and this time when he woke up, she was still there, cradled in his arms with her head tucked under his chin. The dark red banner of her hair lay in a tangle around them. He lay there, playing with the silky strands until she came awake.

It was a slow, sinfully sweet affair, with Renee making soft little purring sounds in her throat and wiggling against him until he was ready to push her onto her back and come inside her.

So he decided to do just that, snagging the last condom from the bedside table, rolling her onto her back and coming into her even as her eyes started to flutter open.

"Good morning," he whispered, dipping his head to kiss her.

She smiled against his lips, a breathy sigh escaping her as he made love to her.

It was slow—softer, sweeter than anything he'd ever felt. She arched under him, rising to meet him, his name a ragged whisper that he caught with his mouth.

There were no demands this time, no commands, nothing but slow, lazy sex that was too sweet to be called anything other than lovemaking. She arched into him and came with a cry and he followed her, catching one of her hands and twining their fingers, palm to palm.

As it faded, as their breathing slowed down and their heartbeats returned to normal, Deacon lay sprawled between her thighs and wondered if this was what it was to fall in love.

Was it waking with a smile because she was there? She . . . not just any woman, but *the* woman. In his case—Renee.

Was she the reason he'd always been so vaguely dissatisfied with each and every relationship he'd had in life?

Her voice was husky and morning-quiet as she spoke, intruding on his thoughts. "You know, it's way too early in the morning for this kind of heavy thinking."

Shifting around, he pushed up onto his elbows so he didn't keep crushing her as he asked, "What makes you think I'm thinking heavy?"

Combing her fingers through his thick hair, she replied, "Aren't you?"

"Yeah."

"What are you thinking about?"

Too honest to mess with lies or stalling tactics, he said simply, "You."

Her brows arched up. "Me, huh? I dunno if I like being responsible for early-morning thinking. It sounds kind of dangerous."

With a soft laugh, he shifted around, resting his head on her belly again. She wrapped her arms around him and cuddled into him, soft and sweet. "Thoughts about you sound pretty damn dangerous period."

That made her laugh. "Thoughts of me? Dangerous?"

"Hmmm." He pressed an openmouthed kiss to her belly and wished he had the strength in his legs to move up and cover her again, push inside her body. He wondered if he could spend the next eighteen hours doing just that . . . making love to her, making her sigh, and then making her beg and plead, and then making her sigh all over again.

It was a tempting thought.

Too tempting.

So instead, he rolled away from her, flopping onto his back and staring at the ceiling. As much as it appealed, he couldn't spend the day with his dick buried inside her sweet pussy or snug ass.

He was out of rubbers, for one.

He wanted to have a word with Seth, for another—see if they had any clue who'd broken into Renee's home. He wanted to make damn sure his friend didn't try to write this off as some random act of vandalism.

Plus, if he didn't spend some time with his mother, she just might have Callie get her out of bed and come looking for him. *That* could get embarrassing.

5

WITH HER HANDS tucked into her pockets, Renee studied city hall. "You really don't have to do this, you know."

He reached out and caught one of her wrists, tugging on it and lacing their fingers together. "Yeah, I do."

From the corner of her eye, she studied him. He had a pair of simple sunglasses, a button-down shirt worn untucked over beat-up blue jeans and a pair of tailor-made leather loafers that cost more than some people made in a month. So damn gorgeous, he made her mouth go dry. Gorgeous, and just all-out wonderful. She could get into serious trouble with him, she suspected.

"Why?"

A smile curled his mouth upward and he replied, "Has something to do with those heavy thoughts earlier."

He'd been quietly pensive half the morning and from behind the shield of those sunglasses, she knew he'd spent a decent amount of time staring at her as she drove them to the sheriff's office, using one of the cars that had belonged to her mother—and now they were hers.

Her mouth went dry under the weight of that intense, unseen

scrutiny. "You going to share these heavy thoughts with me anytime soon?"

"Yeah. Once I muddle through them a little more." Jerking his head toward the stately old building, he said, "Come on. Let's get this done. I'll let you buy me lunch."

"Oh, gee . . . thanks. I'm so flattered."

"You should be. I don't let women buy me stuff—well, unless it's my mother."

"She buy you a lot of stuff?"

"Hell, yes. She can't do much shopping outside the house anymore, but Callie has turned her into an Internet junkie. Clothes, shoes . . . golf clubs." He sent her a grin and said, "I hate golf. But I won't tell her that."

"That's . . ." She searched for the word. "Sweet." And it was. Her mother may have bought Renee plenty, but it always came with a price tag, and not a monetary one. *You should wear this dress to the Arbor Club dinner dance. Here, this should do for your date with JD—and do try to be a lady, Renee. No, you mustn't wear that—what will people think?*

None of it had been bought simply to please her, but she suspected that was exactly why Deacon's mom bought things. Because she liked to give them, because she wanted to make her son happy.

He interrupted her ponderous, slightly envious thoughts with a tug on her hand. "Now who's doing the heavy thinking?"

She shrugged. "Maybe it's contagious."

"I'm hoping so," he said, an odd note in his voice. "So, where you living now?"

"Fishers. It's a suburb of Indianapolis—hey."

He came to a halt and since he didn't let go of her hand, she had to stop, too. Shoving his glasses back onto his head, he squinted at her. "You serious?"

"Yeah. I moved there a couple of years ago."

Something moved through his eyes—a flash of something she

couldn't decipher, and then it was gone, replaced by a pleased, rather smug-looking smile. "I live in Carmel."

Renee blinked and then she laughed. "Well, hell. It's a small world, huh?"

Whatever he had been about to say was abruptly cut off as his hand tightened on hers. "Maybe a little too small." His voice went hard and edgy and he moved closer to her. Something about the movement struck her as protective—possessive, too. For some reason, that didn't rub her the way she would have thought.

The look in his eyes had the skin on the nape of her neck crawling and Renee didn't need to turn around to know whom he'd seen.

Who was probably headed their way.

Grimly, she turned.

JD, in the flesh.

She hadn't seen him since that summer, the day after Boyd had died. It had been right here, just inside the town hall, where she'd spoken with law enforcement. Although her mother had tried goading her into what to say, Renee had explained exactly what had happened. None of them had been happy with her explanation and she knew why.

They'd wanted to hear that Sherra was somehow to blame.

They hadn't wanted to hear that JD and Boyd had been getting ready to rape the girl. God, she could still remember the look on her mother's face as she explained what she'd seen. As she'd insisted that she hadn't made a mistake about what she'd seen.

She'd told the truth, as hard as it had been with her mother breathing down her neck, and she'd hoped that maybe something would happen. JD shouldn't get off scot-free.

But he did.

No charges were pressed against him.

Of course, as much as it had disappointed some people around town, they weren't able to press charges against Sherra, either.

Blowing out a sigh, Renee said quietly, "I could have gone my whole life without ever seeing him again."

The world definitely was too damn small.

He had aged, and not well. Call her petty, but the sight of him as he headed up the brick sidewalk did her good. He'd put on maybe twenty-five or thirty pounds and he wore it all around his middle.

His perfect, pale blond hair was receding from his forehead. Back in high school, he'd had that cool, polished blond-and-blue-eyed prince look down pat, but it just wasn't a look that suited him as well now. His tan looked entirely too fake, his teeth looked entirely too white and perfect and every single one of them showed as he aimed a curious smile at her before focusing on Deacon.

"Deacon, it's been a long time."

Deacon's lip curled. "Not long enough." He pointedly ignored the hand JD held out, reaching instead for Renee's.

"Is this your . . ." Then he looked at Renee.

She saw the moment he figured out who she was. She hadn't changed quite as much as he had, she didn't think. Longer hair, more casual clothes, but most of her changing had been done on the inside.

The grin on his face spread. "Renee."

He slid an insulting look over her, from head to toe, his gaze lingering on her chest before traveling on downward. There was something deliberately insulting about the way he looked at her. Trying to get some sort of reaction out of her, but he wasn't going to get one. Judging from the tension in Deacon's body, though, Deacon just might give JD a reaction.

One JD wouldn't like.

She squeezed Deacon's hand and hoped he was a mind reader. She didn't run from confrontation anymore and she didn't let other people handle them for her.

Now wasn't the time to change that.

Deacon said nothing, but the tension in his body eased and when she tugged her hand from his grasp, he let her. Shifting forward, she cocked her head and returned JD's stare with lazy insolence, lingering on the excess weight he'd picked up, down to his feet and then back up to study his hairline before she met his eyes.

With a smirk, she said, "Well, JD, I almost didn't recognize you."

"Renee, you look wonderful."

He shifted forward, too close, close enough that she could smell garlic on his breath, and the sweet, cool scent of a breath mint he'd used to try to cover the smell. Close enough that she could see the pores in his skin—and close enough to see the way the pulse in his throat jerked as she replied, "Sorry I can't say the same about you, JD. Doesn't look like the years have been entirely kind."

She stepped back, giving him a look of mocking pity before focusing on his hair. "You know, I've heard a lot of good things about the Hair Institute for Men."

He went white—then red.

Behind her, she heard an odd choking sound coming from Deacon—laughter, she suspected.

JD's voice had a hard edge as he replied, "I'll keep that in mind. I'm sorry about your mother. Business kept me from attending the funeral. I'd hoped to see you afterward, but I heard you didn't want to stay in town."

She blinked. If he thought he was going to take jabs at her using a dead woman's memories, he was wrong. Very wrong. "I saw no reason to stay after the funeral. Mother's lawyer is very efficient."

Efficient. Yeah, that about described it. The scandal of her dad's suicide may have stung Claudia Lincoln's pride, but that hadn't kept her from making very good use of the family money. Charitable bequests, incentives to the current staff to remain until Renee decided what to do with the house. Hell, the will took care of damn near everything with no interference from anybody.

"Yes, your mother was one hell of a business woman. The way she handled things after your father's death was quite admirable."

A look flashed across his face, one she recognized quite easily. The need to hurt. It was something he excelled at—finding a sensitive spot, digging his claws in. But Renee had stopped being a target years ago. With a chilly smile, she shrugged and said, "I don't know. The times I came home and found her drunk on the floor and crying about how he humiliated her, I don't really think you'd call it *admirable*."

He gazed at her, assessing, wondering. She didn't know what in the hell he was trying to find. She didn't blink, didn't look away. He finally broke the stare, focusing once more on Deacon. "Deacon, I've been trying to get in contact with you."

Bored, Deacon said, "Yeah, I know. You've been keeping my assistant busy—she really does hate to keep writing all the phone messages when she knows I won't return the calls."

"Won't return . . ." JD's brows pinched together; then his eyes narrowed. The outraged mask lasted only a minute, and then it was gone.

He'd gotten better about hiding the ugliness inside him, Renee decided. The friendly, appealing charm was going to make up for what age was slowly leeching away. People were still going to be fooled by him.

His voice had only the slightest edge as he said, "I really won't take up much of your time. I just wanted to ask if you'd consider—"

Deacon snorted. "You want me to add my name, my family's name, to the list of your supporters. Tell me something, JD, is your memory really *that* short, or do you just think mine is?"

A canny, crafty smile curled JD's lips. "Of course not. Important things are always remembered. Those who help us. Those who hurt us. I don't forget those who help me." The rest of it—*I don't forget those who hurt me*—went unsaid, but still, it came through loud and clear.

"The only thing I'd be interesting in helping you do as far as your career goes would be ending it. And don't waste your time making threats at me." Deacon smirked. "I'm not one of your lackeys, and I never have been. You're wasting your time."

Renee followed the conversation, did what she could to sum it up—JD wanted Deacon's support, whatever that meant. Probably JD had followed Daddy's footsteps and gone into politics. Hell, why did all the perverted fucks go into politics? How did they do so well?

JD's eyes slid her way. She could tell what he was thinking just by that look. Wrinkling her nose, she took one slow, deliberate step backward. "Whatever in the hell you're thinking, the answer is no. No, let me correct that. The answer is *hell*, no."

The cool, friendly facade fell away. His smile went from friendly to cold, devious. "Hell, no. You always did like those words. You really should learn to say yes; might warm you up, make you relax a little more." He leaned closer and whispered, "I'd be happy to help."

Deacon grabbed him. He probably would have done more than haul JD away but as he cocked his fist, Renee laid a hand on his shoulder. He tore his eyes from JD's face long enough to look at her, and she saw the icy rage brewing deep inside him. Squeezing gently, she said, "Don't waste the energy on him."

Aware that JD was watching, she gave Deacon a sassy smile and winked. "I'd much rather you waste it on me later."

Deacon didn't want to let go, he realized.

He wanted to pound his fist in JD's face, repeatedly. Beating the shit out of the arrogant prick was something that had occurred to him more than once over the years, but he hadn't ever wanted it this bad. Instead of pounding on him, he jerked JD close, fisting his hand in the bastard's expensive shirt.

Lowering his head, he said quietly, "You better be very careful how you talk to Renee from here on out. And if you ever touch her . . . I'll rip your balls off and feed them to you."

Once more, the memory of the bruise he'd seen on Renee's face years ago came up to taunt him.

JD went a very gratifying shade of white, followed by an ugly, mottled purple. Jerking against Deacon's hand, he snarled, "Get the fuck off me."

Deacon took his time about it, reaching up to pat JD's cheek, a little too hard to be considered anything other than insulting. Then he let go with a shove and watched as JD stumbled until he caught his balance.

"You son of a bitch."

Laughing, Deacon glanced around. "Better be careful there, JD. Your earnest would-be constituents could be listening in. You don't want them to see you get into a fight in the town square, do you?"

"You don't want to fuck with me, Deacon."

"Damn straight. Even if I did swing toward guys, snakes and scum aren't on the list." He held out a hand for Renee. As she laced her fingers with his, he gave JD one final warning. "Remember what I said, JD. I've got no problem taking you on. You aren't a threat to me—remember that."

Renee didn't say anything until they were almost to the sheriff's office. "You don't think he's going to just let that go, do you?"

With a shrug, Deacon held the door open for her. "I don't really give a damn if he does or not. He can't do a damn thing to me. He knows it. If I know him, he's going to focus his attention on somebody he has half a chance of controlling."

"JD does love to control things—but I know from experience, when he can't control something, he doesn't let go very easily." Her pretty face darkened with a grimace as her fingers brushed her cheek. "He doesn't handle 'no' well."

She went to brush past him, but Deacon caught her arm. Part of him told him to let it go, but he couldn't. Guiding her back away from the door, he led to a recessed alcove along the porch. He touched her cheek, tracing out the long-faded bruise. "So what did you tell him no about?"

Her green eyes darkened. "What do you think?"

"You wouldn't sleep with him."

"Give the man a prize," Renee said, reaching for a mocking tone, but falling flat. She tried to go around him, feeling too confined, too tense.

Deacon pressed his hand to her cheek and she sighed, slumped back against the wall. He rubbed his thumb over her lip, stroked it down over her chin and then under, using it to guide her head back. He didn't say anything, just lowered his head, brushing his lips along her cheek.

Kissing away a long-faded bruise, kissing away the pain and humiliation of it. Tears stung her eyes at the gentleness of it. Without saying another word, he lifted his head and took her hand.

As he guided her into the sheriff's department, Renee realized she was shaking.

Not from lust—although it burned through her.

But from fear.

She had the worst feeling that she was falling in love with him. *Not good. Not good at all . . .*

Mute, she followed Deacon into the county sheriff's office and stood in silence as one of the deputies from last night saw Deacon and came up to speak with him.

Blood roaring in her ears, she barely heard a word the man said and then silence fell, an odd silence. Feeling them watching her, she looked up and realized somebody had been speaking to her. "I'm sorry; my mind is wandering."

The deputy smiled. "That's understandable. I don't imagine you slept well."

Renee blushed and averted her head, her hair falling to shield her face. "I slept well enough, I guess. Just still a little frazzled by yesterday, Deputy . . . Morris." She had to glance at the badge to remember his name. He'd been the first one to respond yesterday after she called 911, she thought.

Morris took that explanation easily enough and chatted with Deacon for a few more minutes. Renee made herself pay attention and when he offered to go find the sheriff for them, she smiled politely and thanked him.

On the inside, she wasn't smiling, though. Inside, she was a *wreck*.

By the time Seth Salinger appeared and led them back to his office, Renee's gut was a mess of nerves, fear and confusion. She was falling for Deacon Cross—damn it, how stupid was she? She'd suspected from the get-go this man could cause her problems, but had she done the wise thing and gone in the other direction? Hell, no.

Shaking and nervous, she settled on a chair in front of the beat-up, salvage-store reject of a desk as Seth settled down behind it.

As if her turbulent thoughts weren't enough, memories from last night started to intrude as Seth reached for a manila file folder on his desk.

Beat-up, scarred as it was, the desk was meticulously neat. Not even a paper clip out of place.

"Given any more thought to who might have torn your place up last night?" Seth asked.

In a waspish voice, she said, "I've got about as much an idea today as I did yesterday, Seth. No fucking clue."

He glanced up, brows raised. A look of surprise crossed his face and then slowly, a grin curled his lips. "No fucking clue. Miz Lincoln, if your mother heard you . . ."

Renee narrowed her eyes. "I'm pretty sure I'm past the age of having to worry about what my mother might think."

Seth lifted a shoulder in a restless shrug. "I wouldn't know myself—my mom never was much for worrying, but I know there are some moms out there that just love to keep on mothering." He glanced at Deacon. "Isn't your mom like that, Deacon? You still worry about what she thinks?"

Renee might not recognize the conciliatory tone in Seth's voice, but Deacon did. He let himself smile back a little as he answered, "On a regular basis. I don't leave the house even to check the mailbox unless I've got clean underwear on and I don't go to work without making sure my socks match."

Crossing her legs, Renee smiled humorlessly. "Worrying about clean underwear, matching socks, swearing. The joys of motherly love. I'll try to be more ladylike, Sheriff. Now, can we get this over with?"

Seth leaned back in his chair. In his hand, he held a black ball-point pen and instead of replying right away, he started rolling the barrel of the pen back and forth between his hands. Five seconds dragged into ten, then thirty—a minute passed before he spoke. "I owe you an apology, Ms. Lincoln."

Renee blinked.

Across from her, Seth sat up straighter in his chair, staring at her. "I acted like an ass last night. I need to apologize for that."

"Why?"

Seth scowled. "Why what? Why am I apologizing? I already explained why."

Tucking a strand of deep red hair back behind her ear, Renee said, "No. Why do you give a damn if you acted like an ass? You don't like me. Why do you feel the need to apologize for that?"

Shoving back from the desk, Seth hooked an ankle over his knee. "You very pointedly told me that I don't really know you—sort of hard to decide if I like you or not, based on that. Last night was the first time I've seen you in fifteen years."

For a moment, she was quiet. Quiet enough that it started to make Seth edgy, quiet enough that Deacon wasn't entirely sure she was going to respond to Seth's apology any more than she already had—he was right.

"Fine. You're sorry. Apology accepted. *Now* can we get this over with?"

6

THE HOT, HUMID heat of an Ohio Valley summer had sweat trickling down her back. The huge sprawl of land that made up the Cross family's backyard was equipped with shade trees, lawn furniture placed here and there and some very, very nice misting fans. Renee lifted her face to the breeze and sighed with pleasure as a fine jet of mist sprayed out and then the fan oscillated in her direction, enhancing the cooling sensation until she actually felt half comfortable.

Their backyard had been designed to be enjoyed. Unlike the lands around Renee's childhood home. The Lincoln estate was meant to be admired, coveted, but never enjoyed. What little furniture was placed on the grounds was that awful metal kind that was uncomfortable as hell—and this time of year, hazardous. The blistering sun quickly turned it into something that would brand whatever poor soul was dumb enough to sit on the damn things.

Maybe—

No. Not going down that road of *maybe*. Her life didn't belong in Madison anymore.

Granted, she had been quietly going insane with her life. Running a kitchen, being the head chef, it just wasn't enough for her anymore. She wanted to have her own place—and if she wasn't such a damn coward, she might actually go for it. Wasn't like money was an issue . . .

"Heavy thoughts, dear?"

Renee dragged her attention back to reality. The land of *maybe* was a fairy tale, anyway. She met Immi Cross's gaze, eyes the same amazing blue as Deacon's, and she smiled. "My mind is just wandering. That's all."

With an understanding smile, the older woman nodded. "I can understand. What a frightfully upsetting homecoming you had. How did the visit to the sheriff's office go?"

With a restless shrug, Renee said, "About as I expected. They want to pick my brain for possible suspects, but I have no clue. Except for my mother's funeral, I haven't been home in fifteen years. Hell, I don't recognize hardly anybody."

"Fifteen years is a long time to be gone. You weren't here very long after your mother passed, were you?"

Renee shook her head, wishing she could feel a little bit of regret for the loss of her mother. But she didn't. Couldn't. "No. I just didn't see much reason to stay here. Mother and I weren't very close. What family I have left are the cousins from Father's side of the family and most of them no longer live around here."

"It's hard not having close family," Immi murmured.

Renee thought she heard a hidden message in those words, but she couldn't be sure. She forced a smile and said, "I really wouldn't know."

"Does it seem strange, Seth being the sheriff?"

Grateful for the change in subject, Renee grinned. "Oh, yes." Once the man had pulled the stick out of his ass and relaxed a little, she could actually focus on something else and she had to admit, he was definitely putting some thought into who could have trashed her home. "Definitely not what I would have expected."

"He does a good job. Some of the town council was a bit concerned, given his age and all. A few of them mentioned that perhaps another man might be a better choice for sheriff after Luther Williams retired. I think Grady Morris was mentioned, one or two others. But Luther had recommended Seth, so that's who they went with."

Immi's gaze drifted over Renee's shoulder. A smile curled her lips. "I have to wonder . . . how much of those wandering thoughts of yours have to do with Deacon, though."

Unable to resist, Renee glanced over her shoulder. There he was, striding back across the well-manicured lawn, a tray laden with iced tea, glasses . . . and cookies. Renee's belly rumbled even as she grinned at the sight. She wondered what some of the women he'd been with would think if they saw him now, catering to his mom's every wish.

Immi Cross had wanted to come outside, so Deacon lifted the woman out of her bed and carried her outside.

She had wanted iced tea and cookies—Deacon fetched iced tea and cookies.

"He's a good boy."

Renee smiled. "A good boy?"

"Well, perhaps not a boy—not in your eyes, dear." Immi chuckled. "He'll always be my boy, though. A good man—much like his father. He looks so much like him, acts so much like him."

Blood rushed to Renee's cheeks and she thought of Deacon's father. Leonard Cross—Leo—had been a doctor. Somehow, the thought of that smiling man in his white lab coat having much in common, besides looks, with Deacon was enough to have Renee squirming uncomfortably. But the sad, wistful note in Immi's voice had Renee's heart twisting with sympathy. Shifting in her seat, she looked back at Immi and said, "You must miss him terribly."

"Every day. But I wouldn't undo a moment."

Deacon drew close enough to hear. "Undo a moment of what? You better not be relating embarrassing preschool moments or something," he said as he lay the tray on the table in front of his mother.

"No. I wouldn't do that. At least not *yet*," she said with a wink. She accepted the glass he poured her and took a sip, smiling at him over the rim. "I was telling her about your father."

The smile on his face became sad, almost bittersweet. "Oh, now there are some stories." He settled on the seat across from his mother. "Mom and Dad had a whirlwind-type courtship. If you're the romantic type, you'd probably love the story. They met and married within five days." He reached out and took his mom's hand.

Immi squeezed and covered his hand with her free one. "When it's right . . . you know." Her eyes slid toward Renee.

The speculation there was enough to have Renee blushing and once more fighting the urge to squirm.

But it was nothing compared to what happened when Deacon looked at her. The heat in his gaze—that she could handle. She was almost adjusting to seeing that heat there, even though it had been only a few days. No, it was the softer emotion that was harder for her to handle. "I'm starting to believe that."

The words were spoken more to his mother.

But they were meant for her. Renee knew it.

Her mouth went dry, her hands started to sweat and blood roared in her ears.

Somebody's hand touched hers. Renee stiffened and just barely managed to keep from jerking away. Forcing herself to look up, she saw Immi watching her with concern. The older woman's lips moved but whatever she was saying, Renee couldn't hear any of it. Surging to her feet, she stammered out something—what, she couldn't have said, but hopefully it made a little bit of sense.

As she headed for her car, Deacon called to her.

But Renee couldn't stop. She felt like a class-act idiot—a rude one. A cowardly one, running away from something that probably wasn't even real. He hadn't outright *said* anything. Besides, he was too smart for that. The two of them had no chance. Once upon a time, she'd played the sub. A Dom like Deacon needed a real one. Somebody who wanted what he wanted.

She was about two seconds away from a full-on panic attack. She'd much rather *not* have it here.

The tinny, canned music sound from her phone came as one very, very welcome distraction. Behind her, she heard Deacon call to her again. Flipping open the phone, the first thing she said was, "Whatever in the hell you do, please don't hang up the phone in the next five or ten minutes."

Lacey didn't say anything for about five seconds. Then she started to laugh. "Why? Has some geeky nerd from high school got you cornered or something? Told you that you shouldn't be in such a rush to get back to Madison."

Renee chanced a look back over her shoulder. Deacon was standing by his mom, glaring in her direction. Immi had a hand on his wrist and Renee caught a glimpse of him dipping his head to listen to whatever she had to say.

"Geeky nerd?" Renee muttered. Her hand shook as she pushed a stray lock of hair back from her face. "No. Not a geeky nerd."

"Hmmmm. But it is a guy? Shoot, if it's a guy has *you* flustered, maybe I should have gone back home a week early so *I* could meet him before you had a chance. You haven't let a guy fluster you . . . in . . . Geez, Renee, *has* a guy ever managed that?"

Blushing, she strode toward the navy Mercedes she was still driving. It would be another week before her car was done, thanks to the lack of materials on hand. "Do we have to talk about this?"

Lacey was grinning. Renee didn't even have to see her friend's face to know the other woman was grinning. "I dunno. I'm still not exactly sure what we are talking about. Why don't you enlighten me and then I'll decide if we have to talk about it or not?"

Enlighten you—okay, how's this? I had one very wild, wicked encounter with the Dom from my dreams. He wasn't convinced he had to browbeat me into the ground, but he somehow knew every little fantasy I've ever had and sex with him is earth-shattering. Then I find out it's a guy I kind of liked in high school, but he never noticed me. Then I realize this guy is every bit as wonderful as I'd imagined he probably was back in high school. And he starts acting like I'm somebody who matters—to him. As a person. I can't handle this.

By the way, it's your old boyfriend.

Enlightened?

"It's a long story," she mumbled, digging for her keys.

Unlocking the door, she started to climb inside.

From the corner of her eye, she saw something.

Her house.

The front door was standing wide-open.

Frowning, she shut the door.

On the other end of the line, Lacey said, "Don't you go giving me that *it's a long story* bit. You got me curious, now spill."

"It really is a long story," Renee replied. A shiver raced down her spine as she checked the road, crossed it. In the back of her mind, a rational voice told her it would be a good idea to just hang up on Lacey, call the sheriff's office and wait. No.

Not wait. Go back to Deacon.

One thing was certain. Going into her house was a stupid idea. Standing at the base of the steps, frozen in place, she stared inside the open door.

She saw nobody.

It's probably just somebody following up from the sheriff's office.

Logical.

Except Renee didn't see a car.

Get in the car. Don't go in that house—

"Somebody's in my house," she said to Lacey.

Lacey's amusement died. "What?"

"Somebody busted the door open the other day, vandalized it, tore my car up—and the front door is open."

"Are you *in* the house?"

"No. I was over at Deacon's . . . going to my car. Saw the door."

She shifted from one foot to the other at the bottom of the steps. "I'm in front of it now."

"Don't go in the damn house. I'm hanging up. Call nine-one-one."

Yeah. Swallowing the knot in her throat, she said in a rusty voice, "Good idea. Hanging up—" She started to back away, still staring at the open door with some sort of morbid fascination. "Hanging up now."

She lowered the phone but before she could end the call, she heard tires screeching.

"YOU NEVER DID understand patience, baby."

His mother sat there, staring up at him with sympathy. Her hand lay on his wrist and she had a sad, wistful smile on her face. Glancing back toward Renee, he watched as she disappeared around the corner of the house. With a grimace, he said, "Lacked subtlety there, huh?"

"Subtlety was definitely off. So was your timing." She patted the seat next to her and said, "Sit down for a few minutes. Take a deep breath. Let her settle down a few minutes, then call her or go after her."

"Go after her?" Deacon repeated, amused.

"Isn't that what you want?" Immi Cross smiled at him, a world of wisdom in her gaze.

He settled on the seat next to her and she reached up, patted his cheek with a hand that shook. They'd had him late in life. His mother had been nearly forty, his dad forty-three. In the years since her husband had died, life had seemed to weigh heavily on her. It seemed as if she'd aged two decades but only nine years had passed since Leo passed away.

"I haven't seen Renee in fifteen years," he said quietly. "Back then, I barely knew her. What I did know, I don't think I liked."

"Renee's a good girl. She always has been—her parents weren't the kind of parents I would have wanted. They didn't understand love."

"*I* don't understand love."

"You know it when you feel it, don't you? Your father and I, you know we love you. You know you love us."

Love—not loved. Even though his dad was gone, the love was still there.

Deacon smiled. "Yeah. I know that."

"And what about her? Do you love her?"

Slanting her a look, he said, "Now who has some patience issues?"

She laughed. "Baby, I don't have time for patience. Besides . . . it's not like I'm trying to get water from a stone. I see something in your eyes when you look at her."

"We're practically strangers."

"So were your father and I—or so it would seem to others. But I felt like I'd known him my entire life, been friends with him my entire life . . . been waiting for him, my entire life. In our hearts, we weren't strangers. In our hearts, we knew each other—because we'd been made for each other." She patted his hand. "Ahhhh. Here comes Callie. And she has my chair."

Deacon glanced up, saw his mother's nurse pushing the wheelchair toward them.

"You go find your lady now. If she's the one you've been waiting for, you don't want to wait any longer, I'm sure. Just don't rush *her*—she might need more time."

Time.

Yeah. He needed to give her time.

He could do that, he told himself as he left his mom with her nurse and headed around the house at a trot. Shit, it wasn't like he needed to be proposing right now anyway—*proposing*. Why didn't that terrify him?

Because it fit. Plain and simple. Just like she fit him, although

Deacon would bet his next breath that Renee wouldn't see it as easily. He could even hear her arguments. He suspected she had some hang-ups about a serious relationship with a Dom—the way she liked to push, the way she seemed more interested in playing and thrills than anything—but he suspected a lot of that had to do with her past.

They could work with that. Hell, it wasn't like he wanted some woman who'd be happy to spend her life kneeling at his feet. That would bore the hell out of him.

Bored—so many of the women in his life had bored him. There were even times when he wondered if *he* knew what he wanted in life. How could he keep a sub happy when he wasn't all that happy himself?

But Renee didn't bore him.

With her, he didn't just feel happy. He felt whole.

Whatever the problems were, they could work them out. If he could just keep her from disappearing on him.

He saw Renee's car sitting in the driveway and he heaved out a sigh of relief. Okay, so she hadn't taken off running.

But as he drew close, he saw that she wasn't in the car.

He looked up.

Across the street.

Shit—the door to her house was open . . . Then he saw her, heading down the drive. He started working on what to say. He'd freaked her out. He could get that. But he just needed to make sure she knew he wasn't going to rush her.

Even if that was what he wanted, he wasn't going to do it.

Time.

They had time—

That was when he heard the screech of tires. That was when he looked off to the side and saw the car—a dark sedan that looked like ten thousand other dark sedans—come flying around the side of the house, whipping around the curve of the driveway. Heading straight for Renee.

Time.

He didn't have any.

The car was heading straight for Renee and somehow, he knew it was intentional. He took off running for her, screamed her name.

She dove to the side and the car screeched to a stop. Feet pounding on the pavement, he rushed for them as the driver went into reverse, angling around until the rear bumper was directed right at Renee. She shoved to her feet and took off running, across the driveway this time, heading for the porch.

She didn't make it, though.

It was a moment he'd see in his head for years. It would haunt his sleep. It would sneak up out of his subconscious to taunt him. The driver whipped the car around again, tires screeching as the gas was hit. She was almost to the porch—maybe almost safe. She dodged to the side as the car sped up, but she couldn't move fast enough. It clipped her hip and she stumbled, fell.

The car stopped. Backed up—slowly.

Deacon was finally close enough. He lunged, leaping for the car, but just as his fingers brushed off the trunk, the driver went back into drive.

He shouted her name.

Renee screamed.

Over the roaring in his ears, all he could hear was her. All he could see was her.

Even when another car came roaring up, shooting between Renee and himself, knocking the sedan away, Deacon could see only her. Sprawled on the ground, face as white as death, her hair in a tangle around her shoulders.

Distantly, he heard the crash. Heard the screech of metal on metal. Heard somebody saying his name—familiar voice. A car door slammed. An engine revved—the sedan disappeared, those damn tires screeching out yet another warning. He heard his name again.

But he didn't turn to look.

Not even when a second car pulled into the driveway.
The only person that mattered was lying on the ground.

RENEE LAY ON the narrow, confining hospital bed and tried to find a comfortable position. Her hip and thigh were one nasty, ugly bruise. According to the X-rays, neither was broken and that, in and of itself, was a miracle. Her left wrist was broken, fractured when she threw out her hands to catch herself after the car scraped against her hip and sent her flying. She also had a mild concussion, knees scraped so raw they looked like raw hamburger.

Still, all in all, she wasn't going to complain.

At least not while she drifted in a sweet haze of Vicodin. The curtain brushed aside and she scowled, convinced it was going to be Seth Salinger once more. But the scowl melted away as she saw Deacon peer around. When he saw that she was awake, he came and sank down to his knees by the bed. Without saying a word, he slid one arm across her belly and dropped his head down. His forehead pressed against her right arm. She wanted to touch him, but even with the Vicodin cruising inside her veins, she wasn't about to move her left hand to do so.

"Hey."

For the longest time, he was quiet. Then he finally lifted his head. "If Seth asked me one more question, I think I would have pounded him into the ground."

With a grin that felt foolish even to her, she said, "That would have gotten you thrown in jail."

"Would have been worth it," he muttered. His blue eyes went dark as he studied her wrist. He pushed the sheet aside, eyed her bandaged knees; then, despite her slapping at his hands with her uninjured one, he pulled up the ugly hospital gown and inspected her bruised hip. It looked like a dark rainbow, all black, blue and mottled red. "Is anything broken?"

Rolling her head on the pillow so she could see him better, she lifted her splinted wrist. "Just my wrist. The impact when I hit the ground. I don't know how I didn't break something else. " She licked her lips. "Man, I'm thirsty. These drugs . . ."

"Are you hurting?"

She smiled at him.

Deacon couldn't think of another word to describe that smile but *loopy*. Loopy—and her eyes were bleary, almost glassy from the drugs she'd been given.

"No. Not hurting a bit." Then she squirmed, winced—swore. With a lot more variety and color than he would have expected to hear from her.

She closed her eyes and dropped her head back onto the pillow. When she looked back at him, the pain had washed some of the fog from her gaze and she looked more lucid. "Well, I'm not hurting if I don't go moving around."

"Probably going to be a lot of fun to get up and go to the bathroom in a little while," Deacon said, trying to hide the rage burning a hole inside him.

A faint blush colored her cheeks. "Oh, yes. Loads of fun." She sighed and reached up with her good hand to push her tangled hair out of her face. "This has been the weirdest damn day of my life."

"I bet." Without looking away from her, he reached out and snagged the stool, hauled it next to the bed so he could sit down beside her, as close as he could considering the tubes attached to her body, the bed and the rail. The rail. He scowled at it and started fiddling with it until he managed to push it down.

She eyed him sleepily. The jolt that pain had given her was fading fast; he could tell by the way her forest green eyes were clouding up again. "Not every day some lunatic tries to run me over."

He stiffened. As her gaze cut to him, he tried to make himself relax once more but couldn't quite manage it. Bracing his elbows on the bed, he took her good hand and held it between both of his, focused on the warmth of her skin, the way her chest rose and fell with each soft, steady breath. Alive. She was alive.

And right now—she was safe.

"So Seth doesn't know who it was."

"No." He laced their fingers together, recalled those few minutes that seemed like endless hours.

It had been Lacey who came flying out of nowhere—he'd just talked to her a few minutes ago and realized that she'd been on the phone with Renee when it happened and after she hung up, Lacey had ended up calling 911. In town early for the reunion as well, she'd been on her way over to the Lincoln home, looking for Renee. She had driven up in time to see what was happening and had responded in typical Lacey fashion—stomping down on the gas and plowing her Volkswagen Beetle into the side of the sedan. The smaller car hadn't done much damage. The driver managed to get away before Seth and his deputies arrived.

But it had most likely saved Renee's life.

Lacey was damn good about diving into things feet-first. It was one of the things that had alternately amused or irritated him when they had dated in school, that ability to make up her mind to do something in a split second—and nothing made her deviate once she made up her mind. That lack of hesitation had saved Renee's life.

"Doesn't make any sense." Her voice grew softer, quieter, heavy with sleep, and when she blinked, her lids remained down for a few seconds longer each time. "None of it. Why would somebody try to run me over?"

"I don't know, baby," he murmured.

But he had a bad feeling in his gut. Right now, it was just a feeling, but he couldn't shake it, either. Didn't help that Seth's thoughts were running down the same path. He shoved it aside. Right now, he couldn't think about that. He needed to focus on Renee because if she had any inkling of how damn murderous he felt right now—she needed rest, not his rage.

It looked like she was going to get it, too. She cuddled against his hand as he brushed her hair back. With a soft sigh, she closed her eyes.

Let her sleep. Go talk to the doctor. Pushing up from the stool, he tucked the blankets around her slender form and then turned to go. Once she was ready to leave, she was going home with him. He didn't know how she'd feel about it, but he wasn't letting her out of his sight until she was safe—

"Deacon."

He looked back, found her staring at him. Her eyes were heavy with sleep, but clear. "Is it right?" she asked softly.

He blinked—confused, for two seconds—and then remembered. *When it's right . . . you know.* Leaning a shoulder against the wall, he studied her, just barely resisted the urge to wrap her in his arms and never let go. Ever.

"If it was, how would you feel about that?"

She smiled. It was a self-deprecating smile. "Good enough that it scares me at how much I want that." But then her smile faded and she shook her head. "But Deacon, no matter how right it might seem now, it can't be. You have to see that."

Nerves jangled inside his gut, running high with the adrenaline that still coursed through him. "Actually, I'm not seeing that. Why can't this be right?"

"Because you're you," she said simply. "And I'm me. You live a life that I don't want . . . not all the time. You have needs that I won't be able to fill."

Deep breath, man. You can do this. He took one slow, deep breath and then one more, just to be sure. "Maybe your needs and mine aren't so far off, Renee." He reached out and traced a finger along her lower lip. "You and me work together just fine in the bedroom."

"Or the hotel room?" she added, smiling a little. But it was forced. "Yeah. There, we work just fine. But . . . Deacon, outside the bedroom, I can't live that way. I don't *want* to live that way."

Her eyes flashed and she added, "And I don't want an arrogant

Dom who's going to tell me he knows what I want, what I need. That's up to me to decide."

"Yes. It is." He caught her uninjured hand, careful of the IV tubes and laced their fingers. "Just like it's up to me to decide what I want . . . what I need. Renee, I don't need a woman who thinks she has to serve me night and day. I don't *want* that."

She blinked, startled. "You don't?"

"No. I want you." He studied her pale face, the small scratches and scrapes, a bruise coming up on her cheek. "I want what I think we can have together."

"And what's that?" That sarcastic edge creeped its way into her voice, but he saw the fear in her eyes, side by side with the desperate desire to believe. "Me being your little bedroom sub, but outside the bedroom, we're equals?"

"You make it sound impossible. It's not, baby. Plenty of people make it work. Plenty of people *want* it to work . . . and it does."

Her eyes fell away from his. "The guy I was with in college . . . he seemed to think we could make it work. But it didn't last. He wanted more and more—and I didn't want to give it to him."

"Then you two didn't want the same things. That doesn't mean it can't work for us." He placed a hand on her thigh, desperate to touch her, to get closer. But not yet—not right now. "If it's right, Renee, it can work. If it's right, it's *meant* to work." He squeezed the firm muscles under his hand gently, watching her closely. "If it's right . . . it works. So now you have to tell me—does this feel right to you? Do *we* feel right?"

For a moment she didn't respond. Didn't speak. She closed her eyes and didn't even look at him. But then, right about the same time Deacon felt his heart start on a freefall down to his knees, she opened her eyes.

With a hesitant smile, she held out her hand.

Relief punched through him. He went to her, kicking the stool out of the way and stretching his body out next to hers. It was a damn awkward position, forcing his body onto a bed that was barely big enough for one. But he did it, and although she didn't turn into his body, she relaxed against him and made a satified little hum deep in her throat. "Yeah, Deacon. We feel right."

Then she cuddled a little closer and sighed. She fell asleep, tucked against him. Perched on the edge of the narrow bed, he buried his face against her hair and breathed in the scent of it. Warm. Soft. And as long as he could keep her this close, she'd be safe.

BOOK TWO

Lacey

CHAINS OF LONGING

1994

GRIMACING, LACEY STOOD on the steps of JD's huge house and looked back at her best friend. "I don't feel like doing a party tonight, Missy."

Missy didn't bother even looking at Lacey. "I already told everybody we'd be here." As Lacey watched, Missy fiddled with her hair, tugged on her skirt and basically stood there primping like she was on her way into the prom instead of JD's party.

JD's parties were notorious. His parents went out of town a lot and more than a few of these parties had resulted in the cops being called. But he was JD Whitcomb, son of the mayor, and as far as his family and most of the other well-to-do families were concerned, JD could do no wrong.

Small-town life, Lacey's mom had said once. And if Lacey's mom knew she was here—she'd be lucky if she was allowed out of the house to go to her own graduation. Lacey had thought they were going into Cincinnati to see a movie. Not coming out here. Damn Missy sometimes.

Missy slid her a glance and frowned. "I can't believe you're wearing that."

Rolling her eyes, Lacey said, "I thought we were hitting a movie—not a booze fest." Automatically, she glanced at her T-shirt and jeans. It was no different from anything she'd wear to school—or even to a party if she'd planned on going to one. Lacey liked nice and casual.

Lacey loved Missy—the girl was like a sister—but Missy didn't do nice and casual. She was more into skin, skin, more skin . . . She checked out Missy's clothes. "Your clothes should have clued me in. No wonder you didn't come to the door."

With a laugh, Missy looked down to check herself out.

Lacey thought her friend looked like a major skank, a thin, white tank top that showed the black lace bra underneath, a skirt that was just barely legal and boots that went up over her knee. Lacey would bet anything those boots belonged to Missy's older sister. Tina could wear clothes like that and pull it off without looking cheap. But Missy just looked like she was out to get laid.

Sighing, Lacey admitted to herself that was most likely the case. Getting laid, often, was Missy's goal in life. It had been since ninth grade. Lacey would have thought that three pregnancy scares would help Missy get a clue.

Not.

"Lace, you need to lighten up a little. I mean, we're *seniors*. We start college in a few months—although I still can't believe you're going to Tulane." Her smile turned a little ugly. "You'll be hitting plenty of keggers there, I bet."

Pushing her hair back from her face, Lacey said softly, "I'm going down there to get an education, play some ball. I'm not going to party."

Missy's brows dropped low over her eyes, a sullen pout forming on her face. "Yeah, I bet. You're going to be partying it up at one of the coolest schools around and I'm going to be stuck here going to community college. I'd love to be loaded like you are."

It was an old argument, and not one that Lacey really felt like having again. She wasn't loaded—she had parents who worked hard jobs and they got paid pretty decent for it. But she wasn't loaded—and damn it, she'd *worked* for those scholarships. Busting her butt to get good grades, to look good out on the court so she could get an athletic scholarship, taking the SATs as often as she could just to improve her scores and better her chances at an academic scholarship.

As it was, her scholarships would pay for most—not all—most of her school. The college fund her dad had started when she was little would cover most of what was left, but it wasn't like Lacey had everything handed to her.

"Money isn't what got me into Tulane. *I* did it, Missy. I worked for it." She wanted to say more, but then her cell phone rang. Digging it out of her pocket, she hoped it wasn't Mom. The main reason her mother had bought her the phone was so Lacey could check in when she was going to be out late. It wasn't that her parents didn't trust her, but they worried.

Of course, if Mom heard the party music, Lacey would be busted.

But it wasn't her mother—it was Deacon. She almost hung up on him. Almost. He'd been so pissed off when she told him she was accepting the scholarships to Tulane. Deacon would be starting his sophomore year at the University of Kentucky. He'd been so certain that Lacey would be coming to Lexington with him.

Instead of hanging up, though, she said softly, "I don't want to keep fighting with you, Deacon."

His voice was warm, gentle, as he murmured, "I don't want to fight with you." Then his voice hardened and he swore. "Damn it, Lacey, tell me you aren't at JD's party."

Sending Missy a dirty look, Lacey said, "I am. Unfortunately. But I don't feel like hanging around. Why don't you come pick me up?"

Missy scowled, but Lacey ignored her. She'd agreed to the movie to get her mind off the fight with Deacon. But if he wasn't in the mood to argue, she'd much rather be with him.

MISSY HAD ABANDONED Lacey the minute she hung up with Deacon.

Lacey didn't really care. If her friend wanted to get wasted, wanted to get laid, fine. She slid up the back stairs, away from the main party. It was quieter here and a lot less annoying than the party taking place downstairs.

One thing about JD's parties, people managed to keep on the main level. A few people would sneak up the steps, but the staff usually emerged from the shadows to usher them back to the first floor.

So far, nobody had come out to chase Lacey off and she was glad. She much preferred the relative quiet over the noise. Enjoying it, she roamed up and down the halls as she waited for Deacon to get there.

Well, she *had* been enjoying it, up until a little while ago. She'd seen Renee Lincoln, and the bruise on her face was still giving Lacey a bad time. Part of her just couldn't believe JD had hit Renee. But the other part . . . the other part wasn't surprised at all. JD had a mean streak in him. It was the main reason Lacey had always steered clear of him.

She had half a mind to track Renee down, just to make sure the other girl was okay, but before she could act on it, a noise caught her attention.

Hearing a weak, breathy little moan, she stopped in the middle of the hallway, frozen. There was a squeal. Panting. Wood banging against a wall and the squeak of bedsprings. Blood rushed to Lacey's face as she realized she was hearing somebody go at it.

Apparently a few others had decided to abandon the party, too.

Just when she'd managed to uproot her feet, she heard her name. Turning her head, she smiled at Deacon as he cleared the stairs. Relief crashed through her. Being here was enough to put her on edge—too many kids got into trouble and she'd heard rumors about all the drugs and drinking. Maybe it was her parents talking, but it just didn't seem the best place to be.

"I'm going to kill Missy," she said, slipping her arms around his waist once she drew near enough.

Deacon snorted. "Is she how you ended up here?"

"Yes." Tipping her head back, she smiled at him. "We were supposed to go see a movie so I could forget I was pissed off at you."

Golden brown brows arched up over his eyes. Deacon had the most amazing eyes . . . She could drown in them. He cupped the back of her neck, his fingers digging into tense muscles. "So are you still pissed off at me?"

"I dunno. Are you still mad I'm accepting the scholarship?"

Deacon grimaced. "Mad? Yeah. But . . ." He sighed and dipped his head, pressed his lips to hers. "I think I understand why, though. Tulane is a great school."

Heat rippled through her as he kissed her, taking it from light and sweet to deep and hungry. Her knees went weak and when he lifted his head to stare down at her, all she could think of was him.

All she wanted was him.

A HALF HOUR later, they lay in one of the guestrooms, the door locked, cool air dancing in through the window to drift over their sweat-dampened bodies.

"So you really want to go to Tulane?"

He lay on his side, with her body tucked into the curve of his. Brain half numb from the past hour, it took a few minutes to process his words. "Yeah. I really want to go."

"What about us?"

She squirmed, wishing for a minute they hadn't come in here. It was private; it was quiet—there was no way she could avoid this conversation.

"Deacon . . ." Searching for an answer, she rolled onto her belly, putting a little bit of distance between them.

He rested a hand on the base of her spine and even though her heart was still racing from the last time, it skipped again. She licked her lips, tried to figure out what to say. What was there *to* say?

She wanted to grab this chance she had—grab it and run. She didn't even care what she was leaving behind. At least, not a lot. From the corner of her eye, she saw him watching her and she felt absolutely awful.

She liked Deacon—sometimes she thought she even loved him. But sometimes she suspected he felt more for her than she did for him. Blowing out a sigh, she stared down at the sheets and wished that sometimes she didn't feel like such an outcast.

Most of the girls her age would have been thrilled to have a guy like Deacon. He was good-looking; he was funny—he was in *college*. He didn't feel the need to impress people and he wasn't a jerk like half the popular guys were.

And man, what he could do to her when he touched her . . .

But when she looked at him, Lacey couldn't see changing her life, changing her plans, just to stay close to him. She didn't want to. What she wanted was to do something about the edgy, impatient boredom that flooded her, filled her, threatened to drive her insane.

She wanted away from here, even if it meant leaving Deacon.

What kind of person did that make her?

If she loved him like she should, then wouldn't she *want* to stay closer?

"What about us?" he repeated.

"It's not like I'm leaving the country, Deacon. It's just a little farther away."

He watched her, his eyes grim. Finally, he sighed and stroked his hand up her back. "Yeah, I guess. I was just . . ." His voice trailed off and he sighed. "Never mind. You ready to get out of here?"

"Yeah." Together they climbed from the bed and got dressed. Deacon went to leave, but Lacey, blushing to the roots of her hair, stripped the bed and put the linens in the hamper in the bathroom. Hoping like hell none of the house staff had seen them come in the room, she followed Deacon out into the hall, pulling the door closed behind her.

The hallway was empty and she started toward the stairs. Deacon reached out, caught her wrist, and she stopped, looked at him and smiled. He smiled back and for a minute, her world seemed right again.

Straight.

He dipped his head and kissed her, then brushed her hair back from her face. "We'll work it out," he murmured.

World went all wobbly again. But she said nothing. Throat too tight to speak, she just nodded. She started to follow him down the back steps and then she stopped, looked back over her shoulder. Thought of Renee. "Let me go check on somebody, okay?"

Lacey hadn't seen Renee since their brief conversation earlier. She didn't know why, but for some reason, she had to go check on the other girl.

"Who? Missy? You know you aren't going to get her out of here until she passes out." Deacon grimaced. He didn't like Missy all that much—hell, if Lacey hadn't grown up with her, she doubted she'd like Missy much, either.

Shaking her head, she said, "No. Not Missy. I saw Renee in here earlier—she had a bruise on her face." Pausing, she looked back at Deacon. "I think JD hit her."

Brows dropped low over his eyes. "Are you serious?"

Shrugging her shoulders, Lacey said, "It sure looks like it—and she didn't tell me I was wrong when I said something." Rising on her toes, she kissed his cheek and then patted his chest. "Wait for me, okay?"

He opened his mouth, closed it. Sighed. Then, crossing his arms over his chest, he leaned back against the wall.

Halfway down the hall, the party going on downstairs intruded. Apparently the staff was taking the day off or they'd just gotten tired of trying to corral the messes JD's parties caused. The halls were half full of people and from the corner of her eye, she could see Melinda Benton shove her hand down the front of her boyfriend's pants.

Renee wasn't anywhere on the second floor, unless she'd found a room to hide in, and Lacey wasn't about to start opening doors. She came to the end of one hallway and turned, following it deeper into the house.

It was quieter here. Darker. The boisterous sounds of the party became faint and as the strains of music and laughter faded, she heard something else.

Something weird.

Stopping in her tracks, she glanced back down the hall. Nobody there. Not a soul, and that was *weird* considering the hall had been full of people, kids looking for a private room—or in one case, just looking for a bare wall.

Frozen, she closed her eyes and listened, straining to hear whatever that faint, strangled sound had been. There it was again—then, a guy's laughter muffled it and she heard another voice. With her heart pounding in her throat, she walked to the door where the noise was coming from.

It was a library—JD's father's library. Lacey knew that only because Missy had told her a few hours ago that she'd made out with JD on the desk in there once. If that was all that was going on in there now, then she was going to be so embarrassed.

But that didn't keep her from moving closer. Closer.

For some weird reason, fear choked her. It wanted to paralyze her, immobilize her. A voice screeched at her, demanded she turn around, just turn around and go find Deacon. Another voice, quieter, softer, whispered a warning.

Your life is getting ready to change on you. Big time.

Change in a way she couldn't even begin to understand.

Hearing footsteps, she looked up, saw Renee standing just a few feet away. Two minutes ago, there hadn't been anybody there. "Do you . . ."

Renee nodded. The bruise was an ugly, dark shadow on her pretty face. Her eyes glittered with fear. Lacey knew just how she felt but she didn't let her own fear keep her from reaching out and pushing the door open.

It took a few seconds for her brain to process what she was seeing. Her body was already acting, though—as was her mouth. "Leave her alone, JD. Now."

He snarled at her. "Get the fuck out, bitch. Unless you wanna join the party."

The look he gave her had Lacey's skin crawling, but she'd be damned if she walked away. Instinct had her screaming Deacon's name. The same instinct had her kicking JD's unprotected side—*hard*. He was crouched atop Sherra's pinned, struggling body and he swore, swung out with an arm, but Lacey evaded the blow easily. Boyd was crouched on the floor, holding Sherra's wrists so tight his knuckles had gone white. Like the idiot he was, he stared at Lacey with dumb, uncomprehending eyes.

Something caught her eye and she turned her head just in time to get a full, unobstructed view as Renee brought a heavy lamp down on JD's head. His body went limp, collapsing on top of Sherra's and pinning her to the floor.

She glared at Boyd. "Get off of her."

Boyd just sat there, staring at her while he held Sherra's wrists pinned to the floor—staring at Lacey as though he couldn't figure out what the problem was.

The sound of Deacon's voice was a welcome relief.

"*Move. Now.*"

As Boyd went to do just that, Deacon glanced at her. "Call the cops."

Digging out her phone, she said, "I'd love to."

"What the hell for?" Boyd asked. His forehead was wrinkled

and the guy looked utterly confused. "The little slut was looking to party."

Deacon moved, striking with a speed that left Lacey's head spinning as he lashed out and caught Boyd in the jaw.

Lacey flinched instinctively as she punched in 911. Dispatch came on the line but Lacey didn't have a chance to say anything more than *"We—"* Before she could manage even more than one word, too many things happened. JD surged to his feet, rushing her. He tore the phone away and tried to backhand her. Instinct kicked in and Lacey threw up her forearm, blocking the blow. It was a hell of a lot harder than the practice punches she blocked in her tae kwon do classes at the Y. Pain flared but she gritted her teeth, ignored it and struck, pulling fingers back so that when she hit JD in the nose, it was with the palm of her hand. The palm-heel strike hit him hard and she heard bone crunch, saw the blood spray, splattering on her shirt.

"Stupid bitch," JD howled, stumbling away.

Lacey knelt to grab her phone from the floor. Boyd moved toward her. She dodged away, saw Deacon moving toward them. Heard Renee's voice, panicked and harsh.

She heard the word *gun* and her mind went blank. *Gun?*

Dumb, dazed, she turned her head and watched as Boyd knelt down to pick a gun up from the floor. Where had that come from? She didn't remember seeing it . . . Deacon had JD on the floor, pinned down.

Off to her left, she saw somebody moving. Sherra. She held something—

Then there was blood.

A lot of it.

Hot and metallic, the scent of it flooded the air. It was quiet in the library now, save for the harsh sounds of breathing.

Nobody said a word.

Nobody made a sound.

They just stood there, staring at the jagged piece of the broken

lamp Sherra had grabbed from the ground. Blood dripped from the
tip to the floor and as Lacey stared at it, the puddle of blood grew
larger and larger.

Drip.

Drip.

Drip.

1

DRIP.

Drip.

Drip.

Lacey tried to block out the sound of the leaky water faucet, closing her eyes and resting her back against the wall.

Drip.

Drip.

Drip.

Muttering under her breath, she surged out of the hard, ladder-back chair and stomped across the waiting room, into the bathroom. It was small, with nothing more than a toilet, a mirror and a sink. A sink with a faucet that kept going . . . Drip. Drip. Drip.

Clenching her jaw, she turned the knobs until that infernal dripping stopped. "There." Spinning around, she headed out of the bathroom—and crashed straight into Seth Salinger's chest.

Seth—shit.

One of the main reasons she rarely came back home for more than a day or two. Enough time had passed. Lacey would have thought that maybe she could handle seeing him.

Obviously not.

Get over it. It was one fucking night. Five years ago!

One long, blissful night . . . one night . . . and the last damn time a guy touched me and made me feel much of anything—

A night when her brain had actually shut down on her. A night that haunted her dreams. A night that still had the power to make her belly get all hot and shaky. *There you go, making things seem bigger than they really are. It was one night—the earth didn't move, you didn't fall head over heels in love, and there's no reason you can't act like an adult here.*

No reason. Adult. Got it. She forced herself to look in his eyes and reminded herself, *It's been five years since that night, kid. It was a fluke—*

She might have even succeeded if he hadn't touched her. His hands came up, cupped over her upper arms and steadied her, and heat flared along her skin. Her heart skipped a few beats and started to slam in a sexy little rumba against her breastbone while she tried to get her breathing to level.

"Hey. You okay?"

Easing back, she forced herself to smile at him. "Just peachy, Sheriff."

A smile tugged at his mouth. His very nice mouth . . .

"You look exhausted."

But Lacey barely heard the words at first—she was too busy focusing on that mouth and remembering. Lacey groaned inwardly and gave herself a mental kick in the ass. This was why she hadn't come back home much since then. At Christmastime, always in and out, a few quick weekends where she stayed with her parents and didn't leave the house.

Because of him.

What had he been saying . . .

Oh. Yeah.

Exhausted . . . Smothering a laugh, she edged around him and said, "I *am* exhausted." Just barely, she managed to keep enough distance between them so that her arm didn't brush up against his. She felt his heat, though, caught a trace of his scent and wanted to press her face against his neck and just breathe him in.

Instead, she settled back in that hard, uncomfortable, miserable excuse of a chair and drew a knee to her chest. Resting her chin on her knee, she asked, "Any luck finding the driver?"

Seth gave a disgusted snort. "Hell, no. Even in a place as small as Madison, there are a ton of *dark sedan* type cars." He slid her another look. "You sure you didn't get the make? A Ford emblem on the back? Anything?"

Lacey shook her head. "Sorry. I'm not exactly car-minded under the best of circumstances." Her mouth suddenly dry, she licked her lips and reluctantly thought about just *why* it hadn't been the best of circumstances.

A minute ago, she'd been trying to focus on anything other than Seth, but now she would have been very happy to think of him. Or that one night she tried damn hard to forget.

Anything but what she'd seen earlier.

It was a terrible thing, seeing somebody on the ground, helpless while a couple of tons of metal plowed straight toward her. Even worse when it was a friend.

Seth nodded, taking the chair across from hers. She was glad— at first—that he hadn't sat down next to her. But then she realized that sitting across from him made it damn hard not to look at him. He'd always been too damn easy on the eyes and the past fifteen years had only improved that fact of life.

It was a fact she didn't want to enjoy, either. She didn't want to notice that he'd started cutting that midnight black hair, but not all the way. It was still long enough for a woman to run her hands through, framing that narrow face, just long enough to brush the collar of his shirt. His eyes were the color of dark chocolate and his eyelashes were almost ridiculously long and curly. What kind of guy needed eyelashes like that?

Unlike his twin, Sherra, who had to slather down with SPF 50 whenever she went out in the sun or ended up looking like a lobster, Seth was tanned. Very nicely tanned—and she knew it was because he spent a lot time outside.

At places like the lake outside of town . . . where she liked to go to shoot pictures, where he liked to go to fish—or at least pretend to fish, wearing nothing but a pair of jeans and beat-up tennis shoes.

Her brain went back on its little stroll down memory lane and she remembered that day. A hot, muggy summer day when she had come home for a short visit five years ago. Her trip had been a last-minute one and she hadn't realized until she got home that her parents had taken a quick trip of their own and she was alone in the house. Instead of heading back to her empty apartment in Yonkers, she'd decided to stay in Madison and just relax a little. After sleeping in late and helping herself to some of her mom's homegrown tomatoes for breakfast, Lacey had gathered up her gear, climbed on her sadly neglected mountain bike and headed for the lake.

Hot days like that one usually had a bunch of people gathered at the southern end for swimming. The northern end wasn't as easily accessible and that was where a lot of guys headed for fishing. That had been her destination, too, but she was more interested in the area around the lake than any fish in it.

Seeing Seth there had come as a surprise. In high school, Seth had been the typical bad boy, practically straight out of a good girl's fantasy, dark eyes, a wicked smile, a way of watching you that turned the insides to molten lava. The years since graduating had only increased his appeal.

She'd seen his bike first, a big, mean-looking bike that he had built with his own hands. Even though she'd recognized the bike, it had been a surprise to see him there, a fishing pole in hand.

All that nice, golden skin probably came from days spent out on the water.

Like he'd been that day . . .

Stop it, Lacey! She jerked her attention back to the present, but it didn't help her focus much. Well, it didn't help her focus on anything *besides* Seth.

Lacey wasn't entirely sure it *was* possible to focus on something else or somebody else when Seth Salinger was around. At least not for her.

Back in high school, he had been tall, on the thin side, with that brooding, sexy aura that drove teenaged girls nuts. He was still tall but not what one could call thin—lanky, maybe. Lean, definitely. Muscles strained at the shoulders of the simple, white cotton button-down he wore, long, lean legs in faded denim. As he absently pushed his hair back from his face, she noticed his hands and wrists.

Bony wrists—one of them adorned with a simple watch with a black band, an ordinary piece that could be bought at Sears for $25. Beautiful hands, no rings, nails clipped neat, but not manicured— she was getting damn tired of looking at men who spent more time on their appearance than she did.

Seth was sexy as all get-out, but it didn't come from a two-thousand-dollar suit, hours spent at the gym, baking under some hot lights to get that warm, golden tone to his skin. It was just him.

Damn, she bet he'd be fun in front of a camera. She already knew he photographed very, very well . . . although Seth wasn't aware of it. Those pictures were something she hadn't ever shown anybody, and they were her best work.

If she had the chance to do it again, do it right instead of sneaking pictures from a distance, she wondered what would happen. Were those pictures another fluke? Like that night?

The pictures she'd taken of him were sheer magic, but it wasn't a fluke. She could do it again. Something inside her, that nagging, itchy need for her camera, started to burn. A couple of hours—if she had a couple of hours, Lacey could do it.

She knew she could. A few hours and she could find it. Find that elusive magic that had danced just out of her reach for so long.

That was what she wanted—what she needed. Finding that magic, that heat, that heart.

Heart . . . A memory, this one much more recent, rose up to taunt her.

You do beautiful work, Lacey. But it lacks heart.

It wasn't her work that lacked heart—it was her.

Closing her eyes, she suppressed a sigh.

Yeah. She lacked heart. She lacked heat.

Passion . . .

Lacey, you're a beautiful woman, you're a lot of fun, and you're a great photographer. But you're cold. Yet another ghost—this coming from the guy she'd been dating off and on for two months, the guy who had just dumped her less than a week ago. The same day she'd been told she hadn't gotten the job down in Brazil.

Scowling, Lacey drew her legs up to her chest and buried her face against her knees. That way, she wasn't forced to look at Seth's way-too-nice face, remember the last time she'd really felt heat.

You're cold.

You lack heart.

Oddly enough, it was losing out on the assignment in Brazil that really stung. Luis had bruised her pride, but his leaving hadn't really hurt—the guy had dumped her, gone on to bigger, better things—namely a photographer who could help his career in ways Lacey couldn't. Or more, in ways Lacey didn't *want* to.

She knew Luis hadn't been all that interested in *her*, but he'd made her feel something, at least. But not enough. After two months of dating, she still hadn't been interested in sleeping with him and she wasn't going to have sex with a guy unless she really wanted him. She had no desire to fall into bed with a guy who didn't make her want it.

She wasn't to blame for that. It wasn't like she was frigid or anything. She could give herself an orgasm just fine—usually while thinking about Seth. The lack of heat wasn't something that could be blamed on anybody, not the guys. Not her.

But she was to blame for the abysmal failure in her career. She'd chosen photography because it was something she loved, had always loved, and was good at. But in the past seven or eight years, the life that had always been in her pictures started to fade, then disappear altogether, and she couldn't get it back.

"Are you here?"

Seth's voice, low and amused, tugged her out of her reverie and she chanced a quick glance at his face. "Yeah. I'm here. Just thinking."

A wry grin tugged at his lips and he shook his head. "Considering how pissed off you look, I'm not sure I want to know what you're thinking about."

I'm not pissed—I'm depressed. But all she did was smirk and wondered what he would think if he knew she'd been thinking about getting him in front of a camera. That she'd been remembering a day that he'd probably forgotten. That she'd run away from her life because she was tired of feeling like a failure.

Chances were, he'd laugh.

She narrowed her eyes thoughtfully, studying his face. Those grooves around his mouth, they'd deepen when he laughed. He hadn't been much on laughing that she could recall during high school, but it wasn't like they ever really hung out together. He hadn't laughed that day, either . . . not when she crashed into him after . . .

His voice intruded on her drifting thoughts. His eyes narrowed on her face, then he grinned, shook his head. "You're getting ready to zone out on me again."

"Sorry." She shrugged and lowered her feet back to the ground, looking off to the side so she didn't keep looking back at him and either try to picture him in front of a camera—or remember him over her body, that beautiful face so close to hers, his dark eyes rapt on her face . . .

You're obsessed, babe. O-B-S-E-S-S-E-D. You need to get away from him before this gets out of hand.

With that thought in mind, she glanced at the clock and asked, "You think they'll let me talk to Renee for a few minutes?"

He shrugged. "Let you? Probably not, but I can probably stall them for a few minutes, if she's not asleep. There aren't any serious injuries, but she's pretty banged up and they gave her some pain medicine a while ago." Shoving out of the seat, he offered her a hand. "Come on. We'll go look. If she's awake, you can slip inside for a minute and I'll fend off the nurses."

She acted as if she didn't see it, rising and edging around him.

"I hadn't realized you kept in touch with Renee."

Sliding him a look from the corner of her eye, she shrugged. "It wasn't exactly a planned thing. We both came home for Christmas later that year, ran into each other at the store. Starting talking . . ." Lacey sighed. "Started talking and we couldn't stop. That night totally screwed with our heads."

He was quiet, a frown on his face. They came to a halt in front of a curtained-off section and Seth peeked inside. "She's asleep," he murmured, blocking her with his body.

Lacey moved past him to peek inside for herself. Then she stopped in her tracks, her jaw dropping in stunned surprise.

Damn.

Deacon and Renee.

She'd thought she glimpsed something between them earlier. But it had been sheer chaos, cops, paramedics, all sorts of curious people emerging from their houses to gawk. She hadn't had that much time to really put two and two together.

It was as clear as day, though. An unconscious smile curled her lips and she glanced at Seth before looking back at Renee. The other woman was asleep all right. And lying pressed up against her body was Deacon Cross. Torso propped up, weight braced on one elbow, he stared down at Renee. Lacey had a feeling he'd been doing just that, staring at Renee, for quite a while.

In her head, something clicked. Lacey knew about the guy Renee had dated in college—knew about the kinky stuff Renee was experimenting with. She'd worried about her friend for a while, just because everything Renee was getting into seemed so—*not* Renee.

Likewise, Lacey also knew about Deacon. He'd always been big on being in charge when it came to sex when they'd started sleeping together, a little too confident for the typical teenaged boy. His appetites had gotten darker. Even though he had been able to make her feel so damn hot, he had ended up pushing her past a line she was comfortable with. The more he needed, the less she could give.

During Christmas break her freshman year, they'd just decided to walk away.

Deacon and Renee.

She snickered. "I should have seen this coming."

Deacon glanced up at her from the bed. A grin tugged at his lips and then it faded as he once more focused his attention on Renee.

Like she was the only thing in the world that existed—no. Like she *was* his world.

How did that happen so fast?

Longing moved through her as she watched for another minute. She wanted that.

Not Deacon—he had been the first guy she'd ever gotten serious over—hell, actually, he was the *only* guy she'd ever been serious over. But she hadn't loved him.

He might have loved her, probably had, but he hadn't ever looked at her like that. Never looked at her the way he looked at Renee, as though she was the center of his universe.

That was what she longed for.

Some sort of connection that went deeper than heat, deeper than need.

Something that would fill the empty hole in her heart. Seemed sappy as hell, but some people were fine playing the crowd or just going it alone. Lacey wasn't one of them. She wanted *someone*.

She just couldn't find him.

While envy burned quietly inside her heart, she backed away from the curtain. Turning on her heel, she headed down the hall.

"Hey."

Seth caught up with her, eyeing her with unreadable eyes. "You still got a thing for him?"

Lacey shoved her hands inside her pockets and focused on the empty hallway in front of her. She wanted out of here. "No."

Seth smirked. "You sure about that?"

Stopping in her tracks, she turned and faced Seth. "Is it really any of your business? No. It's not. But yeah, I'm sure."

"Then why do you look like Renee just stole something from you?"

Lacey blushed. Did she feel like that? No—not exactly. Renee hadn't taken anything from Lacey. But she did have something Lacey wanted—coveted. Needed. "It's not that she took something. It's that she has something. Something I want and can't find." Glancing back down the hall, she heaved out a sigh. "If she's got something going with Deacon, I'm happy for her—she deserves somebody who'll make her happy. But I'm still jealous."

2

"JEALOUS."

Seth could understand that.

He'd lived with jealousy for most of his teenaged years, because the girl he wanted was going out with somebody else—and she didn't even know he was alive.

Sometimes he felt like he'd been born loving Lacey Talbot. Back in high school, she'd been so far above him, it had been a waste of time to even dream about her. But he'd done it anyway.

That one day they'd had together had been enough to convince him he'd been right—she was definitely out of his reach. The best damn night of his life—and while he had been reeling and trying to convince himself he hadn't been dreaming, she'd been trying to convince herself it *had* been a dream.

I don't believe this . . .

Three simple words. And they stung like hell.

She had slept with him and turned his life upside down. He imagined that she'd either forgotten it altogether or wished she could.

Even knowing that, even the way she hadn't said a damn thing when he stormed out of her room, unable to look at her and see the shame on her face—even though he had no pride when it came to her, he still loved her.

Quietly, desperately loved her—and at times, he hated himself for not being what she needed.

Now she was looking at him with misery in her eyes and once more, he'd failed her. He'd tried to keep her from seeing Deacon and Renee like that, but when she went to go around him and look for herself, there wasn't much he could do unless he wanted to bodily stop her. Unless he put his hands on that smooth, long body with its sleek muscles, soft skin, beautiful blond hair . . . no. Not much he could do.

He'd wanted to put his hands on that body for years.

Years.

Since high school.

Hell, since *before* high school. He'd been mooning over Lacey Talbot from the time she and her family had moved to Madison when Lacey was six years old. She'd walked into his class on the first day of first grade and he'd fallen head over heels in love. First, it was the schoolboy crush deal, teasing her in the desperate hope that she might notice him, and as he got older, smarter, watching her and pretending not to—hoping that one day, maybe she'd look back.

It hadn't ever happened.

Time went by and he went from mooning over her and teasing her in front of classmates to hot, sweaty dreams and sneaking his way into the high school during a game just so he could watch her play.

All throughout high school, she'd been the focus of more dreams and fantasies than he could possibly recall. But he'd loved her even before that.

Deacon Cross came into the picture and Seth had hated the bastard throughout high school. Even beyond that, until he found out through Sherra—thanks to a few well-placed questions—that

Lacey and Deacon had broken up a few months after she left to go to college in Louisiana.

Years passed and he saw her only sporadically, but even those brief encounters still made his heart race—still made his heart ache. Then that summer five years ago—he could remember the terror in her eyes when she came bursting out of the woods down by the lake. She'd crashed into him, stared up at him, her face scratched and bruised, bruises forming on her pretty neck, leaves and dirt and twigs tangled in her hair. Somebody had grabbed her from behind in the trees.

It didn't make any sense in his mind and if it was anybody other than Lacey, he would have suspected either a prank, a domestic dispute that had gotten out of hand—maybe she'd been drinking and her imagination got away from her. Because what she described sounded unlike the norm for Madison, Ohio.

A mask, a hood, a freaky black robe.

Somebody grabbed her but she managed to get free and ended up squaring off with a sick fuck dressed like a Hollywood horror-movie reject. Whoever it was hadn't been prepared for the fact that Lacey knew how to defend herself—thank God for that—and when it didn't go the way the bastard had expected, he'd ended up taking off running.

But not until he'd rushed Lacey again, knocking her to the ground. He'd wrapped his hands around her neck. Squeezed. Lacey, though, hadn't panicked. She had struck him in the throat, so her attacker ended up being the one gasping for air. While he tried to breathe, she shoved him off and took off running, crashing into Seth at the edge of the lake.

By the time she had guided him back to where it had happened, whoever had attacked her was long gone.

Seth had no idea what might have happened to her if she hadn't known how to take care of herself.

They never did find out who had done it. Lacey did go and file a report, but nothing ever came of it. After she finished the paperwork, he'd taken her back to her parent's house, but it had been empty. Her parents had taken a quick trip to Gatlinburg, Tennessee.

She'd told him she'd be fine.

But he hadn't been able to leave her alone . . .

Don't think about that right now, man. Won't do you a bit of good.

Instead of reliving a very vivid memory, he focused on her, focused on the here and now, instead of then.

He didn't even have to ask what she was jealous of, because when he'd looked in and seen Deacon with Renee, he'd felt a few pangs himself. Seth didn't really spend much time thinking about white-picket fences, a wife, kids—a family. Lacey was the only woman who'd ever managed to evoke those kinds of thoughts inside him and he knew the feeling wasn't mutual.

But since she was all he wanted, he didn't bother trying to find some sort of connection with another woman. He wasn't going to go into a relationship knowing it was a sham. He knew from experience what an ugly mess that could lead to.

And how empty it could make a person.

He'd shied away from commitment, but up until that one day he'd had with Lacey, Seth had done whatever he could—or rather, *who*ever he could, trying to fill the void inside him.

It hadn't worked. The empty hole inside his heart was there and nothing eased it.

So he didn't keep trying. He looked at some of his friends, happily married, settled down, and he felt envious. He wanted that—but with only one woman.

Yeah, he understood the sadness in her gaze.

"Just because you don't have it now doesn't mean you won't ever have it," he told her, after he finally managed to swallow the knot in his throat. Even thinking about her with some guy was enough to make him want to punch something. But thinking about her sad and lonely at night was almost as bad.

She glanced at him from under her lashes and then looked away. "Whatever."

She started to walk away from him. Seth waited long enough to enjoy the view—her slim hips, that tight ass, her confident, easy stride and the way her blond hair bounced against her shoulders as she walked—and then he shook off thoughts of lust and need and focused on duty instead.

WITH HER ARM braced against the door, Lacey tried very, very hard not to look at Seth, not to breathe too deeply, not to think about him. The entire damn car smelled of him—warm, sexy, male. Why in the hell couldn't he at least not smell so good? Plenty of guys had a less than pleasant—or at least, not enticing—scent that had nothing to do with deodorant, cologne, aftershave, soap.

But could Seth be one of them?

Nope.

He smelled of grass. Sunshine. Hunger shuddered through her. An onslaught of memories swamped her—his hands on her body, the front door of her parents' house hard against her back as he kissed her. Touched her as though he just couldn't get enough. Kissed her as though he was dying and she was the only thing that could save him.

She sneaked another glance at his hands and then jerked her gaze away, stared outside the window. "I really don't see why you think it's necessary for you to come check out the house."

Not necessary at all. She didn't need him in that house, or even near it. It was hard enough to function there, remembering those few hours with him. She couldn't go home for a visit without remembering how they'd gone at it on the porch. Then inside on the floor just beyond the door. On the couch—or rather, behind it, with her bent over it. In her bed, in the bathroom . . .

Oh, hell. This wasn't good. Need was an ache down low in her belly and heat throbbed inside her pussy, a tormenting series of pangs. In an effort to ease the ache, she pressed her knees together and tried to convince herself this wasn't a big deal.

She could do this.

She was an adult.

She wasn't going to lose it just because Seth was coming out to the house with her.

To a very empty house.

Her parents were on their annual trip to Maine. Every year, like clockwork, they went and stayed in a beach house for three weeks, ate lobster, walked on the beach and came home talking about how they should consider moving back there. Except neither of them wanted to deal with New England winters anymore. Neither of them really wanted the hassle of moving, either. They'd be back next week and Lacey had originally planned to take a few extra days so she could visit with them.

But for now, the house was empty.

"It's necessary."

His voice jerked her attention back to the present and she scowled. "What?"

"It's necessary," he said again. "Because of what happened with Renee." Seth glanced at her from the corner of his eye and then focused back on the road. "Today somebody tried to kill her and a few days ago, her house was vandalized."

Oh. Yeah. She remembered. Frowning, she pushed her hair back and shifted on the seat to look at him. "What does this have to do with me again?"

Seth shrugged. "Don't necessarily think it has anything to do with you." *Yet.* He kept that part quiet. He had a weird feeling in his gut, but he wasn't going to say anything until he had something more than feeling. He'd get Lacey to her house, take a few minutes and check the place out, then get the hell out of there.

Easy as could be.

Except he hadn't planned on his gut feeling being right.

Or at least not this dead-on.

Next to him, Lacey still hadn't noticed the house as he slowed
to a stop in front. She was staring out the window as though she
wanted nothing more than to forget he existed. Worry churned inside him, running neck in neck with fury.

Her house had been torn to hell and back.

Unlike Renee's, which had been a quick, haphazard deal, somebody had taken his time on Lacey's house. The big, old house
was set back from the road, situated on a heavily wooded cul-
de-sac. The old neighborhood had huge yards, lots of trees, lots
of room . . . lots of privacy. Whoever had done this had definitely
taken his time.

He blew out a sigh and reached for his phone, putting in a call
to dispatch. As he requested a unit, Lacey's gaze moved toward
him. Then beyond.

Her eyes went wide.

Her jaw dropped.

Disconnecting, he tried to come up with something suitably
comforting, suitably calming, but she wasn't aware of a damn thing
he said. Color drained from her face, leaving her pale under the
smooth, golden glow of her tan. The confusion in her eyes lasted
only a few seconds, and then it was gone, replaced by fury. Her
summery blue eyes narrowed and she swore, long and hard. She
freed her seat belt and went to climb out of the car. Seth caught her
wrist and said, "Not so fast."

She jerked away and Seth let her go with a sigh. He climbed out
of the car and cut her off just before she could take off running for
the house. "Lacey. Stop it."

He was going to have to do it.

He was going to have to touch her, and not just a quick, light
touch on her wrist, either.

Reaching out, he caught her upper arms as she would have
darted around him. "Lacey, you can't go in there."

She snarled at him and jerked against his hands. Seth couldn't
help but think about how much he wanted to kiss that snarl off

her mouth. Couldn't help but notice the smooth, lean muscles working under his hands as she tried to pull away from him. Couldn't help but notice that she still smelled the same—like honeysuckle.

"That's my house, damn it. The hell I can't go in there."

"Somebody broke in there, tore it to hell. For all we know, the guy is still there. Right now, you need to get in the car. I'll have my men here in a few minutes and then—"

"No *and then*. I hope the bastard *is* in there. I'm going to beat the shit out of him . . ." Her voice trailed off as her gaze landed on the flower beds off to the right of the house. "Oh, no. Mama's roses."

He wouldn't have thought it was possible, but the wrathful light in her eyes burned even hotter. Seth followed the line of her gaze, lingered just a second on the mess of uprooted or smashed rosebushes before he focused on her face again. "Lacey, the roses can be fixed. All of this can. But first we need to figure out if he's still here."

"Damn it, Seth!"

She planted her feet, swiveled her hips—a clever, damn-near-successful takedown. He countered and just barely managed to keep his feet as she tried to wrench her weight away. Moving in, he wrapped an arm around her waist and locked her against him. "Stop it," he growled. Fury and concern tangled inside him and something of it finally showed in his voice. She stilled, glaring at him, but no longer fighting to get to the house.

"Think for a minute, Lacey. Somebody did this to Renee's house. Then he tried to run her over. Now your house gets torn apart . . . You're a smart woman. Put it together."

Lacey's tense, struggling body slowly relaxed. She glanced from his face to the house, then back. Shaking her head, she murmured, "You can't be serious."

"Do I look like I'm joking?"

She shoved against him, and this time, he let her go, prepared, ready to grab her if she tried to go for the house again. Her voice shook a little as she said, "Why?"

"I think you've already figured that out."

Lacey blanched and shook her head. "That doesn't make any sense." Her mouth opened. Closed. Then she pressed her lips together, closing her eyes. When she looked at him again, the blue of her gaze was clear. "You can't *know* that. It's been *fifteen* years. Why would somebody wait this long . . . ?"

Her voice trailed off and she fell quiet, remembering.

Absently, Lacey reached up and brushed her fingers across her cheek. Fifteen years . . . but was fifteen years really that much time? That night was still vivid in her memory.

That day at the lake, somebody had come up at her from behind. She'd managed to break his hold and turn around to face her attacker, but the sight of the hooded, masked figure had almost made her freeze.

It was like being caught in some dumbass, badly written horror flick—he'd worn some sort of black, hooded robe and a mask. Bizarre, surreal, but the rage she felt coming from the man was all too real. Seeing that nightmare face in front of her, for a second, it had frozen her.

Enough that she hadn't moved away in time when he rushed her. Took her down. Adrenaline and instinct had kicked in and she'd struck the vulnerable, soft flesh of the neck, obscured by cloth, putting all the strength in it that she could.

It had worked, well enough that she had gotten away. As she ran away, she'd looked back. Only once, long enough to see that her attacker had also taken off running—this time in the opposite direction, disappearing into the woods before she got much more than a glimpse of his black-shrouded body.

A stupid teenaged prank—that was what she'd convinced herself it had been.

But now . . . *No. No "but."* "Fifteen years," she repeated, but it was more for her benefit than anything, and she knew it.

3

THAT DOESN'T MAKE *any sense.*

You can't know that. It's been fifteen years. Why would some-body wait this long . . . ?

Shit, the way she was looking at him was like getting a vicious sucker punch. Seth almost wished he hadn't said anything at all. It wouldn't change anything, though, if he'd kept quiet on his suspicions. Plus, if she knew, she'd be cautious—he hoped.

He forced himself to smile and say, "It could be nothing. But we're going to be careful anyway."

Her eyes were dark, huge in her face, full of fear and anger. Before he could give in to the urge to try to comfort her, Seth made himself look at the house, made himself focus on the trampled, destroyed flower beds.

Nothing, my ass.

He'd had a bad feeling in his gut even when he stood in front of Renee's house, taking note of details from the shattered garden statuary down to the bits of dirt tracked onto the porch.

Lacey didn't need to know how certain he was, though. There was no reason to tell her—not right now. It wouldn't help. Right now, he needed her calm—needed some distance between them so he didn't have to keep fighting the urge to reach for her. Fight the urge to pull her against him, stroke away the tension from her body, calm the first edges of fear he could see dancing in her eyes.

He couldn't do that. Hell, she'd probably laugh at him or pat him on the head for being a "sweet guy." And if she did that . . . He snarled, swore silently.

He took a deep breath and rolled his shoulders, forcing the tension knotting his muscles to relax. He couldn't do a damn thing to help Lacey until he focused on the job. The job . . . not on her.

It would be easier if his men would get here, though. Give him a distraction—something to think about besides *her*.

You got something to focus on, man. Like somebody might try to hurt her?

Yeah. That did it. Even though the need to comfort didn't fade, it was overridden by the need to protect.

Renee.

Lacey.

. . . and maybe Sherra.

Shit, he needed his men here and *now*. Because he needed somebody to watch Lacey for a few minutes so he could make a call to his sister. If he had any luck, Sherra would change her mind about coming. It wasn't like she really loved coming back to Madison for any reason anyway.

The big, hotshot book tour she had lined up could go on just fine. All she had to do was cancel the stop here. Why on earth they had to do this big kick-off deal in Madison, he had no clue.

It wasn't enough that he had to come face-to-face with his fantasy after she'd been avoiding him for five years. No, he had to have an attempted murder get dumped in his lap and he knew that was exactly what he was dealing with as far as Renee Lincoln was concerned.

Now he had to worry about Lacey and Sherra, too. Worry about the fact that somebody might have been waiting for the opportunity to get these women—and probably Deacon—ever since that night.

Shit. Things like this shouldn't happen in his town.

Hell, it shouldn't happen *anywhere*.

You've seen what kind of shit happens here—even in Small Town, USA, he reminded himself. He'd *lived* some of that shit, and his twin sister, younger by eight minutes, had, too. Their dad had used the two of them for punching bags until Seth got big enough and mean enough to stop him. Sherra was nearly raped and had ended up killing one of her would-be attackers.

Small Town, USA, wasn't any kind of Utopia, and he should know it better than most.

But still . . . this was *his* small town and with the exception of what happened to Sherra that night, Madison was a nice, quiet little town—about as close to Utopia as one could probably hope to find in this world.

They had the occasional drunk driver, the random domestic dispute, and the normal problems with teenagers and troublemakers, but mostly, Madison was quiet.

For fifteen years, it had been peaceful—

Except for Lacey's attack. Why it came to him then, he didn't know. From the corner of his eye, he saw Lacey shove away from the car and approach. Slowly, he turned to face her. Ready to stop her if she took off running for the house again, but she didn't. She turned and looked at him, her head cocked, that beautiful mess of hair tangling around her shoulders. Being this close to her still hit hard, stole his breath away completely. He braced himself against it and waited until his voice would be steady before he spoke.

"Do you remember the day at the lake?" He kept his tone level, neutral, kept his face blank—and steeled himself for the possibility that she'd forgotten it.

Forgotten the day. And the night.

Quietly, she murmured, "Yes."

Seth nodded slowly, ran his tongue along his teeth. "Anything like that ever happen again? Anything weird going on at home?"

"Home?" she repeated. "This is home. I assume you mean in New York, though, and the answer is no. Nothing. Well, unless you count me losing what could have been one hell of a job . . . and that's not weird. That's just my luck."

"What about on your trips back here? Anything else happen here? Maybe something that keeps you from coming back too often? You hardly ever come back here anymore."

At Christmas, a few weekends—and you never leave the house. I never see you . . .

She shook her head. "No."

Absently, he shoved a hand through his hair. He had an itch deep in his gut that wouldn't go away. This was all connected. He knew it. The attack on Renee, the vandalism at her house, what was going on here . . . the attack on Lacey five years earlier.

Nothing had been directed toward Sherra—at least that had better be the case or he'd have his twin sister's hide. But she rarely came back to Madison, other than a book signing at the Book Shelf every now and then. The odd weekend home. She rarely stayed more than two days and lately, she rarely left Chicago.

Lacey shifted on her feet and he found himself looking at her, seeing the nerves she worked hard to hide. "It will be okay," he said quietly.

He wasn't one to offer false assurances. But he wasn't giving empty comfort—it would be okay. He'd damn well see to it. Seth hadn't been there to take care of Sherra fifteen years ago, and he hadn't been much good to Lacey when she was attacked five years ago. But he wasn't going to let anything else happen to either of them.

He focused back on the house, eyeing the mangled flower beds. Somebody had taken a great deal of time there—and pleasure. He could all but feel the malice that had driven such a pointless, destructive act. "You know you can't stay here tonight."

Lacey shivered and rubbed her hands down her arms. "That's not a bad thing. I'm not so sure I want to *ever* go back in there." A scowl darkened her face. "Damn it, I've lived in this house since I was a little kid. Damn whoever this was—bastard has no right making me afraid of this place."

The fear pushed out altogether, as anger took a good, tight hold on her. Seth would much rather have the anger than the fear.

At the sound of an engine approaching, he heaved out a sigh of relief. Finally. He turned toward the drive as the first of two squad cars drove up.

Over the next few minutes, he was busy explaining things, barking out orders and jotting down notes. Lacey watched from the side, leaning against the car and watching with unreadable eyes. Seth's gaze kept drifting to her and he had to make himself focus on the job.

But in the back of his mind, she was all he could think about.

HER STOMACH WAS in knots.

Wrapping her arms around her belly, Lacey stared at the gravel drive under her feet and tried not to think. There was enough going on that she should have been able to zone out or least find something to focus on besides her mom's trashed rosebushes and memories of a pool of blood spreading out from under Boyd's body.

She couldn't, though. All she could do was lean back against a squad car and brood. Brood. Worry. Fight the urge to chew on her fingernails, a habit she'd broken back in middle school. Her mind kept going back to that night.

It's been fifteen *years*.

She could hear the echo of her own voice and kept fighting the ridiculous urge to laugh.

Fifteen years—yeah. So what, though? What did time matter?

It was still as vivid in her mind as it had been the night it happened—hell, *worse*. As it happened, she hadn't had any time to think, any time to recoil in horror. Her body had taken over and she had acted on instinct with no input from her conscious mind. But in her memories . . . different story.

Flash forward ten years—the day she'd gone out to the lake with the intention of getting some half-decent pictures taken. What she got were some drool-worthy pics of Seth—and an attack. The panic as she fought back, the fear when he got her on the ground and wrapped strong hands around her neck, then the rush of air as she struck him in the throat and he let her go.

She could remember staring up at that masked face and feeling the hatred.

They couldn't be related . . . could they? Was there somebody who was pissed off enough over that night to come after them? Pissed over Boyd's death? The smear on JD's name?

Not that the smear had lasted long. Within a few days, it was all business as usual and Sherra had been to blame for whatever had happened. The way she dressed, the way she "invited" trouble . . .

No. It wasn't about JD. Boyd. Had to be.

But why would somebody wait fifteen years? And who in the hell could it be?

JD sure as hell wasn't behind this. He didn't have the cool-headed thinking it took to lie in wait like this. Besides, JD hadn't really given a damn about Boyd.

"Oh, God . . ."

She wasn't even aware she'd spoken until she heard her voice. Wasn't aware she'd started to rock back and forth as she leaned against the squad car, wasn't aware that she was shaking.

Or that Seth had emerged from the small crowd of cars and deputies, moving up until he stood just a few inches away. He reached up, touched his hand to her face. "Lacey, are you okay?"

She blinked. Stared at him, focused on his face as she tried to see past the memories. This couldn't be connected to that—couldn't. Because that would mean it wasn't over, and she desperately needed it to be over.

The heat of his hand on her face felt ridiculously good and she started to turn her face, press her cheek against his palm. The fear crowding her mind receded and she found herself breathing deeper than necessary just to breathe him in.

Then the phone at her waist went off, the tune of "I'm Here for the Party" blaring out into the silence of the night. She jumped, pulling back as she realized she'd been swaying toward him. Jerking her phone from her belt clip, she glanced at the display. "It's your sister."

Seth fell back exactly two steps.

Which suited her just fine. She really didn't want him any farther away than that.

The weight of his stare, the warmth she could feel radiating off of him did something weird to the jangled nerves swarming through her. Flipping open the phone, she pressed it to her ear. "Hey."

"What the hell is going on?"

Lacey slid Seth a glance. His face was unreadable.

"Ahhhh . . . Whaddya mean?"

"Don't give me that." Sherra's voice was short, brusque—her normal. But there was an edge under it that made Lacey's heart ache in sympathy.

Fear.

"Somebody vandalized my parents' house." Lacey shoved off the squad car and started to pace. But she didn't go far. Five steps. Then, as if something were tugging on her, she turned, retraced her steps. Back and forth in front of Seth and the entire time, she could feel him watching her. Feel the weight of his stare, feel the warmth of his presence. It soothed her, eased back the acid burn of fear, even as it caused an entirely different burn in various parts of her anatomy.

"Ya know, I really don't see my brother calling me and telling me not to come back home because some stupid kids tore up your mama's rosebushes."

Rolling her eyes, Lacey stopped in place. "You're a pain, Sherra."

She pinched the bridge of her nose as the headache pounding behind her eyes swelled to massive proportions. "Somebody broke in, tore it up to hell and back from what I can tell. A few days ago, somebody did the same over at Renee's house. And . . ."

Her voice trailed away.

She couldn't say it.

Even though she had sat in the seat of her car and acted on pure instinct, she couldn't quite wrap her mind around what she'd seen. The knot in her throat and the bile churning inside her, it would choke her if she tried to say it.

"Seth said somebody tried to run Renee over. You played Dame Galahad again. Is this right? Did somebody try to kill Renee?" Sherra asked, her voice soft.

Dame Galahad—Sherra had referred to Lacey like that more than once. Sherra had a very caustic sense of humor. Even those she loved weren't safe from it. Lacey licked her lips. Her heart skipped a few beats and then started to pound against her ribs in hard, heavy thuds, and nausea churned in her gut. "Yeah. I think so."

"Shit."

"Yeah."

Turning, she met Seth's eyes. The impact of that penetrating black gaze left her reeling, and she was already unsteady.

Look away—self-preservation demanded she do just that. She needed to look away. Very badly needed to look away. She couldn't, though. All she could do was stare at his face, into those dark velvet eyes.

Softly, she said into the phone, "Sherra, I don't know, but maybe you shouldn't come home right now."

"Fuck that."

Then Sherra disconnected.

Scowling, Lacey lowered the phone and stared it.

"I guess she took it about as well coming from you as she did from me."

Lifting her head, she smirked. "She hang up on you, too?"

"Yeah. After she told me to get my head out of my ass."

"Sherra. Charming as ever." Sliding the phone back onto the clip at her waist, she smothered a yawn.

"You need to get some sleep."

"Yeah." It had been a longass drive from New York. She'd debated about flying in, but then decided she really would be better off saving the money it would cost to fly back and rent a car. Even though it took a chunk of change to fill the gas tank, it had saved her several hundred dollars and since she had no immediate plans to work for the near future, saving cash seemed like a good idea.

But it had been a long, monotonous car ride, followed by the gut-wrenching spectacle of seeing somebody try to run Renee down. Combined with the shock she'd received at the hospital, seeing Deacon curled around Renee, and the far less pleasant shock of seeing what somebody had done to her parents' house . . . Well, suffice it to say she'd had *enough*.

All she wanted was a nice, spicy Bloody Mary, a big, messy burger and some hot, salty fries, followed by a very long, hot shower and oblivion in a nice, soft bed. But she wasn't sleeping here. She knew that without even asking. Not that she really wanted to sleep in that house just yet, anyway.

"You got anyplace you can crash?"

Lacey sighed and rubbed a hand over the back of her neck. "Not really." The few obvious choices were out. Renee's house didn't strike her as the best choice. She wasn't about to call Deacon and disturb him, see if he'd let her spend the night at his place—hell, even if he wasn't at the hospital, that would be just too awkward. She supposed she could call Missy, but the thought of showing up at her old friend's doorstep and explaining why she wasn't sleeping at home . . . Nope, she didn't want to do that, either.

"Guess I'll call the Inn."

Seth shook his head. "They don't have any rooms open."

"Well, hell."

He laughed. "Look, I've been staying at the Inn's guesthouse for the past couple months. Renting it."

She started to ask why and he shook his head. "Don't ask. Long story. Anyway, Sarah Landry is letting me rent the place. It's got two bedrooms . . ."

"No."

A black brow cocked. "Why not?"

She opened her mouth to explain why. But the spit in her mouth went dry and the only thing she could think about was the last time she'd spent a couple of hours in close proximity to this guy. The last time she'd ever felt more than a slight spark coming from a guy.

"What about Sherra? Isn't she going to need a place to crash while she's here?"

Seth shrugged. "She's got a room reserved at the Grainger B and B. You know how she is—if a place has *history*, she wants to be there. Nothing weird ever happened at the Inn. Plenty of weird at the B and B." Then he scowled. "Of course, if she had any sense, she wouldn't come at all."

"Sherra's not real big on common sense," Lacey said, her smile halfhearted. A breeze kicked up, blowing her hair into her face. Brushing it back, she moved her shoulders restlessly. "I appreciate the offer, but I'll figure something out."

"At almost ten? Lacey, you need to remember you're in Madison, not New York City."

She slanted him a gaze. "I don't live in New York City."

"Yeah, you live in Yonkers—close enough. I bet it doesn't shut down at nine there. You're not going to find a whole lot of choices right now. You're either going to have to crash with a friend or sleep in your car." His eyes narrowed and he said, "And if you go with sleeping in your car, I'll have it towed."

STUPID, STUPID, STUPID.

His hands were sweating.

The drive to the guesthouse passed by in a blur. He'd been renting the small cottage at a ridiculously low price for two months now and he really needed to focus on finding a new house. He was in no big hurry, but right now, he wished he had a little more room than a two-bedroom cottage.

Thanks to an electrical fire, he no longer had a home. Not that it was a big loss, the small, run-down house where he had grown up. And at least with the cottage, he had a bed—besides his own—to offer Lacey.

There was no way he would have invited Lacey to his old house. He'd inherited the rat trap from his mom after she'd died—well, he and Sherra inherited it. Sherra wanted nothing to do with it. She'd ended up deeding it over to him, after arguing with him for months to sell it. Or at least fix it up.

Something.

But Seth hadn't much cared.

It had a roof.

It had running water.

It had electricity. Very faulty electricity as it turned out.

But he wouldn't have ever taken Lacey there. He would have been too humiliated to let her inside the near hovel he'd grown up in. Of course, this wasn't anything he'd ever seen happening, either. Him offering a bed to Lacey.

If he was a smart man, he would have called his assistant and seen if she couldn't come up with some alternative. Hell, Luann could easily have offered Lacey a bed, and probably would have. Seth would have been spared the sweet torment of knowing she'd be sleeping feet away. Brushing up against her in the hall. Breathing in her scent, honeysuckle and woman.

But Seth wasn't a smart man. He was *stupid, stupid, stupid.* Because Lacey was sitting next to him, completely oblivious to his inner torment—and his raging hard-on from hell.

Lacey . . .

From the corner of his eye, he could see her leaning back against the headrest, eyes closed, golden-tipped lashes resting against her cheeks. She was exhausted. He needed to remember that.

Yeah, as long as he focused on the fact that she was exhausted, stressed-out, probably scared, it would be easier to get through the night.

"You got anything to eat at your place?" she asked abruptly. Two seconds later, her belly growled.

She gave him a sheepish smile and covered her stomach. "Sorry. I get stressed, I want food."

"I've got some stuff. What did you have in mind?" *Whatever it is, I'll get it for you* . . . He did manage to refrain from blurting that out. Just barely.

You're such a fucking loser, he told himself.

"A burger. Fries. A drink."

He smiled. "I can do the burger and fries." Then his smile faded and he shrugged. "I don't have much to drink beyond water, Cokes or tea, though. I don't . . ."

"Shoot." She straightened in the seat and slid him a glance. "I'm sorry. I wasn't thinking."

"Don't worry about it." He glanced at her, shook his head, silently wishing he could kick himself. "Seriously. Don't worry about it."

He shifted restlessly on the seat and then flicked his gaze to the rearview mirror before changing lanes. Nervous, he beat a tattoo out against his leg with his fingers as the silence stretched out between them. "My dad was the town drunk and Mom wasn't much better. You know it, I know it, everybody knows it—it's a fact I've known for years. They're both gone, I'm not harboring a bunch of stored-up resentment over it and I don't see liquor as the root of all evil. But I don't like to tempt fate, either."

"Makes sense. Sherra doesn't drink, either, I know. I don't know what I was thinking—"

"You were thinking you've had a shitty day and a drink would probably make it a little easier to close your eyes here in a little while," Seth said, cutting her off. "Like I said, don't worry about it."

He'd like to tell her that he could offer her something much more relaxing than a couple of drinks, but he refrained. The last time he'd offered her much comfort, he'd had the best night of his life, followed by the worst day.

Days.

Weeks.

Months . . .

It had taken him months to get over the humiliation of that morning, when she woke up and stared at him, sleep and lust clearing from her eyes. Talk about the cold, hard light of morning. Whatever had moved her to sleep with him the past night wasn't some sort of unrequited need like Seth had hoped.

All the unrequited need had been one-sided, no doubt about that. She'd stared at him, eyes wide, mouth working but no words coming out. When she finally did find her voice, she had been sitting with her knees drawn up and her face buried against them. *I don't believe this.*

That was all she'd said.

All she'd needed to say.

He hadn't bothered asking for any clarification and in less than five minutes, he'd been out of there.

She'd called after him.

He remembered that clear enough, too, and he was pretty sure she'd realized what she'd said, how it had come off, and there was some pretty, polite apology she wanted to offer. But he didn't want to hear it. She wasn't the first member of the female species to spend a few hot, sweaty hours under him and then wonder what in the hell she'd done. Some need for a thrill drove it. Seth definitely came from the wrong side of the tracks and when he'd been younger, he'd raised more than a little hell, gotten into more than a few fights, and worked his way through more than a few women.

Women looked at him and saw some sort of bad boy. Even now.

It had been fifteen years since he'd been in any sort of trouble, and for the past ten years, he'd been working in law enforcement—first for the Cincinnati Police Department and then serving as a deputy here in Madison. He'd worked his way up to second-in-command and when the old sheriff had to retire abruptly due to health concerns, Seth had stepped in with no opposition from his fellow deputies and none from the city council.

But it didn't matter that he wasn't the same rough-talking, troublemaking kid he'd been before his twin sister was attacked. People looked at him and saw exactly what they wanted or expected to see. Nobody, not even Lacey, looked deeper.

Seth didn't know why in the hell he was still so damn hung up on her, but he was. He had a feeling he always would be. Inviting her to spend the night at his place where just a few feet and a thin wall would separate them . . . not smart.

Of course, she didn't seem at all perturbed by it. Hell, the way she looked at him, he wasn't even sure if she remembered. The thought stung his pride, but when it came to Lacey, he had next to no pride anyway. She didn't seem at all concerned about it, though, so there was no reason he couldn't get through this night without losing any more of himself to her. Right?

He could do this.

He hoped.

4

It shouldn't look so right, she decided.

Shouldn't feel so easy, either.

But it did.

Seth stood at the counter, by the stove, slicing up a couple of big, fat Idaho bakers. There was a pot of oil steaming heat up next to him. There was stuff for a salad, lettuce, cucumbers and tomatoes neatly sliced, chopped and bagged up, just ready to serve. All rather domestic. Almost too domestic.

"You do much cooking?" she asked, breaking the silence as a nagging thought started to dance in the back of her mind. To her knowledge, and definitely in her experience, a lot of people didn't bother going to the work to cook for one person.

"When I'm in the mood." He glanced at her, a smile tugging at his lips. "Mom wasn't much for cooking and I learned early enough that if I wanted a decent meal, I'd have to cook it."

She grinned. "Apparently that's not a lesson that Sherra ever figured out or learned well."

"Oh, she figured it out. But she had another choice—make me do it." Seth shrugged. "She knew I'd make sure she ate. Didn't see the point in doing it for herself. Now she lives in a place where she can get food delivered or just throw something in the microwave. Has nothing to do with not being *able* to cook and it has everything to do with not wanting to bother."

That didn't surprise her. Sherra was the type who could do anything she set her mind to. Cooking wasn't one of the skills she wanted to acquire, so she never bothered to learn and anytime she messed with it, it was a halfhearted attempt that ended up with undercooked chicken and overcooked vegetables.

"Anything I can do to help?" Not that she really wanted to get up and move around. The kitchen was small—too small. They'd bump into each other, brush against each other . . . Her heart skipped a few beats as one thought led to another and she found herself recalling the last time she brushed and bumped against him.

"No. I've got it." He looked up, met her eyes.

Her breath locked in her throat as their gazes connected. Blood rushed to her cheeks. Everything inside her went all hot and liquid. Damn it—

Then he focused back on the task at hand, looking away from her.

The moment shattered.

"You've had one hell of a day. Just take it easy."

At least she thought that was what he said. Over the blood roaring in her ears, she couldn't be completely sure. Lacey swallowed and licked her lips.

All in all, it was a good thing he had it under control. If she tried to get down off the stool and go give him a hand, her knees just might give out the minute she stood up. How in the hell one simple look could hit her so hard, she didn't know. One look, a few seconds . . . and now she was remembering that night all over again.

———————

SHE ATE TWO hamburgers. Had one huge serving of fries, liberally doused with salt and ketchup. A salad. One of the brownies that Sarah Landry made by the dozens and always shared with him.

As she leaned back from the table with a satisfied sigh, he asked, "Where in the hell do you put all that?"

With a sleepy smile, she said, "I've got good metabolism." Then she wrinkled her nose and said, "Plus, I still torture myself with a three-mile run four or five times a week. Don't play ball much anymore, but I've been active all my life. Can't get out of the habit."

Tortured herself with running? Okay, kind of like he was sitting there torturing himself with images of the way she looked when she ran. Not that it was a sight he got to see often. Those long limbs moving, sweat gleaming along her flesh, the swell of her breasts retrained under a tight-fitting tank that ended a few inches above the waistband of her shorts.

Hell, he wondered if Lacey knew anything about self-inflicted torture.

The longer he looked at her, the worse it got. Shoving back from the breakfast bar, he grabbed his plate and glass. He'd already played the host bit and shown her the spare room. Now he just needed to lock himself inside his own room and stay the hell away from her. Maybe take a nice cold shower.

Or ten.

As he stalked around the bar, Lacey slid down from her stool, plate and glass in hand. Seth dumped his dishes in the sink and turned to go get hers, but she was standing right behind him. Their bodies crashed together and she dropped the plate. It hit the hardwood floor and broke, but Seth barely noticed.

She was close . . . too close. Lids drooped low over his eyes, he stared at her face, watched as she licked her lips and murmured a quiet, "Sorry."

He had his hands on her arms, he realized. Under his touch, her golden skin was buttery soft and satin-smooth. He flexed his fingers unconsciously, pulling her closer. Her eyes widened.

Swearing, he went to let her go.

But then she broke eye contact and looked down, her gaze traveling down, lingering on his lips. She licked hers again and the sight of her tongue stroking over that glistening, pink curve was a little more than he could handle. Groaning, he dipped his head and covered her mouth with his, tracing the path her tongue had taken with his own. He trailed the outline of her mouth, nibbled on her lower lip and then sucked it into his mouth. When he bit down, she shuddered and pressed her body against his.

Reaching up, he threaded a hand through her hair and cupped the back of her head. The glass she still held slipped out of her hand, and water splashed against their legs, puddling under their feet, but neither noticed. What he noticed was her body—as soft, sleek and sexy as it had been five years ago. Her small breasts went flat as she rose onto her toes and wrapped her arms around his neck. He could feel her hard, budded nipples and just like that he was desperate to see them. Desperate to taste them.

Taste her.

Wrapping an arm around her waist, he hauled her up. Glass crunched his feet as he turned and carried her over to the kitchen counter. He set her there, her hips at the edge. Looking into her eyes, he held her gaze as he reached for the waistband of her T-shirt. Her face flushed pink as he stripped it away but she never once looked away from him.

She wore a lacy, white bra, a barely there confection of silk, so sheer he could see her nipples through it. Between her breasts, there was a simple little bow. He lowered his head and pressed his lips to that bow as he reached around and freed the clasp. He stripped it off and tossed it onto the counter beside her.

She was gold and pink, all-fucking-over, he thought, dazed. The soft, smooth skin of her breasts was golden tan, the same sun-kissed gold as the rest of her, and her nipples were berry pink and tempting as sin. He bent over her and caught one tip in his mouth. She arched back with a cry. Seth slid his arm around her waist, holding her lower body tight against him as her upper body twisted and strained.

Sanity tried to prevail as she reached for his shirt, tugging until he straightened up and let her strip it away.

With his breath heaving in and out of his lungs, he stared down at her and demanded, "We doing this again, Lacey? You sure you want this?"

"Is there a reason we shouldn't?"

Only a million of them—

I can't have you walk out on me again.

I won't ever get you out of my system if I don't get you out of my life.

I need more than a couple of hot fucks.

But he didn't give voice to any of them.

Instead, he straightened and shoved away from her.

She blinked, confused—and a little hurt, he thought. Without putting her bra on, she jerked her shirt back on, concealing her pretty little tits, that lithe, lean torso. Clutching her bra in her other hand, she folded her arms around her middle and went to push past him.

He wanted to call her back.

Instead, he snorted and crossed his arms over his chest, leaning against the refrigerator. "I guess sweet, sensible Lacey figured out a reason of her own why she shouldn't do the nasty with me. Bet you wish your common sense had kicked in five years ago. Could have saved yourself the hassle."

She glared at him over her shoulder. "Excuse me?"

Seth shrugged. "Don't give me the innocent act. You wanted the same thing a bunch of other women want. A walk on the wild side—or at least a pretend one. I'm not all that wild, Lacey, and never have been. Sorry to disappoint you."

"You think I had sex with you out of some need for vicarious thrills?" she demanded.

"Didn't you?"

Slowly, Lacey turned back around. Her summery blue eyes narrowed and she planted her hands on her hips, giving him a murderous glare. "You know, oddly enough, I don't really remember *thinking* anything. And unless I'm mistaken, *you* touched me *first*."

He shrugged. "Don't recall you running away screaming." He didn't know what was pushing him—maybe the remembered humiliation of that morning as she rolled away from him and muttered, *I don't believe this.*

Maybe the emptiness that filled him as days passed without seeing her, days that stretched into weeks and months . . . until five years had gone without him so much as catching one decent look at her.

Maybe it was jealousy because he knew that she hadn't said something like that to any other lover she'd had.

He just knew he wanted to strike out at her, even though he had no justifiable reason. Something that drove him to smile at her tauntingly and say, "Matter of fact, the only time I remember you screaming was when you wiggled that sexy ass of yours and pushed back against me, begging for more. Screaming it."

Blood rushed to her cheeks.

"You scream like that for other guys, Lacey?"

Now the blood drained out of her cheeks and something entered her eyes, a look, stunned, a little stricken—and hurt. Seth could have kicked himself. Swearing, he went to push past her. "Sorry," he said tersely. He grabbed his keys from the small table in the hall and stalked to the door.

But he made the mistake of looking back at her.

She stood there, staring at him with wounded eyes. Blowing out a breath, he said again, "I'm sorry. Get some sleep. Go to the damn reunion. Get back to your life, find some nice, polite guy, somebody who won't leave you feeling humiliated in the morning."

He turned back to the door, grabbed the doorknob.

But her quiet voice stopped him.

"You think I felt humiliated?"

Unable to look back at her, he listened, speechless, as she sighed. "You don't know a damn thing about me, Seth. So keep your assumptions where they belong—inside that obviously empty head of yours."

Then she headed down the hallway, away from him. A moment later, he heard the door to the spare room shut behind her.

Leave.

Just leave.

But he couldn't listen to the voice in his head this time. He'd done it five years ago. He wasn't doing it again.

At least not until he had a better understanding about the hurt he'd seen in her eyes.

The door to the spare bedroom was locked.

However, she obviously hadn't bothered to check the connecting door in the bathroom. He went in that way. She wasn't on the bed, wasn't sitting in the chair by the window . . . No, she was sitting on the floor, right in front of the door with her back braced against it and her face pressed to her knees.

She still held her bra fisted in one hand and as he watched, her shoulders rose and fell, hitched a little as though she was trying not to cry.

"Lacey."

She jerked her head up and the sight of the tears gleaming in her eyes hit him right square in the solar plexus, stealing his breath.

"Leave me alone," she said, her voice hollow—empty.

But that wasn't going to happen.

He'd made Lacey cry.

If the guilt in his chest didn't kill him, the pain he saw in her eyes would do it. He went to her, crouched down in front of her. "I'm sorry."

She looked away. "So you said."

"I . . ." He stopped, took a deep breath and blew it out. "Look, I won't lie and say I didn't mean it. I can't. I was trying to piss you off . . ."

She glanced his way from the corner of her eye. "Why?"

Seth winced. *Because I love you . . . and you'll never love me. Because I know I don't deserve you—and I know you'd laugh if I ever told you.* He couldn't tell her that. He wasn't going to strip himself bare like that, not in front of her. "I dunno. Pride, I guess. Last thing a guy wants to hear when he wakes up with a woman is *I don't believe this.*"

Somehow, even though he was only inches away, she managed to stand up without touching him, not even the lightest brush of her body against his. She edged around him, keeping a careful distance between them. "I know that. And if you hadn't taken off like I'd tried to kick you in the balls, I would have apologized. What I said had nothing to do with *you.* It had to do with me."

Rising to his feet, he tucked his hands into his pockets and studied her averted face. "Okay. I'm confused. Exactly *what* did it have to do with you? If it wasn't sleeping with trailer trash that had you reeling, what was it?"

She shot him a narrow look. "That's an ugly name, Seth. If you have a low enough opinion of me to think that's how I view you, then why in the hell did you bother touching me to begin with?"

Seth shrugged. "I've been called that most of my life."

"Not by *me,*" she snapped, jabbing a thumb at her chest. "You forget, your twin is one of my best friends. You actually think I'd think that of *her*?"

Blood rushed to his cheeks. "Why in the hell do I feel like apologizing again?"

"Because you apparently like to make assumptions?" she replied sarcastically.

"Then help me out—shed some light on the subject. What the fuck were you talking about that morning?"

She shook her head. "Just leave me the hell alone, Seth." She went to push past him but he caught her arm and used her body's momentum to whirl her around. She crashed into his chest and immediately brought up her hands to wedge against his chest and force some distance between their bodies. "Leave. Me. Alone. I'll find someplace else to crash."

"I'm not leaving you alone until you tell me." And the more she avoided answering, the more he needed to know the answer. Cupping her chin, he forced her to look up and meet his eyes.

She glared at him.

Seth glared right back.

"Damn it, I was talking about the fact that up until you touched me, I haven't been able to have a climax with a man in close to ten years!"

Shit, I didn't just tell him that!

The words startled Lacey every bit as much as they startled him. His hands went slack and she took advantage of it to pull away from him. But she didn't get far. Two steps—two steps, and then she was back in his arms and then up against the wall, trapped between the drywall and his long, lean body as he leaned into her and kissed her like he wanted to swallow her whole. His hand cupped her chin, his thumb and forefinger seeking out the sensitive spots along either side of her jaw that forced her to open her mouth for him.

His tongue swept into her mouth, stroking, rubbing, teasing . . . devouring. He wedged his knee between her thighs until she was all but riding the muscled length.

Lacey's heart was pounding so damn hard, she thought it might explode. Harder, harder, stealing her breath, stealing her ability to think, even breathe. All she could do was twine her arms around his shoulders and arch against him as he kissed her.

His mouth left hers, briefly. Very briefly . . . just long enough for him to kiss his way up to her ear and mutter, "You're going to regret telling me that, darlin'."

Uhhh . . . possibly, Lacey thought—if she was ever able to get air, she just might regret how she'd just told him the most humiliating, personal secret imaginable.

But then he lowered his leg to the ground, the leg she had been rubbing and rocking against like a cat in heat. And he laid his palm against her belly, trailed his fingers down, down, unbuttoning and un-zipping her jeans . . . pushing them down to just below her hips. Then he dipped his hand inside her panties, and his fingers inside *her*.

"Ten years, baby?" he muttered against her lips. "You climaxed for me, so fucking easy . . . again and again . . ."

His thumb circled her clit and he pumped one finger in and out of her pussy, slow, teasing strokes that had her panting and gasp-ing, rocking her hips against his hand. "So easy . . . just like . . ." He added a second finger, twisted his wrist, screwed his fingers deep. "That . . ."

"Seth . . ."

"Lacey . . ." he growled against her mouth. He pulled his fingers away, left the tight, wet embrace of her body so he could strip her jeans and panties away. He knelt at her feet, untangled the denim from her ankles, tugged off her shoes and sent them flying. When her lower body was naked, he paused at her feet, staring up at her body with stark, hungry eyes. "I want you. I want to spread your thighs and lick that pretty pussy until you scream my name. Then I want to fuck you so bad, I'm hurting with it. Then I want to lay you down and make love to you until you can't see, can't think of anything but me. But if that isn't what you want, you need to tell me now."

Lacey didn't say anything.

What she did was shift her stance, spreading her thighs ever so slightly as she cupped the back of his head and tugged him closer.

Just before he would have pressed his mouth back to that sweet pussy, reality intruded for one harsh second.

Damn it. He resisted and pulled away, hating every second. She whimpered and tried to draw him back to her and he shook his head. "Just wait here a second." Pressing her back against the door, he cut through the bathroom to his own bedroom, heading for the bedside table.

Condom. He needed a damn condom— Fuck, did he even have any?

Yes. Relief hit hard. Stopping now just might kill him. He grabbed the box and took it with him. He took one foiled wrapped packet out and tossed the rest on the bed. Then he turned and stared at Lacey. Watching her, he crossed back over to her and knelt down in front of her.

He slid his hands up her thighs, grasped her hips. Rolling his eyes upward, he watched her over the expanse of her body as he licked her. Watched as he flicked her clit with his tongue and watched as he spread the lips of her pussy with two fingers and then pushed his tongue inside her. The tight walls clutched at his tongue, squeezing down, and his eyes almost crossed as he thought of shoving his dick inside that sweet, silky, wet sheath.

But—not yet.

Not until she screamed his name.

Not until she came for him, came against his mouth.

Letting go of her hip, he caught her thigh and brought it up, draping it over his shoulder so that she stood with her weight balanced between one leg and his hands. It opened her more fully to his mouth and he groaned. She was so sweet, so fucking hot and responsive . . . She cried out his name as he slid his free hand up her thigh and pushed two fingers in her pussy.

He circled her clit with his tongue—pushed his fingers deep, deep, until he could go no deeper—and she came. *Just like that . . .* he thought, a little dazed, as she rocked and moaned and whimpered against his touch.

Red-hot need ate at him, had him shooting to his feet, shoving his pants down, and he grabbed her as she stumbled, off balance. "Shh . . ." he murmured aginst her brow as she reached for him and moaned. It only took a few seconds to tear open the foil packet and slip the rubber on, but those few seconds were hell.

Sheathed in the thin latex, Seth went to her, pressing his body against hers. Lacey kissed him, hot, desperate, hungry. He boosted her hips up, hooked his arms under her knees and opened her.

The pink, swollen folds of her pussy were wet. He could smell her, could still taste that soft, sweet rain. "Watch," he muttered gutturally as he pressed against her.

Those sweet, wet folds resisted him at first—tight, snug, clenching down on him as though that would keep him from going any deeper. All it did was make him hotter, though. Made him burn hotter, made him need her more. "You're so fucking tight."

He pushed deeper, deeper, so focused on every subtle cue—when she flinched and tried to recoil, he slowed, stilled within her. "How long, Lacey?" he whispered against her mouth. She was tight. Too damn tight.

Her breath caught in her throat, hitched as she answered him, "Five years."

Five . . . five years?

His control snapped and he swore, his hips recoiling and then slamming against her, his aching cock forging through the satin-wrapped vise of her pussy until he'd buried himself to the balls. She cried out and he heard the harsh pain in that broken sound. "Shhhh . . ." he whispered against her lips, jerking his body back under control. "Shhhh . . . relax for me, Lacey. Relax . . . Yeah, that's it, baby. Fuck, you're so tight, so hot and sweet . . ."

Staring at her, he watched her cheeks flush pink, watched as she averted her eyes.

Seth smiled, a pained, strained expression, as he put two and two together. "You like it, don't you? When I talk to you . . . tell you how sweet it is to be inside you, how hot and perfect your pussy is."

Her breath caught. It didn't seem possible, but she tightened around him and her body temperature skyrocketed. She was so damn hot now, she practically burned him. "Yeah." He laughed, dipped his head to rake his teeth down her neck. "You do like it." He reached between them, stroked her clit until her tense, tight body relaxed just a little more. Seth rocked inside her, keeping the strokes slow and easy, determined not to hurt her anymore.

Five years—she hadn't been with a man in five years. Yet even as he tried to jerk himself back under control, thinking that she hadn't slept with anybody since then was akin to throwing gasoline on a bonfire—explosive.

He stroked her slick, wet flesh and teased her more. "How about if I tell you that your pussy tastes like honey and rain? Hot, sweet, slick honey . . ." Reaching up, he painted her mouth with the slick moisture on his fingers and then he kissed her, licking the taste away, plundering her mouth until they tore away from each other, gasping for breath. He rested his brow against hers and shuddered as she clenched around him, the muscles in her pussy rippling, clutching, convulsing around him. He gritted his teeth and held still until her body relaxed a little more. Sliding a hand down her sweat-slicked back, he palmed her ass.

Seth looked up, met her eyes. She arched against him, rubbed her breasts against his chest and purred deep in her throat like a little cat. He stroked his hand up, gliding it over her back, shoulders, neck until he could tangle his fingers in her hair. Angling her head back, he kissed her, deep, rough—devouring.

Damn it, he could eat her up. He bit her lower lip and she whimpered. He pushed his tongue into her mouth and she caught it, sucked on him. Her taste flooded him, the hot, hungry scent of her body overwhelmed him. Leaning into her, he started to shaft her, slow, deep digs of his cock, fucking his way through her tight, wet pussy.

Five years—

It moved on her far too soon—Seth could feel the orgasm building inside her, the way her pussy clamped down even tighter, fighting his entry and at the same time gripping him, holding him when he withdrew. He felt it as her limbs started to stiffen, saw it in the way her eyes flew wide and her mouth parted on a mewling cry.

Too damn soon—but he couldn't fight it any more than he could fight the rising of the sun. She exploded in his arms and he followed her, groaning her name against her lips as she cried and whimpered, shuddering her way through orgasm.

It ended. Too soon. But he wasn't done.

No way in hell.

When she pressed against his chest, eyes averted, he caught her chin and guided her face to his. *Not this time,* he thought, slanting his mouth across hers.

This time, she wasn't walking away until he had a chance to figure out what in the hell was going on—whether there was any chance in hell for them.

He'd loved her his entire life.

Unconsciously or not, he'd worked his entire life to try to make himself ready for her, worthy of her. But it wouldn't do him any good if he couldn't work up the balls to go after her.

If she slipped away from him again, this time, he *would* go after her.

LACEY WOKE UP in his arms.

Whoa . . .

Silvered moonlight streamed in through curtains neither of them had bothered to close. Against her back she could feel the slow, steady rhythm of his breathing. His arm rested around her waist, holding her snug and close. Cool air danced over their flesh, the sheets tangled around their legs and waists. The blankets had been shoved to the foot of the bed. She shivered, but there was no way she was going to pull away from Seth's arms just to grab a blanket. Instead, she cuddled closer, wiggling backward against his body.

He grunted in his sleep and obligingly pulled her closer. Although if she got too much closer, their bodies would have to merge. Against her butt, she could feel his cock, thickening, hardening, pressing into her flesh. She was tempted to turn around in his arms, nudge him onto his back and then crawl on top of him and ride him until she exploded. She just might do it, too—in a few minutes.

But for now, she was content to lie there and be held.

Content—

A disbelieving smile curved her lips and she huffed out a soft breath. Lacey hadn't realized she could *feel* content. Most of her life, something had kept her from it. Growing up, she'd been in such a hurry to do as much as she could, as well as she could—just too damn busy to slow down and take it slow, enjoy life a little. Lately, a nagging sense of restlessness, a need for something she couldn't quite define had kept her from being able to just sit back and enjoy, even when she tried to do just that.

An emptiness, she realized.

She'd felt empty for years.

But that nagging, restless emptiness wasn't there now.

Behind her, Seth sighed in his sleep. Then, as her heart did a slow, lovely spin inside her chest, he murmured her name. Tears stung her eyes. He was sound asleep, but thinking of her. Aware of her. It probably didn't mean anything, right? No reason for her heart to melt inside her chest.

Laying her arm over the one he had banded around her waist, she covered his hand with hers and linked their fingers. He squeezed, nuzzled her neck and slowly drifted into awareness. Part of her wished now that she had turned around. She wanted to see his face, those sleepy, melted chocolate eyes and that slow, almost reluctant smile on his face. Then he rolled his hips forward, his cock hot and throbbing, pressed against her bottom and demanding attention.

The mattress shifted under his weight as he pushed onto his elbow, staring down at her. Their gazes locked and time slowed down. The moment stretched out forever as he lowered his head. Lacey craned hers around and met his kiss, her breath catching in her chest. Sweet . . . perfect. How could anything feel that sweet, that perfect . . . that right?

He lifted up and reached behind him, fumbling on the nightstand. Lacey heard foil tear as she started to shift around and look at him. Seth stopped by, sliding a hand down her hip, along her thigh. He caught her knee and lifted it. Opening her—her breath caught in her throat as his fingertips glided over her slick, swollen sex.

She was sore.

After he'd carried her to the bed, they'd had sex again—no. It hadn't been sex. It had gone deeper than that. Even acknowledging that was enough to shake her to the core, but she wouldn't lie about it, not even to herself.

Twice in one night, and neither time had been exceedingly gentle. This was more bedroom sport than she'd had in years. Even the light brush of his fingers against her pussy was a cross between pain and pleasure. But she couldn't have pulled away, even if she'd wanted to. Something held her there—not Seth. She knew that if she tried to pull back, he'd let go without a word. She knew that if she told him she was sore, he'd stop—and it would probably make him feel guilty as hell.

But as he pushed inside her from behind, his body blanketing hers as he held one thigh high and open, she was spellbound. The position of their bodies should have been awkward, but she didn't care. She couldn't look away from his eyes as he slowly sank his shaft inside her. He looked as enthralled as she felt, his gaze burning into hers, a sexy little snarl forming on his lips as she clenched down around him.

He couldn't take her as deeply this way, but there was something almost painfully intimate about it as he made love to her with the silvery light of the full moon spilling down on them through the big window.

"I've needed this," he rasped. He hunkered down over her body, one hand braced on the mattress by her head. He blocked out the light, casting his features into shadow, but she could still feel the burn of his stare. "You can't know how many times I've thought about us like this."

She pressed her ass back against him and clenched down. A fist wrapped around her heart. "As often as I have?"

He stilled above her, his body tensing. Then he shifted his weight back, settling on his haunches and withdrawing from her body. She clenched down, trying to hold him within her, but he continued to pull away. He flipped her onto her back, grasped her hips and pulled her close, lifting her bottom up, grasping his cock and tucking the flared head against the entrance of her body. "Have you thought about it?" he asked, his voice hoarse—throbbing with some underlying tension that made her body go hot and cold, shaky and tense all at once.

"Yes."

"For how long?" His penis rested there, right at the entrance of her body, but he didn't enter her.

She whimpered and rolled upward, tried to entice him closer, but the hand gripping her ass tightened, stilled her movements. "How long?" he repeated.

"Ever since that day."

He sank some of his length inside her body—some. Not all. She whimpered and wiggled, reached out and tried to pull him closer.

"Five years." He reached down, petted the flesh of her pussy where she was stretched tight around the head of his cock. "You've wanted me for five years."

The air went hot, tense—then he spanked her, swatted her clit with his hand. She jolted and cried out, startled. He growled and slammed into her, his cock cleaving through her tight, swollen pussy mercilessly, until he had buried himself inside her. His hands caught her ass, lifted her up and tucked her more closely against him, guiding her legs around his waist. Her upper body bowed back. Her nipples, tight and aching, throbbed, stabbing into the cool air and aching for his touch.

"Five years," he rasped as he fell forward, his heavier weight crushing her into the mattress. "I've fucking wanted you my whole damn life."

His mouth slanted over hers. His tongue plundered her mouth. His hands stroked, teased and caressed. His cock throbbed and jerked, his hips slammed against hers, driving the swollen stalk of his cock deep and hard. "All my damn life," he muttered, growled, lifting his head for a second, staring down at her.

His eyes glittered. There was a fierceness in his shadowed face, combined with a painful vulnerability that wrapped around her heart and squeezed. Something . . . something important was happening—she could feel it, shifting around inside her, realigning—pieces of herself falling into place and making her whole.

For once.

She felt whole.

Then he kissed her, caught her hands and drew them over her head, twining their fingers. He fucked her, hard, fast, desperate—and she shattered into a million pieces around him. But he shattered with her. She felt it. Not just a physical release, but something more solid, something deeper.

"Don't walk away this time," he whispered against her lips, their breath mingling as they fought for air.

She reached up, cupped a hand over the back of his neck. "I wasn't the one who walked away."

Seth buried his face against her neck, his lean, powerful body shaking. "Then don't let me do it again."

THEY ATE BREAKFAST in bed.

It wasn't anything fancy, just a big box of Krispy Kreme doughnuts Seth had picked up and a quart of milk they shared between them.

He watched as she licked the glaze from her fingers. Some of the sugary flakes drifted down to linger on her breasts and he kept thinking about rolling onto his knees and crawling over there to lick it off.

But just the thought was enough to have his cock begging for attention and he hadn't missed the wince she'd tried to hide when he pulled out of her the last time he'd made love to her. She was sore and he knew if he put his hands on her again, he'd be inside her the second he had the chance.

So he kept his hands to himself and wondered if he'd been wasting the past five years. Curiosity—no, not just curiosity, but a gut-deep burning need to know had him asking, all nice and casual, "If you're still hungry, we could hit the café. It's only about a block away. Or I bet Sarah will let us come in for breakfast."

She glanced up, one finger still captured between her lips. She gave it one last, lingering lick—it was enough to have him all but on his knees—and then she dusted her hands off. "What kind of breakfast?"

"At the Inn?"

She nodded.

He hadn't exactly been serious. She'd eaten two doughnuts— he couldn't have more than that without the sugar hitting him hard. He'd just wondered how she'd react to going someplace with him. "Ahhhh . . . the big kind. Ham, eggs, bacon, pancakes, fruit, cereal. You name it."

Lacey glanced at the box of doughnuts, empty now except for little bits and pieces of the sweet, sugary glaze. Then she wrinkled her nose and muttered, "Last thing I need is to put more food on top of that."

Seth shrugged. "I dunno. The protein might not be a bad idea with all that sugar."

What in the hell was he rambling about? He didn't give a damn about protein or sugar. Well, not exactly true. The sugar dusting her breasts looked real damn tempting. Her soft laugh caught his attention and he looked up, found her watching him with a grin. He grinned back. "Sorry."

She smiled at him, a slow, seductive curve of her lips that had his already heated blood set to a boil. His cock jerked, throbbed against his lower abdomen as she reached down and caught a sugary flake on one fingertip. From under her lashes, she gazed at him and slipped her finger into her mouth.

"You're a cruel woman," he muttered, shaking his head.

She laughed and rolled out of bed. "Yeah, well, if I stay in that bed much longer, I have a feeling I won't be able to walk out of here."

"Is that a bad thing?"

She paused, glanced over her shoulder. There was a soft smile on her lips. "Doesn't sound bad to me at all. But if we never leave the bed, you're going to have a hard time figuring out what's going on around here. And I want to know who tore my parents' home apart so I can break his nose."

A few minutes later, the shower kicked on and Seth fell back against the sheets, uncaring of the doughnut crumbs and sugar flakes that were no doubt getting in his hair, sticking to his back. He was pretty damn sure he had a foolish, Dopey-like smile on his face, but he'd be damned if he could do a damn thing about it.

She felt something. It wasn't all one-sided.

And it went deeper than just sex—he knew it. One of those gut-deep instincts of his, but this one didn't have him going grim with foreboding or edgy with adrenaline. Similar symptoms—racing heart, body tense and ready. But what he felt right now was something he really didn't have a name for.

It wasn't something he'd experienced a whole hell of a lot before.

He thought it just might be hope.

5

"DAMN."

Lacey stood in the foyer of the renovated Inn and took it in.

And there was a lot to take in. Highly polished wooden floors, dotted here and there with rugs. A huge stained glass window on the landing spilled multiple hues of color onto the floor. The subtle, sweet scent of roses hung in the air—nice, not too overpowering, not too faint. Off to the right was a large, open area with a gleaming mahogany bar that took up one entire wall.

"It's something, huh?"

"How long has she been working on this?" Lacey asked. She'd been here once or twice, never to stay, usually just with her mom for a couple of baby showers or bridal showers back when she had still lived in Madison, but there was little similarity between what she saw before her and what she remembered.

"Ever since her parents died and left the place to her and her husband," Seth said, his hands tucked into his back pockets. He watched her, a faint smile on his face, his eyes hidden behind a pair of sunglasses.

She stopped in the middle of the foyer, stared up at the stained glass. "Ever do weddings here? That window would make one hell of a backdrop."

Seth pushed his sunglasses up on top of his head, squinting at her. "Weddings?" He shot the colored glass a glance and shrugged. "I don't know. I'm not the wedding type. They expect you to wear a suit. A tie. Bring a present."

"Oh, the horror." Lacey smirked and rolled her eyes. "A guy who can cook shouldn't be too disturbed about going to a wedding."

He aimed her a narrow look. "Obviously you've never been a single guy at a small-town wedding. Every mother keeps trying to introduce you to her unattached daughter." He broke off, a thoughtful look on his face. "Well, maybe not every mother. But enough."

Tongue in cheek, Lacey replied somberly, "You're right there. I've never been a guy at a wedding, attached or otherwise. At a small town or in the city that never sleeps." She gave her chest a pointed glance and then smiled at him. A door opened, then closed, somewhere off in the back of the house and the aromas of breakfast came drifting back to them.

"Oh, that smells good."

A few minutes later, she was seated at a table, a plate piled high with hash browns, bacon and toast. A cheese omelet soon joined the food, along with a tall glass of orange juice. Her belly rumbled demandingly, despite the two doughnuts she'd eaten. "I'm really going to have to run sometime soon," she muttered.

Seth glanced up. "Pardon?"

She smiled. "Just talking to myself. Man, there is no way I can eat all of this."

"Sarah doesn't do things in small measures. Just eat what you can."

She could have managed a few bites, she figured. No more. But ten minutes later, the plate was all but empty and if her cell phone hadn't started to vibrate at that moment, she might not have stopped until the plate was all but licked clean.

Pushing back from the table, she left Seth and the other diners in peace as she turned the phone on. It was Sherra. Blowing out a breath, Lacey wondered what Sherra's reaction would be if her best friend knew that Lacey had slept with her brother.

"Damn, takes you long enough to answer the phone," Sherra drawled.

"Hi to you, too, Sherra."

"Hi. So what's the deal?"

"What deal?"

"The deal where somebody breaks into your house and then my brother gets it into his head that he needs to talk me out of a book tour. *That* deal."

"Didn't we already talk about this?" Lacey glanced back over her shoulder and headed toward the huge foyer. Settling on the bottom step, she braced her back against the wall.

"Yeah. But I'm still not seeing a connection here, not seeing any reason why I shouldn't do my book tour or come to the reunion."

"You know about Renee. You know about my house . . ."

Sherra heaved out an aggravated sigh and Lacey could hear the frustration coming through the phone line loud and clear. "So we've got a stupid teenager pulling some pranks. That explains your house. Renee—shit. I don't know what explains that. The prom queen might be a little stuck up, but I don't see her attracting somebody with that big a hate-on for her. But it *has nothing to do with me.*"

"I think maybe it does." Lacey closed her free hand into a fist, fighting the urge to start gnawing on her nails. Disgusting habit, one she'd broken years earlier, but right now . . . "Sherra, something weird is going on, okay? It might just be a bunch of stupid kids, and who knows? Maybe Renee went and picked up a stalker—"

"A stalker? What in the hell makes you say that?"

The angry edge in Sherra's voice caught Lacey by surprise. "Ahhh . . . well, because it's the only other thing that makes sense

why somebody would decide to try and kill her? What's the problem,
Sherra? You're crabbier than normal—and that's saying a *lot*."

"I'm not—"

A pause.

"Look, it's just . . ."

A harsh sigh.

"Look, Lacey, I just don't see what the big deal is with me coming home. It's not like I never come to Madison. If somebody was
looking to get at me, they wouldn't have waited. Same with you.
Renee, maybe I understand. She came home for her mom's funeral,
stayed two days and that's it. She hasn't come back since she left
for college. But I come back once or twice a year. You come home
regularly to visit your parents. Nothing's ever happened before."

"You're almost always with Seth, honey. Most head cases still
have the sense not to go after somebody when her brother the sheriff is at her shoulder." A shiver raced down her spine as she thought
of the day five years earlier. Sherra didn't know about the attack,
mostly just because Lacey didn't talk about it. That day was one
she tried to block out of her memory. Unless Seth had mentioned
it . . . "You're wrong, though. Something has happened before."

"What kind of something?"

Lacey told her. Or tried to—every other sentence, Sherra interrupted, wanting to know why in the hell Lacey hadn't ever told her.
Because I didn't want to explain what happened after. Sherra was
too insightful. Something Lacey said, or did, would clue the other
woman in.

Of course, right now, Lacey was trying to figure out why she'd
even cared. She was a grown-up. Seth was a grown-up. Neither of
them was married.

Sherra's voice sounded off in her ear and Lacey winced, holding
the phone away until the decibel level dropped to something just
under ear-shattering.

"I can't fucking *believe* you never told me this! What in the hell
is the matter with you?"

Lacey didn't have a chance to answer before Sherra took off again. Blowing out a breath, she waited until Sherra had run empty before she bothered trying to make an explanation. "I don't know why I didn't mention it, Sherra. Maybe I just wanted to forget about it. Maybe I convinced myself it was some stupid high school prank, I dunno."

"Somebody attacks you, tries to strangle you and you tell yourself it's a high school prank? Damn it, Lacey, I thought you had some common sense!"

"Compared to *you*, I do," Lacey drawled. "Look, I'm sorry. It—it's not something I try to think about too often, okay?"

"No." Sherra's tone was waspish. "Not okay."

Silence stretched out between them, Lacey unsure of what to say and Sherra brooding. A floorboard creaked and Lacey lifted her gaze from the polished floor to watch as Seth walked quietly into the foyer. *Sherra*, she mouthed.

He grimaced. Tucking his hands into his pockets, he waited in silence.

"Sherra, look, maybe none of this has anything to do with . . . that night. Hopefully it doesn't. But the coincidences here? Getting a little too odd. My house gets trashed. Renee's gets trashed. I get attacked; then somebody tries to kill Renee. Too many coincidences."

Her friend sighed. It was a disgusted, aggravated sound, and oddly—rather full of despair. "Yeah. Maybe."

OF COURSE, ALL the coincidences in the world weren't going to convince the woman to change her plans.

An hour later, Lacey was still dealing with the side effects of Seth's irritation. It sprang from worry, she knew. Worry about her, worry about his sister. Even though people were better off not taking personal concerns to work, this personal concern bled onto Seth's work a little too heavily. Must be hard to leave it completely at home.

And if she kept telling herself that, she just might manage to keep from killing him.

"There's no reason for you to be here," Seth said—it was the fifth time in five minutes.

She'd been counting. Giving him a sweet smile, she said, "Oh, there's definitely a reason for me to be here." Jabbing a thumb at her chest, she said, "I *live* here."

"You live in New York."

Narrowing her eyes, she responded, "That is my parents' house."

"That is a crime scene."

"It's not like I'm going to go traipsing through the damn flower beds," she snarled. "For crying out loud, what do you think I'm going to do? Lose a hair in the topsoil and contaminate the forensics? Oh, wait a second. This is Madison—we don't exactly have a crime scene unit on hand, do we? And if we did, wasting them on a case of vandalism would be a bit ridiculous."

His eyes flashed and he took a step toward her, looming over her. He loomed pretty damn good, too, considering he had only about three inches on her.

She didn't know what made her do it. He had another deputy on the scene with him, and more than a few neighbors had shown up, drifting down the driveway and lingering until they got bored or saw their fill. Definitely nowhere near alone. Nowhere near private. But she didn't let that stop her from reaching out and tangling her hands in his hair, hauling his face down to hers.

Rising on her toes, she leaned into him and slanted her mouth across his. His hands came up, tightened convulsively around her waist. A groan rumbled out of him. She smiled against his lips as he ran a hand up along her side, up until he could cup the back of her neck. His other arm slid around her waist, hauling her closer. Against her belly, she could feel him, the ridge of his cock lengthening, hardening, throbbing behind the confines of his jeans.

Somebody made a catcall.

She heard it, faintly. But she didn't let it stop her. Not until she knew that if she didn't pull back, they were going to end up taking it too far. Then, slowly, she withdrew, first easing back her body, then sliding her hands from his hair. Finally she pulled her mouth from his and smiled into his eyes. They'd gone opaque with desire, opaque with heat.

"Part of why I'm here," she whispered, "is because you are. So if you don't want me here . . . hurry it up already."

Then she stepped back.

Five minutes later, Seth still kept playing those words over in his head. Over and over . . . and over . . . *Part of why I'm here is because you are.*

Okay, he was in the middle of a serious situation—no reason he should be grinning like a fool.

Jerking his attention away from her, he made himself focus on that serious situation—unofficially serious, of course. The deputy assisting him seemed to think this was a waste of time. Not that he'd said it out loud but Seth could read between the lines pretty well.

As long as it didn't concern Lacey.

She'd kissed him—*damn it, stop. Get your head out of your fucking pants and think.*

Blowing out a breath, he stood on the porch, hands braced on his hips, and studied the door. No clues there. It had just been busted in. Standard locks, even the dead bolt wasn't going to be that much of a deterrent. Somebody had put some muscle behind it and just kicked the damn door in. Splintered wood and the busted locks taunted him as he looked for some clue as to who had done this.

There had been no fingerprints. Didn't mean there was absolutely no evidence to be found, but so far, his guys hadn't found a damn thing. Considering that all he really had was evidence of a break-in, he doubted he could even get some outside help from the State. Of course, that hadn't kept him from making the attempt.

He *knew*—down to his bones, he *knew*—this was connected to that night. Either to Boyd and his death, or to JD. He just didn't know *how* it was connected. No. *Who*. Not how. There was a person connecting this. He just barely suppressed the urge to swear. He had an attempted murder, one break-in, two acts of vandalism—all connected to the night his baby sister killed one of the men who had tried to rape her.

Damn it, this was going to be a serious bitch—and talk about the fucking timing. Lacey was here—and not just *here* in town, but a few feet away from him, and he'd spent half the night with her soft, wet pussy wrapped around his dick. If he had his choice, he'd spend the next few weeks like that. Well, not nonstop. He'd try to figure out a way to . . . well, court her or something. Romancing a woman had never been high on his list of things to do. Since she was the only woman he'd ever wanted to romance and he'd just now gotten the opportunity—

Sherlock, you had that opportunity a few years ago. You just never took advantage of it.

The sarcastic inner voice was definitely not one he wanted or needed to hear just now. He'd be regretting the fact that he had walked away from a chance with her for quite some time.

He glanced at her, felt his heart stutter in his chest as he watched her. She was talking to Grace May, nodding from time to time. A smile came, faded, replaced by a more intent expression. She looked up and their gazes locked for a split second. That fevered need reached out, grabbed him, and he tore his eyes away from her before everybody and their brother noticed that he was standing there with a raging hard-on and entertaining sexual fantasies instead of actually *investigating*.

Timing. Damn the timing. Lacey was here, but until he had this mess taken care of, he was going to have to focus on it. And her being here was the reason the mess existed—her, Renee—and Sherra.

Sherra was just another reason.

He headed inside the house, resisting the urge to glance at Lacey again. Few more things to check out—he wanted to take a look at her room, a little more in-depth look than he'd had the night before. Get that taken care of and then he'd call it quits. For now.

"THIS WOULD DEFINITELY work."

Grace beamed at Lacey, her face glowing and not just because it was pushing ninety-six degrees. Her boyfriend had just proposed to her, and the wedding was being done on the fast track, because he was shipping out to Iraq in a month. Problem was, summer was a booming month for weddings and all the churches in Madison were pretty much booked. As were the photographers.

Thus the reason Lacey had followed Grace down a narrow path through the hedges to check out the Mays' backyard. "You realize it's going to be hot, right? Even an evening wedding . . ."

Grace shrugged. "I don't care. We'll get some of those big fans, a tent, whatever. I can't get a church here and I'll be damned if I go someplace else to get married. We both met here. We grew up here. We want to be married here." She rolled her eyes and gave Lacey a sheepish smile. "That probably sounds really corny, doesn't it?"

"No. It sounds beautiful." So beautiful it had little wisps of envy dancing through her.

"So can you do it?"

Lacey shrugged. "I'm not exactly booked at the moment. I don't have all my equipment with me but I can get it here."

"Oh, wow." Grace spun around in a circle, laughing giddily. "Oh, fricking, wow. I'm going to have a real-life professional photographer take the pictures at my wedding. I mean, you've . . . you've, like, done photography on professional models and movie stars, right?"

Blood rushed to her face. "I'm no photographer to the stars, Grace. I've met a few interesting people, and yeah, I work with professional models, but you're not going to see my work in *Vogue* or *Cosmo*."

"Still . . . you're good, right?"

"Yeah." *When I want to be, I guess.* Not exactly a ringing endorsement. Too often the jobs she did lately were so . . . bleh. She couldn't work up much interest in them, no matter how good they would look in her portfolio. Oddly enough, she was actually more excited about taking pictures at a backyard wedding here in Madison than she'd been over a lot of jobs lately. With the exception of Brazil—but she'd mainly wanted Brazil because it was different.

"Lacey!"

She jumped when she heard Seth calling her, then gave Grace a wry smile. "Sorry; I'm jumpy." Raising her voice, she called back to him. A few minutes later, she heard him coming through the hedge.

"I bet you're jumpy. I can't believe somebody did that to your house and nobody saw or heard anything."

With a noncommittal *hmmm*, Lacey tuned Grace out as she turned to look for Seth. There was a look of relief—and aggravation—in his eyes. She batted her lashes at him. He paused, then shook his head, a reluctant smile tugging at his lips.

She'd gone and turned into a flirt, she realized.

"I'M TELLING YOU, Seth, I can't think of a damn person from that night who would have anything to do with this." She leaned against the booth's padded back, staring at the Bloody Mary she'd ordered, watching as condensation formed and rolled down the glass. She'd taken exactly two sips.

Then Seth had dropped this in her lap, and now she could feel acid boiling up in her throat. She really didn't want to start hurling tomato juice and Smirnoff. Her hands were sweating.

Rubbing her damp palms down the legs of her jeans, she made

herself look at him. "I know how close you and Sherra are. I can't
imagine how hard it was for you—I know you suffered right along
with her. But you weren't there. You can't understand what it was
like to see somebody trapped, pinned, helpless, while a couple of
sick fucks tried to get their kicks. She didn't matter, not to them.
That still gets me, that there are people who value others so very
little." She had to stop, swallow all the spit pooling in her mouth.
"None of us mattered. JD would have had Boyd shoot us, and he
wouldn't have cared. Hell, he probably would have just gotten a
slap on the hand, considering who he is. Boyd would have ended
up in jail, the dumb fuck, while JD walked. And Boyd never did a
damn thing without JD telling him how to do it and when."

She sighed, tucked a loose strand of hair behind her ear. "I came
this close to having some brainless follower put a bullet in me, all
because somebody told him to. This close. What they tried to do to
Sherra, having him point a gun at me—you know, that isn't what
still wakes me up at night. It's the blood. I can still see it, pouring
out of his throat, splattered on Sherra. Dripping from that piece of
glass . . ."

She closed her eyes and pressed the heels of her hands against
them. "For the longest time, hearing water drip from a faucet would
put me back there. I finally started to get over this, move past it. I
still can't stand the sight of blood, can't do scary movies—"

Abruptly, she stopped, lowered her hands and made herself
look at him. "Movies . . . I used to love scary movies. Loved
them. Then Boyd died and I couldn't watch them anymore. One
of my breaks in college, I came home, hooked up with some of
my friends from high school, and they wanted to go see *Scream*
when it came out. I didn't really want to go, but I felt like an idiot
getting so freaked out—and I think I was a little mad, aggravated.
I lost something that night. Didn't have anything to do with horror flicks or anything, but something inside me. I never used to be
afraid and after that . . ." She trailed off, unsure of how to explain
it. "I wanted it back. Maybe I thought I could take it back. I went

and saw that movie and I ended up running out almost as soon as it started, spent the next thirty minutes puking my guts up."

She covered her face with her hands, remembering how humiliating it was to be so distressed over a dumb movie. "Until that night, I hadn't ever really been afraid. Never understood what it was to be weak." She lowered her hands to the table and stared at him over the scarred, battered Formica table. "I've felt weak and afraid for fifteen years and I hate it."

He was quiet as he reached across the table and caught one of her hands. Holding it between his, he said softly, "You're not weak, Lacey. You're one of the strongest people I've ever known—and you're one of the smartest. Smart enough to know that being afraid just goes along with being human."

"I know. I just . . . well, *knowing* it and actually accepting it are two different things."

"You're too hard on yourself. You always have been." He leaned forward and brought her hand upward, pressing a kiss to her palm.

He stared at her from under his lashes and she swallowed, mouth going dry. "You know, if you want me to actually concentrate, you can't look at me like that."

Seth laughed. "If I want to concentrate, I can't keep looking at you period. I need blinders or something." He let go of her hand reluctantly and then leaned back against the seat. "Did you ever hang out with Boyd? Can you think of any friends or anybody else that might be doing this?"

Lacey shook her head. "Boyd didn't *have* friends, exactly. He was like JD's shadow. Whoever JD hung out with was who Boyd hung out with. Hell, you know what Boyd was like."

Seth grimaced. "Yeah. I know. What about the party? Did anything else weird happen?"

Unspoken were the words about Sherra's near rape and Boyd's death. But it hung between them. Sighing, Lacey murmured, "No. I wasn't even planning on being there, Seth. Missy said something about a movie—I'd had a fight with Deacon and a movie sounded like a good way to not think about him or the fight. Then we show up at the party . . ."

"But Deacon was at the party."

Somebody had scratched a heart into the Formica tabletop. Lacey traced it with her finger, eyes staring off into the distance as she replied, "Yeah. He came to pick me up—he called right after I got there and we were on the verge of making up. I didn't really want to be there anyway."

"So Deacon shows up."

Lacey shrugged. "Took him a little while to get there. I just wandered around until he showed up. I saw Renee—so did Sherra. We all bumped into each other upstairs. Renee, she had this big bruise on her face. JD had belted her because she wouldn't have sex . . ." Lacey winced. "Shit, probably shouldn't have mentioned that."

"JD hit her because she wouldn't sleep with him?"

Lacey scowled. Folding her arms over her chest, she said, "Renee will kill me if she knows I'm talking about this."

Drumming his fingers on the table, Seth said, "It's not like I plan on going around writing it on the wall in the boys' room, Lacey. But if all of this is connected . . ."

With a grimace, she muttered, "Yeah, yeah. I get the point. Yes, JD hit her. He kept pushing and pushing, but Renee didn't want . . . She . . ." Blood rushed to her cheeks and once more, she buried her face in her hands. "I can't believe I have to go through all of this. Look, Renee hadn't had sex before. She didn't want to do it for the first time at one of his parties—and she didn't want to sleep with JD at all. She couldn't stand the guy, just went out with him so her mom would leave her alone. When she told him no, he made fun of her and she walked off. Boyd saw her and said something like, *Man, that was fast, JD.* They started messing with her, JD pushed her at Boyd and told Boyd he oughta have a go at her. She said something to JD and he hauls off and slaps her. I don't know the exact details—she didn't tell me any of that until a few years later.

I didn't see any of it or anything. I just remember seeing the bruise on her face and . . . well, I wasn't surprised, you know?"

"JD's the kind of guy who likes hurting people—it's not surprising at all," Seth said, his voice absent. He glanced at her and then back down at the table, frowning. "You already know I'm good at making assumptions. I went and made a few about Renee—pissed her off, wasn't entirely fair toward her."

Lacey shifted on the seat, resignation and irritation warring together. She imagined she knew what sort of assumptions Seth had made about Renee—probably the same ones that Lacey had made once upon a time, so it wasn't exactly fair to get irritated. "You know that saying about still waters running deep?"

"Yeah."

She licked her lips and shrugged. "Think of Renee as an abyss. She's got depths to her that most people couldn't even begin to guess at." Making herself look him in the eye, she said levelly, "I look at you and feel things I'm not used to feeling, Seth. I want to see what happens with that . . . but Renee is one of my best friends, and I'm very protective of my friends."

With a self-deprecating smile, Seth said, "Yeah, that doesn't surprise me, either." He braced his elbows on the table and pinned her with that direct, intense stare. "I don't know Renee and I'm a little too quick to make assumptions; I know that. But I also know that she didn't have to go in that room; she didn't have to help Sherra. Whatever else I *don't* know about her, it can't matter as much as the one thing I do know, and the one thing I should have remembered."

The weight pressing down on her chest eased and she smiled. This time, she was the one to reach out and catch one of his hands. "None of us are going to be at our best when it comes to thinking about that night. Or how we react to it."

He squeezed her hand and laced their fingers together, pressing his palm to hers. He cleared his throat and although he didn't pull his hand free from hers, his voice was once more all business. "So what else can you tell me about that night? What else happened after you saw Sherra and Renee?"

"Deacon showed up." She blushed to the roots of her hair, debating about what to say next. In the end, she just blurted it out. "We made up, ended up finding a room on the second floor and had sex; then we were going to leave."

A muscle jerked in his jaw. "You and Deacon slept together that night?"

"Yeah." She shrugged. Reflexively, she went to pull her hand from his, but he showed no inclination of letting go so she stopped. "We were in the room a half an hour or so. We were going to leave and I wanted to check on Renee, asked Deacon to wait for me."

"Is this when you heard Sherra?"

"Not right away—I went looking for Renee. Heard Sherra a few minutes later. I didn't know what it was . . . just heard this weird noise. Like a scream." Shaking her head, she said, "I—look, after I saw Renee right outside the library, my memory isn't the most reliable. I don't know if I can help too much here. You can ask Deacon. Guy doesn't forget the small details."

"That's a lawyer for you," Seth murmured.

There was an odd note in his voice, one she couldn't quite put her finger on. Before she could puzzle over it, though, he asked, "Did you see anybody while you were looking for Renee?"

Sighing, she rested her elbows on the table and tried to think. "Yeah. I saw a few people, but I can't remember who. There was a couple going at it in the hall. Didn't bother trying to find a room. After that, I don't remember really seeing anybody until I saw Renee. It was right outside the library."

The nausea churning in her gut was getting worse. The more she thought about that night, the sicker she felt, and the harder it was to breathe. "I gotta get out of here." She dug through her purse and fished out a ten, threw it down to cover the drink she'd barely touched and a tip. Without waiting for a response, she strode out of the restaurant.

Seth was right behind her. She could feel him, even before he spoke, even before he said anything. She kept walking, not really caring where she was going. She just had to keep walking—needed some space. Space. Silence. Time to get her thoughts under control—

Shit. Just ahead she saw Missy climbing out of her car in front of the bookstore. Without thinking, Lacey made a sharp right turn and headed into the boutique. Divas was a fairly new addition to the square, a hodgepodge of sleek, sophisticated styles, the ever-popular Goth look and vintage clothing dating back to the seventies and earlier.

The girl at the desk was too busy listening to her iPod and reading a book—written by Sherra Salinger, no less—to notice Lacey and the sexy sheriff following along behind her. She riffled through the clothes, not really looking for anything, just trying to keep her hands busy and not let him see how badly she was shaking.

Something silky and ocean blue caught her eyes and with an overly bright, false smile, she turned to him. "I'll be right back."

She snagged the halter-styled dress off the rack and headed toward the fitting rooms. The fringed, beaded curtain kept that area cut off from the shop and she'd assumed she could get a little bit of privacy behind it.

Not. Bells and beads chimed merrily as he slipped right through behind her. She frowned at him as he herded her into one of the closet-sized fitting rooms, took the dress from her and then slid his arms around her waist. She jerked, tried to pull away from him. Damn it, she wanted to get her head on straight, not get comforted—

A harsh breath escaped her.

He stroked a hand up her back, cupped the back of her head and eased it against his chest. He lowered his head and brushed a kiss across her cheek. "I'm sorry."

Tears burned her eyes, threatened to spill over. She blinked them back, determined not to cry. She'd stopped letting that night in high school control her a long time ago—she thought. She hoped. But if she let herself start crying over it . . . "This is so damn stupid. Am I still going to freak like this in another fifteen years? Another thirty years?"

His arms tightened around her waist and he dipped his head. He nuzzled her neck and murmured, "So what if you do? You get to thinking about it, it gives you a few bad moments, and then you move on."

"Move *on*?" she demanded. "I *haven't* moved on. I feel like I'm still stuck there. Everything fell apart after that—I can't find anything, anybody, who makes me happy. I pushed Deacon out of my life. I can't keep anybody in my life—hell, I can't find anybody I *want* in my life except—"

She clamped her mouth shut, refusing to let the words spill free. She couldn't think about that yet. She didn't even know if there was even a *that* to think about.

Seth wasn't too interested in letting it drop, though.

He reached up and cupped her chin, angling her head back. Their gazes locked. "Except who?"

She swallowed the knot in her throat, mind racing as she reached for something to say that would answer his question, without stripping herself bare. But there wasn't anything—at least nothing she could say without lying about it. Blowing out a breath, she reluctantly said, "Except for you."

Trying for flippancy, she added, "And how messed up is that? I haven't seen you in five years and the last time I *did* see you, we spent more time sweating and panting than we did talking—"

Well, not entirely true. They'd talked. Throughout that night, they'd actually talked quite a bit in between the panting and sweating marathons. "Other than that, we've known each other our whole lives and we *might* have talked once or twice a year."

His hands tightened, his fingers on her face digging in almost to the point of pain. Something flashed across his face—too hard to define and she had no time to try to define it, either, because the world started to spin—

No. *She* was spinning. They were, Seth whirling their bodies around and pressing her up against the wall, his mouth coming down on hers. He had his tongue in her mouth, his hands under her shirt. Oxygen dwindled and her thoughts started to go dark, but she couldn't stop kissing him back. Her hands tangled in his hair, clutching him close, and when he tore his mouth from hers, she could have screamed in frustration.

He bit her lower lip. "I can't even touch a woman without seeing you—can't sleep without wishing you were there with me."

. . . what . . .

Something important—that nagging sense—rose up to taunt her, whispering to her. Something . . . something important here, but she couldn't grasp it. Couldn't and she needed to. She knew it. But she couldn't think past the heat swamping her to try to figure it out. "Seth," she whimpered, tugging his head back to hers.

He came, but he didn't kiss her. Instead, he raked his teeth down her neck, bit her where her neck curved into her shoulder as his hands jerked her thin cotton skirt up to her waist.

"Seth, we can't . . ."

"Can. Damn it, put your hands on me," he rasped, his voice harsh, hoarse.

She did—how could she not? That long, lean body that felt so damn perfect against hers. They fit—she'd never *fit* with anybody before. She'd noticed it before, that first time five years ago, but she hadn't let herself think about it too much. If she survived this, she was damn well going to think—

But she may not survive.

Suddenly Seth stopped, swearing viciously. "Damn it. I don't have anything with me."

"Anything?" She stared at him, dazed. What was he talking about?

He reached up, trailed a finger over her lips. "A rubber. I didn't bring any." He gritted his teeth and the look of frustrated longing on his face echoed what she felt inside as he pulled back.

"I don't care." Lacey reached out, trailed her fingers down his cock, then cupped him, stroking up, down.

He covered her hand with his and pumped himself into her hand. "You'd better be careful what you say, Lacey."

A grin curled her lips and she squeezed the rigid shaft. "I don't care . . ."

A few seconds passed and she didn't know what he was going to do. Then, abruptly, he grabbed her and lifted her, once more bracing her against the wall. "You sure about this, Lacey?"

"Hmmm." She arched, rubbing herself against him.

"Witch," he muttered. Then he pulled her panties aside. "Wrap your legs around me."

She did, gasping for air. He was hard, hot—bruising her, pushing into her with no preliminaries, no pause—pushing deep, deeper, until he'd completely seated his length inside her. Lacey groaned and squirmed against him, wriggling around and trying to adjust to the sudden invasion.

"Am I hurting you?" Seth rasped, his brow pressed to hers. She shuddered and bucked in his arms, her pussy tightening around him in a convulsive caress. The need to fuck her, hard and fast, slammed into him. "Hell, Lacey, don't do that . . . Be still, baby. Please, just be . . . still. Am I hurting you—damn it, tell me if I am."

"No . . . Seth, please . . ."

"Shhh . . ." It didn't matter what she said; Seth knew he was hurting her. He could see it in her eyes, but he couldn't pull away from her any easier than he could cut off his own arm. Hell, it might be easier to cut off a limb than pull away from her. He adjusted his arms, moving her around and hooking them under her knees. It opened her wide, took away her leverage so she couldn't keep wiggling and twisting around his aching dick, threatening to drive him insane.

Then he leaned into her, moving on her body so that he could caress her clit with each deep thrust. Her lips parted and he caught her scream before it could bounce off the walls—a dressing room.

Damn it, he was fucking Lacey Talbot in a damn dressing room and he couldn't have cared less.

All he could think about was how damn perfect she felt in his arms, and that naked vulnerability in her eyes as she laid herself bare. Slanting his mouth over hers, he deepened his kiss. Although it took every last bit of control he had left, he slowed his thrusts, stopped demanding, started to tease and seduce.

She moaned into his mouth, her fingers fisting in his hair.

"You have any idea how often I've thought of this?" he whispered against her lips. "Every damn day. For years. I wake up wanting you, I go to sleep thinking of you and then I finally get a taste of you—it isn't enough, Lacey. It's never going to be enough."

The smooth, soft golden glow of her skin had gone rosy and it was like stroking his hand down wet silk as he guided one of her legs to his waist. It wrapped around him, strong and limber, freeing his left hand. He stroked it up, up, up . . . cupping her ass and squeezing. She shivered, arched into his touch. Lifting his head, he stared at her, stroking his fingertips along the crevice between the cheeks of her ass.

She tensed as he touched her there, her eyes going wide as he pressed against the tight pucker of anus. Sweat slicked their bodies, eased his way as he pushed inside. "Want you . . . all of you." He dipped his head and licked her lips, nipping at the lower one until she opened for him. "Can I have you? All of you?"

Can I keep you?

But he didn't let himself voice that question . . . not yet.

He pushed deeper, deeper, watching as she flinched, groaning as she clenched and fought to accept the foreign touch. It was a new thing for her; he could tell just by the half-embarrassed, half-scared look on her face. He withdrew and then pushed back in and this time, she took it a little bit easier. "Can I have all of you, Lacey?"

She slammed her head back against the wall, whimpering. "You can have whatever you want, Seth. Whatever . . . ohhh . . ."

He rotated his finger, rotated his hips. She clenched down around him, tightening around his dick, tightening around the finger he had buried in her ass. The last threads of his control broke and he growled, slammed into her, lost himself in the swollen, wet depths of her pussy, the hot silk of her ass and her soft, strong arms.

She came, shattering around him, and as she clenched and convulsed around him, he couldn't hold back. Burying his face against her neck, he climaxed with a harsh groan. Until she answered, he didn't even realize he'd spoken, didn't realize he said the words out loud . . . "Can I keep you?"

Lacey rubbed her cheek against his shoulder, his T-shirt damp with their sweat. "Only if I get to keep you, too."

6

WITH A GOOFY grin, Lacey fought to smooth her clothes and hair.

Seth had slipped outside, and she only hoped he was distracting the sales girl. Of course, if the girl was still listening to her iPod, chances were she hadn't even realized anything had happened.

Blood rushed to her cheeks as she looked around the small cubicle. It smelled of them, of her, of him, of sex. Closing her eyes, she breathed it in.

She'd just made love with Seth Salinger in the changing room at Divas. She hadn't ever lost her mind like that before, but there wasn't a bit of regret. The only thing in her mind was *Damn, can we do it again?*

Lost in the memory of the pleasure, she slipped out of the dressing room, following a sign that pointed to the ladies' restroom. She left the turquoise silk halter dress on the small bench in the changing room.

Just inside the restroom, she realized she didn't have her purse. Blowing out a breath, she muttered, "Damn it." She felt like her brain had gone and overheated on her.

She turned to go back out and didn't have time to scream as a hand came up and shoved her back inside, kicking the door closed. Turquoise silk was wrapped around her throat, jerked so that it cut off her air supply.

"Is Lacey getting lucky?" a distorted voice asked, pitched low, too low to alert Seth just on the other side of the door.

Black dots danced in front of her eyes. Instinctively, she clawed at the hands that had the silk wrapped around her throat, kicked at the legs hidden by a shroud of black. Panic settled in, chasing out training, chasing out any and all rational thought. The black dots were converging together, forming a black veil, and in her gut, Lacey knew that if she passed out, it was done.

She could feel the hate, the malice, rolling from her attacker. Could taste her own death on the air. He wanted her dead and if she didn't get a grip—

She stilled, stopped fighting. Her lungs screamed for air, but she reached deep, found a reserve of strength she hadn't realized she had. She didn't go for the throat this time. She struck straight out, hand stiffened, fingers straight, as she plowed forward into the soft, vulnerable area where the ribs joined together just below the solar plexus.

Through the roar of blood in her ears, she heard his harsh grunt. The makeshift garrote at her neck went just a little slack. But it was enough. She twisted and jerked away. Her legs wobbled and went out from under her, but as she hit the floor, she kicked, sweeping his feet out from under him as well.

She screamed Seth's name. It bounced off the walls and she heard him immediately.

"You're going to fucking *die*, bitch. Die screaming."

With that menacing threat dancing through her mind, he took off running, throwing the door open so hard it smashed into the drywall and the framed pictures hanging in the restroom went crashing to the floor.

Is Lacey getting lucky . . .

"Lacey?"

Dragging her eyes upward, she watched as Seth came rushing into the room. He had a gun and she could see agony in his eyes. Waving a hand toward the emergency exit, she rasped out, "I'm fine. He ran—there."

Her voice was garbled, half broken, but he seemed to understand well enough. She saw the indecision in his eyes and she grunted out, "Go. Hurry."

Without wasting another second, he took off running.

The belled, beaded curtain shifted and a pair of large eyes peeked through. It was the employee, sans book and iPod. She stared through at Lacey and then glanced down the hall. Seth was already gone, the door left wide-open.

"You okay?"

Lacey snorted and then winced as it made her throat scream in pain.

Okay? She'd just been fucked within an inch of her life inside a changing room. Then some masked lunatic tried to strangle her with a silk dress.

And she suspected she was falling in love with her best friend's brother.

Okay?

Not in a million years.

LACEY SWALLOWED GINGERLY and then made herself smile at Seth as he stood looming in the doorway. "Hey."

"Hey, yourself."

He came in but instead of settling on the stool by the bed, he stretched his body out along hers on the hospital cot. "There's not enough room for this," she whispered. She couldn't talk much louder without it hurting.

"Don't care," he muttered, burying his face against her air and inhaling.

Smelling her hair . . . she might have felt self-conscious, except she realized she was turning her face into his chest and breathing in his scent as well. "You didn't catch him."

"No."

He swallowed. She could hear his throat clicking, and heard the bitter anger in his voice as he said, "I'm sorry, Lacey. I keep fucking this up, don't I?"

"You're not fucking anything up. And don't be sorry."

He swore. "The hell I'm not. Fucking bastard gets that close—and I didn't even know until it was too late. Can't catch him. Have no idea who it is. Believe me, I'm fucking up in the worst possible way."

"No." She swallowed, ignored the pain in her throat as she made herself speak up. "I knew you'd get there. If I could just get him off of me so I could scream, I knew you'd come. And you did. That's why he ran, too. He knew you'd come."

It didn't make him feel any better. Lacey knew it didn't, and she wasn't surprised. Cuddling into his arms, she sighed.

Seth stroked a hand down her back and said, "The doctor said you could leave as soon as the nurse gets the paperwork to you."

"Hmm. Come home with you?"

"Bet your ass," he muttered, cupping her cheek. "Although I bet you're real damn ready to get the hell out of Madison—and not come back, either."

She reached up, wrapped her fingers around his wrist. "Not so much. Not leaving." She lifted her head and smiled up at him, smiled despite the pain in her throat, despite the fear crowding her mind, despite her own confusion. "Can't leave . . . not unless you come with me."

That look again—that one she'd seen flash through his eyes, too deep, too intense for her to be able to define. But for some reason, she caught something in it this time and it left her head spinning. Lacey wasn't completely sure, but she thought . . . maybe, just maybe, it might be love.

"I've spent the past five years dreaming about you, Seth. I've never dreamed about a guy like that, never thought about what it would be like to go to sleep with him at night, wake up with him in the morning. Not in such a hurry to walk away from that."

She reached up and stroked her index finger across his lip. He caught her hand in his, squeezing tight. "Lacey . . ." He opened his mouth, closed it, opened it again, but he didn't say anything else.

Forcing a smile, she said, "Unless you feel like walking again?"

"No way in hell," he growled. He moved fast, too fast, sitting upright and pulling her into his lap. With his arms wrapped around her, his face buried against her neck, he said it again, "No way in hell."

Then he lifted his head and stared at her.

She saw it again and this time, the look in his eyes made sense.

It was love.

It was longing.

As she leaned into him, pressing her lips to his, she realized that she felt complete.

BOOK THREE

Sherra

CHAINS OF MEMORY

Madison, Ohio, May 1994

"DAMN IT, SHERRA, what are we doing here? Come on, let's go see if my cousin can give us a lift into town."

Ignoring Leslie's whiny voice, Sherra continued to walk toward the brightly lit house. Damn it, she was going to *kill* Jonah Simmonds. The idiot might be one of her best friends, might be her sometimes-on, sometimes-off boyfriend.

But he was a fucking *idiot*. If he got caught at JD Whitcomb's house with one of these parties going on, his parole would be revoked and he'd end up serving the rest of his sentence—and damn it, *this* time, it wouldn't be some two-month stay in juvie. No, he'd be serving out two years in a state penitentiary.

Sherra couldn't let it happen. So what if Jonah knew the risks, knew how much trouble he could get in? He might technically *know* the risks, but she knew *him*. He'd think he wouldn't get caught.

Just like he thought he wouldn't get caught "borrowing" the car from his next-door neighbor.

Just like he thought nobody would notice or miss the electronics he'd gotten caught stealing from RadioShack last year.

Just like he thought he wouldn't get caught when he broke into the high school two years ago so he could spray paint all over the trophy cases as the football team won the state championship again.

"I can't believe you're going in *there*," Leslie said, her voice taking on a snide tone that made her high-pitched twang even more annoying. "You *hate* JD."

Sherra rolled her eyes and slid Leslie a look. "I don't *hate* JD. He's not worth that kind of energy. But I'm not here for JD. Has nothing to do with him. I just want to get Jonah out of here before he gets caught."

She mounted the steps and had to literally elbow her way through the crowd. The air was ripe with the stink of marijuana and alcohol and she said a quick, hopeful prayer that nobody had called the cops yet. If she could just get out of here with Jonah before that happened, she'd be happy. Thankful, even. Thankful enough that maybe the next time sweet old Mr. Baker asked her to join him and his wife for church, she just might go.

Just please let me get out of here before the cops show up . . .

She wasn't walking as fine a line as Jonah. The one and only time she'd gotten into major trouble, she'd been put on probation for one year and that year had officially ended six months ago. But she really didn't want to get into any more trouble.

A few more months and she could get the hell out of Madison and never look back.

After twenty minutes of wading through people, discarded paper cups and empty beer bottles, Sherra still hadn't had any luck finding Jonah. Behind her, Leslie was getting more annoying by the second and Sherra had to grit her teeth together to keep from telling the other girl just to leave her the hell alone.

Heading out of the huge living room, she searched the rest of the main floor and then headed for the stairs. They cleared the landing and Sherra shifted from one foot to the other, trying to decide where to look first. A hand came up, caught her elbow, and she paused, looking back at Leslie. Leslie was staring off to the side, a wide grin on her face, a mean light in her eyes.

"Somebody belted the prom queen."

"Huh?" She followed Leslie's line of sight, seeing Renee easily enough despite the dimmer lighting on the second floor.

The prom queen didn't look quite so elegant just then, her hair messed up, her pretty, perfect white dress wrinkled—and one ugly bruise already swelling on her cheek. She walked past, staring straight ahead, but something about the way she held herself, the way she moved, told Sherra that Renee was completely unaware of what was going on.

" 'Bout fucking time somebody hits her one," Leslie sneered as she started to edge around Sherra.

Nausea roiled in Sherra's gut and she stopped in her tracks, lifting an arm to block Leslie's way. The hot light of glee in Leslie's eyes made Sherra feel like puking.

And it also made her damn mad.

Sherra knew what it was like to get hit, knew what it was like to have somebody bigger, stronger, use their hands on you and leave marks behind. Leslie, though, was clueless. She came from a "nice" family and her parents shook their heads and wrung their hands over the kind of people Leslie liked to hang out with.

Although she already knew the answer, Sherra said, keeping her voice low, "You got any idea what it's like to have somebody a hell of a lot bigger, a hell of a lot stronger belt you across the face, Leslie?"

Leslie blinked. Then she cocked her head and pursed her lips, studying Sherra. Very obviously confused. "It's *Renee Lincoln*. Shit, who hasn't wanted to hit her a time or two?"

"I don't care who it is. You've never had somebody pound on you—you don't know what it's like to crawl off the floor, hurting so bad you want to die, and the entire time, you're thinking . . . *What did I do?*"

"It's *Renee*."

"So you being jealous is enough reason for her to get whaled on?" Sherra bit off.

Leslie's jaw dropped open. "I ain't jealous of the little rich bitch."

"Only thing that makes sense to me."

Eyes narrowing, Leslie took a step toward Sherra. "I'm not *jealous* of that stupid bitch. She's a brainless, self-centered, pampered princess and I just think it's time somebody gave her a taste of her own medicine."

"Yeah, because I see that pampered princess going around and pounding on people smaller than her." Sherra shook her head and shoved past Leslie. "Do us both a favor, Leslie, and stop trying to think."

Leslie's hand flew up, catching Sherra's arm. Sherra stopped in her tracks and looked down at Leslie's hand. The black-lacquered nails bit into Sherra's skin, but she didn't flinch, didn't show any kind of emotion, didn't pull away.

Instead, she stepped in a little bit and got in Leslie's face. Leslie had a good three inches on Sherra and with the shiny, fake patent-leather boots and their four-inch platforms, she towered over her. But Sherra had been short all her life and she was past the point of being intimidated just because somebody was taller than her.

Narrowing her eyes, Sherra said, "Problem, Leslie?"

Leslie swallowed, eyes darting around the hall. There was nobody around, though. Renee had disappeared and most of the kids here for the party were caught up in the party and they hadn't yet started trying to wander up the stairs. "I just don't see why in the hell you're so bent up over somebody slapping that bitch."

"Yeah, well, there were several times my dad put me in the hospital because nobody saw any reason to get bent out of shape over him hitting me." She glanced down at Leslie's hand, a slow, deliberate look, and then she lifted her gaze and pinned it on Leslie. "You really want to let go right now—and you really want to leave me alone about this."

Leslie did just that and as she headed downstairs to lose herself in the crowd, Sherra sent another look down the hall after Renee.

She didn't follow, though.

She had problems of her own, and the main one was finding Jonah before the jerk ended up in trouble.

AN HOUR LATER, she was pretty damn sure that she'd checked just about every room in the house. And it was a big-ass house, too. Sherra kept having to dodge into rooms when she heard some of the house staff coming.

No wonder the second and third floors were mostly empty. Some stiff-necked guy and a cadre of maids were making regular rounds and politely requesting that JD's "guests" remain on the lower level. Apparently, these people had a vested interest in keeping the party downstairs, but that was their main concern. None of them seemed to give a damn about the liquor or drugs being passed around.

Blowing out a sigh, she slipped down the back staircase and started toward the front of the house. She needed to just cut her losses and get out of there.

Her belly rumbled demandingly. As always, there hadn't been much of anything in the house to eat for breakfast, nothing to take for lunch, and there was no way she was taking the free lunch that was offered for students in the public school system. She hadn't eaten much of anything since dinner the night before, but she knew if she could get home, Seth would have something for her to eat.

He got paid on Fridays and he always snagged some food to cook at home. Ever since Dad had died a few years earlier, their mother had been living off a mostly liquid diet—the liquids being beer, whiskey, vodka and anything else that could put her in a haze. She rarely spent money on anything beyond booze and when she did, she didn't worry about making sure the twins were fed.

But Seth worried about it. He'd have food for her.

A hand stroked down her back as she pushed through the crowd. She didn't bother looking back, just drove her elbow backward, plowing it into an unprotected stomach. Somebody swore; a few others laughed.

Her neck went hot, but she didn't stop to look back.

Being talked about, being laughed at, whispered about, it was nothing new to her.

Sherra had very, very few friends. Most of the guys thought she was just a slut. Most of the girls probably agreed, but they wouldn't dare say things like that to Sherra's face.

The Salinger family was known for being trouble. Neither Seth or Sherra had escaped that curse. Neither of the twins was afraid to fight, although Sherra was more likely to do it than Seth. Up until last year, she actually went out of her way to look for a fight.

As she pushed through the crowd now, some of them fell back, giving her a little bit more room, and she had to hide her smile. No, she wasn't afraid to fight. And sometimes, that reputation actually came in pretty damn handy.

From the corner of her eye, she saw a familiar dark head and she narrowed her eyes, tracking Jonah as her boyfriend headed out of the room.

"Finally." She followed him, determined to catch up with him and let him have it.

Too many people in the way, though, and she lost sight of him. Swearing, she hit the stairs once more. One more look through the house. That was it. After that, she was *done*. And if Jonah got in trouble, it wouldn't be because she hadn't tried.

She never did find him, though.

What she found was Renee. Sliding out of a room. Heading down the hallway. And Lacey Talbot—going to block her.

Renee tried to hide it, averting her face, but she didn't move quickly enough. Besides, it would take a platoon of Hollywood makeup artists to hide *that* bruise.

"Hey, are you okay?" Lacey's voice was concerned.

A polite, false smile started to form on Renee's mouth and

Sherra could already hear it. Already hear the polite lie she'd told herself over the years. *I'm fine—*

The words ripped out of Sherra's throat before she could stop them. "He hit you." Leaving the shadows of the hallway, she went to confront Renee, all but daring the other girl to deny the truth.

"I'm fine."

Renee said the words—but her pale face, her shadowed eyes, and that ugly bruise revealed the lie. She wasn't fine.

"JD hit you?" Lacey asked, incredulous.

Sherra watched as Renee tried to shrug it away, her eyes dark, glinting with tears.

"I'm fine," Renee said again, trying to go around them.

Sherra blocked her, laying a hand on Renee's arm. Her hand looked vampire-pale against the soft, smooth tan of Renee's, her bloodred nail polish near black. "Guys who like to hit don't stop too often, Renee. Believe me, I know."

How many times had her dad beat on her or her brother, their mom . . . and then begged for forgiveness a day later? A few weeks, a few months later, it would start again, an ugly, vicious cycle. There were a few things that could end that cycle—his death had been one of them.

Lacey spoke up, her voice no longer so heavy with surprise. "Has he done this before?"

The prom queen somehow managed to get her crown on, lifting her chin and glaring at Lacey and Sherra down her nose. "This doesn't really concern you, does it?"

IT WAS THE fourth time somebody had tried to push a glass of punch into Sherra's hand. She was tired. She was hot. She was damn ready to get the hell out of JD Whitcomb's house, and if Jonah ended up getting his ass hauled back to jail, it was his own fault.

Thirsty, her belly grumbling, she took the punch and tossed it back. It hit the empty, aching pit of her stomach with a sweet, sweet warmth—too damn sweet.

Shit . . .

Some of that night would forever be lost to her. The last thing she remembered clearly was somebody calling her name—she thought it was Jonah, but she wasn't sure. After that, everything was a haze. She had a vague recollection of one thing, and one thing only— finding someplace dark and quiet, where she could hide.

Even under chemical influence, her natural instinct was to pro- tect herself and that was what she did, stumbling, shuffling and dragging herself away from the party, ignoring the voice that called her name, ignoring everything as she found a flight of steps, stum- bled up them, and then up another flight. The noise below faded down to a muted roar.

In a dark, quiet bedroom, she hid, stumbling to her knees and even- tually crawling across the floor, through a doorway into a closet.

Under the impact of the alcohol-and-drug-laced punch, her belly revolted and she ended up puking up what little remained in her stomach. And then, drawing her legs to her chest, she buried her face against them and fell into oblivion.

Sherra woke to total darkness, confused, unaware of where she was or how she'd come to be there. The rancid stink of vomit hit her nose and she could taste it in her mouth as well. Easing her way upright, she felt her way along the wall until she came to a light switch. Flipping it up, she stared down at the ugly red stain marring the pristine, ivory carpet.

She swallowed, her belly twisting itself in hot, slippery knots. She really should clean it up—

But if she didn't get out of here, she was going to get sick again.

Backing out of the closet, she found herself in an unfamiliar room. She could still hear the music pumping downstairs and as she opened the door, the cacophony of voices blended with the music until it was all an indistinguishable blur.

Tugging up the sleeve of her close-fitting black shirt, she squinted at her watch. Midnight. She'd gotten here around eight—she thought. Last time she remembered looking at her watch it had been just a few minutes after nine, right when she was mentally complaining about being hungry, thinking about going home and getting Seth to make her something to eat.

The thought of eating anything now was enough to make her break out into a sweat. No way in hell was she eating a damn thing.

A couple hours—gone.

Her mind was cloudy, almost like she'd slept just a little too long, and the taste of vomit in her mouth was making her feel even worse. She glanced back in the room she'd just left, spied another door. A bathroom—she hoped.

Thank God—yep, it was a bathroom. Done in gold and ivory, ferns set up on shelves along the back of the sunken Jacuzzi tub. If she hadn't felt so damn nauseated, she might have stood there staring at the tub in wistful envy.

But what caught her attention was the toothbrushes. Neatly wrapped, tucked into a basket that rested on a shelf near the sink. Toothbrushes, and toothpaste. Five minutes later, teeth brushed, face washed, she felt almost human.

Not an improvement, though, because now that her head was a little bit clearer, she was starting to figure out what had happened. Sherra knew she was more than a little paranoid. She knew that her imagination usually worked overtime. But she knew what had happened.

Somebody had drugged that fucking punch. People had kept pushing more and more of it toward her. Each time, she'd either refused to accept it or just set it back down. But at some point, she must have taken a drink—and damn it, the shit had been spiked.

What with, she didn't know.

She wanted to hit somebody.

But her memory was one big blank; she barely remembered

drinking the damn punch. She had no idea who had given it to her.

The anger snarled, struggled inside her, but she knew there wasn't a damn thing she could do about it. Hell, if she called the police, chances were JD's parents would make *her* out to be the bad guy here.

Still—

She left the bedroom, furious, her legs wobbling underneath her and her head spinning around like she'd just climbed off the Tilt-A-Whirl. Home. She just needed to get home.

Preferably without Seth seeing her stumble inside.

He'd know something was wrong and she knew as mad as she was, she wouldn't be able to keep her mouth shut. Her twin would go ballistic.

Walking through the dim hall, she found her way to the steps and headed down. Halfway down, she saw JD and his favorite tagalong, Boyd. Ignoring them, she didn't pause as JD called her name.

He laughed and reached out, grabbed her arm. She could smell the liquor on his breath, but it wasn't until she looked at him that she got scared. She wouldn't let him see it, though. JD was an asshole—and a hyena, the kind that went after anything that showed weakness. She'd be damned if she let him see she was afraid.

But then he glanced over her shoulder at Boyd—strong arms came around her and before she could even scream, a big, hard hand was clamped over her mouth.

No no nonono!

She fought, but neither of them cared as they dragged her away from the stairs and into a room. Boyd shoved her to the ground as JD shut the door behind him and turned.

He laughed as she tried to come off the ground and Boyd shoved her back. "Ready to party, you ho?"

She wished she hadn't woken up.

Wished she hadn't left that closet until somebody found her hiding in there.

Wished she were anywhere but where she was, held to the floor, struggling and swearing, screaming as JD shoved her long black skirt to her waist. She kept screaming, fighting, cussing until he took off her panties and shoved them in her mouth.

What little fog left in her brain evaporated under the rush of fear as adrenaline kicked in, but other than that painful clarity, the adrenaline surge didn't help much.

Sherra lay on her back, struggling against hard, cruel hands and trying to breathe past the makeshift gag, choking on her damn panties.

"Quiet, bitch. Quiet, or I shove my dick down your throat until you choke," JD panted as he knelt between her thighs.

She reared up with her lower body. Being short sometimes had its advantages. She was able to get her legs between them and kick him back.

"Stupid bitch!"

He backhanded her. Head spinning, disoriented, she moaned. JD's hands bit into her thighs and she fought to keep them closed, locking her knees together and praying for a miracle. JD swore and then he hauled off and slugged her in the belly. The resulting pain and breathlessness pervaded her body but she didn't stop fighting him.

Above her head, Boyd held her hands pinned down and he was panting, breathing on her face. The smell of the beer he'd been drinking fogged her brain.

"Damn slut—" JD panted. He gave up struggling to pry her legs apart and instead lay on top of her, his weight grinding her into the floor—and his forearm came up, pressing against her throat. She couldn't breathe—couldn't breathe—

His cruel laugh just barely reached her through the gray fog that came up and wrapped itself around her as he choked her. She felt him between her legs now, her skirt tangled around her hips, leaving her lower body naked and vulnerable as he jammed his fingers inside her. "Shit, bitch. You're dry as a damn bone." Then he laughed. Weakly, she tried to pull her legs together again, but couldn't. The rasp of his zipper was loud, very loud.

"What the . . . ?"

It was a new voice. One that intruded on the fog and the fear and Sherra's eyes popped open. In the doorway stood Lacey Talbot, her eyes wide and shocked, her mouth open.

"Get the fuck out, Lacey," JD snarled over his shoulder.

Under him, the gag rendering her mute, Sherra pleaded silently, *Please don't . . . Please help me!*

Lacey rushed in and as she did, she screamed something out. Sherra didn't know what she'd said. She still couldn't think.

"Leave her the hell alone, you son of a bitch!" Lacey shouted. She shoved against his shoulders, but it didn't do any good.

She didn't give up, though, and if it wasn't for the gag, Sherra might have sobbed in relief. Even when JD swung around and tried to hit Lacey, the other girl didn't stop.

Then Lacey kicked at JD again and he snarled, swore at her.

Their voices bled together and Sherra couldn't tell one from another. Somebody shouted, "Get the fuck out of here!" And then blinding pain as JD backhanded her again.

A furious grunt, the hands pinning her wrists to the ground slackened just a little and she tried to tear herself away. Boyd didn't let go, though.

A flash of movement caught her eye and Sherra wheeled her head around to see Renee creeping inside the door. The ugly mark on her face had started to bruise and she stared at Boyd and JD with horror. Later, Sherra would think back and realize that while horrified, Renee hadn't been surprised to find her boyfriend trying to rape a girl. Renee grabbed a lamp, moved up around Lacey and then lifted it over her head.

It crashed down on JD's head and broke. Little slivers of glazed pottery rained down and Sherra could feel some of them hitting her on the face. The bruise on Renee's face stood out against her pale skin, but all Sherra could see was her eyes as the other girl backed away.

"Get away from her." Who was that . . . Lacey? Was it Lacey?

Sherra still couldn't move. Boyd still held her pinned and JD's deadweight had her lower body trapped.

Another new voice joined in, deep, furious. Who was it . . . Her head, damn it, it was spinning, fear and adrenaline churning together with the lingering effects of whatever she'd drunk, and she couldn't *think*.

Escape. That was the only thing she could think about. She had to escape . . .

Too many voices.

Too much commotion.

Then she was free, wiggling out from under JD and scrambling to her feet. Her skirt fell into place but it wasn't enough. She still felt naked, vulnerable. With a shaking hand, she took the panties out of her mouth and threw them on the floor.

Raised voices. Shouting.

Stumbling away, she fell against the wall and wrapped her arms around her middle. She was going to be sick—going to pass out—

No. No, you're not, she told herself. She wouldn't let herself get sick. Wouldn't let herself pass out.

Get away.

She had to get away.

The blur of voices, the people around her, none of it mattered. Huge chunks of pottery from the broken lamp crunched under the soles of her heavy, ugly combat boots. JD was moving again and instinctively, she flinched. *Run. Run. Run.* She had to get away from him, but before she could make her body move, somebody spoke.

The words made no sense—save for one.

Sherra didn't recognize the voice, had no idea what they were talking about, who, none of it.

But that one word—it leaped into her mind, branding her, burning through the fear-induced fog.

Gun—

Half numb, Sherra turned, watched as JD rushed to the huge desk that took up half of the wall. Deacon Cross—where had he come from? Deacon was there, running toward JD.

JD jerked on one of the drawers, grabbed a gun just as Deacon reached him.

The gun went flying.

She watched it, tracking its arc through the air with her eyes, watched as it landed on the ground in front of Boyd. He looked up. His eyes met hers. JD shouted his name. Lacey and Renee appeared in the corner of her vision and Renee said, "We need to get out of here."

But she couldn't move. Couldn't even blink as Boyd looked down at the gun, watched as he started to grab it.

Without thinking, she bent over and grabbed a big, jagged shard of pottery from the ground. It was part of the busted lamp, big, sharp—and it had a handle. She curved her hand around it and moved, her body reacting even though her mind still felt frozen with shock.

She struck, watched as Boyd's eyes widened. Watched as blood sprayed out, watched as he sagged to the ground.

Empty, numb, she stared down at him and watched as one of her would-be rapists breathed his last.

1

May 2009

"Not going to happen."

On the other end of the phone, Sherra Salinger's agent, Monica Green, blew out a quiet, controlled breath.

Sherra knew what her friend wanted to do was yell, but the two women had known each other for years, had been friends for years. A friendship that went deeper than the agent/author deal. Because of that friendship, Monica knew how Sherra would react if Monica yelled. Sherra didn't react to yelling very well. Under most circumstances, she could be cajoled, coaxed and kindly coerced, if it was done right.

Yelling accomplished nothing with her.

Monica knew this.

So instead of yelling, she took a deep breath and tried a ploy more likely to work. "Look at it this way—you'll have somebody to yell at if you don't have coffee in the morning."

"Not going to happen," Sherra repeated, staring down at her desk.

There were two pieces of mail there.

One was an invitation to her fifteen-year reunion. Right now she wished she'd burned the damn thing, but she'd made plans around that stupid reunion and she'd be damned if she let some psycho stalker make her alter those plans in any way.

She'd been waiting all her life for this.

Going back to Madison a success.

All those people who'd sneered at her, all those people who'd whispered behind their hands that she'd asked for what had almost happened to her—and all those people who said she should have gone to jail for killing Boyd.

White trash—you're nothing but white trash and you'll never amount to anything.

How many times had she been told that?

Too many to count.

She'd already proved them wrong. She'd hit the bestseller lists for the first time eight years ago, only seven years after she'd graduated high school. She'd never gone to college, had worked as a waitress, a bartender, a taxi driver, worked in housekeeping through several hotels, and all the while, she'd tried to burn the horror of her memories out by writing them down.

Memories that took on lives of their own and no longer even resembled anything remotely her own, becoming stories of their own, happening to somebody other than her.

She'd proved them wrong—but this time, they were actually going to see how damn wrong they were.

Monica's voice dragged her attention back to the conversation—and the *favor* that Monica was trying to get out of her. "Sherra, sweetie, you have to understand, this is serious."

"I know it's serious, but I'm not naive. I'm not stupid. I'll be careful. I don't need some hulking bodyguard standing in the background while I sign books in order for me to be careful."

"He's not there to make sure *you* are careful. He's there as a deterrent."

"No . . . if I allowed this, he'd be there as a deterrent, but I'm not going to allow it."

"Sherra. Be sensible."

"That's your job, not mine." She reached for the other piece of paper, this one a letter. Written using bits and pieces cut out of newspapers and magazines.

Waiting for you.

That was all it read.

That was all each of these had read.

Over the past five years, she'd received hundreds. At first, they went through her publisher, forwarded on to her, but then they started screening her fan mail—thanks to her agent. Monica told her editor about these letters and they'd started weeding them out. But within a few months, the stalker managed to track down her home address and they'd started arriving in her personal mail.

Once a month. Then twice a month. Over the past year, they'd come once a week.

Every week.

Even when she moved, he found her again.

There were no fingerprints.

The postmark zip code changed on a regular basis.

There was nothing to identify the sender.

Sherra could have handled the letters. They didn't even really give her bad moments at night. She had a good security system, and an even better dog—a German shepherd she had raised from a puppy and who guarded her like nothing else.

Three months ago, things had escalated to the point that the FBI was now involved. The first few e-mails had been innocuous enough, but then he'd started sending her pictures. Pictures of Sherra. Or her head at least. Photoshopped onto the bodies of other women. Amateur porn pics, most likely, considering the lousy quality.

The subject line always read:

Waiting for you.

And each successive e-mail was getting worse and worse. Going from kinky and spookily weird to downright depraved and terrifying. The last few, the police believed were stills from pseudo-snuff films. Sherra hoped and prayed they were pseudo, at least. It was bad enough seeing her face in those images, images where somebody held a knife to her neck as he sodomized her. Images where hands wrapped around her throat and choked the life out of her while he raped her.

The FBI was working on it, but Sherra knew they weren't having much luck as yet. The e-mails never came from the same server, not even in the same city.

"... listening?"

Sherra carefully turned the letter facedown and leaned back in her chair. "Yes, I'm listening. Monica, listen, I understand how serious this is—"

"Has the letter come this week?" Monica asked, interrupting her.

Reluctantly, Sherra said, "Yes."

"And . . . ?"

"And I opened it."

Monica's control snapped. "Damn it, Sherra!"

"Monica, what does it matter if I open it or if the FBI does?"

"Have you bothered to let them *know* you've gotten another?"

"What, they don't have my mailbox wired?" Her smart-ass quips weren't going to help any, but she couldn't stop. Sherra got nervous, she got mouthy.

"You gave me your word you'd take this seriously." Monica's voice leveled out, grave, serious—and just the slightest bit reproachful. "After that last e-mail, you told me that you would do what was needed to make sure you were safe."

Sherra winced. "Look, I was going to call Agent Mueller today.

I promise. I even have it on my list," she said, hastily adding it up on the very top.

"Yeah, and I bet my morning cup of coffee that you just now put it on your list," Monica said with a snort. "Sorry, sugar. It's not good enough. If you go on the book tour, you are going to have a bodyguard with you."

Unable to stop it, the words slipped out. "You can't make me."

Monica laughed, but it wasn't a happy, *oh you're so funny* kind of laugh. It was hard, brittle and humorless as she said, "Oh, yes. I can. You either agree to the bodyguard, or I'm going to call every single one of the booksellers and tell them that because of threats to your safety, your publisher feels it would be best to cancel each stop unless the bookstore is willing to have uniformed policemen at each event."

The pit of her stomach dropped out. "Monica . . ."

But her agent continued, her voice taking on a happy, entirely forced, chipper tone. "You know, most of them will be happy to do just that. And most of them, if not all, have media lined up for this event. This is big, you know. Very big. The media is going to want to know why there are cops at your signings, and you know how gossip goes . . ."

Sherra dropped her head forward, letting it thunk down on the desk. "I can't believe you're doing this to me."

"I CAN'T BELIEVE you're doing this to me," Dalton Green snarled, glaring at his big sister. Big in chronological terms, not literally. In literal terms, she was about average, but not too many women looked average next to him.

He stood six feet five in his bare feet, weighed two-sixty and even on his best day, he looked liked trouble waiting to happen. A perpetual five-o'clock shadow darkened his features. Unless he carried a razor with him and shaved two or three times a day, that shadow was going to be there. He had pale green eyes, his skin was naturally dusky and he only bothered to cut his brown hair when it got in his way.

Over the past few years, he'd finally figured out that if he grew it long enough, he could wear it in a ponytail and then he could cut it even less. The long hair added to the roughness of his appearance and came in handy on his job—or rather, what *used* to be his job. He was no longer a narcotics detective, didn't want to have anything to do with that old life, no reminders, no jobs working a security detail—*including* playing chaperone to some fluff writer his sister took care of.

"It's just for a little while, Dalton. And look at it this way, you'll make enough money that you can take your time trying to figure out what you want to do."

"I'd already made that decision," he snapped. "I'm going down to Miami. I'm going to get drunk, sit on the beach and watch girls walk around in dental-floss bikinis. Then, I'll go to bed, get up and do it all over again."

"And you'll get money . . . where?"

So he hadn't put *that* much thought into his plan yet. "Bartending. Bouncing. I dunno. I don't care. I don't want to play bodyguard for some prep school Barbie doll romance writer. I ain't doing it."

Four weeks later

I AIN'T DOING it.

Famous last words, Dalton decided as he climbed out of Monica's way-too-small convertible Jaguar. He'd practically had to eat his knees on the drive over and it wasn't helped by the fact that his darling sister loved to drive too fast and brake too hard.

"I can't believe I'm doing this," he muttered. He smoothed a hand back over his hair, caught it into a tail at his nape and secured it with a rubber band he'd snagged from Monica's console.

She gave him a strained smile. "You're doing it because you love me," she said, striving for a light tone.

And failing.

Frowning, he glanced at the house and then back at Monica. "Exactly how serious is this stalker problem?"

Monica licked her lips and then reached into the briefcase she never went without. "She doesn't know I have this. Please don't tell her."

Dalton took one look at the picture and his gut went cold. "You've called the police about this, right?"

She nodded. "Police. FBI. We're doing everything we're supposed to. I tried to talk Sherra out of this book tour, even though her editor would have killed me. Sherra won't cancel. It's her first one—I *know* it's a big deal, but . . ." Monica blew out a breath. "Dalton, I'll be honest. I'm *terrified* for her. The last thing I want Sherra doing is going on this damn book tour right now."

Sherra . . . He frowned, tried to place the name. Monica rambled on about her writers endlessly, but most of them wrote romance or fantasy, nothing he had much interest in. There were a couple, two mystery writers, a horror writer, that he liked, though. Narrowing his eyes, he searched his memory until he came up with the right name.

This wasn't one of the romance writers.

It was the horror writer. "Sherra. Sherra Salinger is the one with the stalker?" he asked.

"Yeah."

"This is her?"

"Some of her, at least. The guy likes to play with Photoshop."

It was hard to tell what she really looked like in the picture. A black mask hid her face, one that probably had been airbrushed on—looked too fake for anything else. The body was very obviously not hers, bent over a bench, chained in place. The knife being used in the image—shit, Dalton really hoped it was just some staging going on in that picture.

"How long has this been going on?"

"The pictures come via e-mail—they started about three months ago. But she's been getting letters for years. They always read the same. '*Waiting for you.*' That's all they say."

Carefully, he folded the picture and handed it back to Monica. "Is she aware how serious this is?"

Monica grimaced. "Aware, yes. In a way. But she has blinders on."

He blew out a sigh. "All right. Let's get this over with."

He was broke. He needed the money. More, he needed to stop sitting around and brooding and thinking about the complete waste of his life and how much he hated dirty cops. He'd figured playing babysitter for some fluffy romance writer was an easy way to make some money—he'd even figured it was entirely likely this was some publicity ploy that Monica had been suckered into, knowingly or otherwise.

He'd planned on being bored out of his mind for the next couple months, but earning a decent amount of money doing it. Now he was doing some mental rearranging. This *was* serious. He wasn't going to be sitting on his tail or just a roughed-up version of arm candy, either.

"You could have let me in on how serious this was," he muttered as he followed Monica up the artfully laid-out brick walkway.

She shot him a look over her shoulder and said, "Dalton, if it wasn't serious, I wouldn't have asked." She used her own key to let them in, telling him that Sherra Salinger was a lot more than a client to his sister.

Pausing just inside the door, she reset the security system. Clawed feet came clattering over the tiled entry way.

"Hi, King."

Dalton remained where he was, eying the big Shepherd as Monica bent over and petted him behind the ears. "King?" he repeated.

"As in Stephen," Monica said, grinning at him over her shoulder. "King and me are going to be housemates while you two are on the tour. I'm keeping him for Sherra." She scratched the dog between his ears for a few more seconds and then straightened.

"I'll let Sherra introduce you to him. He's a great dog, but he takes his responsibilities seriously."

Yeah, Dalton could see that, eyeing the dog while the dog eyed him right back. King didn't make any threatening moves, didn't pull that growling-and-raising-his-hackles bit, but Dalton wasn't fooled. Somebody had trained that dog, and damn well.

"Where's your mama, boy?" Monica asked.

The dog barked once and headed off down the hall, Monica trailing along behind him. Dalton brought up the tail end of the procession, walking through the house and taking everything in with a little bit of surprise.

But the biggest surprise came when Monica led him into an office.

Dalton wasn't entirely sure what he'd been expecting, either Wednesday Addams or maybe Elle from *Legally Blonde*.

What he found was Snow White.

The woman sitting behind the desk looked delicate. It was hard to tell with her sitting down, but he guessed she was no more than five-five in her bare feet. The low-scooped neck of her tank revealed firm, ivory mounds and he caught a glimpse of black lace as she reached up and pushed her hair behind one small ear. That hair was blacker than midnight and her mouth was a lush shade caught between red and pink, a full-lipped, sexy mouth that made him think of just one thing.

Sex.

She lifted her eyes from the pile of paper in front of her and looked at Monica. Then her eyes flicked his way and the only thing that Dalton could think was . . .

Oh, hell.

All the blood drained out of his head, headed south. As she leaned back in her seat to give him a disdainful stare, he realized his mouth was watering.

"Who is he?"

At least he *thought* that was what she had said. He couldn't be entirely sure because he was too interested in imagining that pretty, cupid's-bow mouth under his to worry about what she was saying.

Talk about complications.

Off to his side, Monica was smiling, talking, gesturing toward Dalton and making all those soothing, mama-hen noises she made so well. They seemed to have about as much effect on Snow White as they did on Dalton.

Little to none.

She leaned back in her seat and propped her feet on the edge of the desk. Her eyes, dark, dark eyes, flicked his way again and then she looked at Monica, smiled sweetly. "Hell, no."

Dropping the mama-hen act, Monica planted her hands on her hips and said, "Don't you *hell, no* me, Sherra. You already agreed to this. You damn well *will* be taking him along with you on this damn tour of yours. If you absolutely refuse to cancel it, then you'll have somebody at your side. Twenty-four/seven."

Usually, when Monica used that tone, people meekly agreed to do whatever she wanted. She might look sweet and unassuming, but when she was pissed off, any intelligent soul who knew her took pains to steer clear of that temper.

Either Sherra wasn't all that intelligent, or she was every bit as stubborn as Monica. Neither option boded well for him, because he was in this for the long haul—either spending the next few weeks with a woman who looked like sin and had about as much substance as cotton candy, or spending six weeks with a woman who looked like sin and fighting her over every damn thing.

The light snapping in her eyes pretty much eradicated the cotton candy possibility.

He still hadn't spoken, keeping his hands tucked into his back pockets, focusing on her face so his eyes didn't trail down over all that white, creamy skin exposed by her scoop-neck tank top. A faint smile curled the corners of her lips as she reached up and took off the horn-rimmed glasses she'd been wearing.

How in the hell could such an ugly-ass pair of glasses look so damn sexy? He had to know.

"This isn't going to happen, Monica. I love you, but I'm sorry. This isn't going to happen."

Monica smirked. "Yes, Sherra. It is. I love you, and I'm sorry, but it *is* going to happen."

"You can't make me agree to this," Sherra said, a thread of steel working its way into her voice.

Lifting a shoulder, Monica said, "You already did. And if you're thinking you can change your mind, too bad. Don't think you can fire him or run him off, either. I'm paying him. And believe me, I'm paying him well enough that your surly attitude and your bitching isn't going to chase him off. He's going to stay on your ass—"

Oh, damn, the imagery on that one . . . yeah, he'd be more than happy to stay on her ass. Dalton found himself wishing she'd get out of that chair, come out from behind the desk. He wanted to see if she was as pretty a picture as he suspected she was.

Sweat broke out on his forehead as another image worked its way inside his mind, thanks to his sister. *He's going to stay on your ass . . . Damn, would I like to stay on your ass . . .*

Sherra surged up out of the chair and slapped her palms down on the desk, glaring at Monica.

He just barely resisted the urge to drool. He still couldn't see all of her, but he could see enough. He could see a perfect hourglass figure with full, round hips, the curve of what promised to be a very delectable ass, plump breasts that would fill his big hands perfectly . . . Damn it, he was so completely fucked.

"If I don't want some big, brooding jackass following every step I take, you can't make me agree to it," Sherra gritted out between her teeth. She flicked the big, brooding jackass in question another glance and flushed, realized he was staring at her breasts.

She braced herself against the rush of disgust that always came when men looked at her—but it didn't come. Frowning, she looked at him again, a little longer this time. He wasn't looking at her tits anymore, thank God, but when his gaze connected with hers, she realized it might be easier if he'd just continue to ogle her.

His pale green gaze looked entirely too dreamy, entirely too beautiful in that harsh, rugged face. But she could see the intelligence snapping in that gaze, felt the force of his personality radiating out from him.

He wore jeans, faded and worn. A T-shirt that molded to big, powerful arms and a wide chest. His golden brown hair was long, easily shoulder length, she decided, possibly longer, but it was hard to tell with it secured back from his face in a tail at his nape. The dark, swarthy cast to his skin was most likely natural and although it was fairly early, he had a heavy growth of five-o'clock shadow going.

He looked like sex and sin.

He felt like a cop.

All in all, that was just too much trouble waiting to happen.

Sherra didn't like cops.

Sherra didn't like sex.

She wasn't opposed to a little bit of sin now and then, but she generally found it in driving a little too fast, swearing when she was mad and shopping in excess. Gluttony and recklessness suited her a lot better than any sort of carnal pleasures.

His eyes moved over her again.

She wasn't even looking at him and she felt the heated, leisurely weight of his eyes as he looked her over again, from the top of her head and down as far as he could go until her desk blocked her from his view. Every inch he touched with his gaze seemed to heat and she clenched her teeth, fought not to blush.

Over the past fifteen years, her knee-jerk fear to any sort of male interest had slowly faded, going from a vicious, ugly wound to a faded scar that hurt only every now and then. Too much interest made her nervous, but she was bitchy enough, aloof enough that most men didn't bother didn't displaying anything beyond a passing interest that quickly faded after she ignored them or cut them down.

She'd ignore him. Best way to handle it. If she ignored him long enough, he'd get bored . . . and she suspected she was going to need him bored, because the look in Monica's eyes was unmoving. Implacable.

Taking a deep, slow breath, Sherra tried one more time. "Monica, I don't need some full-time bodyguard watching over me for this."

Monica smiled sweetly. "Yes, you do need it. You just don't want it."

ARGUING WITH MONICA Green was like arguing with the Rock of Gibraltar. Sherra knew this from experience. If Sherra fought having that . . . that *cop* following her around for the book tour, then Monica damn well would call every single bookstore and explain the hows, whats and whys of Sherra's nasty little stalker. Cops would be brought in. Questions would be asked.

Sooner or later, somebody would slip up with the details and Sherra would find herself the target of attention she didn't want.

So, fine. She'd deal with it.

Deal with him.

But there was no *way* she was going to deal with this, she decided a few minutes later. She watched him saunter through the door with a duffel in one hand and a garment bag slung over one big shoulder.

"What's this?" Sherra demanded, stopping in the doorway and glaring from him back to Monica and then back.

Damn it, he still hadn't said even two words to her. Did the guy know how to talk?

He stared at her from under heavy-lidded eyes, a sardonic smile curling his lips, but just as he had earlier, he let Monica do the talking for him.

"Dalton's going to be staying here for the next few days. You leave in a little over a week—you're going to be running all over the place, so I'll feel better knowing you have somebody watching out for you while you're doing it, all those last-minute shopping trips you're so damn fond of. Besides, I figure now is a good time for you two to at least get half comfortable with each other."

Sherra blinked.

Comfortable?

With *him*?

No.

Couldn't happen.

He was too big. He was too male.

Too *real*.

Even from ten feet away, even though he hadn't said anything at all to her—*not one damn word*—she could feel the weight of his personality beating against her and she knew that ignoring him wasn't going to work.

Snide, bitchy comments weren't going to work.

Worse . . . the longer he was in the same vicinity, the more aware she became of him. Too damn aware. She could feel him watching her, could feel his growing interest.

The book tour was going to be six weeks of practically non-stop work, at least once the stop in Madison was done. She had interviews lined up, book signings, visits to a couple of different colleges, and several Q&A sessions that were taking place at libraries or with reading groups. It was going to be busy enough that she could focus on work, keep herself occupied—hell, that was her preferred state anyway.

Work. Focus on work. Focus on the story, because if she wrote enough, the screams that still haunted her nightmares didn't send her clawing and struggling into wakefulness—or at least, not as often.

But how could she focus with some stranger living in her house with her?

She hadn't had anybody living with her since she'd left home. Even when she'd been so damn broke, finding a roommate would have made her life so much easier, she hadn't lived with another person. She didn't *want* anybody else in her living space.

She wanted her privacy, needed it.

Shaking her head, she told Monica, "I didn't agree to this."

But . . . just like so many other times, it was as if Monica didn't even hear her. She rolled right over her, a friendly, smiling steamroller, and it wasn't until Monica was walking out the door that Sherra stopped trying to change the inevitable.

The door clicked shut behind Monica, and Sherra stood, gaping at the door, her head spinning, panic and nerves clawing at her gut.

He spoke—*finally*—and his voice was like whiskey-soaked velvet, rough, raw and entirely too sensual. "You should probably let me know your security code. That way you don't have to reset it if I go for a run or something."

Crossing her arms over her midsection, she snapped, "What, you're actually allowed to leave me alone? I thought I was getting a twenty-four/seven babysitting detail."

He smiled—shit, what in the hell was his name? Monica had told her, she knew it. But for the life of her, she couldn't remember. "You haven't needed a babysitter for a while, I bet."

His eyes slid over her again and she hunched her shoulders, hugged herself tighter. She might not like men, she might have to fight not to let her instinctive fear overtake her, but her body sometimes had a mind of its own, and this guy's sexuality was pulling a very unfamiliar response from her. Her nipples peaked, her belly was awash with heat and her legs were weak, wobbling underneath her.

Sherra knew what she was feeling—she understood sexual arousal even if she wasn't familiar with it in much of a personal sense. She preferred to keep it that way—understanding in the abstract was tolerable. Actually feeling it, the few times it had happened, was the beginning of an emotional avalanche for her.

A guy touched her and something would send her back. Didn't

matter how good she'd been feeling, didn't matter how carefully he moved, it happened every time. She'd find herself back on the floor of the office in JD's house, struggling under his weight, against Boyd's hands—and then like a flash, she was free—and she had that broken, jagged piece of the lamp in her hand and stood in front of him, staring at the gun in his hand.

A wash of blood.

Then his lifeless, hazel eyes staring sightlessly, frozen in a mask of death.

In her mind, sex equated death—violent death, and a death she caused.

Sherra was a fucking basket case and she knew it.

But she'd happily existed without sex and she preferred to keep it that way, thank you very much. So this big, rough, sexy guy was a complication she didn't want or need. His pale green eyes slid back up and connected with hers. The heat in that gaze left her shaking and her mind cringing with instinctive fear. She had to get away—

Tearing her eyes from his, she rattled off the code. Then, without looking at him even one more time, she backed away and mumbled under her breath, "I've got work to do."

SCOWLING, DALTON WATCHED as she disappeared down the hall, arms crossed over her chest, head tucked low.

A world of emotion had danced through her eyes in that brief moment when their gazes had locked. Just the quickest flash of heat, gone almost before it formed, nervousness, anger, regret—and a horrified fear that had the cop inside him going on alert.

Worse, it had an unfamiliar sense of protectiveness washing through him.

Shit.

He blew out a breath and set the alarm, fighting the urge to trail after her and see if he couldn't figure out what was running through that mind of hers. He wasn't going to do that. This was a job. Just a job.

And even if there was a real-life, grown-up, way-too-sexy version of Snow White hiding away in her office, it didn't change anything. He was here for a job. Just a job. One that would get him enough money to get him the hell out of Chicago, away from the memories of a life he no longer wanted.

SNOW WHITE NEVER left her cave.

Four days into his "assignment," he was a lot bored, a lot curious, and way too ready for this damn book tour that Miz Sherra Salinger had lined up. He was staying at her place for now because the lease had ended on his apartment exactly five days ago, the day before he walked into his sister's office and told her he'd take the damn babysitting job if it was still open.

He'd planned on crashing at Monica's for a few days.

But Monica had the brilliant idea that he should get to know Sherra a little before the tour. At least that was what Monica claimed. Dalton knew better. His sister was scared. Scared of the threats her friend had received, and scared that Sherra wasn't taking the threats as seriously as she should.

Monica would have to come to grips with it, because people generally didn't have bodyguards with them nonstop. Deals like this, a book tour where she was going to be very visible, yeah. Bodyguards were more a visible deterrent than anything else. Inside her home, they could keep her secured. She had that big-ass dog; she had a very decent security system. It was a controlled environment and in his mind, it was a safe one.

Once this job was over, Sherra wasn't going to have somebody watching her nonstop. Right now, Monica would take what she could get. Hopefully, she'd planned on using the next few weeks to try to figure out another solution—Dalton knew his big sister, knew how her mind worked.

He could give her some peace of mind for a while by sleeping here and watching over Snow White. He could do that. He needed the money; he needed some time to think about what he was going to do next. Something that had nothing to do with being a cop. A beach bum actually sounded pretty damn okay to him.

Wasn't exactly a hardship staying in a nice, big house. She had every fricking channel under the sun, a killer entertainment system, plenty of books.

Of course, right now he couldn't focus on a damn thing. It was eleven o'clock at night and he was slowly going out of his mind from boredom. It was quiet save for the thunderstorm raging outside and Dalton felt like he was going to come out of his skin if he didn't do something to relieve the monotony. He'd flipped through one of the many books arranged on the shelves. Nothing had held his interest—well, not entirely true. There were a few that had done more than hold his interest.

But he had forced himself to set those down—it would be seriously embarrassing to wake up from the nightmares that those books could induce. She looked like Snow White—but her imagination rivaled that of the wicked stepmother. He'd read enough of her books over the past few years to know just how beautifully twisted her imagination was.

The woman could write. Her books were a strange blend of horror, urban fantasy and suspense.

But he was already on edge, already tense. He was still trying to get over his own nightmare. Four months had come and gone and he still wasn't level. He wasn't entirely convinced he'd ever be *level* again.

Shit, Zeke . . .

He scrubbed his hands over his face, raked his nails through the thick stubble on his chin and tried to shut his mind down before it went down that road. He couldn't go there, not right now.

Never sounded best to him.

He had too much shit in his head, was too damn edgy right

now. As much as he'd like to lose himself in a good book, he knew that if he lost him himself in one of her nightmare worlds just then, it might be enough of a push to have his own nightmares flaring to life, and he could live without that. Yeah, he could do just fine without that.

There was no sound, no change that he could see, but in the span of a heartbeat, Dalton's instincts flared to life. Somebody was close—too close. Had somebody gotten in? His skin prickled; his senses went on red alert. Automatically, his hand moved to his side only to fall into a useless, impotent fist at his side as he remembered that he'd laid his weapon down months ago.

Then, as he heard a faint, disgruntled mutter coming from the kitchen, he blew out a breath. Following the sleepy, grouchy voice, he came to a halt in the doorway and leaned against the doorjamb, eyeing the view before him with a grin.

Sexy? Hell. *Sexy* didn't even begin to define Sherra Salinger. She wore a black pair of panties that rode low on her hips, stretching across her plump, round ass in a way that had his mouth watering, his hands itching. Inches of bare skin were visible above the waist-band of the panties, revealed by a strappy, cotton tank top done in bright, vivid purple. She straightened and nudged the refrigerator door with her hip before turning. That razor-straight black hair fell in her face, her hands full with enough sandwich supplies to feed an entire family.

"Midnight snack?" he asked, his voice a little lower than normal.

She didn't jump.

Didn't yelp in surprise.

Her gaze cut to his face and as the bottom of his stomach fell out, he realized he would have been a lot happier if she'd jumped or yelped when he startled her. Because the look in her eyes didn't come from being startled. It came from being terrified. She slowly lowered the stuff in her hands to the counter and stood there, staring at him with unreadable eyes while all the blood slowly drained out of her face and left her even paler than normal.

From the corner of his eye, he saw her hand shifting, moving across the countertop. Her hand closed around the wooden handle of a big butcher knife but he didn't look away from her face.

"I'm sorry," he said, his heart banging against his ribs as she stood there, clutching a knife in one small hand and staring at him like he was a modern-day version of the big bad wolf. "Didn't mean to scare you."

Her breasts rose and fell as she took a deep breath. He could see her knuckles go white as she tightened her grip on the knife and then, as quick as that, it was done. She let go of the knife and that blank, expressionless mask was replaced by one of grouchy exhaustion. "What do you want?"

The moment of fear might have passed for her, but his throat was still tight. The puzzle of Sherra Salinger was one that he knew he'd have to solve. Had to—the same way he had to breathe, the same way he had to eat—and the same way he had to do whatever he could not to see that lifeless, expressionless look in her eyes even as he felt the fear tearing at her insides.

2

HE'D TAKEN A turn and somehow found himself caught up in Mayberry, Dalton thought, staring around in bemusement. He knew from Monica that Madison, Ohio, was a small town. He'd been prepared for a distinct lack of the things he was used to seeing in Chicago.

Skyscrapers for one. He could handle not seeing the huge structures that jutted into the sky, blocking out everything but what was directly overhead. Traffic jams were another. It wasn't a big loss not to sit in a snarl at a red light and wait for his turn to go as cars clogged the intersection.

But he hadn't quite expected . . . *this*.

There were no traffic jams, because downtown Madison consisted of an old-time town square, complete with a courthouse that looked as if it had been built in the middle of the 1800s, a roundabout in lieu of stop signs and traffic lights.

There was a gazebo set up on the lawn in front of the courthouse, surrounded by picnic tables and stone benches. Half of them were occupied, some by people eating lunches out of brown paper bags, others by kids or teenagers. A kid came zipping by on a skateboard and Dalton sidestepped as a couple of friends quickly followed.

He heard the low chatter of voices, but even weirder, he heard birds chirping overhead. He lifted his gaze to the leafy green trees that dotted the square, squinting as he tried to make out the birds he could hear from within.

"Feel like you've fallen into the Twilight Zone?"

Glancing at Sherra, he smiled. Waited to see if she'd smile back. But she just gave him that same expressionless stare. Where in the hell was that sassy brat who had faced down his sister? Monica had come by twice before they left, called several times, enough for him to see that Sherra acted differently around him. Normally, she was flippant, just this side of bitchy, with a caustic sense of humor that Dalton loved.

But not with him.

With him, she was quiet, almost too quiet, watching him with wary suspicion.

He hated it.

Blowing out a sigh, he made himself respond to her question. Talk to her. That was what he needed to do. If he talked to her enough, maybe she'd relax a little more around him. "Yeah. Kind of strange. I counted all of three stoplights driving into town."

Sherra shrugged. "Madison's come up in the world. When I left home all they had was a flashing red light at the intersection of Main Street and the old highway. Three stoplights is major news for this town."

"I bet you're bigger news," he said, cocking his head and studying the huge banner on a storefront. The banner had Sherra's name on it and a huge book cover—her latest. Over the past few days, he'd spent some time learning as much as he could about the reclusive woman.

He knew how many books she had out, how much money she'd made last year, knew about the speeding tickets, her rather disturbing love of shoes—and about her past.

Knew she'd gotten into trouble damn often as a kid.

Knew that she was near genius level and had been offered no less than three free rides to a couple of very decent colleges when she'd graduated from high school. Three—and she'd walked away from them, choosing to wait tables and, once she'd gotten older, bartending, driving a cab in several different cities. After she'd sold her first book—something she described as a stroke of very weird luck, because she hadn't been trying to sell the book—she'd continued to work her odd jobs for another year. The second one hit the bestseller lists and she became an overnight phenomenon.

There were entire websites devoted to her books, fan sites, message boards.

Some of them referred to some of her darker secrets—although they weren't exactly secret. He'd found the information when he did a background check and he'd run through the information caught in a mix of fury and disgust.

At seventeen, she'd almost been raped.

And at seventeen, she'd taken a life.

Somebody had tried to quiet the part of the story dealing with her rape, but there were too many witnesses and nothing could whitewash the facts he'd read in the police report. Those witnesses had saved her from the rape and then a gun was brought into the story, and she'd used a broken piece of pottery, killing one of her attackers before he had a chance to use the gun.

How many of her nightmarish stories stemmed from that night? Dalton knew what a scar it left to end a life. He had his own scars to deal with, but it came with the job, the knowledge and the willingness to end a life if it was necessary.

He dealt with it. He had nightmares, and more than a few thousand times, he'd questioned the choices he'd made. Even knowing he'd do it all over again, the three lives he'd ended left a mark on him. He'd killed before—he'd hated it, but he knew he'd done the right thing, possibly the only thing. He could live with it—he could even live with knowing he'd taken his partner's life, his friend's life.

Zeke was the reason he'd put down his gun, and even though Dalton hated the choice he'd made, he could handle it. He could deal with it.

But Sherra had just been a kid. A scared kid who'd almost been raped by a couple of rich, privileged, pretty-boy bastards with serious entitlement issues.

Hell, between her past and the perverted freak now stalking her, it was no wonder she'd looked at him with absolute terror the night he'd scared her in the kitchen.

She was a puzzle, all right. One he had every intention of solving. She'd looked at him with terror in her eyes and a knife in her hand, as if she'd do whatever she had to do in order to protect herself. But she got sick e-mails from a guy who obviously had her starring in very violent, sexual fantasies and it didn't faze her.

The latest had come that morning, just before they left her house, loaded down with enough luggage to clothe an entire platoon of females.

If he hadn't been in the office, he had no doubt she would have kept quiet about the latest e-mail. But he'd been in the office, acutely aware of her, watching her so closely, she had no chance of hiding her reaction from him as she opened up the e-mail.

The subject line had read, *Waiting for you.*

The body of it was composed of nothing but one image after another. All of them Photoshopped, Sherra's head placed on the body of another woman. Various poses, various vices, all of them featuring pain and debasement, and more than a few of them including sexual torture, like being sodomized by a glass bottle, a knife handle—

And in the sickest one, a knife blade.

It was faked.

Many of the more gruesome images had been faked, but it took an experienced eye to see the clues and he doubted Sherra knew what to look for. These were better than the one that Monica had shown him. The guy was really getting into his work, smoothing out the rough edges, and if Dalton hadn't known what to look for, he might have been fooled.

She had stared at the e-mail with unblinking eyes and when he'd asked her if he should contact Monica, she'd stared at him blankly.

"What for?"

"You serious about this book tour deal?"

She had snorted derisively. "The bastard has been sending me these little love letters for five years now. You think I'm going to let him scare me into not living my life?"

Dalton in her kitchen at night had terrified her. Considering her past, it was understandable.

But somebody else was threatening her, in a very graphic, very gruesome way—and she continued merrily on, making plans for this city and that, jotting down notes, making phone calls and writing like a fiend every second she got.

In ten days, he'd come to realize that the woman worked like a demon, slept less than any one person should, made killer coffee— and the sadness in her eyes broke his heart. He'd be damned if he let anything add to that.

The book tour kicked off on Tuesday, the day her new book officially released. There was going to be some kind of "open house" at the bookstore throughout the afternoon, and that evening, she'd be signing books and having some sort of discussion. Already forty-some-odd people were down on the list to attend and those were just the ones who had thought to sign up. Monica had informed him that there would probably be quite a few more who just showed up.

From a cop's point of view, it was a logistical nightmare.

"What are we doing here again?" Sherra asked irritably. She'd piled most of her hair into a clip on top of her head, but a few strands had worked free. With one hand, she tucked a loose strand of hair behind one small ear, revealing long, silvery ropes that dangled from her lobes, hanging almost to her shoulders. She had a love of shoes and jewelry that rivaled his sister's.

He found himself seriously loving it. He remembered expecting either Wednesday Addams or Elle, but he realized Sherra was actually a mix. Dark and brooding, sexy and soft female, all mixed into a package that was driving him nuts.

She moved liked sex, smelled like sweetness and sin—and she watched him with nerves and distrust in her dark brown eyes.

"We're here so I can take a look at the bookstore and see what kind of nightmare we're dealing with."

Sherra rolled her eyes. "It's a book signing. The nightmares will come after people read that crappy book I wrote. Or when people ask what I do for research. The booksellers will have their own little catastrophes going when I sign. But all I gotta do is sit there, smile and answer questions while you stand behind me and brood and glare. That's what bodyguards do, right?"

"We're taking a look around," he said, ignoring her comments. "Then we're going to head to the police department or whatever passes for one in this town so I can talk to some of the locals and let them know what's going on."

Sherra's eyes popped wide. Her jaw dropped. "Why?"

Dalton rolled his eyes. "You've got a stalker, Sherra, and from what I can tell, some out-of-town people are coming in just for this book signing. Seems like a perfect time for a stalker to try and pull something. It's kind of a courtesy to let the locals know there could be trouble."

"You tell the *locals*, I can guarantee you there will be trouble." Her soft mouth turned down in a frown and she sighed, rolled her shoulders restlessly.

"Meaning . . . ?"

She sighed again. Before she answered, she reached up and pulled the clip out of her hair. His mouth went dry as all those midnight strands came tumbling to her shoulders, almost drooled as she combed through it with her fingers. It wasn't a move done to drive him nuts; he knew it wasn't—it was a stall for time, more than anything else.

But she *was* driving him nuts. By the time she had gathered her hair back up and resecured the clip, he was rock hard.

Her hair looked exactly the same, sexy and disheveled, and all he wanted to do was grab the clip from her hair and watch those raven strands fall all around her pale shoulders, shoulders left bare by the silky black camisole she wore.

He was caught up in that fantasy and had to jerk his attention back to the matter at hand. Her rosy mouth—a natural color, he knew it—parted on yet another sigh and she took a deep breath, squared her shoulders. "I know the sheriff. And trust me, we tell him that I've got a stalker, I'm never going to hear the end of it."

Jealousy ripped through him. He couldn't put his finger on it, but he knew it, the same as he knew the color of his eyes. There was a connection between her and some small-town sheriff. "Know him how?" he asked bluntly.

If there was something there, he wanted to know ahead of time. Plain and simple. He wanted to know, and he would.

She opened her mouth to respond, but before the words got out of her mouth, he heard a war whoop coming from behind him. Sherra's face broke into a smile and she took off at a run. He turned just in time to see a man catch her in his arms, a tall, lean man with dark eyes, a wide smile and a look of utter adoration of his face as he spun her around.

Sunlight glinted off the badge at the guy's waist and Dalton had the answer to his question.

The sheriff had arrived—and shit, was there a connection.

As he lowered Sherra to her feet, Dalton closed the distance between, something dark and ugly twisting through his gut. Jealous—shit, he really was jealous. Jealous over a woman who had never shown any interest in him at all, one who looked at him with a combination of fear, dislike and distrust.

The guy had his hands on her waist. Was smiling down at her.

But that smile faded as Dalton drew near and Dalton watched as the cop took over. Okay, so he might be in Mayberry, but the local sheriff looked like he took his job pretty seriously. His eyes flicked over Dalton, took him in, measured him up and made the same assessment that Dalton would have made, even if the guy hadn't been wearing his badge.

Dark eyes narrowed, slid from Dalton's face to Sherra's with curiosity. "What kind of trouble are you in, sis?"

Sis?

He was too busy taking that in to fully appreciate her response. At least not right off the bat. Her eyes went wide, her mouth parted and she planted her five feet five inches in front of the sheriff, demanding, "Me? What makes you think I've gotten into trouble?"

Her brother grinned down at her. "Because you're you." Then he stepped around her and held out his hand for Dalton. "Seth Salinger."

Dalton took it, shook once and let go, remaining silent as he went through his mental file. Yeah, there had been something about a brother—no. Not just a brother. A twin.

He could see the similarities now, the same dark eyes and hair, the same wide, mobile mouth. But where Seth was long, lean and rangy, Sherra was a petite powerhouse of curves and softness. He was dark where she was pale.

He also had no problem being blunt or messing with niceties, Dalton realized about two seconds later. Seth faced Sherra, legs spread wide, thumbs hooked in his front pockets as he asked, "What gives, Sherra?"

She blinked and wasted about ten seconds of wide-eyed innocence on him. Then she snorted and muttered, "The hell with it."

Dalton crossed his arms over his chest as Sherra faced her brother and said, "Seems I've got a stalker, Seth."

Seth's eyes narrowed. "When did this start?"

She shrugged evasively and mumbled, "A while ago."

Seth's voice dropped warningly. "How long?"

She winced. "Five years."

BLOOD RUSHED TO her face, her belly was an ugly, tight knot and her lip was sore from biting it, but she kept quiet.

If it wasn't for Dalton standing by, quiet and watchful, she would have laid into Seth a good thirty minutes ago. Shit, if it hadn't been for Dalton, she never would have let Seth drag her into his office so he could fuss at her, either.

Having Dalton there was a deterrent to the temper she could feel sparking inside. She didn't know why. Normally she didn't care if people saw her temper in all its wicked, razor-sharp glory.

But she didn't want to react like that around him.

She didn't want him to see any reaction from her at all.

She couldn't quite understand that, but she wasn't about to try to figure it out right now, either. Not with Seth all but breathing fire down her neck. His eyes bored into hers as he took his seat behind his desk, glaring at her the same way he'd done back when they were kids and he'd caught her doing something dangerous and stupid.

Dangerous and stupid might be okay for *him* to do, but he couldn't have his little sister doing it. "Why haven't I been told about this?"

Sherra shrugged. "Up until recently, I hadn't thought it was anything to worry about."

Seth's eyes narrowed down to mere slits, but his voice remained calm. "And when did you decide it was worth worrying about? When you decided to get a bodyguard for your book tour?"

She licked her lips. "I . . ." *Lie.*

But she wasn't going to lie to her twin. Hell, he knew when she lied. She blew out a breath and admitted, "I didn't exactly make that decision. Monica did. Told me I could either agree to a bodyguard or she'd make my life a living hell—*and* she'd end up getting a bodyguard on my tail anyway."

Without realizing it, she glanced at Dalton and that weird heat fluttered in her belly as a smile tugged up the corners of his mouth. Mouth dry, she swallowed. Her palms were sweating. Wiping them down the short denim skirt she wore, she shifted on the chair and looked back at Seth. Even if her twin was absolutely furious with her, he was definitely the safer subject to look at. Definitely safer than Dalton with his beautiful eyes, his sexy mouth and his way of making her think about things she didn't want to think about.

The past ten days had been so damn stressful she'd almost looked forward to the start of the book tour. It meant she wasn't trapped in her house with him nonstop. Granted, sitting next to him on a plane, in the cab, wasn't much easier. Not much easier at all. In those small, closed spaces, she was too aware of a few too many things. Like the way he smelled. She'd caught traces of that masculine, woodsy scent in her house, when he walked past her, when he stood across from her at the counter while he sipped coffee with her first thing in the morning.

But sitting next to him in the cab had been hell.

Now, trapped in Seth's small office was almost as bad.

He smelled good.

Too good.

And he watched her. All the time. Wasn't exactly something she could put down to his "job," either, because he made no attempt to hide the male interest in his gaze, even if he was careful to keep his distance.

The way he watched her should have freaked her out, but instead it made her tight, edgy—nervous, but in a way that was too unsettling and too unfamiliar. The way he watched her made her heart race, made her palms sweat, her nipples ache and her pussy weep. Hell, there had been three times in the week and a half when she had lain in bed and masturbated—something she very, very rarely did. Sexual arousal just wasn't her thing.

Or at least it hadn't been until he came into her life.

Now he had her living on the knife's edge of it and she didn't like it at all. On edge. Irritated. So turned on she hurt.

Now she could add *pissed off* to the mix. Seth was furious and it had her temper sparking as well.

Definitely not helping any.

"Let me get this straight," Seth growled. "You've got somebody threatening you, sending you sick, perverted e-mails, and has been around for *five* years—"

"The e-mails started three months ago, brother dear," she drawled.

He glared at her. "Okay, you've had a stalker for five years, been getting fucked-up e-mails for three months but you didn't really think you needed a bodyguard while you go traipsing around the country. You really didn't think you needed to tell me about any of this. Sherra, aren't you the least bit scared about this?"

Scared . . . She blinked, stared at him as though he were speaking a foreign language. "You think I'm not scared?" she finally said.

He snorted. "Sure as hell don't look scared to me. You don't even look *worried*."

She swallowed, her throat gone dry and tight. "I'm worried, Seth. Believe me, I'm worried plenty. I've let fear take too much from me, though. I'll be damned if I let it chase me inside my house and keep me trapped there. He *wins* then, Seth. He wins—and I lose."

Unspoken were the words, *I've already lost enough*. Seth heard it, though. She rather wished he hadn't because whining irritated her, even her own—especially her own. Her life didn't suck. Her life hadn't ended that night. Even when it felt like it had for a long time.

Seth blew out a harsh breath, deep flags of color staining his cheeks as he leaned forward and braced his arms on the desk, staring down at the scarred surface. "Damn it, Sherra."

She crossed her arms over her chest, crossed her legs. Automatically, she started to swing her foot, her sandal catching on her toes, going back and forth. "Seth, I don't want to fight with you over this. I *am* being careful. I've got a great security system, I've got a big dog and I know how to fight."

"Yeah. You've also got a brother who you neglected to share this with—for five years."

She caught the hurt in his voice and felt something clench inside her. Rocking forward, she rested her elbows on her knees, laced her hands back behind her nape. "Look, I'm sorry, Seth. Honestly, up until recently, I figured it was just some quack. I ignored them. There's nothing else I could have done. When the e-mails started, I did what I was supposed to do, e-mailed him back and told him to stop contacting me. I got the dog. I had the security system installed. I did what I thought I needed to do and I don't take unnecessary risks." She swallowed and lifted her head, stared at her brother. "But I knew what you would do. You'd worry. You'd nag me about coming back here—or worse, you coming there to play watchdog over your flighty, foolish sister—"

With an edge in his voice, Seth said, "I don't think of you like that."

"Yeah. Sure you don't." Leaning back in the seat, she crossed her arms over her chest and asked, "What if it was you, Seth? If you had somebody sending you weird e-mails, even threatening ones, would you hide yourself away?"

"I'm not saying you should hide away," he replied. "But damn it, you should have told me."

She blew out a ragged breath and closed her eyes. "I know."

She felt the start of surprise move through him and opened her eyes in time to catch it before it completely faded from his face. He covered it with a forced, fake cough and then reached up, wiggled a finger in his ear. "Excuse me? Didn't quite catch that."

Narrowing her eyes, she said, "I should have told you. I'm sorry."

A slight smile tugged up the corners of his lips but it didn't erase the worry in his eyes; neither did the attempt at a joke. "Man, Sherra, admitting she might have made a mistake. Not something I hear every day."

"Better write it down," she advised. "Might not happen again."

He studied her for a long, quiet moment. "I don't doubt it." Finally, he looked away from her and focused on Dalton. "So. What makes you think you can take care of my little sister?"

Sherra muttered, "I'm only younger by ten minutes, Seth."

But she didn't look up, even when Dalton spoke in that low, whiskey-rough voice that made shivers dance down her spine. "Fifteen years on the job with the Chicago Police Department. Spent the last eight working narcotics. Did that up until I quit a few months ago."

Seth cocked a brow, angled his head. "Quit? Why?"

"Personal reasons."

"If it's something that can affect your job, I have the right to know. That's my sister."

Sherra rolled her eyes and shifted in the chair, sitting sideways with her arm braced along the back of it. She lowered her head and studied her nails, even though the red nails with white tips really weren't all that interesting to her. However, the pretense let her study the men from under the fringe of her lashes without them realizing she was watching.

"I said it's personal. That means it's something that won't affect my job," Dalton replied, his voice level.

"If you're watching over my sister, I need a little more detail than that," Seth growled, coming up out of his chair and leaning forward, his hands planted on the desk.

"Then when I leave, you can run your little background check—which you're going to do anyway. That's all you're getting from me."

Seth straightened up, crossing his arms over his chest. He eyed Dalton appraisingly in silence for a minute. "How seriously are you taking this?"

Dalton's pale green eyes went cold and flat. "More seriously than your sister is."

Sherra scowled. "Hey, I agreed to let you tag along, didn't I?"

He shrugged. When he did, his shoulders stretched the seams of his faded blue T-shirt.

Sherra realized she was way too distracted by the way his muscles moved under that worn cotton. Tearing her eyes away from his body, she stared straight ahead as Dalton said, "Yeah, you let me *tag along*. You're doing this because Monica would have made your life hell for the next month or so and you didn't see the point in arguing over it. You didn't agree because you felt you need to have somebody watching your cute little butt; you did it to shut her up. So no, I don't think you're taking it all that seriously."

She was adorable when she blushed, Dalton decided. He had a feeling he'd be doing what he could to make her blush often, because when she was flustered, she couldn't quite manage that blank look she showed him way too often. He shifted a little, bracing one shoulder against the wall, watching the siblings. The sheriff was glaring at him, but there was a bit more of the older-brother look in his eyes now than that of a concerned law enforcement officer.

"I've gone through the letters and I spoke with the FBI agent assigned to the case." Shoving off the wall, he faced Seth. "I've seen the e-mails. Whoever is doing this is a sick son of bitch. But whoever it is, they'll have a damn hard time getting through me, I can guarantee you that."

"You bulletproof?" Seth asked, his voice mocking.

"No more than you."

Seth dropped backed down into his chair and switched his attention to his sister. She shot him a look from under her lashes and softly said, "Don't start in on me, Seth. I've got too damn much on my mind already. Being back in Madison does not put me in a good place. I don't need you getting pissed at me and adding to it."

"Low blow," Seth muttered.

Effective, though, Dalton noticed as Seth took a couple of deep breaths and willed the tension to leave his body. "You been to the bookstore yet?"

3

AFTER LEAVING THE bookstore, Dalton climbed into the compact car, keeping his long legs folded, and braced himself for another miserable ride. Sherra wasn't exactly easy on the brake or the gas pedal.

It wasn't a long drive, though. Hell, if it wasn't for the suitcases in the trunk, he wouldn't have even seen the point of driving.

The bed-and-breakfast was less than a quarter mile from the town square, set up in an old residential neighborhood where most of the houses looked as though they were built back in the early 1900s. The bed-and-breakfast itself had been built in 1876—he knew that because it was on the bronze plaque mounted by the door, announcing the house's standing as a historical landmark.

Sherra glanced at him as they went inside. "I don't know how we're supposed to do this. I only requested one room."

"One room is all we need. Place like this will have a rollaway or something and there's no point in me being here if I'm not close."

Something in his chest knotted as a look flashed across her face. It was quick, there and then gone again, but he was getting too familiar with that particular look. Fear. Nervous apprehension; then it was wiped away, replaced by that blank mask Dalton despised.

Her throat worked as she swallowed and he wanted to pull her up against him, cuddle her and stroke her, promise her that nobody would ever hurt her again. Foolish promise, one he had no way of keeping. The urge to do so was one that made even less sense, but Dalton wasn't the type to try to analyze his every thought.

He was more interested in acting than analyzing and if it was any other woman but Sherra, he knew he would have already put his hands on her. As it was, it was getting harder and harder *not* to put his hands on her. He wasn't going to last six fricking weeks without touching her; he already knew that.

His sister was going to kill him.

He didn't much care, either, and he was damn tired of fighting it.

That was the sole thought in his mind as they checked in. A smiling redhead introduced herself as the manager, eyeing him quizzically as she studied Sherra's reservations. "We only had you down for your stay, Ms. Salinger. I hadn't realized you were bringing a guest."

She glanced at him from the corner of her eye and said, "Up until a few days ago, it was only going to be me. He was dumped on me at the last minute."

Dalton could have pointed out that she'd known for ten days now, but he didn't see the point. Instead, he smiled at the manager and said, "I've been asked to keep her out of trouble while she's on her book tour. I think she's had too many wild nights and her agent got tired of bailing her out of jail and paying for property damage."

The manager's jaw dropped.

Sherra snorted. "My agent only *wishes* I had wild nights. Trust me, I won't be doing any property damage while I'm here."

"Ahhh . . . hmmm." The manager stammered a little bit, looking back and forth between the two of them as though she wasn't sure which one could be taken seriously.

With a surprisingly charming smile, Sherra said, "Ignore him—that's what I do."

Not for too much longer, Dalton thought. She had maybe ten more minutes.

Ten more minutes should get them to their room, through whatever little welcome spiel the manager had lined up and then some privacy. Privacy—and then damn it, he was going to taste that mouth of hers.

The manager gave them a smile, falling back on professional courtesy. "Well, fortunately, you requested the Coleman suite and it is the largest one we have available. It has its own entrance, a master bedroom with a king-sized bed. There's also a sofa bed in the living room . . ."

He half listened as the manager led them to the room, pointing out other areas along the way, the breakfast room, a lounge, a library. He took them all in, made mental notes of some security issues he really didn't care for and wondered how many nights they were going to be spending in places like this.

Hotels were informal, but they were a bit more secure than this.

Three minutes later, after the manager had left them alone in the room, he had the answer to his question and had to bite back the urge to swear. "Let me get this straight—over the next six weeks, half of our trip is going to be in places like this."

Sherra glanced at him from the desk as she went about setting up her laptop. "Yes. That a problem?"

"Depends on how easy you want to make it for somebody to get their hands on you." But as soon as the words left his mouth, he wished he could yank them back.

She paled. Her chocolate brown eyes went nearly black. "I've stayed in places like this a lot and I've never had trouble."

"Just because you've never had trouble doesn't mean it won't ever happen," Dalton muttered, rubbing a hand over the back of his neck. "This place isn't at all secure."

She glanced around. "I don't see anything wrong with it."

"For starters, anybody with a key can get in the front door. Doesn't take much to make a copy. There are too many windows, no security—"

"There is security. *You*. Isn't that why you're here?" Sherra interrupted as she bent over the desk and fiddled with the cables.

She said something else—he heard the husky cadence of her voice, but the words didn't make any sense. Nothing made any sense right now, except the fact that he was practically drooling, his hands itched to touch her and his cock ached as it sprang to rampant, full attention. Bent over the desk like that, Sherra's skirt had drawn tight against her plump, perfect ass and the black shirt she wore rode up, leaving inches of bare, creamy skin.

He held still, knowing that if he moved, his feet were going to take him over to her and he'd end up touching her.

He was going to touch her anyway, but he didn't want to scare her. Grabbing her from behind, pumping his cock against that perfect ass, that would most definitely scare her. The caveman bit wasn't going to get him very far. He could do better than that . . . he hoped.

She straightened and turned, facing him. She had her arms crossed over her chest and that familiar scowl sat on her pretty face as she said, "If the point of having a bodyguard is the physical, visible deterrent, then it shouldn't matter if I'm staying in a hotel or a B and B. Hell, I could camp out at the lake and whoever it is watching me would see you there with me, right?"

Ignoring what she'd just said, he took a step toward her. He fucking had to kiss her. Had to.

Her eyes widened.

Dalton moved slowly, giving her plenty of time to move away, but she stood completely still as he reached up and cupped her face in his hand. "You've got the prettiest damn mouth," he whispered, stroking his thumb across her lower lip.

Sherra blinked. "Ahhh . . . what's that got to do with the bed-and-breakfast?"

"Nothing." He stroked her lip again, this time pressing down until her mouth parted just the slightest bit. "It's just that I've been staring at your mouth for ten damn days and it's driving me crazy."

She shifted her face, just enough to dislodge his thumb from her lip. She dipped her head. He recognized the instinctive attempt to hide behind her hair, but she still had it pinned up off her neck. "Looking at my mouth is a waste of time, Dalton," she said quietly.

Her voice was soft, low, but he caught the edge of sadness there and wondered at it, even as it twisted his heart. "I don't see how admiring something so damn pretty can be a waste of time."

"If all you plan on doing is looking at my mouth, maybe it's not." She glanced at his face, then down.

He felt the weight of that look explode through his veins like dynamite. His cock jerked, all but begging for more attention. But all she did was look back at his face. "But if you might have something on your mind besides my mouth, it's a waste of time. I'm on a business trip, not a pleasure trip. You're here because your sister thinks I need a babysitter. That makes our relationship a business one. I don't mix business with pleasure."

"Nice lie," he said, taking a small step forward. Closer now. Close enough to kiss her, close enough that her scent, midnight and roses, filled his head and he was ravenous to see if she tasted the way she smelled. It was intoxicating, made him think of hot, wicked sex and dark, desperate needs. Sweet, mysterious and oddly innocent. "But I'm thinking this has nothing to do with not wanting to mix business and pleasure . . . and more to do with you shying away from pleasure on a regular basis."

She blushed. It started low on her chest, that charming pink visible first on the mounds of her breasts and then spreading upward until her cheeks glowed with it. "And you know this . . . how?" she asked, that cutting, sarcastic humor edging into her voice. A defense mechanism.

"I'm a quick study," he told her. He knew her well enough to know she often used that biting humor as a weapon to keep people at bay. Of course, this was the first time she'd really directed it at him. Usually all she did was ignore him. Maybe she'd figured out that wasn't working with him, so she was trying the sarcasm instead.

It worked pretty damn well with most people. But it wasn't going to work on him any better than ignoring him had worked. "If you had enough pleasure in your life, I wouldn't keep seeing that sad, lonely look in your eyes when you thought nobody was paying attention." He slid his hand down, curved it around her neck.

Just there.

It was the only place he touched her as he lowered his head and brushed her lips with his own. She gasped, her lips parting. Dalton shook, damn near overwhelmed by the urge to push his tongue inside her mouth, almost shattered under the urge to haul her against him and explore all those soft, lush curves.

Instead, he traced the outline of her lips with his tongue, trailed a line of kisses across her cheek. He nuzzled her neck and whispered, "You need a little bit of pleasure in your life, Sherra."

If her heart beat any faster, it just might explode. Keeping her arms wrapped around her middle, she swallowed the moan building in her throat and kept her legs locked under her. Kept herself locked in place.

Being completely still was the only safe option.

Part of her wanted to jerk away.

Wanted to run.

But the other part, the larger part, wanted to sink against him and, fist her hands in his shirt, curl against him and let him run those big, callused hands all over her. She sighed shakily and when she did, his mouth came back to her. When he touched his tongue to her lower lip, she opened for him.

He stilled, lifting his head and staring down at her with glittering eyes. She had the weirdest damn feeling he was treading cautiously and as that thought circled through her mind, something ugly and ashamed started to form. But before it could, his mouth was back on hers, his tongue pushing inside her mouth. He groaned, a harsh, rough sound that vibrated out of him and made her knees go weak and soft.

"Put your arms around me," he muttered against her lips.

Part of her rebelled, wanted to jerk away—but her body reacted, before her mind had even processed what he'd said. Before she could even think if she *wanted* to put her arms around him, she had already done it, rising up on her toes and twining her arms around his neck. She had to stretch just to reach him. He towered over her, all long limbs, hard muscle and big hands.

Big hands that stroked down her back, touching her with exquisite gentleness. One of those hands slid under the hem of her shirt and she hissed into his mouth, startled by the heat that streaked through her veins at that simple, light contact. "Fuck . . . you're so damn soft," he rasped. "So damn warm . . ."

Warm?

No. She wasn't warm.

She was burning . . . burning . . . Whimpering into his mouth, she arched against him, half mindless. His kiss tasted like coffee, chocolate and man, something entirely too addictive, she realized. Something she could start to crave. He started to pull away and she tightened her arms, following his head with hers and shocking the hell out of herself as she kissed him back, tracing his lip with her tongue, just like he'd done to her. Then pushing inside, seeking out more of that addictive, drugging taste.

He shuddered against her. His hands clenched, tightened. "Damn it, Sherra," he growled, tearing his mouth away.

Who in the hell knew that a pair of brown eyes could burn like that? Dalton thought, staring into her wide, dazed eyes and trying to jerk his body under control.

He hadn't been prepared for this.

He'd been prepared for nerves, anxiety, even outright fear when he touched her. He hadn't been prepared for the hunger and heat burning inside her. He'd been prepared for the fact that she might pull away, might struggle against him, and he'd have to let her go.

He hadn't been prepared for her to kiss him back, for her to arch against him so he felt those sexy, plump curves in all their glory. He hadn't been prepared for that soft, female whimper as he kissed her neck. And no way in hell had he been prepared for her to kiss him back.

His head was spinning, his hands were sweating and all he wanted to do was strip her naked and climb on top of her, fuck her until she was hoarse from screaming his name. Would she let him?

He had to know . . .

Clenching his jaw, he lifted his head and stared down at her, watched her face as he laid his palm on her hip, slid it around and flattened it against her rump. Urging her lower body into close contact with his, he watched her face as he rocked against her. "I want you. The first time I saw you, I wanted to strip you naked, bury my face between your thighs and lick your pussy until you screamed for me, and then fuck you until you couldn't scream anymore."

She blushed furiously, her mouth falling open. The tip of her tongue appeared as she licked her lips and he groaned, dipping his head and covering that slick, red mouth with his own. He kissed her, deeper, harder, and then forced himself to lift his head. "Your call, Sherra. Do I let you go or should I show you just how well I can mix business with pleasure?"

She didn't have a chance to answer.

In that moment, somebody started pounding on the door. She froze, that heartbreaking stillness taking control, and that heat in her eyes died as her mind caught up to her body.

Blowing out a harsh sigh, he fell back. "Saved by the bell."

"Sherra?"

It was a woman's voice calling through the door, an unfamiliar, angry one. Turning on his heel, he strode across the room and looked through the Judas hole. Tanned, blond, pissed. He could tell that much. "Yeah?"

"Open the damn door," their unwelcome visitor demanded. Through clenched teeth, if he wasn't mistaken.

Sending a glance toward Sherra, he cocked his head. "You know a tall blonde?"

She took a deep breath, one that had her shoulders rising and falling. She licked her lips and then, in a husky voice that made the ache in his balls so much worse, she murmured, "It's Lacey. A friend of mine."

4

I'M SO NOT up to this, Sherra thought despondently as Lacey paced her room. Dalton stood quietly off to the side, not saying anything, but every once in a while, his gaze would move to hers and she'd feel it stroke over her body like velvet.

Sherra was in a very uncomfortable, very unfamiliar position, her body aroused, aching and needy. She felt empty inside, and she was slick and wet between her thighs. So damn wet, she'd have to change her panties. So damn wet, she could even smell it. She blushed and squirmed on the couch, crossing her legs and squeezing her knees together in an attempt to ease the ache inside her.

Her nipples beaded and she jerked her head up, realized Dalton was staring at her again, his pale green gaze lambent and hot. He slid his eyes along her body, lingering on her legs as she pressed them together. A knowing look entered his eyes and she could have melted right then and there as he looked back at her face. He knew she ached, he knew why . . . and *she* knew he could fix it.

Never before had a man made her ache like this. Never before had one long, slow look from a man made her feel like melting at his feet. If she wasn't trying to follow Lacey's tirade, she just might have spent a few moments in speculative wonder over the fact that not only had a guy gotten her this turned on, but he'd done it without once giving her a bad moment as he touched her.

Hell, even now that he wasn't touching her and her mind was once more functioning, more or less, she was okay. She kept poking, prodding at herself, deliberately trying to see if she could bring something about, but all she could focus on was the heated bliss that had wrapped around her when he touched her.

Well, when Lacey's tirade wasn't interrupting and intruding on her memories. Her friend kept jerking her attention back to the here and now, her voice climbing a notch or two.

Sherra shifted on the chair yet again and crossed her arms over her chest, hiding the way her nipples pressed against the soft, filmy material of her shirt, hard and erect. "Lacey, could you turn it down a little?" she asked.

Lacey whirled on her heel, glaring at Sherra. "Turn it *down*? I just find out you've had some sick bastard stalking you for *years* and you want me to turn it down?"

"Well, screaming about it doesn't do any good," Sherra said reasonably.

"Screaming about it makes me feel better," Lacey screamed.

Sherra rolled her eyes. "Fine. Scream away. Let me know when you're done."

"Damn it, Sherra. Seth was right; you're *not* taking this seriously at all."

Narrowing her eyes, Sherra shoved up off the couch. "The hell I'm not. Just because I'm not hiding in my house and wailing to everybody I know doesn't mean I'm not aware of how ugly this could get. Just because I'm not biting my nails and cowering doesn't mean I don't get the fact that I've got a sick son of a bitch fixated on me." She shot Dalton a dirty look and added, "I'm getting sick and tired of people telling me I'm not worried enough about this. It's *my* ass that bastard's after and I'm well aware of it. But I'm not going to hide away until he's caught, either. That could be years and I'm not going to let some monster have that much control over my life."

"You should have told us," Lacey said, forcing the words out through gritted teeth.

"Yeah, maybe I should have," Sherra agreed, crossing her arms over her chest and glaring at her friend. Sherra had very, very few close friends—Seth, of course. He was her twin; he was half of her. They had that weird, indescribable bond so many twins had.

Other than Seth, there were Monica and Lacey.

Lacey knew Sherra in a way that others didn't. They had their own bond, one forged in a night of horror, and Lacey understood things about Sherra that nobody else could. Sherra *did* understand why Lacey was upset. She didn't know if she'd do it differently, but she understood.

"I didn't . . . because I knew how you would react. I knew how Seth would react. I don't need you two breathing down my neck and hovering over me. I've had enough of that from him, and I'm not going to put up with it from you."

"So we aren't entitled to worry?"

"Worry all you want . . . but let me live my life," Sherra said, swallowing the knot in her throat.

"Hell, I didn't realize my worrying about you was going to keep you from living your life," Lacey drawled, her voice heavy with sarcasm. "You can't get up, drink three pots of coffee a day and write until you fall asleep at your desk if I'm worrying about your safety?"

Sherra flinched.

Lacey hadn't said anything less than the truth. All she did was sleep, write and eat when she remembered. Well, she shopped. She did love to shop. But she didn't have much of a life outside her writing.

For the most part, she didn't want anything beyond her writing and the few friends she had. Old habits died hard. She didn't make friends easily because she had a hard time trusting people, had a hard time liking many of them, and an even harder time letting people get close to her.

Tears blurred her eyes but she averted her head before Lacey could see them.

Dalton saw it, though, and his eyes narrowed. Shoving off the wall, he planted himself in front of Lacey. "Back off."

Lacey glared at him. "Sorry. Private conversation. You weren't invited."

"She's got enough to deal with right now without you laying into her."

"I'm just worried about her. We've been friends for fifteen years and she hides this from me, and then thinks I'm not going to be upset? The hell with that."

Blood rushed to Sherra's cheeks as Dalton said, "I don't give a damn if you've been friends with her since birth. You got no problem jumping on somebody when they're down, fine. But I do have a problem with it and you're not doing it with her, not while I'm around. Now *back off*."

Blowing out an unsteady breath, Sherra said, "Dalton, just let it go, okay? Lacey's got a right to be upset." So what if Lacey's words left an ugly ache in her chest? Sherra was used to feeling empty inside.

He glanced at her, his mouth pressed into a flat, hard line. "No, not okay. She wants to be upset, fine. But she doesn't need to dig her claws in and hurt you."

"I'm not hurting her—damn it, it's not like this is the first time we've ever yelled at each other," Lacey snapped, circling around him and sending him a glare. Then she looked at Sherra.

Sherra didn't know what Lacey saw, but it must have been the same look that Dalton had seen, because Lacey's eyes widened and she stopped in her tracks. "Hell." She opened her mouth, snapped it closed.

Blue eyes locked with brown. "I don't get how you can expect me to *not* be upset over your keeping this from me. Shit, it's got you so damn worried that you're upset because I'm yelling, but you expect me *not* to worry?"

Despite the knot of pain in her chest, Sherra managed a sneer. "The day I get upset because you yell is the day they bury me."

"Something sure as hell got you upset."

"Let it go," Sherra said.

"I'm not going to let it go." Lacey crossed her arms over her chest and glared at Sherra.

Sherra glared right back, frustration burning through her. Frustration, the worry and fear she tried not to show—and now, her confusion over Dalton—it all brewed inside her. Top it off with the fact that she was back in Madison, feeling the memories piling up and waiting to pounce, her temper was shot.

It wasn't like she had a level temper even on a good day.

Today wasn't proving to be a good day.

"You want to know what's got me upset?" Sherra ground out. "I stay in my house, I write my books, I leave when I run out of coffee, food or I feel an insane urge to buy shoes. Once or twice a year, I do book signings. I don't date. I don't have that many friends. As far as social lives go, mine pretty much *sucks*. I'm aware of that. But I sure as hell don't need *you* to rub it in my face."

The red flush of anger slowly leeched out of Lacey's face, leaving her pale under her tan. Her eyes went dark and she deflated, her head dropping forward, hair falling to hide her face. "Shit. Sherra . . ."

Shaking her head, Sherra said, "Just let it go, Lacey. I'm not in the mood for this. Not in the mood for any of this shit."

Growling under her breath, she spun away from Lacey and Dalton and stomped over to the window. "Why in the hell did I ever come back here?" she muttered.

In a strained voice, Lacey said, "Well, Seth tried to warn you." She huffed out a sigh and Sherra glanced over her shoulder in time to see Lacey flop down on the couch. "This is the last thing any of us needs right now, ya know. Already have a mess here. Renee doesn't even get out of the hospital until this afternoon."

Renee . . . Memory crashed into Sherra with staggering force. Turning, she leaned back against the wall and watched as Lacey covered her face with her hands. She lowered them back to her lap and the two women stared at each other, both of them fighting their own torrent of memories.

Huge shadows lay under Lacey's eyes and Sherra could see signs of fatigue and worry laying heavily on her friend. "Are things really that bad?" she asked quietly.

She hadn't wanted to think that they were. Her twin was protective of her. He always had been, but her near rape had just made it even worse and she knew he worried about her coming back here. The first few months after Boyd's death had been hell, people whispering under their breath how girls like Sherra either didn't get raped or they asked for it when bad things happened to them. People who had outright confronted her and called her a killer, people who didn't believe it when they heard that JD and Boyd would have raped her if Lacey, Renee and Deacon hadn't been around.

Those first few months had been almost as traumatic as the night itself.

Sherra came home rarely because visiting here set off a cavalcade of memories she didn't want to deal with, and she hated fighting the depression that too often followed.

Seth knew all of that. Lacey knew it. Sherra had assumed it was their protectiveness that had each of them urging Sherra to stay away—consciously or unconsciously. But the look in Lacey's eyes was one of serious, sincere worry.

Her voice unsteady, Lacey said, "Bad? Yeah. Yeah, Sherra, they really are that bad." She reached up and touched her neck and for the first time, Sherra noticed the raw-looking abrasions on Lacey's neck.

Licking her lips, Sherra asked hoarsely, "What happened to your neck?"

Lacey dropped her hand. Pulling her knees to her chest, she met

Sherra's gaze and said, "Somebody grabbed me, tried to strangle me—it's kind of classic, used this silk dress I'd tried on. Now isn't *that* fucked up?"

"Are you serious?"

Closing her eyes, Lacey rested her head against the back of the couch and murmured, "Serious as a heart attack."

Bile burned its way up her throat and she shot Dalton a look from the corner of her eye. Something told her he wasn't going to be happy about this added complication.

His eyes moved from Sherra's face to Lacey's. "What's going on?"

A knock sounded at the door. A ghost of a smile curled Sherra's lips up and she said, "Saved by the bell, again."

She wasn't getting a reprieve, though. At least, not much of one. Seth entered the room, glancing at Sherra, but then his eyes bounced away from her and locked on Lacey. A little dumbstruck, Sherra watched as her brother crossed the room. Lacey was on her feet before he reached her and while Sherra stood there watching, Seth pulled Lacey against him.

His mouth slanted over hers and for a few seconds, the room was quiet, full of sexual tension and an emotion so poignant, it had Sherra's throat knotting up again. She'd always known how Seth felt about Lacey. He was her twin; there was no way she *couldn't* know. She'd kept it quiet, figured if Seth ever wanted to do anything about it, he'd do it on his own.

Apparently, he'd done just that. He stroked a hand up Lacey's back, his touch familiar, gentle. Lacey arched against him, sighing against his lips as they slowly broke apart. They didn't pull away from each other, though, not yet. They lingered, staring at each other with naked need written all over their faces. Then Seth rubbed his thumb over one of the red marks on Lacey's neck, dipping his head to press his lips to it.

Sherra cleared her throat and waited until Lacey looked her way. Narrowing her eyes, she glared at Lacey. "Gee, apparently I'm not the only one not talking about certain important issues. How long have you been sleeping with my brother?"

Lacey blushed.

SHE HAD A reprieve, but it was short.

Once Seth and Lacey had unlocked their tongues, Dalton had wanted some answers, but Seth bought a little bit of time with the explanation that it was a long story, and one that was easier told only once.

Apparently, that once was going to take place over dinner—at Deacon Cross's house. Renee had been discharged from the hospital and was going to be staying with Deacon. There was another story there, Sherra could feel it, but she wasn't quite ready to ask about that one. She was too busy trying to wrap her mind around what was going on between Lacey and Seth.

She was happy for them, no doubt about that. Seth had been in love with Lacey for most of his life, she knew. Even when they were in high school and Sherra had about as much use for Lacey as she had for a cheerleader's uniform, she'd known how her brother felt about the pretty, popular blonde. They'd be good together. There was a lot more to Lacey than her pretty, all-American-girl good looks, something that Sherra had figured out that night—the night all of their lives had changed.

She was loving; she was loyal; she cared about others. In her own way, Lacey's life had become every bit as lonely as Sherra's. Neither of them could connect with people. Seth could change that for Lacey, and it looked like he already had.

Still, it was weird.

Sherra and Dalton sat in the back of Seth's squad car as they all drove out to Deacon's house. It was quiet, not an uncomfortable silence, exactly, but a weighted one. A waiting one. Once more, Sherra found herself wondering why she hadn't canceled this part of her trip—hell, canceled the whole damn thing. Yeah, she had

readers who were looking forward to meeting her, she had obliga-
tions, she'd busted her ass to get to this point . . . but she also had a
huge, red target on her head with this stalker tailing her.

Staying out of Madison, with its morass of memories, would
only have made things easier. Not to mention coming back here
was just adding another target.

Why couldn't she ever do things the *easy* way? Shivering, she
rubbed her arms. From the corner of her eye, she saw Dalton move
but she didn't realize what he was doing until he slid across the seat,
settling closer to her and wrapping a big arm around her shoulders.
She tensed, her body reacting in one way, her head reacting another . . . while her heart melted. He rested his chin on her head
and whispered, "I don't know what other kind of trouble you're in,
princess, but it will be all right."

A reluctant smile tugged at the corners of her mouth. "Princess?" she repeated, shifting until she could look up into his pale
green eyes. "I'm no princess, Dalton."

"Hmmm. I like the way you say my name." He dipped his
head, kissed her quick and light, then bent down and whispered,
"Princess—suits you better than you think. I'll tell you why . . .
later."

Then he leaned back against the seat, keeping her pressed close
to his body, warming her. As good as his heat felt, though, Sherra
was still chilled. Down to the bone. The moment Seth had shown
up at her door, a heavy wave of foreboding had crashed into her
and with every second, the weight of it pulled at her more and
more.

She felt somebody watching her and looked up, met Seth's eyes
in the rearview mirror.

People who didn't know him wouldn't have been able to pick
up on the fear he had carefully covered. They wouldn't sense the
deep rage he held in check.

But nobody knew Seth Salinger as well as his twin. What she
felt coming from him, combined with her own growing apprehen-

sion, was enough to make her wish she'd listened to the overbearing jerk for once.

Instead, she had done what she always did, and that was ignore everybody else's opinions. She spent the next few minutes quietly kicking herself and probably would have continued to do just that all the way to the house where Deacon Cross lived on the other side of town if one thing in particular hadn't occurred to her.

Dalton had absolutely no idea what was going on.

And he wasn't going to be content with any pat, empty explanation. He would want to know exactly what was going on. All of it. She could either explain it, or he'd figure it out on his own. The guy was a cop—had to be like a Marine or something—once a cop, always a cop. She could see it in everything he did, in the way he moved, the way he looked at people. The reformed hoodlum inside her would have recognized him as a cop from fifty feet away.

He'd figure it out—

If he hasn't already.

The bottom of her stomach dropped out, sank to her knees. Nausea gripped her. Bile churned up the back of her throat and she had to swallow repeatedly to keep it from spilling out of her. Stiffening, she pulled away from him, not bothering to be subtle about it. She moved until she was all but hugging the door.

Either he already knew, or he would know shortly. About the worst night of her life, a night that still had the ability to send her screaming into wakefulness or cringing under the covers as the nightmares attacked.

He'd know about the night she'd almost been raped, and how she'd killed one of her attackers.

The car stopped but she didn't realize it until Dalton slid out and came around to open her door. Staring at him, she was only vaguely aware of Seth and Lacey waiting for them just a few feet away.

She'd know.

Before she walked in there, damn it, she would know.

Without looking away from Dalton's face, she said to Seth, "We'll be up there in a minute."

The second they were alone, she folded her arms over her chest and leaned back against the car.

"What is it?" he asked softly.

"Did you investigate me before you accepted this job?"

His lids flickered. There was no other sign. But that was enough. Nor did he try to lie about it. "Not before, no. Monica didn't give me any information, not even your name, until we got to your house."

"But you did investigate."

"Yes."

Just like that. That simple. That easy. No explanations, no apologies, just that simple answer.

Swallowing, she looked away from him. "Just how far back did you go?"

"Why don't you just ask me what you want to know?" That haunted, bruised look was back, that whipped puppy look that broke his heart and infuriated him. Unable to keep his distance anymore, he went to her, lifted a hand and cupped her cheek. She tried to avoid his touch, but he didn't let her.

She shot him a sidelong look, the thick fringe of her lashes shielding her gaze from him. She licked her lips and then caught the lower one between her teeth, staring off to the side. "You went all the way back."

"Yeah." He wasn't the type to offer explanations when he did something he felt needed to be done, but for some reason, he had to offer one now. "Monica adores you. She's mentioned your name to me probably fifty times in the past couple of years—took me a few minutes to make the connection, but trust me, she talks about you a lot. And not just because you're one of her authors, but because she cares about you. Something that affects you is going to affect her . . . and I wanted to know just what I was getting into when I told her I'd do this for her."

A glimpse of the cocky attitude she hid behind made a quick appearance. "I bet you had no idea you'd be watching over a confessed killer, did you?" It faded quickly, though—like keeping up the facade took more energy than she had to spare.

He cupped his hand over the back of her neck and this time, when she tried to avoid his eyes, he wouldn't let her. "You killed a punk who tried to rape you, one who had a gun. From the reports I read, it sounds like he would have killed you and everybody else involved if you hadn't done what you did. That doesn't make you a killer."

"You sure about that?" She wrenched away from him and the panic in her eyes kept him from following. Even though that was what he wanted to do.

She strode away from him, heading up to the house with her arms wrapped protectively around her middle.

He caught up with her as she mounted the steps. Crowding her back against one of the huge pillars that marched along the verandah, he caged her in with his arms. "Yeah, I'm sure about it. What's the deal here, Sherra? You've got a hot/cold switch that I can't quite figure out."

"I have no idea what you mean," she said, her voice icy.

"Don't give me that. You spend ten days ignoring me. Then two minutes all but melting in my arms. We get in the car, same thing. First you pretend I don't exist; then you melt against me, and now you're pulling away just as quick. What, did you think I'd get disgusted over the fact that you were forced to kill a guy before he could kill you?"

Something flickered in her dark eyes but then she focused on the ground, staring at the sexy sandals she wore as though she was utterly amazed by them.

He'd seen it, though. Saw that very belief in her eyes. She *had* expected him to freak over her history. But that wasn't all of it. Not by a long shot. "Come on, Sherra, help me out here."

She lifted her eyes from her feet and stared at him. "I don't know exactly how I'm supposed to help you out. I don't waste a whole hell of a lot of time with guys, Dalton. I don't like them."

Stroking a thumb across her lower lip, he muttered, "You seem to like me just fine."

A sexy scowl darkened her face and she snapped, "I don't even *know* you. I can't like you that much."

Unfazed, Dalton reached for the clip holding her hair up and tugged it loose. Dark, gleaming strands fell halfway down her back. She tried to grab the clip back as he pushed his fingers into her hair. "I think you like me just fine. If you didn't, you'd call Monica and tell her she needed to find somebody else for this. No matter how much she bullies you, you wouldn't have me around if you couldn't stand me. Good thing—I sure as hell like you." Tugging on her hair, he angled her head up and back, taking her mouth.

As he pushed his tongue into her mouth, he wrapped his other hand around her waist and pulled her close. She felt small against him, damn small, almost fragile. Fury lit inside him, back in the recesses of his mind, as he thought about what had almost happened to her—she'd been seventeen, still a kid. That night had scarred her and the scars ran deep, so deep they still interfered with her life fifteen years later.

Normally, Dalton's inclination would be to back away from a woman with the kind of baggage Sherra carried around. He wasn't the most soothing person; he didn't know jackshit about comforting a battered soul, but his natural inclinations weren't coming into play here.

No, what felt natural with Sherra was to get closer. *Much* closer. He wanted to soothe, wanted to stroke and ease the fear he saw in her eyes. Then he wanted to replace it with other things. The hot light of a woman on the verge of climax, the wicked gleam of laughter, and so much more.

Fuck, this is happening too fast . . .

She sighed into his mouth and he could have gone to his knees when she leaned against him, hesitant at first, her hands smoothing up his chest, resting lightly on his shoulders as she arched up on her toes.

Through their clothes, he could feel her—soft, full breasts and nipples already hard, a soft belly that cradled his cock as he brought her more fully against him. He had to feel more of her. Tightening his arms, he straightened, lifting her until her feet left the ground and every last inch of that delicate, dynamite body was pressed against his own.

Tearing his mouth from hers, he kissed his way down her neck, muttering, "See, you like me just fine."

Sherra laughed shakily. "Is that what this is?"

Like didn't quite describe it—although she did have to admit, she did like him well enough. Or at least she had before he put his hands on her. Even if he made her nervous, even if he invaded on her personal space way too much, she'd liked him. But right now, *like* didn't quite describe it.

She liked her agent.

She liked salsa.

She liked a good fantasy, liked a good mystery.

She liked watching the sunset from the deck in her backyard.

She liked fresh, hot bread.

But compared to the way he felt against her, all of those things paled. Somewhere in the back of her mind, Sherra realized she was in trouble. He could become addictive. Way too easily, he could become addictive.

He nuzzled her neck as he brushed aside the strap of her chemise. Raking her shoulder with his teeth, he said, "I love the way you smell. You taste as sweet as you smell, princess?"

An odd noise intruded.

She was too focused on the way it felt to be pressed against his body, her feet dangling off the ground while he supported her weight with one arm wrapped around her waist. Most of her life, she hated her body, too damn short, curves that seemed overripe for her frame, but right now, she had no complaints. Not a one.

There was that noise again.

Dalton groaned against her neck and swore under his breath. She forced her heavy lids to lift so she could look at him. He trailed a finger down her cheek and whispered, "We've got company, princess."

Princess—

Company?

Shit. Her eyes widened as she craned her head to see around him. Blood rushed to her cheeks as she realized there were four pairs of eyes directed her way. Deacon, Seth, Lacey and Renee—all four of them stood in the doorway of Deacon's house and were staring at them with varying degrees of curiosity, surprise, amusement and concern.

Groaning under her breath, she dropped her head forward and rested it on his shoulder. Shoving against him, she mumbled, "Maybe you should put me down."

He chuckled. "If you're going to make me . . ."

He did so, but he did so slowly, his hands lingering, his body brushing against hers in a way that should have had an alarm screaming through her. Instead, all she felt was an empty ache spread within.

But it wasn't the ache of loneliness.

She was familiar with that one, and nothing she did ever eased it completely.

This ache was different and she knew, without a doubt, that Dalton would be more than happy to take care of that ache. What really surprised her, though, was that she had every intention of letting him do just that.

5

DEACON AND RENEE had the hosting thing down to a T. Lacey pitched in, the three of them keeping up a steady stream of conversation, as though they'd made some agreement that they'd eat a nice, relaxing meal before dropping the bomb.

Dalton wished they'd just get it over with.

Everybody had introduced themselves once they got done smiling over the fact that they'd found Sherra on the porch making out with her bodyguard. Dalton kept a mental list of the names, watched each of them. When he had five seconds of private time, he was going to do a background check on all of them. It would come up clean, he had no doubt of that, but he wasn't going to take chances. Not on this.

Not on Sherra.

Especially since it was becoming very obvious that Sherra could be facing a whole different level of threat here.

One from her past.

Somebody had made an attempt on Renee's life. She was a chef, single, never married, not involved in any serious relationships— well, up until recently. Dalton read between the lines quite well and there was definitely something serious going on between her and Deacon Cross.

Enter the lawyer. He worked as a victims' advocate, and while Dalton knew Cross could have easily picked up enough enemies in that line of work, he couldn't see a connection between what had been going on here and his business life.

Lacey was a photographer, moderately successful, only very recently attached to somebody. There were several breakups in her past, but nothing ugly, and when Dalton pressed, she'd just smirked and said, "I got dumped because I bore the hell out of the guys I date. Believe me, there's no angry, obsessed lover behind this."

Seth had stroked a hand down her back as he told her, "You don't bore me."

A wise man might have taken off running at this point. There was either something in the water, or Cupid was working overtime and well into the summer, and an unattached guy looking to stay that way wasn't going to be interested in being around all the rampant emotion in the air here.

Dalton apparently wasn't wise—either that, or he'd already drunk too much of the water, been shot in the ass with an arrow or something, because he had no desire to get away from the emotion-heavy atmosphere. Hell, all *he* wanted to do was have Sherra curl up next to him the way Lacey was curled up next to Seth. Renee was sitting on the couch, leaning against Deacon to keep him from waiting on her hand and foot.

The bruises, scrapes and cuts on her body and face didn't detract from the woman's elegant, sophisticated beauty. It also didn't hide the worry in her eyes as Seth explained everything that had been going on since Renee and Lacey hit town.

Both of them had been attacked, had their homes vandalized.

Shoving up off the couch, Dalton started to pace, listening to Seth, filing everything away even as he muttered, "Shit, what are the odds?"

"Excuse me?"

It was Deacon—the lawyer. Hell, even if he hadn't mentioned what he did for a living, Dalton would have pegged him for a lawyer. He stopped in midstride and studied the other man. "Just thinking out loud, Counselor."

"Odds of what?" Deacon asked. He narrowed his eyes on Dalton's face, consideringly. Then he glanced at Sherra. "Sherra, why do you have a bodyguard? I didn't realize they were the standard thing for an author, even a hotshot bestseller."

Sherra gave him a sugary smile and replied, "What can I say, Deacon? I'm a law unto myself."

"Always have been, but that's not exactly an answer." He jerked his chin toward Dalton. "Call me paranoid but with the mess we have going on, I'd rather know exactly who he is, and why he's here. I'm not buying that you regularly have off-duty cops following you around."

Dalton didn't bother to correct the mistaken assumption. He wasn't an off-duty cop. He wasn't a cop period, but an ex-cop probably wouldn't make much of a difference to the lawyer. He remained quiet, curious about how Sherra was going to handle this. She sighed and shoved a hand through her hair—he still hadn't given her the clip back. He didn't plan to, either. He loved seeing all that midnight black lying against her pale shoulders, framing that pretty face.

"I have a stalker," she said, shifting on the couch and crossing her legs. It made the denim skirt she wore ride just a little too high on her thighs for Dalton's peace of mind. Instead of focusing on her words, he was focusing on a fantasy where he pushed that skirt higher, completely out of the way, and then pressed his mouth to her.

He had to focus, though. Needed to stay in control. At least for now. Right now, he had to look at the bigger picture.

Later, though . . . once he got her out of here, he had every intention of fucking her. Might be best if he went about it with a little bit of care—that meant staying in control, which was going to be very hard to do if he kept obsessing about pushing that skirt up over her hips and pressing his mouth to her sex.

Control.

Across the room, Renee's eyes widened at Sherra's statement.

Deacon showed no change in expression and his voice, hell, he could have been discussing the weather for all the reaction he showed. "A stalker."

Sherra grimaced, sliding her brother a quick look. "Yeah." She sighed and pushed her hands through her hair, linking them back behind her neck. Leaning her head back, she stared up at the ceiling. She'd dealt with this mess for the past five years by not letting herself think about it too much. As long as she thought about it in the abstract, she was good. She wasn't in denial about it exactly, but she was displacing, acting as though it were happening to somebody else.

In a way, that was exactly what was happening—the stalker was after Sherra Salinger, bestselling author. Yeah, that was *her*, but it wasn't how she saw herself. She was just Sherra. Reformed troublemaker, grew up on the way-wrong side of the tracks, more aware of the stories inside her head instead of the world around her. It was easier to think about if she kept the two parts of herself separate. It was the author the stalker was coming after, and in her mind, as long as she kept separating herself into the two separate personas, she could handle this.

But the more she talked about it, the harder it got to keep her different selves separated. Shoving out of the chair, she started to pace. She jammed her hands into her pockets; it was either do that or start biting on her nails. "It started about five years ago. At first, it was just letters. They came regularly, about once a month. Then they started coming every two weeks, then every week."

Her mouth, shit, it was so damn dry. She swallowed, dragged her tongue across dry lips. "A few months ago, he somehow got my private e-mail address, started e-mailing me." She shot Seth a look but jerked her eyes away from him at the fury brewing there.

She was cold.

Too damn cold.

Then Dalton was there.

He caught her arm, guided her back to the couch and eased her back down on it, settling next to her and wrapping his arm around her shoulders. He was warm. Strong. Too damn big. She ought to be terrified; she hated big men, hated men period, except for Seth, hated for them to touch her . . .

But she liked having Dalton touching her. Liked—no. That wasn't right. She *needed* him touching her. The cold inside her receded, the fear gnawing at her gut eased and she managed to take a deep, slow breath, then another. In another minute, she just might be able to talk without jabbering like a maniac.

It wasn't necessary, though. Because Dalton started to speak. That deep, whiskey-rough voice could go cold. Ice-cold, almost clinical as he relayed the facts as he knew them. And he knew them pretty damn well. As he wrapped it up, she said softly, "You've been talking to Agent Mueller."

He glanced at her, a humorless smile curling his lips. "Yeah. As well as anybody else with information. The cops—I know one of the detectives who handled your original complaint. We were at the academy together."

Academy—man, how was she so comfortable around him? He was a *cop*. Why did she feel so safe around him? The only man she ever felt completely safe around was her brother. Anybody else, even her few male friends, she still had to fight a knee-jerk instinctive fear and it could creep up on her without any warning.

Unaware of the haunted look in her eyes, she watched as he lifted a hand, cupped her cheek. "It will be okay," he murmured, looking at her as though they were the only people in the room.

She smiled sadly. "You can't promise that."

Dalton dipped his head and rubbed his mouth against hers.
"Yeah, I can." And he meant it. He didn't think he'd made a conscious decision about this, but he wasn't going anywhere until this
threat against her was resolved. Ugly images kept sneaking up on
him, catching him off guard, and he found himself imagining what
could happen if her stalker decided to escalate things.

No. Not *if*. Staring at her, seeing the fear she'd hidden from
finally showing naked on her face, he knew there was no *if*. As certain as he knew his own name, as certain as he knew his own need
for her, he knew it was going to happen. The stalker would make a
move on her. Dalton was going to be there when it happened. He
was going to take care of her. He was going to protect her . . .

An ache settled in his chest and it felt as if he were standing
on the verge of a cliff he'd avoided his entire adult life. Attach-
ments weren't his style. Caring for people outside his immediate
family—namely some of the guys he knew from the force—just
wasn't his thing. Dalton was a loner, and he was happy being that
way. Especially considering that one of his closest friends had lived
a lie for years—his partner, Zeke, had been dirty. About as dirty as
they came.

Zeke had been dirty for years and Dalton had never guessed.
It wasn't until he stumbled across some irrefutable evidence that
Dalton began to realize his partner was on the take.

Years. They'd been best friends for years.

Of course, that friendship hadn't kept Zeke from trying to kill
Dalton once he realized his partner knew, that Dalton was working
with Internal Affairs to help bring the dirty cop down. He'd tried
to kill Dalton, and if Dalton had hesitated, it would be him in the
ground now instead of Zeke.

After that, Dalton had decided it was better just not to get attached to people.

But this woman, this bundle of contradictions, she was getting
to him.

She'd already gotten to him. If he was the fanciful sort, he might have imagined that he'd started down this slippery slide the moment he first laid eyes on her—before. Something inside him had looked at her and wanted, but it went deeper than that. It was as though he'd looked at her and found something that was meant to be his. Somebody.

6

SHE WAS STILL cold.

Climbing from the back of Seth's squad car, she stood staring at the B&B. The air was hot and heavy, perfumed with the scents of blooming flowers and wild honeysuckle. Sweat formed at the nape of her neck and trickled downward, but she could have been standing in a blizzard for all she knew.

She was so damn cold.

Dalton stopped in front of her. For a minute, she didn't look up, staring at his chest but not seeing anything. Vaguely, she heard Seth's voice but his words didn't make sense. Dalton's voice rumbled around her and she shivered at the sound. If he would just keep talking . . . Damn, she loved his voice.

"Sherra."

Lifting her eyes, she stared at him, watched his mouth move, forming words that made little to no sense. He sighed and she felt it brush against her skin like a whisper-soft caress. He rested a hand on her waist, let his fingers linger for a long moment. "I need your keys," he murmured.

"My keys?"

He smiled and slid his hand into her front pocket, plucking them out of her pocket. "Oh."

"Sherra."

Turning her head, she met Seth's gaze and shook her head. "Seth, I'm sorry but I'm too tired."

He stood a few feet away, staring at her with worried eyes. The harsh lines of his face softened. His arms lifted and Sherra went to him, slipping her hands around his waist and relaxing against him. For the longest time, this had been the only place she'd felt safe. When they'd been younger and their dad had just looked for a reason to whale on one of them, Seth had always done his best to protect her.

She knew he always would.

"Stop worrying so much about me, Seth," she whispered against his shirt. "I'm not helpless, and I'm not a fool. I can take care of myself."

"You've always taken care of yourself," he muttered. "But that never kept me from worrying before. I don't see it changing now."

She fell back a step, gave him a faint smile before glancing past him to look at Lacey in the car. "You've got somebody else to worry about now, too. I'm not the only one in trouble here," she said, shaking her head. "Go on. We'll talk more tomorrow and see if we can't figure out what in the hell is going on."

Seth scowled. "Figuring that out is my job, sis."

Scoffing, Sherra muttered, "Yeah. Like that is going to make any difference to me."

Ten minutes later, she was curled on the couch at the B & B, staring into the empty fireplace. Dalton came walking across the floor, entirely too soundless considering how damn big he was. She didn't need to hear him, though. She knew he was there. She felt it.

Felt it in the way the goose bumps broke out over her skin, felt it in the way her nipples went tight and the chill pervading her body was replaced by that unfamiliar heat. No longer cold, but she started to shake, minute shudders that increased in strength until she had to clench her teeth to keep them from chattering.

He sank to his knees in front of her, those pale, dreamy green eyes staring at her intently. As though he saw nothing beyond her. "You've had a hell of a day," he said softly.

She swallowed and managed a jerky shrug. "Not really. Nothing much happened."

Nothing much? She'd fought with Seth; she'd fought with Lacey. Dalton had put his hands on her and for the first time in fifteen damn years, she'd actually wanted a guy to touch her and just keep on touching her. She had to acknowledge the fact that her past was quite possibly getting ready to rear its ugly head.

Dropping her chin to her chest, she took a deep, shuddering breath. Hardest of all, she had to face the cold, ugly truth about her own life, and the fact that it was in danger. Thinking about it in the abstract had been so much easier.

But *nothing* had actually *happened*.

A humorless smile creased his face and she suspected she was all too transparent. At least with him. He shifted closer, laying his hands on her thighs. But he didn't look at her. He stared at his hands on her thighs, thighs left all too bare by the short skirt she wore. "You expect too much out of yourself," he murmured. "Tough girl—can't let anybody know you're afraid, gotta handle everything yourself. You had a lot dumped on you; we both know it. If I was any kind of a decent guy, I'd get you tucked into bed and leave you the hell alone."

Her heart leaped into her throat as he lifted his gaze, staring at her through the fringe of his lashes. Hunger burned there.

"Is that what you want me to do, Sherra?"

She swallowed and licked her lips, tried to speak. For the life of her, she couldn't say a damn thing.

She sat there, locked in place, as he bent over her and pressed his lips to one bare knee. "Do I stop, Sherra?"

With her heart pounding in her chest and her breath frozen in her lungs, she reached up. Uncertain of what she was going to do, uncertain of what she wanted, she watched as she cupped her hand over the back of his neck. His lips trailed higher, higher, until the hem of her skirt stopped him.

"Do I stop?"

In response, she pressed against his chest. He tensed and for a moment, he didn't move. Then he did and when he lifted his eyes to meet hers, his gaze was shuttered. But the blank mask on his face fell away as she eased off the couch, ending up with her thighs on either side of his so that she straddled him.

Leaning in, hesitant, slow, she kissed him.

Dalton slid a hand up her back, trying to keep from grabbing, trying to keep from pushing her to her back and climbing on top of her, burying his aching dick so deep inside that lush, perfect body that he lost himself.

Instead, he touched the ends of her hair and eased back away from her shy, soft kiss. "Better be certain, Sherra. This is going to happen—I think we both know that. But if you aren't ready for it to happen now, you need to get off of me and walk away."

What she did was grab the hem of her shirt and pull it off. Under it, she wore black lace. Her soft, ivory skin glowed against the black lace and with a groan, he dipped his face and buried it between the full, plump mounds of her breasts. Damn it, she was perfect.

Her breasts swelled and strained within the confines of her bra. Through the lace, he could just barely make out the deeper pink of her nipples. Her torso seemed almost too fragile for those curves, her waist narrow, her hips full. He reached down, slipping his hands under the hem of her skirt. It had already ridden dangerously high, high enough that he could see more black lace under it. Pushing the denim completely to her waist, he cupped her ass in his hands, squeezed the plump, supple flesh.

She stared at him with a mixture of apprehension and arousal, her pupils dilated, her cheeks flushed. When she licked her lips, he groaned and covered her mouth with his, catching her tongue and teasing her into kissing him. She deepened the kiss—slow, shy strokes that had heat zipping through his body.

Slow, Dalton. Go slow.

Keeping that in mind, he stripped her bra away, eased it down her arms and then lifted away from her kiss so he could see her. "Fuck, you're perfect," he muttered, staring at her swollen breasts.

Her nipples were tight. Wrapping his hands around her waist, he eased her up so that she sat on the edge of the couch, her breasts right on a level with his mouth. "Been dying to know if you taste as sweet as you look," he growled right before he took one perfect pink nipple in his mouth and found out.

No. She didn't taste as sweet as she looked.

She tasted sweeter. Hotter. Completely addictive. He licked and sucked, teased her with his teeth and tongue until she was whimpering, her fingers tangled in his hair as she urged him from one breast to the other.

With a harsh, ragged groan, he tore his mouth away from her and pulled her to her feet. She stood before him as he stripped her skirt off but not her panties—and not her shoes. He didn't know what in the hell the shoes were called—an old girlfriend of his had told him once, but damned if he could remember. Thick, wedge-shaped heels that added about three inches to her height with black laces that wrapped around her ankles.

They were sexy as hell.

Combined with the lacy panties she wore, Sherra looked like a wet dream come to life.

He cupped her hips in his hands and drew her close. Her hair fell around her shoulders, framing her pretty tits, cascading down her back. "I don't want to do anything that scares you," he muttered, his voice harsh and gritty with the effort it took just to squeeze the words out through his tight throat. "I couldn't handle scaring you."

She gulped. "You're doing just fine so far."

"Fine . . ." He laughed. "We gotta do better than fine, baby. I want more, want to taste all of you . . ." He pressed his mouth to her, licking her sex through the lace.

She jerked, a startled breath hissing out between her teeth.

She didn't try to pull away but she held herself all too still, too controlled. Dalton was determined to see that control shattered, even if part of him understood why she kept so much of herself hidden. Slipping his fingers inside the leg band of her panties, he drew the lace aside and blew on her flesh.

She was so fucking wet already, wet, swollen, the folds of her sex glistening. Dipping his head, he licked her, using his tongue to open her before he pushed the tip of one finger just inside her pussy. "You're sweet," he muttered as he shifted up and caught her clit between his teeth, sucking it into his mouth.

Sherra arched up, grinding her head back into the cushions of the couch. She bit her lip to muffle her cry, bit so hard she tasted blood but she didn't even care. He added a second finger, stroking deep, deep, deep. Pleasure raged through her, tore into her with near-painful intensity, twisting through her belly, stealing her breath and leaving her blind and deaf to everything but Dalton.

Then he stopped—stopped touching her, stopped kissing her.

Dazed, Sherra opened her eyes to stare at him as he knelt between her thighs. Warm, callused hands slipped under her bottom, lifting her up. Their gazes locked over the expanse of her body, her flesh ivory white, so pale against the deep, tawny gold of his. "You're going to scream," he muttered. "Scream for me, baby."

He stroked her with his tongue and she whimpered.

He circled her entrance and she moaned.

Then he trailed a hand down the back of her thigh, along her knee and downward. He shackled her ankle with his fingers and pushed it up until it was bent. "Look at that pretty pink pussy," Dalton rasped, stroking the delicate skin of her ankle with his thumb. "So hot, so pink and so fucking wet. Are you wet for me? Is that pretty pink pussy wet for me, Sherra?"

She moaned out his name and reached for him, fisting her hands into his hair and arching up to him, unaware she'd even moved. She just knew she wanted his mouth back on her, wanted him stroking her with that tongue, wanted to feel just the barest edge of his teeth raking over her clit.

He pressed his lips to her upraised knee, trailing them down the inside of her thigh until he reached the mound of her sex. Resting his chin on her pubis, he looked at her. Lashes low over his eyes, he whispered, "Are you wet for me, baby?"

"Yes." She blushed, embarrassed, self-conscious, but she needed his mouth back on her.

Needed it like she needed to breathe. Need blistered through her, cramped her belly, burned through her pussy and left her dazed and whimpering. Mindless, she tugged on his hair and arched up.

This time, when he licked her, she bucked under his touch and he braced an arm across her hips to hold her in place—hold her in place as he circled the entrance to her body with his tongue. He pushed his tongue inside her aching, clenching sex and she cried out.

He growled, pressing his face more firmly against her. He fucked his tongue in and out of her pussy, harder, harder. The empty ache in her belly expanded, stretched, became fire, hot, molten fire that spread through her and had her straining against him. Her breath locked in her lungs. Unable to breathe, unable to think, all she could do was feel.

Feel it as the growth of his beard rasped against sensitive tissues, feel it as he growled against her, vibrations of it shuddering through her, edging her closer—closer—

He shifted, nuzzled her clit with his tongue.

It hit with the force of a tidal wave. She screamed out his name and jerked against him, fighting the arm that held her hips banded in place, fighting the painful need, fighting instinctively for some sort of control.

There was none to be found, though. He pushed her, pushed her, drawing everything he could from her until she collapsed against the cushions of the couch with a broken, exhausted moan.

Exhausted, she was only vaguely aware when he pulled away from her, only vaguely aware of it as he stripped his clothes away. When he came back to her, his hot, hard body was bare. He brushed his mouth across her knee, edging higher and higher, until he could feather his lips across the fiery wet heat of her pussy. "Pretty girl," he whispered against her, his voice soft and reverent. "You screamed for me. Now scream again."

He tugged her off the couch. At the feel of his hot body pressed to hers, she caught her breath. Hot. Hard. Muscled. His gaze caught hers. For a moment, she knew fear. It sank its teeth into her, jagged and cold.

For a moment, she was caught again. Trapped on the ground while hands held her own pinned and a big, heavy body had her pinioned to the ground.

Then Dalton kissed her. Light and soft. His whiskey-rough voice teasing as he murmured, "You gonna scream for me again, pretty girl?"

He took them to the ground, but he didn't place her on the ground, didn't try to cover her. He went to the ground and tugged her on top of him, guiding her until she straddled him. Between her thighs, she felt the heavy, thick column of his cock, throbbing against her swollen sex.

Beneath her, Dalton lay, waiting. She knew he'd wait there indefinitely if he needed to, even though hunger came off him in hot, intense waves and she could see the strain in his eyes. His long, powerful body all but vibrated with it.

Yeah, he'd wait. If he had to.

But Sherra realized she *couldn't* wait. Catching her lower lip between her teeth, she reached down and wrapped her fingers around him, held him steady as she lifted herself up. Awkward, fumbling, she managed to guide the tip of his penis to her entrance.

The look on her face was almost as fucking erotic as the way her pussy clenched around him, Dalton thought. He struggled to hold still, struggled not to do much more than breathe as she slowly sank down on him. The flared head disappeared inside her silky wet sheath and he swore. Reflexively, his hands came up and clutched her hips, but he didn't grab. Didn't arch up and impale himself in all the snug, delicious heat.

He lay there.

Taking each slow stroke downward.

It was a sweet, painful pleasure, watching as she slowly worked him in. Inch by inch. Her pussy squeezed tight around him, the tiny muscles milking him, teasing him, until he was ready to come before she'd even taken all of his cock.

Fuck, he'd been ready to come from the first time he looked at her.

But he wouldn't. Couldn't. Couldn't grab her and roll her underneath him, couldn't bury his dick inside her and ride her until the viselike need in his balls eased. She was killing him. Slowly, bit by bit, she was killing him.

"You're killing me," he muttered, staring at her through his lashes and fighting to breathe. "You're so fucking tight."

She braced her hands on his chest and leaned forward, her silken hair falling like a cloak. A smile tilted the corners of her mouth up and she whispered, "But it's fun."

"Fun . . ." he growled. Unable to resist, he arched his back and hissed as she took a few more inches inside.

Her eyes widened, shock drifting across her face.

Shock—

Tight—

Somewhere in the back of his mind, he made the connection, but he was too lost in her, too lost in the pleasure of seeing her smile, too caught up in the intoxicating delight of having her wet pussy as she glided up, down. "Fun . . . mean woman. You're killing me," he groaned, slamming his head back and grinding it into the ground. "Fuck, more. Damn it. You're killing me. All of me, damn it, take it all."

She sank against him, her breasts pressing flat against his chest, that same mischievous smile curling her lips as she whispered, "You take me."

Beneath his breath, he swore. "I'm trying to be a nice guy here," he bit off, his fingers digging into her flesh. "I don't want to hurt you—I don't want to scare you."

Where had this woman come from? She was full of him, stretched tight around him, and the whisper of pain threatened, but she didn't care. She needed more. Had to have more. She wanted to feel that earth-shattering pleasure when her body and soul split and she went flying apart and she wanted him with her.

Sherra liked being alone. It was easier. Safer. Lonely as hell, but it felt safe.

With Dalton, though, she didn't need to *feel* safe. She was safe.

Hell, where had this woman come from . . . ? Sherra wondered as she kissed him and whispered, "Do I look hurt? Scared? Come on, Dalton . . . you wanted to make me scream. Do it." She didn't need the safety net of isolation. She just needed him.

Catching his lip between her teeth, she bit down softly. "Make me scream."

He growled, that harsh, male sound of ripe hunger, and the hands on her hips clenched, pushing her downward as he arched his back and pushed upward. The thick pillar of flesh cleaved through her, forging deep, deep, deeper.

She arched upward, crying out in shock as he buried himself inside her. Back arching, she fought to breathe past the pain, fought to accept this intimate invasion. Dalton reached up, hooked his hand around the back of her neck and pulled her close. "Relax," he muttered against her lips. "Relax . . . come on, princess; that's it. Relax for me. Awww . . . fuck, you're sweet."

Dalton reached between their bodies, seeking out the tight,

bundled knot of her clit. When he touched it, she shuddered, whimpered into his mouth.

"Dalton . . ."

"Yeah, I'm here. Hold on to me, baby." He wrapped an arm around her waist, bracing her body as he started to shaft her. Deep, slow. His tongue stroked against hers, twined with hers, stroked, rubbed, echoing the movements of his cock.

She sobbed into his kiss as that hot, vicious need tore through her. Harder this time. Hotter. His hands skimmed down her back, cupped her ass and guided her hips in a driving rhythm. She fell into it and ripped her mouth away from his, bracing her elbows on the floor on either side of his head.

She wanted to see him.

Had to.

Their gazes connected. The hands on her bottom gentled and the desperate, frenzied movements of their bodies eased—now they glided. Glided through a wave of molten, liquid pleasure. Brows touching, she stared into his pale green eyes, lost to anything, lost to everything else.

Deep inside her pussy, his cock jerked. She shuddered, instinctively rocking against him. "Come for me, princess," he whispered. He reached between them, once more seeking out the aching knot of her clit. "Come for me . . ."

"I feel like I'm gonna fly apart," Sherra moaned.

"Do it," he rasped against her lips. With his thumb, he circled her clit. "Fly apart for me, princess. I've got you . . ."

She cried out against his lips and Dalton swore as her pussy locked down, clenching around his aching cock, milking him, massaging him, stroking, convulsing, sweet . . . sweet . . . *sweet* . . .

She climaxed and as she flew apart in his arms, he arched up, buried his dick inside her and let go.

Long moments later, Sherra stirred in his arms. Slowly, she lifted her head and stared down at him with bleary eyes. "What are you doing to me . . . ?" she whispered hoarsely. Sprawled atop him, wearing nothing but her favorite pair of espadrilles, her thighs aching, his cock still twitching inside her.

She barely even recognized herself.

"Loving you, pretty girl," Dalton answered, his voice soft and so gentle. His lips brushed against her. "Just loving you, princess."

Tears blurred her eyes. Her heart clenched. "Don't stop . . . please don't stop."

"Shhhh . . ." Dalton kissed the salty tears away from her cheeks. Stroking her silken back, he swallowed the knot of emotion in his throat. "I don't think I could stop if I had to."

SHE CAME AWAKE in the bed with no memory of how she'd come to be there.

That empty blankness was ugly. She hated losing time. It did bad things to her—

From the corner of her eye, she saw something move. Tensing up, she braced herself, swallowing the ugly fear in her throat and shoving the fear, the nerves, the panic, the need to *run*, all of it, deep down inside and locking it up tight.

Only then, only when she had herself under control, did she let herself look.

She turned and found herself trapped in Dalton's pale green gaze. He had his weight braced on his elbow, staring at her.

She gave him a bright, entirely fake smile. "Hey!" Her voice bright and chipper, and she didn't do chipper. Especially not at . . . whatever in the hell time it was. She winced at the overly bright tone, blood rushing up to stain her cheeks pink.

"Why do you do that?" He cupped her cheek in his hand, rubbing his thumb across her lower lip.

"Do what?" She didn't really need to ask. The cheerleader Barbie act just wasn't her.

"Hide."

Sherra shrugged awkwardly, pushing at his shoulder and struggling to sit up and pull the sheet over herself without looking as if she was trying to hide. "I'm not hiding," she said defensively.

"That's your favorite thing to do, princess. Hide."

She felt the bed shift under her as he moved and then he was sitting behind her, pulling her body back up against his. Resting his chin on her shoulder, he tugged her close. "You hide. You were hiding the day Monica showed up with me in tow and you growled and snarled at me. You were hiding those ten days before we left Chicago. You hide when your brother growls at you; you hide from anything . . . everything."

He slid a hand around her hip and reached between her thighs, cupping her pussy in his hand. She was slick and wet, so wet his fingers pushed easily inside, despite how swollen and sore she was. "Even last night you were hiding."

Sherra swallowed, her mouth dry. "After last night, there's not much I have left to hide from you." After they had caught their breath, he had lifted her up in his arms, told her they needed a shower . . . and they hadn't made it into the bathroom for a good thirty minutes. Once they were in there, after they'd soaped each other down, he'd lifted her in his arms and made love to her with her back pressed against the wall as the water streamed down around them.

Three times in one night, she didn't know if she had anything left she *could* hide. He read her too easily and had from the beginning; he looked at her and saw things she was pretty sure nobody else knew.

"Didn't I pretty much expose myself last night?" she whispered, struggling to breathe as he circled his thumb around her clit.

He lifted her up onto his lap, used his knees to open hers and then he angled her hips and pushed inside, pushed his way past tight, swollen muscles. "You're still hiding," he whispered against her shoulder, rocking forward against her. "You're so fucking tight. Why didn't you tell me?"

"Tell you what?" How was she supposed to answer . . . Shit, he was huge, stretching her, filling her so damn full it hurt and at the same time, it was a sweet, hot pleasure.

"That you hadn't had sex before." He cupped her breasts in his hands and pinched her nipples, plumped the full mounds together. "Why didn't you tell me before?"

Tell . . . Her eyes crossed as he raked his teeth across the arch of her neck. "Tell you . . . ?"

Dalton chuckled and placed the flat of his hand against her torso, stroking downward until he could trace the tip of his finger around her entrance, stroking the skin where she stretched so tight around him. "Why didn't you tell me you hadn't had sex before?"

Some of that penetrated. She thought. She wasn't completely sure she understood. "Ah . . . didn't think of it. Damn it, Dalton, don't make me think right now," she groaned, wiggling her butt back against him.

"Fine. You can think later." He bit her shoulder and wrapped his arms around her waist, holding her as he surged up off the bed and shifted them around. "Put your hands on the dresser, princess."

She did, taking a deep breath just before he fucked it right out of her. He stole her breath with slow, gentle strokes and teasing, light touches against her clit, along her sides, across her bottom. It hurt, his thick width burrowing inside her, stretching her, hard, achingly hard, bruising and throbbing.

But it was the sweetest pain. And when it ended and he once more had her snuggled up in his arms as he carried them to bed, she was still struggling to think past the pleasure.

7

I DIDN'T THINK about it.

Dalton scowled into his coffee an hour later, listening to the spray of water from the other room as Sherra showered. He'd herded her in there by herself even as he kissed her and thought about kneeling at her feet in the oversized shower stall and washing that pretty pussy clean so he could taste her again.

Clean—

Fuck, he hadn't worn a rubber, and that was one more thing they needed to talk about, but he was still trying to think about her explanation when she finally managed to give him one.

Why didn't you tell me?

She had blinked at him owlishly and then shrugged self-consciously. *I just didn't think about it.*

Hiding—he'd accused her of hiding, but he had something he was hiding from her, and he wasn't planning on confessing anytime soon. At least not until he could get his mind wrapped around it. He really was in love with her.

He'd fallen in love with Snow White.

Blowing out a breath, he dropped his head into his hands and tried to figure out how in the hell he'd gotten into this mess. He'd just needed a job—needed some money and some time. Time to figure out what in the hell he should do next. All he'd ever been was a cop, but he knew he couldn't go back to that. He'd lost the heart for it and he didn't see that changing.

"I'm supposed to figure out what in the hell to do with my life, not make it more complicated," he muttered.

Linking his fingers behind his neck, he stared down at the table and brooded. He had just needed a job. That was it—

Not quite. You were trying to figure your life out—maybe she's the answer. It was a quiet voice that came from somewhere deep inside him. With it came a sense of peace that managed to wash away all his doubts, all his fears.

How had he ended up in this place?

Because this was where he was meant to be—and she was who he was meant to be with.

Dalton wasn't one for believing in fate, true love, or anything other than what he could see, hear, understand. He didn't understand this, but it felt right. Dalton was big on doing what felt right.

Just behind him, the door to the bathroom opened, letting a cloud of hot, scented air escape. Letting his hands fall to the table, he looked up as Sherra left the bathroom. She was wrapped in a big, fluffy towel just a few shades lighter than her lips. She'd brushed her hair back from her face and there was an expression on her face that reminded him of how she looked when she climaxed.

Her gaze was focused on the coffee cup sitting in front of Dalton. A smile tugged his lips and he curled his hand around his cup, drew it close. "Hey, get your own coffee."

She gave him a charming smile, showing yet another facet of her personality. "But yours is closer."

"You're standing two feet from the coffeepot," he pointed out. "And that coffee is still hot. Mine's been sitting here for the past twenty minutes." His gaze roamed over her, lingered on the tops of her barely covered breasts and then traveled all the way down to her bare feet. He took his time looking back at her face.

When he did, she cocked a brow. "Enjoying the view?"

"Absolutely."

The look in her eyes should have warned him. It was wicked and mischievous. Lifting her hands to the knot in her towel, she tugged it free and stood before him naked. With a grin, she took his cup and settled on the stool next to him. "For coffee, you can look all you want."

He barely suppressed a groan.

Just barely.

He couldn't sit next to her without touching her, though, so he slid off his stool and went to pour himself another cup. He warmed hers up while he was at it, putting a good five feet between them before he looked back at her.

She sat at the bar, drinking the coffee while her nipples played peekaboo with her hair. "You're killing me," he muttered.

Sherra grinned at him. "You keep telling me that."

"And you keep torturing me. You shouldn't tempt a starving man, princess."

Cocking her head, she asked, "Why do you keep calling me that?"

Smiling, he took a sip of his coffee. Over the rim of the glass, he watched her, his gaze lingering on her lips and hair. "Snow White." He shrugged and murmured, "Snow White . . . princess. It suits you."

She choked on a mouthful of coffee, staring at him like he'd lost his mind.

"Snow White? As in the fairy tale, the apple and all that crap? Are you nuts?"

"Lips as red as blood, skin as white as snow, hair as black as night." Setting the coffee down, he circled around behind her and caught a fistful of her hair in his hand, tugging lightly until she looked up at him. Lifting a finger, he traced the line of her mouth with his fingertip.

"I love that pretty mouth," he whispered.

She blushed. That charming pink started at the mounds of her breasts and slowly crept up until she was blushing to the roots of her hair. Knocking his hand aside, she squirmed on the barstool, crossing her bare legs and hunching her shoulders. "You're crazy."

He dipped his head and pressed his face to her hair, breathed in the warm, sweet scent. "I love your hair. I love this soft, pretty white skin." Skimming his fingers along her arm, he muttered, "Soft and silky. Especially . . ." He went lower, lower, lower, until he could cup her sex in his palm.

He didn't penetrate—she had to be sore and he'd be damned if he added to that. "Especially here," he finished, his voice hoarse and raw.

She shuddered. "Dalton . . ."

Regretfully, he withdrew his hand and took a step back. "You don't need to do this again. Not right now."

Sherra tipped her head back and stared at him. "I know what I need."

"You're sore."

Her lower lip poked out even as she blushed. "So?"

He kissed her, quick and light. "We're not making it worse."

Stooping, he grabbed her towel and draped it around her shoulders, hiding temptation. Then, before that sexy, sleepy look in her eyes undid him, he headed for a shower. He needed to shower, needed to get dressed, needed to focus on the job.

And he needed some distance. Needed to get steady again.

SHERRA FOUGHT THE need to fidget as Missy stood two feet away. The other woman went on about the signing coming up on Tuesday, and then bounced to the upcoming reunion, talking in rapid-fire bursts that left Sherra's head spinning.

Dalton waited for her by the door, long, jeans-clad legs crossed at the ankle, big arms crossed over his chest. He watched her, tracking her with his eyes as she followed Missy around the room.

They'd spent an hour at the sheriff's office that morning, along with Lacey, Renee and Deacon. There definitely was a story between those two, energy crackling between them every time their eyes connected, every time Deacon stroked a hand down Renee's back. Which was pretty often.

Restless, itchy, Sherra wandered off to study the new releases when a customer came up to Missy looking for a book.

Deacon and Renee hooked up.

Seth and Lacey.

Hell, the way things were going, one would think it was Valentine's Day and Cupid's arrows were flying around. Idly, she glanced at Dalton and felt the impact of that look clear down to her toes.

It hit her with breath-stealing force, all but knocking her feet out from under her. Blood roared in her ears and she couldn't hear a damn thing. Just like last night, she couldn't see a damn thing. Couldn't see beyond him.

No. This isn't happening . . .

Cupid—hell, yeah, he was working overtime. All of her life, she'd managed to escape any kind of entanglement. Ever since she'd broken up with Jonah, no man had lasted in her life beyond a few days.

Every man she'd met, she kept at a distance. Nothing mattered to her except that distance. She hated the nightmares that came anytime she tried to leave her safety net and actually interact with the opposite sex. Even a simple date was too much. Simple dates usually led to a kiss, and a kiss was all it took to set her down the path of depression. To bring back memories that lurked too close to the surface. Desperate to avoid that, she just avoided guys.

But she hadn't been able to avoid Dalton—and he kissed her without giving her nightmares.

He called her princess.

He let her steal his coffee and his covers and he wrapped his big, hard body around hers at night and stroked away the nightmares.

This can't be happening—

"It already is," she muttered, spinning away from a shelf stocked with paranormal romances and urban fantasy. She plowed straight into Dalton's chest, his big hands coming up to grab her arms and steady her.

"You okay? You went ghost white there," he murmured, cupping her cheek in his hand.

"Skin as white as snow sounds so much prettier than ghost white," she quipped. Humor was better than nerves, right?

"Yeah, but you're a spooky writer of scary stories. You should appreciate the imagery."

"Nice alliteration." She sidestepped around him, but he just moved, blocking her way.

"Nice attempt to change the subject. You didn't answer me. Are you okay?"

Sherra glanced toward the front of the store, flushing.

"She's helping some little old woman with a list of probably twenty different books. Answer me."

Rolling her eyes, Sherra said, "I'm fine—well, mostly fine."

"Liar. You get this big, fake smile on your face when you aren't telling the truth. Or you try a joke or smartassery."

"Assery?"

"Being a smartass—you've perfected it to an unknown level; it deserves special recognition." His voice softened and he moved in, wrapping his arms around her waist. "Come on, princess. What's wrong?"

"A little bit of everything?" she said, not entirely joking. "I'm just jumpy. Restless. Too much going on, too many questions, no answers." She gave him a tight smile and pushed up on her toes, tugging on his shoulders until he dipped his head. She pressed her lips to his cheek and then settled back down on her feet, easing back.

She rolled her shoulders, tried to get rid of the restless tension trapped inside her. She desperately wished she could do something to burn the energy off, but she wasn't much for exercising unless she had to—her idea of exercise was a marathon shoe-shopping spree. She mustered up a smile and wondered if she could talk him into a trip to Cincinnati. A nice, long day of attacking the malls might do wonders for her mood.

The bell over the door jangled and Dalton turned, automatically shifting so that her body was tucked away behind his. Missy called out a greeting from somewhere in the store.

A flash of bright color and vivid font caught Sherra's eye and she reached for a book on the shelf. As she pulled it from the shelf, somebody spoke. At the sound of that voice, a shiver raced down her spine and her fingers went numb.

The book fell to the floor, forgotten, as she turned to look, craning her head so she could see around Dalton's body.

Jonah . . .

JEALOUSY WAS AN ugly, exhausting emotion, Dalton realized some three hours later. Sitting at the booth, only inches away from Sherra, it was like miles separated them.

Dalton hadn't needed anybody to draw him a picture—he figured it out all on his own that these two had been close at some point. *Couldn't have been that close*, Dalton thought darkly. Dalton was the only guy to lay between her pretty thighs and bury his cock inside her sweet pussy.

Jonah's deep laugh boomed out of him and Sherra grinned. Dalton didn't even have to see her to know she was smiling—he could hear it in her voice. He wanted to grab her, haul her out of the booth and away from Jonah. He wasn't a fool, though. Doing that would be a bad, bad idea. So he sat, gritted his teeth and made the occasional grunt or nodded when the rare question was directed his way.

Seth's arrival in the café was a godsend. He came sauntering up to the table, eyeing Jonah. His expression never changed but Dalton got the impression that Seth was about as impressed with Jonah as he was.

"Heard you were coming back to town, Jonah," Seth said as he stopped at the table.

Jonah leaned back, smiling at Seth. Something flashed through his eyes, there, then gone. Dalton didn't know if Seth had seen it, but Dalton sure as hell had.

DALTON WAS QUIET. Too quiet.

The walk back to the B&B was taking forever, and his brooding, chilled silence wasn't helping.

Jealousy? That was what her instincts whispered, but Sherra wasn't entirely sure she trusted them. At least not lately. Too tired. Too stressed—seeing Jonah had helped. They'd ended things amicably enough and still e-mailed a few times a year. He sent her a birthday card every year—always a week late, just like when they were dating.

They were friends. Friends who shared a decent amount of history. If life hadn't changed on her the way it had, she suspected Jonah would have been her first lover. They'd come close, more than once. Whether things would have lasted between them, she didn't know. Didn't really matter, either. Sherra cared for Jonah, but she knew nothing more would ever come of it.

She knew that—but maybe Dalton . . . She glanced at him from the corner of her eye. He stared straight ahead, but she knew he felt her watching him. The guy noticed everything. "I haven't seen Jonah in, like, ten years," she blurted out.

His pale green eyes flicked her way. He shrugged. "Looked like you two had a lot to catch up on."

Sherra shrugged. "I don't know. We were friends—" She broke off when he stopped in his tracks and looked at her. "Okay, we were a little more than friends some of the time. That was back in high school. There . . ."

Dalton took a step toward her, closing up the scant distance between them.

Cupping her chin in his hand, he angled her head back. The intensity of his gaze stole the breath from her lungs. "You never slept with him. I know that. I get that."

He was so close, she could feel the heat coming off his body. If she rose on her toes, she could press her lips to his chin. Somehow, though, she doubted he was going to meet her halfway like he had done just a few hours ago. Scowling, she said, "Then what in the hell is your problem?"

"What's my problem?"

He moved fast. Way too fast. Hooking an arm around her waist, he hauled closed the few inches that separated their bodies. "That guy sits there looking at you and thinking about how much he wants to put his hands all over you, and you just smile and laugh."

"Jonah was *not* thinking—"

Dalton snarled. He cut her words off with a kiss, pushing his tongue deep inside her mouth. The kiss ended quick—too quick, leaving her shaking and wanting more.

He didn't pull away. With his mouth pressed to hers, he rasped, "Don't tell me that. I saw him looking at you. I know what he was thinking, because I think the same damn thing every time I see you."

Swallowing, mouth dry, Sherra didn't know what to say. Part of her wanted to be pissed off—possessive much? But she wasn't having much luck working up the enthusiasm to *get* pissed off.

Pressing against his chest, she tried to get some distance between them. He let her go and she fell back a few feet, staring at him. Confused, worried, that awful restlessness building inside her again.

"You and I haven't had so much as a date."

Dalton gave her a hot, hungry smile. That hard edge still glinted in his eyes. "No, we skipped the date and went straight to the main course. Does that mean I'm not supposed to care if some guy is thinking about putting the moves on you? Especially some guy you've already got history with?"

"Why *should* you care?" she demanded, planting her hands on her hips. "I'm a fucking *job* for you, remember? When it's done, you disappear."

"Says who?"

Caught off guard, Sherra blinked. "Ahhhh . . . you? It's not like you were real eager to take this job. You only took it because you needed money."

"Yeah, that's why I took it."

Mesmerized, she watched as he lifted a hand and caught a strand of her hair, toying with it. "Took the job for the money, but the job, the money, none of that has anything to do with why you and me ended up in bed together."

"I didn't think it did," Sherra said, wincing as she realized how she must sound. "But, Dalton, you don't *know* me. Up until a couple of weeks ago, you'd never even laid eyes on me. We slept together—we had one night. But what does that amount to?"

"For me, it amounts to a whole hell of a lot," he murmured, his voice rough and soft, his hands gentle as he reached up and cupped her face. His lip brushed against hers, warm and gentle. "I'm thirty-eight years old, Sherra. I'm not going to lie and say I've never had casual sex, but I will tell you I've got a decent amount of self-control. If sex was all I wanted, I wouldn't have risked fucking things up by sleeping with the woman I was hired to protect."

Pursing her lips, she drawled, "So because you wanted *more* than sex—whatever that is—you risked fucking things up?"

He crooked a grin at her. "Smartass."

Something about the way he looked at her shook her to the very core. Even more than what had happened between them last night, something about the way he watched her now . . . She swallowed, fighting to speak past the knot in her throat and the way her heart ricocheted around in her chest. Nobody had ever looked at her in quite that way, not until now.

It wasn't just care; it wasn't just concern. Even as isolated as she kept herself, she'd had people in her life care about her. People who loved her, worried about her—even if they were a tad overprotective.

This . . . this was different in a way she couldn't possibly understand.

He lifted his head, brushing her hair back from her face. "I shouldn't have slept with you. It was a tactical error in the biggest way, and it's one I plan on repeating. Often. I don't mix business with pleasure any more than you do, princess. I did it this time because of you—because you *do* matter. And it drives me fucking *nuts* to sit there and watch you laugh and smile with that guy. I want you to smile for me. I want you to laugh for me. Not some punk you dated in high school."

Especially not that punk. Besides, Dalton thought, something about Jonah made his mental radar go off. Granted, it could be just jealousy but until he got a background check done on the man, he wasn't going to trust Jonah any farther than he could throw him.

He pressed his lips to Sherra's. She sighed against his lips and he felt his knees go just a little weak as she relaxed against him. Damn it, the things this woman did to him—it was unreal.

"Soon, you and me are going to have to have a talk," he said, his voice harsh and hoarse.

"We're talking now."

"Different sort of talk." He didn't say anything more, though. He was still trying to figure all of this out for himself.

Soon, though . . . Soon.

8

A MUSCLE JERKED in his jaw as he stood over her shoulder reading the e-mail.

It wasn't just pictures this time.

Or that obscure little message. *Waiting for you.* Not enough anymore.

You let that man touch you.
How could you do it, Sherra?
How could you do this to me?
When I've been waiting.

Without tearing his eyes away from the screen, he reached for his cell phone and dialed a number he'd memorized—Mueller's number. Sherra glanced over her shoulder at him, her skin even paler than normal, her dark eyes gone near black with fear. "If you're calling Mueller, he already has it. They set up some weird program that lets them read all my e-mails." She tried to work up a smile, but it fell flat. "Why is it the victims always end up losing so much of their privacy?"

Resting a hand on her shoulder, he squeezed gently. She covered it with her own and rage spiraled through him as he felt her shudder.

The phone rang twice and went to voice mail. Leaving a terse message, Dalton explained the e-mail and left a less-than-politely phrased request that Mueller call him back.

Still not trusting himself to speak, he continued reading the e-mail, scrolling past the pictures—if he looked at them too long, he was going to put his damn fist through the monitor. Forcing a deep breath past his tight throat, he asked, "Anything like this ever happen before?"

Sherra shook her head. From the corner of his eye, he could see the haunted look on her face and he would have chopped off his arm to take that pain and fear away. "No. He's never really said anything more than 'waiting for you.'"

Dalton glanced at the time stamp. Sent less than an hour ago.

Just a few hours after they'd left Jonah at the café and come back to the B&B. Jonah had his own business—apparently, the guy was a tech genius, had his own company, made a substantial amount of money. How substantial, Dalton would know the minute he accessed his own e-mail, because he was running a complete background check on the man.

Tech genius.

How hard would it be for a clever, computer-savvy guy to bounce e-mails around enough to keep from being tracked? Or maybe he wasn't bouncing e-mail—maybe he was just sending them from all over the place. A good hacker could fool the FBI—not indefinitely, but hackers were constantly coming up with something new. All this guy had to do was stay a step ahead of the FBI. It could be done.

Reaching around, he closed the laptop. Sherra just stared straight ahead, at absolutely nothing. Dalton rested his hands on the back of the chair and spun it around. He crouched down in front of her and lifted a hand to touch her cheek. She'd gone cold, that smooth, soft skin icy under his fingertips. "He won't hurt you. I won't let him."

Sherra swallowed and licked her lips. Quietly, she said, "You can't promise that."

Catching her hand in his, he pressed his lips to her palm. "Yes. I can. He won't hurt you."

She said nothing else, but he could see the doubt in her eyes, saw the fear. He understood the fear, but he wasn't lying. He *would* protect her. He wouldn't let anything hurt her. Shifting to his knees, he slid his arms around her and pressed her head to his shoulder.

"I'm good at what I do, Sherra. Trust me. I'll take care of you."

In his arms, she sighed and snuggled closer.

SHERRA PACED THE floor, the ankle-length ivory skirt tangling around her legs. Her blouse was sleeveless, burgundy lace overlaying pale silk just a few shades darker than her skin. It gave the impression that she was nude under that delicate lace, an erotic effect that had Dalton adjusting himself and resigning himself to a night of discomfort. The past day had been long and tense. Sherra had gotten two more e-mails and he'd spent the better part of the morning trying to talk her into just canceling her tour and going back home.

Or at least skipping this part of it.

She wouldn't.

Seth had warned him that it would be a waste of breath. Dalton had known it would be a waste of breath. But he wasted it for a good two hours before accepting the inevitable. If he thought it would solve anything, he'd make her go. Kicking, screaming, didn't matter; if he thought it would make a difference. But the sick fuck stalking her knew where she lived.

This is your fault, he told himself as he watched Sherra brood and worry—and did some brooding and worrying of his own. If he hadn't touched her . . .

Can't undo it. He crossed his arms and leaned back against the wall as Sherra made her tenth circuit of the room. Since he couldn't undo it, and since forcing Sherra to leave could only make things worse, there weren't too many paths open to him.

The one that made the most sense was the one that set every protective instinct he had on edge.

The cop in him knew, though, that it was the wisest option. Maybe even the only viable option, because here in this small town, the environment was fairly controlled. It wasn't *his* environment— it was Seth's. But Seth had as much of a need to protect Sherra as Dalton did.

Yeah, but his attention is divided. Hell, the small-town sheriff probably dealt with nothing more exciting than a bunch of dumb teens joyriding or the random case of domestic violence. His instincts were humming, twitching, all but driving him nuts as he tried to work his mind around the current, very bizarre mess he was caught up in.

Fifteen years ago, Sherra killed a boy who had been trying to rape her. There had been another kid involved and if two girls hadn't heard her screaming, they would have raped her. He detached himself from that—had to, because he couldn't afford the luxury of getting pissed off, couldn't afford the luxury of daydreaming about finding the other involved party and beating him within an inch of his life.

Renee Lincoln left Madison after that and up until now, she'd come back only once, for her mother's funeral, and she was in town then for two days. Not a great deal of time. Lacey came back often enough, and a few years ago, she had an incident of her own. Then both women came back and the very day they arrived in town, something happened.

Renee was the victim of vehicular assault, nearly killed.

Lacey was attacked.

Both of their homes were vandalized.

Their attacker was local. Had to be—nobody else would have

a reason for stalking two of the three women from that night. He couldn't believe those incidents were unrelated.

Maybe they are all related.

Across the room, Sherra muttered under her breath.

"You okay?"

She shot him a narrow glance. "Oh, I'm just peachy," she snapped.

She resumed pacing, muttering under her breath. If Dalton hadn't been so preoccupied, he probably would have been amused. She looked like Snow White, but damn, she was grouchy.

Instead of grinning at her or trying to kiss her out of her black mood, he resumed his own brooding.

Could they be related?

Jonah—was it possible? Maybe the guy had been harboring some hidden obsession for Sherra all these years—but why the attack on Renee and Lacey? That was the puzzle. If there was a connection, he couldn't see it. Blowing out a breath, he went to shove a hand through his hair only to stop as he remembered he'd pulled it back into a ponytail for the night. The reunion deal was in less than an hour, dinner, dancing, all that jazz at a country club. He'd packed a few things other than jeans and T-shirts and was wearing his own version of "nice" clothes, a pair of black trousers and a black button-down shirt. He kept the top two buttons open. No way was he wearing a tie. He was edgy enough without having some ridiculous tie choking him over the next few hours.

Shoving off the wall, he went and sat behind the desk. Sherra's laptop was still up so he logged on and went to check his e-mail— he wanted to know if anything had shown up on Simmonds's background report. Plus, Mueller had told him that he'd keep Dalton up-to-date on things either by calling or via e-mail.

He had several messages in his in-box and he ignored most of them, making a mental note to e-mail Monica with an update. The only two e-mails that interested him at the moment were the two he'd hoped to find. The first was from a friend from the force who'd agreed to run the background check for him on Jonah Simmonds.

Past few years, the guy had been clean. Some petty crap when he was in high school. Joined the army, did four years. Went to college after that, majored in computer engineering and software development. Dalton's eyes narrowed as he read on. Worked for IBM for a few years. Went off on his own a few years back, was developing his own line of desktops. Knew his way around computers . . . Dalton blew out a breath and settled back in the chair, studying the information.

The possibility was there, he knew. Simmonds definitely had the background needed to hide his tracks electronically. Didn't feel right, though.

Dalton read through the report one more time, making note of a few things, and then he saved the e-mail and pulled up the one from Mueller. A few lines in, a ribbon of satisfaction curled through him. Her stalker had gone and made a slip. The FBI had planted a tracing program that they'd hoped would let them track her stalker, although they'd had very little luck to this point.

But the last message, the guy had messed up.

Hadn't been as careful.

They were having some luck locking on to his signal and in a few days, they might even have an address. A few days—maybe they would get lucky and get something concrete before the big book deal coming up on Tuesday. Logging off, he glanced at Sherra and asked, "You need on here anymore?"

She shot the laptop a distasteful look. "I don't want to look at that thing anytime soon."

Cracking a grin at her, he said, "It's not the computer's fault."

Grimacing, she said, "Hell, I know that. This sucks. I've got a deadline I'm working on, too, but anytime I log on, I see that damn e-mail."

Dalton shrugged. "So get a new computer." Leaning back in the chair, he looked over at the clock. "What time do we need to leave here?"

Sherra shrugged, a jerky motion very unlike the normal, lazy grace she used. "Not for a while yet." She glanced down at her clothes and muttered, "Maybe I should change."

"You look beautiful."

She twitched her skirt, frowning down at herself. "I dunno. I've got this black dress . . ."

Rising from his seat, he crossed over to her and slid his arms around her waist. "You look beautiful."

"I don't feel beautiful."

He cupped her face in one hand, rubbed his thumb along her lower lip. "You're edgy. Restless. Changing your clothes isn't going to help with that."

Sulking, she said, "What *will* help?"

Fisting his hand in her skirt, he drew it upward, bunching the material in his hand until it had cleared her thighs. "I can think of something that will help."

Sinking to his knees in front of her, he caught her panties with his free hand and tugged them down. Sherra stared down at him, her eyes dark and huge in her face. "What would that be?" she asked, her voice soft, almost breathless.

He kissed her, nuzzled her clit with his nose and then licked her. She braced her hands on his shoulders, her nails piercing him through the cloth to score his flesh. Her head fell back. With a weak moan, she swayed against him. Dalton let go of her skirt and slid his hands around to cup her soft, plump ass in his hands, steadying her weight. He licked, teased, suckled, stroked until she was all but melting for him. Her pussy soft, slick and wet, her moans broken and husky, her face flushed, eyes wide and dazed.

Lifting his head, he went to his back, pulling her with him. She straddled his hips and rested her hands on his shoulders as he freed his cock. "We're going to be all hot and sweaty," she whispered.

"Do you care?"

A smile curled her lips. "No."

"Good." Wrapping his hand around his cock, he steadied himself and pressed the head of it to her entrance. Silken soft, wet and sweet, she closed around him. He fed her one slow inch at a time and she wiggled, rocked, and fought against his restraining hold, trying to take him deeper, harder.

She groaned and pushed down with her hips. "More."

The burning in his balls seconded that suggestion, but he kept it slow. Restraining her with his hands, he held both of them back. He didn't want to hurt her—didn't want to scare her . . .

Abruptly, she bent down over him and caught his lower lip in her teeth, biting down. "More," she demanded, her voice harsh, throbbing with the need that burned inside her.

The feel of those sharp teeth scraping over his lip, the hungry, demanding feel of her body atop his, her edgy restlessness, combined with his, worked to eradicate any and all self-control he had. Swearing, he shot a hand into her hair and fisted it, jerking her down to him. He kissed her, hard, rough, all his pent-up hunger coming through in that kiss. "You sure you know what you're asking for, princess?" he demanded.

Sherra smiled at him. Rotating her hips, she intentionally clenched her inner muscles so that her pussy hugged his thick flesh tight. She did it a second and third time, then whispered against his mouth, "I have no clue what I'm asking for . . . but I know you can give it to me."

The moment drew out and he held himself still, held his breath, afraid to move, afraid to blink, afraid to even think. *Control*—he reminded himself.

But control had slipped away from him and with a growl, he flipped their bodies, placing her petite, round body on the hard floor and grasping her thighs. Shoving them high and wide, he thrust deep, burrowing through tight, convulsing tissues, burrowing deep—deeper. She cried out, arching against him, her hands clutching at his shoulders. Snarling, he caught her mouth with his. His tongue swooped into her mouth, seeking out that dark, delicious taste as he fucked his way through the gripping muscles of her pussy and buried his cock completely inside her sex.

"I wanna make you scream," he muttered against her lips when he finally tore away. "I want to fuck this tight, perfect pussy every damn day and listen to you whimper and cry my name as you come."

She whimpered, her eyes locking with his, dazed surrender gleaming in their depths.

"That's it, princess. Let me hear; let me feel it . . ."

Her hands fisted in his shirt and she strained her lower body, trying to ride the thick pillar of flesh piercing her. Trailing his fingers down the soft flesh of her inner thigh, he stroked her clit. "That feel good, princess?"

"Yes . . . Dalton, please—"

Reaching up, he caught one of her wrists and drew her hand down, urging it between her thighs. "Touch yourself."

She jerked against his hold, fighting him at first, but he wouldn't let her. Slowly, reluctantly, she started to stroke herself, her fingers circling the erect nub, quick and light. Slipping his hands under her bottom, he drew her closer and bent down over her. Even as hunger ripped through him, he made himself hold back, watched her eyes for any sign of fear as he let her body take his weight on top of hers. Between them, he could feel her fingers moving, and it was awkward, kept him from getting as close as he wanted, but he didn't care.

He fucking loved it when she rode him, but there was something about the way she felt underneath him that had every possessive, primitive instinct flaring to life. She was close—he could feel her climax building inside, her slick, wet tissues clinging to him like molten silk, perfect, tight and sweet. He growled, raking his teeth down her neck.

Through the layers of their clothes, he could feel the hot, hard points of her nipples, stabbing into his chest. See her—had to see her. Bracing his weight on one elbow, he caught the waistband of her shirt and pushed it up until it tangled under her arms. Her skin glowed against the black lace of her bra. Front clasp—the power of positive thinking. He freed it and shoved the cups aside, staring down at her tits, pale, perfectly shaped, tipped with rosy nipples. Mouth watering, he cupped one in his hand and stroked his thumb over it.

Her breath escaped her in a harsh rush and she arched, clenched tight around him.

"Fuck, Sherra, you're so damn tight," he muttered. Fist-tight, her inner muscles clenching around him, milking him. "Be still, baby . . . Fuck, please be still."

But she didn't seem to hear him. Small, sharp white teeth caught her lower lip and she bit down, muffling a cry. She stared blindly at his face and her fingers continued to stroke her clit, quick, fast, certain. They gleamed wet. With a groan, he caught her wrist and tugged her hand, bringing her fingers to his lips so he could lick that sweet rain away. She pulled against him. Without thinking, he bit her. Her eyes went wide and her pussy vised down around him. A wild cry fell from her lips as she came.

Dalton swore. His own climax built inside him, a warning shiver that whispered down his spine and centered in his balls, expanding—expanding—*Not yet* . . . but then Sherra arched under him, rubbing against him, and the small, strong muscles in her pussy flexed, clutching and convulsing around him.

Bracing his elbows on the floor, he caught her head between his hands and angled her face upward. Dipping his head, he nipped her lower lip before slanting his mouth over hers. The taste of her, sweet and dark, flooded his system.

He couldn't breathe—couldn't think. The need for her filled him, drove him, controlled him. Tearing his mouth from hers, Dalton stared at her, watched as tears gleamed in her eyes and a soft, sobbing cry fell from her lips.

That need, hot and ripe, exploded through him and he lost himself to it. Lost himself to her. His cock jerked as she clenched around him one final time. As he came, that need swirled around them, pulsed through him, and overtook him.

RESTING HIS HEAD on her belly, Dalton fought to catch his breath.

Her hands lay on his shoulders, absently stroking him through his shirt. Her skirt was bunched around her hips, her pretty, lacy top tangled under her arms. With a massive effort, he forced himself up onto his elbows and crooked a grin at her. "You might need to change after all."

"Ummmm. Later. Don't wanna move." Her voice was drowsy and soft, her eyes closed.

"Not moving sounds good to me."

She cracked an eyelid and gave him a moody sulk. "You're not supposed to indulge me."

Chuckling, he kissed her softly rounded belly and then levered his weight back onto his heels. He stroked a hand down her thigh, squeezed her gently just above her knee. She continued to sprawl there, one knee drawn up, exposing her wet slit. Moisture gleamed on the curls surrounding her sex and Dalton felt his cock twitch. Frowning, he looked down at himself. Blinked.

Looked back at her.

Mouth gone dry, he said hoarsely, "Sherra, we keep forgetting something."

"Hmmm. If it involves moving, no reason to remember."

He shifted and settled at her side, cupping a hand over her sex. Unable to resist, he circled his index finger around her entrance and watched as her lids slowly lifted. Her dark brown eyes met his and she smiled mischievously. "We haven't forgotten that—we just did it."

"We didn't use anything."

She squinted at him and then abruptly, understanding it. He could see the realization dawn in her eyes and he said a silent prayer that she didn't shut him out again. "Ummm . . . shit."

He grimaced. "I'd meant to talk to you about this yesterday morning—then again today. Kept getting sidetracked." Trailing his fingers down her thigh, he said quietly, "Selective memory, probably. I didn't want to think about it when I was getting ready to feel that hot, wet pussy wrapped around my dick."

She blushed a bright pink and he laughed, bringing his hand back to cup her sex in it. "I love feeling this hot, wet pussy wrapped around my dick." Then, before he could let himself get sidetracked again, he withdrew his hand. Smile fading, he said, "I can tell you straight-up I'm clean. Had to have a workup done a few months ago and I haven't been with a woman in close to a year. If it will help, I can have the doctor's office fax the info to me."

Sherra made a face. "Hell, that's one way to kill the mood." Heaving out a sigh, she wiggled her skirt into place and then sat up, arranging it so the folds draped over her legs. She took a minute to untangle her blouse and when she looked back at him, most of her blush had faded. Licking her lips, she shrugged jerkily. "That's not necessary, Dalton."

She swallowed and he could see her throat working with the movement. Her voice was soft as she added, "I might have had some blood work done a few years ago, but . . . well . . ." She blew out a breath and slid him a shy glance. "There hasn't ever been a reason to need to do any kind of check. I've never done drugs and up until you . . ."

Her voice trailed off and she ended with a shrug.

Raw, unbridled possessiveness burned in him. Reaching out, Dalton pulled her into his lap. "How insane are you going to think I am if I tell you how damn glad I am there's never been any kind of *need*? How hot I get when I think about being the only man to ever touch you like this, the only man to ever make love to you."

She buried her face against his neck. "Pretty insane. A couple of weeks, Dalton. We've known each other a couple of weeks."

"I feel like I've been waiting for you my whole life," he said. The words slipped out of him without him realizing he'd planned to say them, but he wouldn't take them back, even if he could. "My whole life, Sherra."

She leaned back and stared at him. "*That* is insane."

He rested a hand on her belly and asked, "Does that mean you don't feel it?"

For a moment, she stared at him, frozen and silent. Then, slowly, she shook her head. In a faint whisper, she murmured, "I feel it, too."

Closing his eyes, he wrapped both arms around her and held her tight. She worked her arms around his waist, clutching him to her. "Insane," she mumbled.

"Completely." Nuzzling her neck, he whispered, "But it feels right. So I don't care."

Silence stretched out, the two of them wrapped in each other's arms and holding tight. Loath to break the silence, he whispered, "There is one more thing we should probably talk about."

Sherra shook her head against his chest. "No, there's not. I'm on the pill—had to start taking it for . . . uh . . . female issues. We're safe there."

Dalton let out the breath he was holding, uncertain if it was relief or disappointment—and totally floored by the fact that he wasn't sure. If it was any woman other than Sherra, it would have been relief.

But Sherra changed everything.

Needing her, caring for her . . . loving . . . because he was in love with her. That changed everything. "Okay."

She pressed against his chest, flashing him a false, bright smile. "Nothing to worry about, right?"

But when she went to stand, he wouldn't let her. Cupping her face in his hand, he said quietly, "I wasn't all that worried." He rubbed his thumb over her lip and whispered, "You've gone and changed my whole damn life. How did you manage to do that?"

Keeping her pressed against him with one arm, he braced his weight on the couch just behind him and then shoved them upright. "We need to get through the next few days. Give ourselves some time to settle a little. But we need to have a talk, princess."

He let her go, slowly, hating to lose her touch. Staring at her, he readjusted his clothes and then he closed the distance between them in one slow step. He didn't touch her. If he did, he just might not stop. All he did was dip his head and brush his lips against hers. "You went and changed everything."

9

You went and changed everything . . .

Grim-faced, Sherra stared at her reflection. She'd come to the bathroom under the guise of needing to pee, but what she really needed was a few moments of isolation, someplace where Dalton's all-too-knowing gaze didn't track her every movement. Standing in front of the mirror, she studied herself. She definitely did have to change before they left the B&B. Her clothes had been tangled and wrinkled, her hair a mess and her lipstick all but gone.

She'd chewed some of it off herself, but she'd seen a few red smudges on Dalton's mouth and neck. Kiss-proof lipstick, she told herself. Because she had a feeling she was going to be kissing him *a lot.*

The black dress she wore now was pretty, stark, plainer than she'd wanted, but it would work. She needed panty hose with it, though, and she'd forgotten to pack any.

She also needed to get her head examined. Whimsically, she wondered if five-minute shrink sessions could be bought at the local Walgreens. Although five minutes wouldn't do it. After thirty-two years of celibacy, she had a lover. A lover who looked at her with eyes that made her melt.

It was a weird mess, she decided. She had a stalker. There was another potential problem, although whoever had been harassing Renee and Lacey had yet to direct any attention her way. She had her hands full doing this fricking maniacal book tour—the first one of her career, and the attack of nerves that always hit before a professional engagement were enough to lay her low. This was six weeks of engagement, but she was more eaten up over Dalton than anything.

Even her stalker.

How could one guy take over so much of her mind?

If he's the right guy, maybe that's how it's supposed to be . . .

Sherra wanted to laugh, but it was hard to dismiss something that made so much sense.

We need to get through the next few days. Give ourselves some time to settle a little. But we need to have a talk, princess.

"Settle?" she muttered, shaking her head. Off to her left, she heard a door open and automatically, she leaned in over the sink and studied her reflection, smoothed her hair back. She couldn't settle. Every time she tried, a series of aftershocks rumbled through her and left her once more standing on unsteady ground.

"Is that who I think it is?"

Sherra glanced away from her reflection, distracted. The face in the mirror wasn't familiar. But the voice was.

Forcing herself to smile, she straightened up and turned. "Hi, Leslie."

"I KNEW I'D find you hiding here."

Sherra slid Dalton a wry smile and then straightened, turned to meet Lacey. Lifting her class of Coke, she sipped, catching a piece of ice between her teeth before lowering the drink. "I'm not hiding," she said calmly. "This is the last place I'd go if I wanted to hide."

A high-pitched laugh drifted into the bar from the hallway, audible even over the music that drifted out of the ballroom. "If I wanted to hide, I'd be outside—or I'd just leave." She rolled her eyes and muttered, "And believe me, I've thought it through a time or two."

She glanced toward the doorway as Leslie came stumbling in, clutching the arm of a guy who was only slightly familiar.

Obligingly, Dalton stepped between Sherra and the doorway, blocking her from view. Sending him a grateful smile, she grinned at Lacey and said, "If I have to sign one more piece of paper, napkin, book, matches, *anything*, I'm going to develop a raging problem with carpal tunnel or something."

From Lacey's side, Seth winked at her. "Carpal tunnel takes a while to develop, sis. But we won't tell on you." Then he resumed his slow, thorough scan of the room.

Dalton had been doing the same thing, both of them watching the room, taking everybody and everything in. She wondered exactly what it was they expected to find. If whoever was threatening Lacey and Renee was here, they wouldn't exactly have a neon sign over their head. And if by chance *her* stalker showed up, more than likely they'd stand out like a sore thumb to Seth and some of the others who still lived in Madison.

Big, public event like this, they'd be safe enough. Or so Sherra would think.

The high-pitched grating laugh drew closer. Other than the few minutes in the restroom earlier, she'd managed to evade Leslie for most of the event. Sherra wasn't going to count on her luck holding out.

Grimacing, she slid off the stool and rose on her toes, murmuring in Dalton's ear, "I think I need to go use the ladies' room again."

"I'm coming with you," he replied, moving to do just that, but Sherra slipped through the tight crowd quicker than he did. She heard somebody call his name—Leslie. When her own name was mentioned, Sherra swore and instead of waiting for Dalton to work his way through the crowd, she lost herself in it.

Leslie had been a friend in high school, but after the party that night in May, their friendship had grown strained. A few years ago, Leslie had managed to contact Sherra but Sherra hadn't done anything to try to reestablish a friendship.

Reestablishing a friendship wouldn't be a problem, but she knew that wasn't entirely what Leslie wanted. Leslie was a user and always had been. In school, she'd used Sherra because the bad-girl rep had suited Leslie's purposes. Now it wasn't the bad-girl rep that Leslie was latching on to, but Sherra had no desire to be used for some vicarious thrill or to be used for her money.

If Leslie wanted to glom onto somebody who'd managed some slight level of fame, then she'd have to find it from somebody other than Sherra.

She made it into the bathroom and breathed out a sigh of relief. She really did need to pee this time. Take care of that, loiter in the stall a little bit to make sure Leslie didn't pop in here looking for her. Take about ten minutes or so and Leslie would probably have gravitated elsewhere.

TOO LONG.

Dalton flicked a glance at his watch, disgusted as he realized it was the third time in less than two minutes.

Sherra had been gone too long.

Breaking away from the high-pitched chatter from some lady with an obnoxious cackle of a voice, he made his way closer to the bathroom. Lacey had disappeared into the bathroom after her to find Sherra after Sherra slipped away from him but that had been a few minutes ago.

Seth stood on the other side of the hall, also scanning the crowd.

Nothing out of the ordinary.

Except for the fact that his instincts were humming. Crawling. When the door to the ladies' room opened and Lacey slipped out, her face worried, Dalton shoved off the wall and met her halfway. Seth was closing in from the other direction and judging by the look on his face, he wasn't any happier than Dalton felt at the moment.

"She's not in there."

"You're sure?" Dalton demanded.

Lacey scowled at him and gestured down at her pale peach pant-suit. There were smudges on the knees. "Buddy, I got on my hands and knees and peeked under the damn doors. Yes, I'm sure."

"She wouldn't have just disappeared." Spinning away, Dalton shoved a hand through his hair and fought the urge to put his fist through a wall. "Maybe she saw Renee . . . ?"

"Deacon took Renee home," Seth said, his voice calm, level. It didn't do a damn thing to hide his growing worry or frustration, though. "She was hurting and he wanted to get her into bed, make her take some pain medicine."

"Okay." Closing his eyes, he pinched the bridge of his nose between his thumb and forefinger. "We start checking things out, split up."

Lacey nodded but Seth shook his head. "No splitting up. At least not all the way. Lacey stays with me."

"Fine," Dalton bit off. "Stop wasting time. And you better call Cross, let him know what's going on."

Lacey scowled. "I'm not helpless, Seth. Look, you two go look for Sherra—I'll call Deacon. I can do it from here—and I'll *wait* right here," she said, cutting Seth off before he could argue. "I can see the bathroom and the lounge, watch and make sure she doesn't head back in there. She probably just ran into somebody—or knowing Sherra, she saw somebody she *didn't* want to run into and she took the long way around."

Made sense.

But that wasn't it.

Cold, ugly fear moved through him as he headed off toward the ballroom. The center of the floor had been cleared for dancing, with buffet tables lined up along the sides. As petite as Sherra was, Dalton knew he didn't exactly have a good chance of spotting her through the crowds, but he didn't let that stop him.

She'd changed into a simple black dress, one that made her pale skin glow like a pearl against the dark material. He kept his eyes out for that pale ivory flesh, looked at every dark-haired woman, but no luck. Refusing to waste time, he spent only ten minutes in the ballroom. As he headed back to the center hall, he saw Seth working through the crowd on the opposite end, also heading in the same direction.

His face was grim.

His eyes were dark and worried.

Dalton didn't need to be any kind of mind reader to know what Seth was thinking.

Sherra wasn't there.

His heart leaped into his throat, all but choking him as fear and rage tore through him.

SHERRA COULDN'T BREATHE.

The gag on her face wasn't so tight that it cut off her airflow, but her fear was taking care of that. Being pinned, gagged—even the thought of it was enough to send her hurtling back to that night. But this wasn't a thought.

It wasn't a nightmare.

It was really happening.

Tied to a chair, her head pounding from the blow she'd taken, she sat in the darkened room, trying to make herself think past the fear, think past the pain. It was dark and silent, but she knew she wasn't alone.

She could feel a pair of eyes watching her, all but crawling over her flesh, and it was enough to have a whimper bubbling up in her throat. But she swallowed it back. Even if the gag would muffle most of the sound, she refused to let her terror show. Couldn't let it show—showing fear made it that much worse.

It was a lesson she'd learned as a child and one that had been reiterated the night JD and Boyd tried to rape her—she'd begged and pleaded—and they had laughed and taunted and hit her. Being terrified made no difference, or it only added to their pleasure. She wouldn't show fear.

Can't—can't let him see it. Showing the fear could mean prolonging the pain—

She jerked her mind away from that ugly, awful path. Can't think about that. Wouldn't. It wouldn't happen. Dalton wouldn't let it. He'd come.

He'd promised he'd take care of her.

Inside, a cynical voice laughed, jeered at her. *He isn't going to come. Nobody knows where you are.*

But they were looking. Dalton was looking. Seth was looking.

And how are they going to find you? Magic? Telepathy? They can't. Nobody can find you.

They'll find me. Sherra believed that. She had to. She didn't know *how* but she couldn't let herself consider the alternative.

When the voice finally broke into the silence, she cringed, wishing she could just fold in on herself and disappear.

"I know you're awake, Sherra. You might as well open your eyes and look at me."

That voice . . .

"JUST THE MAN I wanted to see."

Jonah stumbled by, not even acknowledging Dalton's presence.

That didn't stop Dalton from reaching out and grabbing the shorter man, fisting his hands in the lapels of Jonah's designer suit jacket and spinning him around. Jonah's head smacked into the wall at his back, his hands coming up to grab Dalton's wrists as he shifted, trying to dislodge Dalton's hold.

But Jonah was drunk—too drunk. So damn drunk Dalton could smell it on him and the small part of hope that had lit inside him upon seeing Sherra's ex-boyfriend started to wither and die. He deflected Jonah's clumsy attempts to knock him back and brought up a forearm, pressing it against Jonah's windpipe. "Where in the fuck is she?"

Jonah blinked, some of the alcoholic haze fading as he struggled to draw in air. "Who?"

"Don't give me that. Where is Sherra?"

"How the fuck should I know?"

"Where is she?"

Jonah's voice was a ragged wheeze as he gasped out, "Can't fucking breathe!"

Letting up a little, Dalton demanded again, "Where is Sherra?"

Eyes dark and pissed, Jonah snapped, "How the fuck should I know? She came here with you, bastard. Why do you think I've seen her?"

"Because I saw how you were looking at her half the night. I saw how you were looking at her yesterday. Where *is* she?"

"I ain't seen her," Jonah snarled. He managed to work a hand between them and clamped a hand around Dalton's wrist, squeezing down on the nerve endings until Dalton's hand went numb. Then he shoved off to the side, wheeling around to face Dalton as the bigger man went for him again.

"Shit, do I *look* like I'm up to seducing any woman right now?" Jonah snapped. He held out his arms, displaying decidedly rumpled clothes. The stink of alcohol hanging to him would have made a dead horse blanch. "If Sherra saw me right now, she'd go the opposite direction. Why are you foaming at the mouth anyway? She's a big girl—she wants to leave with somebody else—"

Dalton struck. Jonah ended up on the ground and Dalton was

beside him in a second, grabbing his silk shirt and jerking the man up as he cocked his fist, ready to pound him into the ground. "Somebody is after her, you dumb shit."

Jonah squinted, shaking his head, apparently unconcerned that Dalton was more than happy to just keep pounding on him. "After her?"

"You so fucking drunk you went brain-dead?" Dalton growled. "Yeah, after her. As in after her to kidnap her, rape her, kill her. If you know anything . . ."

Jonah paled. "Are you serious?"

In his gut, he knew. Dalton knew it wasn't Jonah. As much as he wished it otherwise, pounding on the guy wouldn't help Sherra. With a disgusted grunt, he let go of Jonah and shoved to his feet, heading for the doors of the country club. Seth was in the ballroom, talking over the speaker and asking for information about his sister. Dalton could hear him and suspected it was a waste of time.

Behind him, he heard Jonah getting to his feet. When the other man called out, Dalton just ignored him, determined to tear apart this damn city if that was what it took. *Sherra—God, let me find her . . .*

"Damn it, would you wait five fucking seconds?" Jonah said, grabbing Dalton's shoulder and whirling him around.

Whether it was fear for Sherra, shock or what, something had cleared most of the haze from Jonah's eyes and in them, Dalton could see a snapping, cunning intelligence—and fury. "Are you serious? Sherra's got somebody trying to hurt her?"

"Don't touch me again," Dalton warned. "Stay out of my way."

He took off again, ignoring the voice behind him.

"STUPID SON OF a bitch," Jonah muttered, shaking his head. He almost went after him, but he wasn't so sure he could stay on his feet if the big bastard took another swing at him. All the alcohol he'd consumed in the past hour was pitching and roiling in his gut, threatening to make a return appearance. Only sheer stubbornness and worry for Sherra made it possible for him to ignore the need to drop to the floor and empty his stomach.

From the corner of his eye, he saw the flashing lights as they turned off the main road and headed down the long drive that led to the country club. The star-shaped emblem on the side, tickling a memory hazed by alcohol. He stopped, and pressing the heels of his hands to his eyes, muttered, "Think. Come on, Simmonds. Think . . ."

Slowly, the fog cleared just a little and he could just barely remember what had sent him stumbling back inside after he'd originally left the bar. He'd seen Sherra—heard her voice, heard her laugh. Watched as she smiled at somebody, shrugged and nodded, tucked that beautiful black hair behind one ear. The man she'd been speaking with mentioned Green. A look had crossed over her face, and it was *that* look that had Jonah stopping in his drunken tracks and heading back into the bar.

He'd come back to Madison for one reason. Hoping to see Sherra. But it was too late. She was with somebody else—*with* in the fullest sense of the word. The hopes he'd harbored over the past fifteen years smashed, he'd gone back into the bar, determined to drink himself into complete oblivion and not just a depressing fog.

"Stupid fuck." He squeezed his eyes shut, concentrating. *Who* . . .

Abruptly, some of the fog cleared and he opened his eyes, stared at the squad car as it came flying into the parking lot with tires squealing. With narrowed eyes, Jonah watched as one of the deputies climbed out of the car.

Seth. Shit. He needed to find Seth.

"YOU REALLY MADE me work, you know."

Sherra squinted in the dim room, trying to see his face, but he stood in shadow. His voice was gruff, but oddly familiar. Familiar enough that it made chills run down her spine. She remained quiet, more out of desperation than anything else. If she spoke, she knew her voice would shake, knew it would show her fear.

Can't show fear. Can't.

"I've been waiting for you. Waiting a long time . . . six damn years, I've been waiting to get my hands on you. You couldn't go and make it easy, could you?"

Waiting for you . . . Her heart froze and the blood in her veins turned to ice. *Waiting for you.*

Shit. He'd found her.

Every single image from the e-mails over the past few months swarmed up from the depths of her memory to taunt and terrorize. Her hands went slick with sweat, a nasty, copper taste filled her mouth and fear burned inside her. Instinctively, she tried to clench her thighs together, but he'd tied her ankles to the legs of the chair, added any extra rope around her calves just below her knee. She was effectively immobilized. Elbows and wrists were also tied, as well as a rope tied around her midsection.

He chuckled, the sound echoing through the silence. "Now that scared you. I take it you remember my letters? Did you enjoy all the pretty pictures I sent you?"

Quiet footfalls sounded on the floor and she cringed, huddling back against the chair as much as she could. *Dalton . . . shit. Why did I go outside?*

She'd seen Leslie again and she had been convinced if she heard that high-pitched, grating voice one more time, her eardrums were going to rupture. *Big fucking mistake. Big. Huge.* She hadn't gone far—she'd stayed right on the path just outside the main ballroom, a path that led to the gardens. She could hear people talking and laughing all around her—safe.

Should have been safe.

He was close now, close enough to touch her, and she flinched as he stroked his hand down her cheek. A gloved hand. Her nose caught the scent of latex and her imagination kicked into overdrive as her mind started to list all the many reasons he was wearing those gloves. "Yes, Sherra, you certainly made me work. But that's okay. All it did was heighten my anticipation. After six fucking long years, I wouldn't want this over too quick. Whoring, murderous bitches like you really should get their just rewards, don't you think?"

Six years?

Murderous—

That pierced the fear that lay over her mind like a shroud. Drove through it like a chisel, hitting her with chilling intensity. Goose bumps broke out along her flesh and she swallowed the spit that pooled in her mouth.

He crouched down in front of her and for the first time since she'd woken up, she saw his face. Dismay flooded her. *You . . . ???*
Doesn't make any sense . . .

He smiled, a friendly, pleasant smile, but his hazel eyes were cold and full of a mad, intense hatred that froze her to the core.

"Neither of the other two made me work as much as you did."

10

JONAH PLOWED THROUGH the onlookers gathered in the hall, trailing after the deputy he'd seen out in the parking lot. He would be heading toward Seth—Seth was still here.

Had to be. Jonah closed his eyes and muttered, "Please, God. Let him still be here."

Breaking through the crowd, he caught sight of Seth just before he would have disappeared out a side door, Lacey and the deputy with him. "Seth!"

Seth shot a narrow look over his side but he didn't slow.

"Shit." Forcing his unsteady legs into motion, Jonah ran after them and grabbed on to Seth's arm.

"I don't have time for this shit," Seth snarled, throwing Jonah's hand off. "I realize you've spent the better part of the night inside a whiskey bottle, but I've got an emergency here."

"I saw Sherra, damn it."

Seth slowed in his tracks, eyes narrowed. Both Lacey and the deputy stopped as well and Jonah found himself the focus of three intense stares.

Taking a deep, harsh breath, he rubbed his hands over his face.

"I saw her. About thirty minutes ago—maybe. Head's still not straight. Too much Jack Daniel's. But I saw her."

"Where? Who was she with?"

"Outside." Jonah grimaced and said, "I needed a smoke. Quit five years ago, but for some reason, coming back here has me indulging in all sorts of bad shit I gave up on. I heard her muttering to herself—she's always done that. I thought about going over to her, but me being shit-faced wouldn't have appealed to her."

"Get to the point," Seth gritted out. "I don't have time to waste, damn it."

Jonah shoved his hands into his pockets. "Sorry. I saw her outside, muttering to herself. Somebody went up to her, started talking to her. Mentioned the guy she's here with, Green. Sherra . . . she got this look on her face."

"I don't give a flying fuck what kind of look she had on her face." Seth took a menacing step toward Jonah. "Who was with her?"

Jonah held his ground and met Seth's furious stare dead-on. "One of your boys, Sheriff."

HIS PHONE STARTED to vibrate, belting out the ring Dalton had programmed for Mueller's number. Jerking it from his belt, Dalton growled out, "Good timing, Mueller. Sherra's gone missing."

There was a pause and then Mueller swore. "Fuck. How long ago?"

"Less than an hour ago." Fear made it hard to speak but he forced the words past his tight throat. "Hell, maybe she got pissed off at me for something . . ."

"Afraid not, Green. Didn't you read the e-mail I sent you earlier?"

Dalton squinted. "Yeah. You were tracking—"

"That was six hours ago. Two hours ago, I sent you a heads-up that we'd narrowed the e-mail's original destination. Southeastern Ohio. And as of five minutes ago, my boys have it pinpointed down to Madison. We won't have a street address for a few more hours but that last e-mail originated from her hometown. For all we know, every single last one of them have come from there."

He went cold with fear. Forcing himself to think past it, he snarled, "And you couldn't have had this brilliant discovery *before* I brought her back here?"

"No," Mueller answered, his voice edgy. "The last e-mail he sent wasn't as carefully hidden as the others. He fucked up; that's what let us trace him this time."

This time . . . shit, what if it's too late?

Icy sweat slicked his hands as he hit the brake and swung the rental car into the parking lot of the B&B. He'd come back here hoping against hope that she was here—but he wouldn't find her here. He knew it without even climbing out of the car—with utter conviction, he knew she wasn't there.

He had her. Whoever in the hell that sick fucker was, he had her. He had Sherra.

"You there, Green?"

"Yeah," he said hoarsely. "I'm here."

"I'm on my way with my team. Once we had the confirmation on location, we were in the air. By the time we get there, we'll have an address and we'll know who he is."

"And if that's too late?"

"It won't be." Mueller paused. "You're a cop—think like one. Somebody put this much time into terrorizing her, he's going to have to draw things out."

"It's already too fucking late. I promised her that fucker wouldn't touch her."

Mueller's response was interrupted by a click and Dalton lowered the phone long enough to glance at the number on the display. Seth. "I'll call you back, Mueller. Local law enforcement's calling."

"Just keep your cool, Green. That's the best way to protect your client and you know it."

Client? Not a fucking client—she's my life . . . Without saying anything, he disconnected. A second later, he said, "Please tell me you've heard something, got something—I just got some very, very bad news from the FBI."

"Can't top mine," Seth said, his voice grim. "You got GPS in that rental?"

Dalton flicked a look at the gadget set into the dashboard. "Yeah."

Seth recited an address and said, "Get there. Now. Don't go in until I get there."

"What's going on?" he demanded as he punched the address in.

"Maybe nothing. Jonah Simmonds saw Sherra in the parking lot—found me after you took off after you threatened to pound him into the ground. Most likely, it was just a few minutes before we started looking for her."

"Was she with anybody?" Dalton demanded.

There was a pause, then Seth's voice, rough and harsh. "Yes. She was talking to one of my deputies, Grady Morris."

"Morris?" Dalton scowled, a memory of the tall, thin deputy coming to mind. He glanced at the GPS's display screen. "Is that whose address you just gave me?"

"Yes."

An automated voice chimed out, *"Turn left in one mile."*

Dread lay in his gut, a cold, heavy weight. "What's going on, Seth?"

"I don't know. But Morris isn't answering his cell phone or his home phone. That's never happened with him—not once. He's been with the department going on six years and I've never once called him and not gotten through. Hell, it's probably nothing—hopefully he saw who she was with . . ."

"I hate to kill your hopes, man." Dalton's hand tightened on the steering wheel. There was a scream building inside him, one of rage, fear and denial. He couldn't give voice to it, not yet. Just like he couldn't let that rage inside him boil out of control. "I just got off the phone with the agent working Sherra's case. The FBI got a lead on that e-mail Sherra got yesterday. The sender wasn't quite as careful hiding his tracks this time, slipped up. They tracked it to this general area, Seth."

Under normal circumstances, Dalton wouldn't have thought much of the fact that Seth couldn't reach one of his deputies. Guy could be sleeping, getting laid, a thousand little things. Today? Not normal.

"I'm hanging up, going to call the agent, give him Morris's name. Hurry your ass up—I'm less than ten minutes away and I'm not waiting for you." With that, he disconnected and dialed Mueller's number. He stomped on the brake just in time to take the upcoming turn without flying off the road, dust kicking up behind him.

Mueller came on the line as Dalton punched it back up to sixty, speeding down the winding country road. "I need you to see if you can find info on a Grady Morris, deputy here in Madison. Seth said something that he's been with the department here for six years."

Mueller didn't waste time with a bunch of questions, just held the phone off to the side and fired off a series of orders before coming back to Dalton. "What's up with the deputy?"

"I don't know but he was seen talking to Sherra right after I lost her."

"THE OTHER TWO?" Sherra forced the words past the knot tightening her throat.

Revulsion lanced through her as he lifted a latex-gloved hand and stroked his fingers down her cheek. "You still haven't put it together, have you?"

Shaking her head, Sherra held herself still as he ran his fingers down her neck, tracing the line of collarbone. His touch was oddly gentle, but that didn't do a damn thing to ease her fear or the nausea burning in her gut.

"I hadn't really expected you to." He shoved to his feet and grabbed a chair, dropping his long, thin body down on it. Elbows braced on his knees, he studied her face.

He was waiting, she realized. Hysterical laughter gurgled in her throat but she just barely kept it trapped inside. They always had to talk—why did they always have to talk? Too fucking clichéd for words.

"Don't you want to know?"

Did she? There was no answer to that. She didn't see the *point* in knowing because the only reason he wanted to tell her a damn thing was to drag her fear out, but at the same time, some logical part of her knew that the longer he talked, the more time it bought her. Time was good. Because Dalton would come. She had no fucking clue on earth how in the hell he was going to know *where* to come, but he'd come. He'd promised—

Jerking her mind away from what would happen if Dalton didn't come, she made herself look at him. She didn't know the man—at least, she didn't know his face. When he'd waved her down outside the country club, she'd hadn't recognized him, but the uniform he wore had kept her from walking away.

One of her brother's damn deputies. His voice was familiar in a way, but she couldn't place why or how. And she didn't *know* him. All of this went back to the night Boyd died. She knew it—what she didn't know was *how*.

How did this guy connect Boyd?

She had to clear her throat twice before she finally managed to speak, and still her voice shook and wavered. "Yes. I want to know why."

"Six years. I've been planning this for six years, but you never came for more than a day or two and you always had your brother there—I'd thought maybe the little love letters I sent you would have had you rushing back home where it's nice and safe, but no. You couldn't make it that easy."

"Six years," he murmured, leaning back in his chair. His eyes took on a far-off look, but she had no doubt he was still completely aware of every last breath she took. "You killed him. I was all he had and when I finally found out about him, he was already dead."

Blowing out a breath, she whispered, "Boyd."

His hazel eyes flashed—hazel. She'd seen those eyes before, she realized. Fifteen years ago. As that fact hit home, she started to shake.

He slapped her, lightning fast. "Don't fucking say his name, bitch." His voice was flat, emotionless.

While her ears rang and her eyes watered, he settled back in the chair, that friendly, affable smile on his face. That friendly smile, paired with the raging hate of his gaze, was completely terrifying.

"I didn't know about him." He closed his eyes.

Having that burning, hate-filled gaze taken off of her made it a little bit easier to drag in a breath of air, but just as she would have let it back out, his eyes opened and the air froze in her lungs. "He was my brother, and I never knew, not until my father died and I found all the letters his whore of a mother wrote my dad. They stopped right before he turned eighteen and I came here, hoping to find him. I find a grave—she stopped writing about him after you murdered him, like we didn't *deserve* to know you'd killed him."

In a smooth, near-boneless movement, he came off the chair and crouched in front of her, his hands gripping the edges of the seat beneath her. "I find a grave, because a fucking little psycho-whore slits his throat."

Psycho? That hysterical laughter was back, threatening to break free. Torn between the laughter, which would probably get her slapped again, the urge to whimper and sob in fear, and the first flames of desperate fury, she bit down on the inside of her cheek so hard that blood filled her mouth.

"Don't you have anything to say?"

"What do you want me to say?"

He shot a hand into her hair, fisted it, jerking so tight pain

streaked through her scalp. "What do I want you to say?" He
shook her, wringing her head like a child shook a rattle. "I don't
fucking want you to say *anything*."

Shoving to his feet, he started to pace around her, the caged pacing of an animal. "I only want two things from you, bitch."

He came to a halt, staring at her.

"I want you to hurt. And I want you to die."

With that, he reached out and flicked on a light switch. Flinch-
ing away from the painfully bright lights, she squinted, tried to see.
But as her vision adjusted, she wished for blindness and oblivion.

In front of her, he started to strip out of his clothes. She couldn't
decide what was more terrifying: the sight of him methodically un-
dressing, the chains hanging from the ceiling or the black table in
the middle of the sterile, white room.

DALTON CLIMBED OUT of the car just as Seth pulled up behind
him.

They were out in the middle of nowhere, it seemed, a good ten
miles outside of town. With the exception of the three deputy cars
that had followed him the last few miles, he hadn't seen another
soul.

The lone farmhouse stood isolated, a big pickup truck parked
off to the side and the deputy's car in front. There were a few lights
on in the house, but no movement, no shadow approaching from
behind the windows to signify that their arrival had been heard.

The deputies stood behind Seth, varying looks of irritation and
confusion on their faces, but none of them spoke. Seth strode toward Dalton, a grim cast to his features. Overhead, the silvery light
of the full moon shone down on them. Around the house and the
tree line, shadows gathered dark and black.

It was far too quiet. They couldn't hear a sound coming from
the house.

"I don't like this," one of the deputies muttered.

Dalton agreed wholeheartedly in silence. "I'm going inside."

Seth swore. "We have no reason—"

A humorless smile curled his lips and Dalton said, "I have plenty of reason—and I'm not a cop anymore." With that, he headed toward the house.

Behind him, he heard some of the deputies speaking to Seth, heard Seth's flat, cold voice cutting them off, although none of the words made sense. Sherra was in that house. Somewhere. Dalton could all but feel her.

The phone on his belt rang. Without answering, he turned it off. Nothing mattered. Nothing but getting in there and finding Sherra.

"YOU'RE NOT JUST another whore," Morris said, coming to stand at her side once he completely undressed.

In one hand, he held a knife. Sherra's eyes fixed on that shining blade, but the knife wasn't the only thing that had her almost too petrified to move.

He was naked and aroused, watching her with a cruel lust that had her cringing back against the hard slabs of the wooden chair. If she could have disappeared inside it, she would have. As it was, all she could do was tremble and try not to flinch as he flashed the blade at her.

"Whores have their uses, at least." He knelt down in front of her and cut the rope fastened around her torso. As it fell to the floor, he went to work on the black dress and her bra. When he reached her panties, he stroked the very tip of the blade along the material. "Like the bitch my dad fucked around with—she had a purpose. She took care of the needs my mom just couldn't handle. Then the bitch got pregnant and decided she couldn't keep having an affair with a married man, that she couldn't keep fucking around on her husband. I think she thought my dad would leave my mom sooner or later. Seemed to think each of them could file for divorce;

then they could be together and raise Boyd like some little happily-ever-after fairy tale. She couldn't see the truth of things. She was a whore—that was her place. I felt bad for Boyd, though. Wanted to make it up to him—that's why I came to find him. I knew he needed me."

He backhanded her and while her head was spinning from that, he went to work on the bonds, releasing her. "I'm going to cut you loose now, and you're going to be good for me. Because if you don't, I've got something special mixed up for you."

The words didn't make sense and as soon as she had her limbs free, she struck out. She caught him unaware and managed to strike him in the throat, but it didn't land dead-center, glancing off the side. It barely slowed him down. She had a second to get out of the chair, but before she managed two steps, he grabbed a fistful of her hair, jerked her tattered, shredded dress away. The dress and her bra fell to the ground, leaving her all but naked. Wearing nothing but panties and a pair of heels, chills dancing over her flesh, she struggled as he dragged her kicking and screaming to the table standing in the middle of the room.

"My dad had a table like this—his "workroom" he called it."

He hauled her up with a strength she never would have believed possible in such a skinny man, throwing her onto the table. She came up, swinging out with her fists, kicking and clawing. Her nails caught skin and drew blood. The scent of it flooded her senses, tickled memories she worked hard to forget, but this time, the onslaught of fear caused a welcome rush of adrenaline. She grunted and swung out again, once more going for the throat.

The time, she connected solidly, felt the soft tissue of the neck and heard him gasp and choke for air behind her as she rolled off the table. Keeping it between them, she backed away from him, scanning the room for a possible weapon with her peripheral vision. Unwilling to take her gaze away from him, she circled the perimeter of the room. There were cabinets lining the walls but she wasn't going to risk searching them. No—she'd just head for the door; fuck a weapon.

Face red, he advanced on her, thin chest heaving as he struggled to breathe. "Warned you, dumb bitch," he grunted.

She got to the door, her sweating hands slipping off the knob as she tried to turn it. Tried without success. She screamed, her voice harsh with denial and rage. So close—

Don't stand there, her mind bellowed.

The coppery taste of fear flooded her mouth, saliva pooling there. She swallowed and once more started to circle away from him. The calm, unemotional facade had disappeared and he stared at her with stark, utter hatred, mouth twisted in a snarl, hazel eyes glinting. He rushed for her, the long limbs giving him the advantage once more.

His hand fisted in her hair and she would have jerked away, even if it meant leaving half of her hair in his fist, but he jerked hard and shifted his grip to her throat, squeezing down. She turned her face into his arm, that slight movement keeping him from fully blocking her airway although part of her wished for oblivion. She felt the hard dig of his engorged penis pressing into her bare back, his breath coming from him in excited pants.

No!

It was her worst nightmare come to life, a nightmare that she had just barely escaped once before. He started to force her to the ground, his greater weight bearing her down. In one last, desperate move, she brought up her foot and smashed down on his instep, driving the spiked heel of her shoe into soft, unprotected flesh. She screamed, the sound tearing from her throat like a clawed beast, leaving her raw.

Bone crunched and he bellowed, hurling her away from him with a force that had her crashing into one of the cabinets lining the wall. Her head smacked into the white-painted wood and her vision blurred, then went dark altogether.

IT WAS FAINT.

Muffled.

If he'd breathed too loud in that moment, he might not have even heard it.

But it was there—

With a silent snarl, Dalton left the living room and followed the direction the faint sound had come from—or at least what he *hoped* was the right direction, because try as he might, he couldn't hear anything else but Seth's quiet footsteps pacing along behind him. He went through each of the bedrooms on the first floor, finding *nothing*. Hearing *nothing*.

But the skin on his spine was crawling, his heart pounding in his throat. His hands were empty, curled into useless fists, and for the first time since he'd turned in his badge, he wished he had his gun.

The last time he'd held it had been to place it on his superior's desk the day he turned in his badge. Only a day before, he'd been forced to draw it on his partner and kill him before Dalton had ended up taking a bullet between his eyes. After that, he'd sworn he'd never use it again. He didn't think he *could*.

He'd been wrong. He could use it, and now he wished like hell he had the option. Seth trailed along behind him while his deputies searched the rest of the house.

Empty office. Dining room that looked like it was never used.

Kitchen—his gaze locked in on the door at the opposite end of the kitchen. Couldn't lead outside, was on the interior of the house . . . could be a pantry.

Could be nothing.

It wasn't, though. Even as he closed his hand around the doorknob, he knew. It was everything.

It opened, revealing sure enough . . . a pantry. A narrow pantry, barely three feet deep and five feet across. And another door, one that looked out of place with its shiny locks and sturdy design. He glanced over his shoulder at Seth and then reached out, grasped the doorknob.

While it wasn't a surprise to find it locked, he snarled in frustration. Taking a step back, he sized it up. "She's in there."

"If you're wrong, and you take that door down, he'll hear. We may not have time—"

Dalton looked back at the door. Shaking his head, he murmured, "I'm not wrong." She was in there. Trapped, alone and counting on him. He'd promised her—

He reached out and grasped the doorknob once more, wiggled, pressed against the door, testing it. It was solid. It was sturdy. But there was just enough give that he didn't think it had been reinforced. It could have been just desperate hope, he knew, and he took a second to say a quick prayer. If it was reinforced—

Stop.

Just stop.

He closed his eyes, took a deep breath. He kicked, putting every bit of fury and fear into the strike. It gave under the blow, almost easily, revealing a set of white stairs, white walls, and blinding white lights. Faintly, just faintly, he thought he heard another scream, followed by a crash, but he couldn't be sure. At the foot of the stairs there was another door and while it didn't give quite as easily, he powered through without pausing to take a breath—

He barreled into the room, taking in the entire scene without pause. Sherra lay in a boneless heap on the floor just a few feet away from him. Across the room was Grady Morris, naked, his eyes crazed.

In one hand, he held a half-filled hypodermic needle, in the other an unlabeled vial. Dalton lunged, howling in rage as he took the other man to the ground. He grabbed Morris's wrist, smashing into the ground until the man's fingers went lax. With his other hand, he pummeled the man's face.

Bone crunched, blood sprayed and still he couldn't stop.

Hands came up, grabbing him, trying to drag him away. From

the corner of his eye, he saw the needle and he grabbed it, shoved the needle into Morris's neck. Just before Seth and his men managed to drag him away, he pushed down on the plunger, pumping whatever poison the syringe held into the bastard's neck.

Dalton tore free from the deputies and ran to Sherra. Heart an icy, frozen knot, he reached out and touched her shoulder. She was mostly nude, the only clothing she wore a pair of panties and her shoes. A soft moan escaped her as he brushed her hair back from her face. The sound of it had tears burning his eyes. Alive—thank God. "Sherra . . . come on, baby, wake up."

He pulled her into his arms, cradling her.

Behind him, somebody swore, but Dalton didn't even hear. He could hear nothing, could see nothing, beyond Sherra.

He didn't see Morris's face go red, then ashen. Didn't see it as thin, bony hands came up to clutch at his chest. Didn't hear as the man struggled to breathe and when the deputy's heart abruptly stopped, Dalton was rocking Sherra, back and forth and whispering to her quietly.

SHE CAME AWAKE to hear his voice.

"Wake up, Sherra . . . come on, princess, talk to me. God, I'm sorry. I'm so fucking sorry . . . Wake up, baby."

There were other noises. Sirens. Voices. She thought she heard her brother, but she wasn't sure. None of the other voices mattered just then anyway. Forcing her lids up, she squinted, half afraid to wake up. What if she was dreaming . . . what if he hadn't come . . .

No. He promised he'd keep me safe.

He was there. She wasn't dreaming. His beautiful pale green eyes met hers, widened and then closed, a deep breath shuddering out of him in a sigh as he muttered, "Thank God."

Her head ached. Her body. Her cheekbone felt battered and bruised and her gut churned violently. But she was so damn glad to be awake—Dalton was here.

He'd come for her. She fought the darkness that pushed in on her, fought to stay awake, fought to think past the sickening throb pounding inside her skull.

In a thick voice, she whispered, "I knew you'd come."

He cupped her cheek, cradled her gently in his arms as he muttered under his breath. None of the words made sense. But it didn't really make any difference. It didn't matter what he said, because he was there.

She wasn't alone, and in that moment, she was damn thankful.

11

"KETAMINE."

Dalton tore his gaze away from Sherra and looked at the doorway to the hospital room.

She had a moderate concussion and the doctors had insisted on keeping her for twenty-four hours to observe her. She'd tried to argue, but had given up halfway through the first sentence—the pain in her head, Dalton figured. Probably hurt too much to talk. He'd had a concussion or three in his lifetime and they were not fun.

Seth stood in the door, staring at his sister with worried, weary eyes. In his hand he held a folder and as he slipped inside, he tossed it onto the chair beside Dalton. He settled in the seat opposite her and braced his arms on the bedrail. "She waking up okay?"

Dalton snorted. "If you count snarling and threatening life and limb unless she gets coffee, yeah." *Keep it light. Keep it easy.* Had to. If he went for anything other than flippancy, he thought he just might break. As it was, his hand shook as he reached for the file folder and flipped it open.

"Ketamine," he muttered, shaking his head. "Nasty shit." His temper and nerves had yet to settle—even after he'd been told Morris had died within two minutes of Dalton injecting him, it wasn't enough. He wanted the man to *hurt*. Needed him to hurt. "Was it a bad dose?"

Seth shrugged. "Hard to say right now. There's a possibility Morris had some undiagnosed heart problem and ketamine was just too fucking much for him. We won't know until the autopsy."

"What about *why*?" Dalton demanded, his voice low and harsh. Shoving up from the chair, he started to pace. It was either that or put his fist through a wall. The fury burning through him felt like it was going to choke him. "The autopsy isn't going to tell us that and I fucking need to know *why*."

". . . Boyd."

Her weak, ragged whisper had both men jerking their heads around. Swearing, Dalton came back to her side and settled his hip on the edge of the bed. "Shit, princess, I'm sorry. You need to be resting . . ."

Sherra grimaced. "Hard to rest. My head hurts." She poked her lip out in a sullen pout and muttered, "Nobody will get me any damn coffee, either."

Her lashes fluttered down, shielding her eyes. A soft, ragged sigh escaped her; then she lifted her lids and stared at Dalton for a long moment. "I knew you'd come." She lifted a hand and he took it, lifting it to his lips.

Feeling useless and guilty, he whispered, "If I'd watched you better, he never would have gotten his hands on you."

Sherra shook her head. "We know better than that." Rolling her head on the pillow, she looked at her brother. "It was about Boyd all along. He was the one after Lacey and Renee, too. Boyd was his brother, or half brother. I dunno, something about his dad had an affair with Boyd's mom, didn't know about Boyd until six years ago."

She frowned and looked at her brother. "He sounded so familiar . . . I've talked with him before, haven't I, Seth? When I've called you at the office?"

"A few times at least," Seth said. A muscle jerked in his jaw as he leaned forward and took Sherra's other hand. "I bet over the past few years, he asked about you ten times easy, wanting to know if you ever came to town for more than a few days. Mentioned wanting to meet you, but the few times I mentioned a signing at the Book Shelf, he couldn't ever come."

"Didn't want an audience." She closed her eyes and took a deep, shaking breath. "Anytime I came home, I never stayed more than a day or so and you were always right there with me. Must have pissed him off, me having a cop as my big brother."

Dalton watched as naked fear danced across her face and wished desperately that he could do something, *anything*, to make that fear go away. To take the past day and just erase it from her life.

She turned her head back to Dalton and asked, "Did I hear right? You said something about an autopsy . . . ?"

Seth started to answer, but Dalton cut him off. "Yeah, an autopsy. Had a heart attack or something, sounds like." Sherra didn't need to know about the ketamine—not yet. When she wasn't half sick with a concussion, he'd tell her. He didn't want to, but if he kept it from her, she'd kill him. She didn't need to know just this second, though.

"So he's dead? Really dead?"

He reached out and traced his fingers down the line of her cheek, feathering his thumb along the bruise there. "Yeah, really dead."

"Then it's over."

He kissed her hand and murmured, "It's over."

She sighed and something about her face softened, eased. That naked fear faded away. "Over." A smile curled up the corners of her mouth and she said, "Looks like you're out of a job, Dalton."

Catching her hand, he lifted it and pressed a kiss to her palm. "The hell I am. I'll work for sex and meals—you aren't getting rid of me that easy."

Across the bed, Seth choked. They both ignored him.

"You know I can't cook," she murmured. "Coffee and sand-wiches, that's about it."

"That's the great thing about takeout, princess. That work?"

Sherra blew out a sigh and whispered, "Deal. But you have to make the coffee." Then she closed her eyes and shifted, drifting back to sleep.